Wryter Gavlin is a writer from Cape Town, South Africa. He has been writing for three years, and this is his first publication. He hopes that you enjoy reading it as much as he did writing it.

Wryter Gavlin

FATHER OF THE FARM

AUSTIN MACAULEY PUBLISHERS™

LONDON • CAMBRIDGE • NEW YORK • SHARJAH

A CIP catalogue record for this title is available from the British Library.

ISBN 9781035814572 (Paperback)
ISBN 9781035814589 (ePub e-book)

www.austinmacauley.co.uk

First Published 2024
Austin Macauley Publishers Ltd®
1 Canada Square
Canary Wharf
London
E14 5AA

Chapter 1

Upon a time once, on a day in 1943, in a country known mostly for its unusually rich soil, and therefore consisting almost entirely of farming districts, 48 make up the country, in one of the smaller of the districts that colour it green and gold, Camel's Neck, on one of the smaller *farms* in the district, a farm that belongs to the sixth generation of a family by the name of Brungle, a name that used to be of much importance in the district as well as a large part of the country itself, 12 farm workers, men and women, all black, dressed in old and worn black jumpsuits, wearing torn and tattered shoes barely holing together, are lined up outside of a cabin, a cabin on the far side of a lawn that separates it from a farmhouse in which the two owners of the farm live, a cabin of very modest proportions, about the length of the 12 workers standing next to each other and the width of about half thereof with two separate builds next to it, one that houses three showers and another that houses three toilet stalls behind it, with their arms tightly pressed against their sides looking down at the ground.

A few feet in front of the workers stands Bees Brungle, one of four last remaining Brungles, and one of the two that live on the farm, a short and stocky man, 49 years of age, with short brown hair uncomfortably curly, hair which has slowly been turning grey and thinning on the top of his head for the last five years, a brown moustache, thicker than all of the remaining hairs on his head put together, dressed in a light brown collar shirt with short sleeves and pants much the same and a pair of dark brown leather shoes—is walking a few feet in front of the workers from one end of the line they have formed in front of their cabin to the other, addressing them in a loud, authoritative voice while lashing a whip.

'Like I've said before and like I'm going to say again, my things, the reason you did not get your breakfast this morning is because you did not complete your work in time, and because you did not complete your work in time, I... did not... get paid, and because I did not get paid, you... get... punished.' Bees lashes his whip at one of the workers, the tip of the whip that 'cuts' through the sky, a noise so loud it seems to crack the air in front of the workers and sends a quick and chilling jolt not only up the worker's spine that Bees lashed the whip at, but the remainder of the workers' spines as well. 'That, my things…' he continues, 'is the way of the world, and the way of the world my things is hard, because the way of the world says when you mess up while working for someone you mess his things up too and that means that the person you are working for can, and more importantly *should*, mess things up for his workers in return.' Bees comes to a standstill and cups his hands over his mouth and yells, 'Am I right in saying that is fair, my things?'

The workers nod. Bees walks toward one of the male workers and stops about a foot in front of him.

The man in front of whom he standing is Petrus; he is 72 years old, making him the oldest of all the workers, he came to the farm 38 years earlier when he was 34 years old. Before he arrived on the farm, he was one of three priests of the church on a settling about half a day's drive away from the farm, the settling was home to not only Petrus but the rest of the workers as well and has been so as far back as any of them can remember, it was a place which they loved very much; and a place—which considering the class divide between the black and white people of the country at the time, they appreciated more than they were able to put into words, as well as a place that they have been missing very dearly every day since the day they were brought to the farm.

Standing in front of Petrus, Bees leans into his bowed head. 'I said is that not right, my thing?'

Before Petrus is able to answer Bees grabs him by the jaw and moves his face upward to look him in the eyes. 'What you say, Petrus?'

Petrus nods. 'That is right.'

Bees squeezes Petrus' face, so hard that the edges of his teeth dig almost into the insides of his cheeks and yells at him, leaving driblets of spit on his face. 'Yes, who you gravel?'

'Yes *boss*,' Petrus answers.

Bees smiles a sly smile and let's go of Petrus' face and takes a couple of steps back to get a clearer view of all of the workers, looking them over with disdain. '*Yes boss* is right,' he says. 'Nothing but *yes boss* is right, do you cave otters understand me?'

The workers nod. Petrus looks up and makes eye contact with Bees who finds this exchange surprising and intrusive to a very unsettling degree and after regaining his prior composure, he looks back at Petrus with furious eyes before taking a step back, digging the back of his shoe into the dirt and bringing his whip over his shoulder and lashing it forward while Petrus and the rest of the workers watch, as the tip of it makes its way through the air and slices through Petrus' jumpsuit and into his right shoulder. Petrus groans through clenched teeth and grabs his shoulder and squeezes the separated pieces of flesh back together in an attempt to numb the pain.

Bees steps to Petrus and puts his hand angry eagerly, though in sarcastically gentle a manner, on his shoulder. 'You know that you must look down when I am speaking to you Petrus, that is how this works, how else can we sustain order here, if you and your lot are not able to remember a request as simple as that?' He puts his hand on Petrus' shoulder. 'Look at me again when you are not supposed to and you will not eat for *another* four days starting next week also, understand?'

Petrus nods.

'Very good,' Bees says. 'And don't think for a second that I am joking because as sure as I am your boss, I will keep to my word about it, even if it means that you drop dead of starvation on Tuesday.' Bees pushes Petrus away from him. 'You see, my things, people only learn when you make them, and that only happens when you behave the way I just did.' Bees rolls up the whip and grabs a hold of it in its newly formed shape... 'Discipline and respect, the only two things more important than the work you do here,' says Bees. 'Always look down when I am speaking to you, not only do you hear me better because there is less to distract you, you also greatly diminish your chances of getting hurt.'

Bees steps onto a plastic crate nearby. 'Now listen closely,' he says. 'In two days, it will be Sunday, then you will be allowed food again, *if* you keep going on with the good behaviour that you have been showing for the last two days now that is. I know that it has been quite some time since you've had anything to eat and that the weaker of you must be on the brink of collapse, but that is okay, because that is what you get for not finishing your work in time.'

Bees steadies the whip and 'rests' it on his shoulder. 'Important lessons can only be learned through suffering, so really I'm doing you all a favour by not allowing you to eat anything for two days now and also for two more days after that, also, back in the olden days, people used to not eat anything for much longer that you have not eaten anything, to win the favour of that which is most up high.' Bees laughs, 'Another favour I am doing for you.'

Bees catches his breath. 'You see, I am a very good guy when you don't piss me off,' Bees says in more calm a manner and claps his hands together and steps off the crate, 'Okay, I've said what needed to be said, now stay in line and walk quickly to the field; my sister is waiting for you in the vineyard.'

The workers make their way over to a small dirt hill at the edge of the plane of grass closest to the cabin that leads down to three fields of crop, the only three thereof on the entire farm, a cornfield, a vineyard and a wheat field, in that order, from the side of the farm on which the workers cabin stands to the other, to meet up with Clarafina. It takes the workers no more than a minute or so, to meet up with her.

Clarafina, Bees' twin sister, is the same height, size and shape as her brother, the only difference between the two of them, other than the length and colour of their hair, Clarafina has thin and straight red hair, is that her breasts are bigger than Bees' and her stomach that hangs over the top of her pants much like Bees', is a little bit smaller. She is wearing a cream-coloured dungaree with short pant legs over a small, white vest covered in red wine stains along with a pair of brown leather boots. As the workers approach her, she is standing in front of a wired gate that leads to the vineyard, one of three gates by the three fields of crop, each leading to a different field of them that forms part of a ten-foot-high fence that surrounds the three of them for safe-keeping.

Clarafina yells at the workers, 'Let's get a move on, my puppets, if you want to eat on Sunday, you will make like you want to be here and pick up the pace!' She flails her arms to exaggerate her feeling of impatience. 'I will not hesitate to mess you up if you mess up today like you did last time.'

As the workers begin to line up in front of Clarafina, she steps up onto an overturned plastic crate next to her to establish a position of dominance. Soon after she steps onto the crate, she bends down with an exaggerated effort to pick up a wine satchel made from buckskin lying next to her feet on the crate. 'Come to your mother, young buck.' Getting back to a standing position takes more effort than it did to bend down and as she does, so a loud crack 'sounds' as a 'knot' in her spine is expelled. 'Ouch!' she yells as she squeezes her back over where her spine is. 'That one did not feel good.' She wipes away droplets of sweat that formed on her forehead while she was busy picking up her wine satchel and flings it off the tip of her fingers with one quick flick of her wrist. When the uncomfortable feeling in her back is gone and her forehead is clear and dry again, she uncorks her satchel. 'Okay my things, let's try this again.'

Clarafina takes a sip of red wine and after 'pushing' the liquid down her throat, she puts the cork back in satchel before flinging it over her shoulder by a strap that she herself stitched onto it when she first got it when she was 12 years old. Clarafina received the satchel as a birthday present from her grandfather, a man known by most solely as Grandpa Brungle. After she had been pestering him for a couple of weeks before her birthday about the red liquid she had been seeing him. Her parents and two uncles drink almost every day and that made them act so much more jolly than what they were before they sat down at the porch table to drink it.

Grandpa Brungle decided it a good idea to give the satchel to her on a birthday as early as he did because for one he wanted her to stop bothering him about what it is and if she is ever going to have one herself, as well as what it is that is inside of his own and why him and the rest of her family act so differently to what they do before after drinking from their own satchels and mostly because he wanted her to know that she has the satchel and that she is not allowed to make use of it for its intended purpose for all years from when she got it up to her 21st birthday, which is the age at which all Brungle children are first allowed to drink alcohol.

'I hear the problem was not hearing right, when you failed to finish your work on time last week,' she continues. 'None of that this time please, and I am saying this not for myself but for you lot.' Clarafina swings her satchel back over her shoulder again and uncorks it before taking another sip, this sends red liquid streaming down her cheeks, chin and neck before it adds to the stains already 'decorating' her vest.

After wiping her mouth and neck with a loud groan, Clarafina puts the cork back in the satchel and continues to address the workers. 'Also, my brother told me to tell you that if you screw up again this time like you did last time each one of you will get screwed in return, and not in the way that we all want to get screwed.' Clarafina claps her hands together. 'Now you have until two o'clock to pick as many grapes as you can, after that you will get a short break as per usual, before going on with your work as you always do until six o'clock.' Clarafina looks the workers over with narrow, awaiting eyes. 'Did everybody get that?'

The workers lightly nod their heads. Clarafina does not like this timid response and cups her hands over her mouth. 'I said... Did everybody hear me, my puppets?' She yells.

The workers respond collectively, 'Yes, Miss Clarafina.'

Clarafina smiles. 'Very good.' Just as Clarafina is about to step off the crate and leave the workers to do their work, she stops. 'Before I leave you be, I thought you might want to know, I heard the other day that monkeys can be and have been taught by whatever people take care of them and do experiments on them and so on to do jobs harder than what you lot do over here? Real life monkeys, my things, I kid you not, think about that while you do your work today, maybe it will help you.'

Clarafina claps her hands together. 'Very good, now get to work!' The workers each pick up a basket from a pile by the gate that leads into the vineyard. When they all have a basket in their hands, they make their way in a single file through the gate and into the vineyard while Clarafina keeps watch, as they begin to disappear in between the grapevines. Clarafina cups her hands over her mouth again and yells after them, 'I will be back to check on you in no more than an hour!' Clarafina steps off the crate and makes her way back to the house to fill her satchel with more red wine, as she slowly empties it on her way there.

While on her way to the house, Marana, one of the female workers, a tall and petite woman in her late forties with her hair in braids down to her shoulders and eyes darker almost than the jumpsuits her and the other workers have to wear while working—taps Petrus on the shoulder.

Marana came to live on the farm when she was only ten years old. She was the youngest of six brothers and sisters and was the only one from her family that was taken from her home to go and work on the Brungle farm. Both her parents were quite a bit older than the average age of parents of a ten-year-old because of the number of children they had and were left behind at the settling because Grandpa Brungle thought they were too old to be able to do the work he wanted them to, as well as for the work to be up to the Brungle standard.

The day she was taken from her home, on her way to the farm, she cried the entire way there thinking about what her life would be like without her family. Once they arrived on the farm, Marana was one of four people that helped Petrus out of the trailer in which they were transported there because of an injury he sustained at the hands of Grandpa Brungle and two of his sons and carried him to the workers cabin, where she helped dress his wound and also the person to which Petrus would become the closest to over the years and come to see as his own.

When Petrus turns around to see who is tapping him on the shoulder, he smiles when he sees Marana standing in front of him, although that same smile quickly fades when he sees how exhausted she is, and before he is able to comment on her tired demeanour, Marana, sweat dripping from her forehead and breathing so heavily that it looks as if she is hyperventilating, says to him: 'I'm not feeling very good, Petrus, I think I need to eat something very quickly or at least have a drink of water, I feel like I might collapse any second, if I don't.'

Petrus sighs. 'Try and put it out of your mind Marana,' says Petrus. 'Before you know it, it will be Sunday morning and we'll be having eggs, bacon, potatoes, sausage and toast.'

'I tried, Petrus…' she says. 'But I don't think I can make it another two minutes, let alone another two days if I don't put something in my body now, I've been feeling like this for almost a day and I don't think I can hold out much longer, I have to eat something, *anything* before I can work further.'

'Maybe you can get away with having a couple of grapes before we start working?'

Marana turns to look at the grapes by her side. 'That might just help.'

Petrus nods. 'Okay then, if you must,' he says. 'But try to not chew them in case Bees or Clarafina comes to smell our breath today.'

Marana nods. 'I won't, but eat I must, Petrus, that I know for sure.'

'Okay,' says Petrus.

Marana picks a couple of grapes from one of the vines and puts them in her mouth and swallows each without chewing them. After swallowing five grapes, Marana picks a couple more and puts them in her pocket to have later, in case she starts to feel faint again.

After a couple of hours, two o'clock, the workers hear Bees calling them from the gate and make their way toward him. Against the gate are about two dozen bags that have been filled with grapes by the workers during the time they spent working. When the workers reach the gate, they find Bees standing on a crate in front of it with Clarafina by his side. 'You can put down your baskets,' says Bees. The workers put down their baskets. 'Marana?' Bees continues, 'Will you come here, please?'

Marana makes her way over to Bees. Once she is standing about a foot away from him, he says, 'A while ago my sister informed me that you looked quite tired and out of breath and almost sickly when she left you to do your work earlier. Looking at you know I have to say that I agree with her,' Bees continues.

'I also have to say that you and your lot brought this on yourselves, so I do not feel sorry for you, Marana, because more so than not eating, the state of you is what you deserve, I'm almost sorry to see that none else of you look the way that you do, having said that, I am not here to sympathise with you, I am here to say that when my sister told me the news, my…' Bees snaps his fingers. 'What's the word I'm looking for?'

'Senses,' says Clarafina.

Bees shakes his head. 'No, that's what a child would say, I'm looking for the grown up one.'

'Intuition?' Clarafina asks.

Bees groans. 'Thank you Clarafina, I did not ask for your help,' he says. 'My *senses* told me that because Marana might be feeling the way, that my sister said she might that she might think that she is allowed to eat something,' he continues.

'After that, my same senses told me that because you are picking grapes today that Marana will probably take *grapes* for herself to eat and because of that, my dear girl, will you please open your mouth?'

Bees steps down from the crate and in front of Marana. 'Any day now, Marana.'

Marana opens her mouth. Bees brings his nose to her mouth and breathes in through his nose. 'Okay, stay here Marana,' says Bees. 'Xhema, will you please step forward?'

Xhema, a female worker who is 42 years old and came to the farm five years after Marana walks over to Bees.

'Now you do the same as Marana,' says Bees.

Xhema opens her mouth and Bees smells her breath. 'A little bit different,' says Bees. 'More dirty, but that's probably because you didn't eat any grapes.' Bees shoves Xhema away from him. 'Back you go, Xhema,' he says. 'Kolos, make your way over here.'

Kolos makes his way over to Bees and opens his mouth. Bees smells his breath. 'The same as Xhema, back you go too, Kolos.'

Bees tucks his thumbs under his suspender straps. 'Can you open your mouth one more time for me please, Marana?' Marana opens her mouth. Bees smells her breath. 'Different from the other two but it still doesn't smell like grapes.'

Bees grabs a hold of Marana by her arm. 'But because you are the one I think to have taken the grapes, because of how you look and how your breath smells different from two other workers, who have been working next to you. Here, I am going to make it that you did take grapes to eat.'

Bees lets go of Marana. 'Go wait by my sister there, Marana,' says Bees. 'Because I already spoke to you about punishment and doing the right thing and everything that goes with it, I am not going to say another thing to shed light on that, what I am going to say is that when you are finished with your day's work go back to the cabin and get in your out of work clothes and meet me and my sister outside of the cabin when you are done,' Bees glances quickly over the workers. 'Is that understood?'

The workers nod.

'Very good, on you go then,' says Bees. 'I'll see you all after work.'

That afternoon when the workers had finished their day's work and had gotten dressed in the clothes they wear when they are not working, Bees and Clarafina comes to meet them at their cabin. Once they were lined up against the front of the cabin, Bees explain to them that they will have to follow him and Clarafina and Marana up into the mountain range that sits next to the three fields of crop for Marana to gather a rock over which she will have to kneel, in order to receive her punishment.

The mountain range is called Camel's Neck. It ranges for the entirety of however much it is long from heights of 100 meters to 250 meters. It reaches out as far as the eye can see, beginning by the edge of the Brungle farm and disappears from view as it reaches the centre of the district two districts away from Golden Heart. Other than being unusually long, rocky and dry in terms of the other mountain ranges that reside in the country, the only other thing that the residents of Golden Heart and some of the surrounding districts know about the mountain range is that Grandpa Brungle came to meet his end on it.

How this came to be, no one is sure of and to this day it remains one of the most popular topics of conversation amongst the people of Golden Heart and other surrounding districts. Some say that he was eaten by a lion, others say that he slipped and fell on his rifle, while some think that he simply slipped and fell off the mountain when he was drunk, which is what he was every time when he went hunting on the mountain. The story that people most like talking about, not because they most believe it to be true but because it is the story they most *want*

13

to be true is that he went up the mountain one night and shot himself with his favourite pistol.

Because of the nature of this story, it comes with many theories as to why it would be, one of them being that he was simply fed up with life and no longer wanted part of it, another was that the guilt of living the way that he did finally got to him and he could live with himself no longer, the most popular though is that one of the workers put a curse on him which made him go up the mountain and point his most prized pistol to his head and pull the trigger. Along with the many speculations of how it might have been that Grandpa Brungle killed himself is another story that he did not die on Camel's Neck, but that he was murdered by one of his family members, the most popular suspect being his wife and that the stories of him dying on the mountain was made up by his family to cover up what really happened. To this day, no one knows how Grandpa Brungle came to meet his end but the topic of how he came to it remains one of the most popular during parties and gatherings in the lounge areas of different hotels in town in the centre of Golden Heart and surrounding districts.

Once Marana had carried the rock which Bees picked out for her back to the farm, she lays it down a few feet in front of the cabin. Bees bends down and puts his hands on his knees to catch his breath. Clarafina laughs. 'Dammit, boet,' she says. 'You should stop smoking that pipe of yours so much, it cannot be good for your workers to see you fall down next to your sister after a little escapade up and down your beloved mountain.' Clarafina opens her satchel and takes a drink of red wine.

Bees looks up at Clarafina from the corner of his eye. 'Dammit Clarafina,' he says. 'You should really stop drinking from that satchel of yours because it's giving you a stomach bigger than the ones on the cows we had on the farm when we were kids.'

Clarafina's eyes widen, she takes a sip of wine, swallows it and forces down from her nasal cavity into her throat, a small amount of phlegm which she spits on the ground next to Bees. 'How dare you speak to blood like you just spoke to me, brother?' Clarafina takes a step toward Bees and stands over him, still bent over with his hands on his knees, and looks down at him with angry eyes.

Bees looks up at her. 'How dare *you stand* over me like that, Clarafina?'

Clarafina smirks loudly and begins to make her way around Bees so that she may come to stand behind him. When Bees is no longer able to see her, he asks, 'What are you doing, my darling sister?'

Clarafina laughs. 'Darling sister is it now,' she says. 'From cow to darling sister, you sure have some nerve, brother.' Once she is standing behind Bees, she puts her hands on her hips and says, 'Look at you, you can't even turn around and face me like the man that you claim to be.'

Bees laughs. 'Facing you like a man has nothing to do with its sister,' he says. 'I am looking away from you for the very reason that I am the man that I claim to be, on this farm and elsewhere.'

Clarafina takes another sip of wine. 'Know this, brother,' she says. 'What I am about to do to you is going to be so much more satisfying than it should be.' Before Bees is able to respond, Clarafina kicks him as hard as she can in his groin. The second the top part of Clarafina's shoe comes into contact with Bees, his face turns white with shock, a shock that greatly precedes the pain because in all of his 49 years he had never thought to experience a humiliation as he is now, especially from his twin sister.

After what felt like an eternity Bees' pale face quickly turns red as the pain begins to supersede the humiliation and he falls on the ground with a thud so loud that it sends a shiver down Clarafina's spine, even though she is standing over him. The sight of seeing Bees wither around on the ground makes her smile in a way that she had never known before and she takes the cork out from her wine satchel and takes a drink from it, so much that she has to swallow three times in order to get it down entirely. Clarafina wipes the spillage from her mouth before putting the cork back in the satchel and swinging it back over her shoulder again. 'Next time you speak to me like that, I'll shoot them off,' she says before holding her hand out to Bees.

Bees takes a hold of Clarafina's hand and lets her help him pull himself up. Once he is standing again, Clarafina wipes the dirt from his clothes. 'Good as new,' she says with a smile. When she looks up at him, she sees a look in his eyes which she has never seen before, on him or anyone else for that matter and her smile fades even quicker than what it came and the muscles in her face settle in an unusually comfortable manner, due to how angry she thinks Bees to be, in a position of strain. 'Brother?' She asks and says at the same time.

Bees stares blankly at her.

'Brother?' Comes her response again.

Bees puts his hands on Clarafina's arms. 'Thank you, Clarafina,' he says. 'I deserved that.'

Clarafina stands staring at Bees' swollen' face. 'I know you did, brother,' says Clarafina. 'That's why I did it.'

Bees smiles. 'I know you did sister, that is why I thanked you for it,' Bees says unfounded as all the manners in which he can exact revenge on Clarafina for what she did to him in front of the workers 'runs' through his mind while Clarafina thinks about how long she'll have to sleep with one eye open after she realises that Bees did not in fact forgive her for kicking him as he would want her to believe.

Bees slaps Clarafina on her arm. 'Now let's get the festivities started, why don't we?' Clarafina points out that in the quickly fading sunlight it will be hard for them to see what they are doing and says that she is going to turn on a spotlight on the roof. While she is making her way to the house Bees takes two pieces of rope out of his back pocket. 'Will you please position yourself over the rock, Marana?' Marana bends down and gets on her hands and knees and leans over the rock.

The moment Bees bends down to tie her hands she begins to cry. Bees holds her face up to him. 'Now, now Marana…' he says. 'There is no need for tears, they are a complete waste in this situation and will only make things worse.'

Marana wipes the tears from her face. Bees reaches into his shirt pocket and takes out a pipe and a small bag of tobacco which he stuffs the chamber of the pipe very snugly with, he prefers to put the tobacco in the pipe that way because it makes it harder to pull on and he enjoys smoking in a manner as that as well as because it makes him feel that he is saving tobacco by it being so tightly pressed against itself in the pipes chamber, before clenching it between his teeth and using a match to light the tobacco before pulling on the tail end of the pipe in quick succession in order to get the tobacco burning in a continuous manner.

After spending a couple of quiet seconds smoking, he takes the pipe out from between his teeth and holds it securely in one hand. 'Do not tell my sister that I said this but I thank you for taking those grapes today, Marana, because if you didn't none of this would have been possible.' Bees holds the pipe to his mouth. 'So, here's to you,' he says before pulling on the pipe again.

When he is done, he puts it gently down on the ground and takes one of the two pieces of rope and begins to tie Marana's wrists together. When he is done, he picks up the pipe and looks at Petrus. 'You know what, Petrus…' He begins. 'You should think about taking this up, at your age and having lived the life you did, you deserve something like this?'

Bees holds the other piece of rope out in front of him. 'Petrus,' he says. 'Take this rope and tie Marana's feet, will you, and make sure that you do not wrap it around her ankles very tightly, make it so that if she tries long and hard enough that she will be able to get loose.' Petrus takes a couple of steps toward Bees and takes the rope from him and bends down and begins to tie Marana's feet together. While he is busy doing so, Bees gets up. 'You being the man of intelligence that you are, Petrus, might find yourself wondering why I told you to tie Marana's feet in the manner in which I did,' he says. 'Are you wondering that, Petrus?'

Petrus nods. 'Good,' says Bees. 'The reason for that is to make it so that she thinks she can escape, to give her just a little bit of hope in the immediate time but also to cover that hope entirely all the while that it is there with the fact that even if she does manage to get free and off farm grounds that she will never be able to get far enough away from me to find freedom.'

Bees takes a drag from his pipe. 'Just to make it more exciting,' he says. 'For all of us, because don't tell me you find not the littlest bit of pleasure from knowing that it is not you bent over this rock.'

Petrus finishes tying Marana's feet and gets up. Bees walks around Marana and tugs on the piece of rope by her feet a couple of times to make sure that it is to his liking. 'Not bad, old man,' he says and makes his way to the front of Marana again. Once there he stands with his arms folded in front of his chest with his head tilted down toward Marana's, falling from it the occasional tear. 'What a pretty picture this is, my things,' he says. 'Is it not a pretty picture?' He turns to the workers asking.

The workers nod in various different fashions of the kind rigid. Bees laughs.

'Very good,' he says. 'Just what I wanted to hear.' He puts the sole of his shoe on Marana's shoulder. 'Let this be a lesson to you all, if your hands become that of a thief's and you take for yourself what you may not; what is about to happen to Marana here will happen to you too, also, if after tonight you do what Marana did today you will get punished twice as bad as she is going to.'

Bees hears Clarafina calling out to him from the middle of the lawn. When he turns around, he sees her running toward him and the workers in the brightening light from the spotlight as it warms up with a bag slung over her shoulder. After quite some time when she reaches him, she is very out of breath and panting heavily and quite loudly. Bees tells her to be quiet. Clarafina puts her finger over her mouth and tries to keep her breathing under control. When she is finished catching her breath, she takes out of the leather bag over her shoulder an old wooden plank.

'What is this?' Bees asks.

'It's a plank, dummy.'

'Where did you get it?'

'From a box in a cupboard up in Granddad's old room,' Clarafina answers. 'It's what him and the boys used back in the day in the olden days to discipline the workers.'

Bees stares back at his sister with a heavy frown 'jammed' onto his forehead. 'Are you joking, Clarafina?'

Clarafina returns a somewhat similar look. 'About what?'

'About how you just spoke.'

'How did I just speak?'

'Simply put, you spoke wrong, sister,' Bees replies.

Clarafina puts her hands on her hips. 'And how did I speak wrong?' She asks.

'You said "back in the day in the olden days", you don't talk like that.'

'Like how do you talk then?'

'There you go again.'

Clarafina frowns, 'There I go again with what?'

'*Like* how do you talk,' Bees retorts. 'You don't say it like that.'

'How do you say it then?'

'Definitely not how you said it,' Bees says. 'And you certainly don't say "back in the day in the olden days", it's a double negative or something like that…'

'Look who's talking now… "A double negative or something like that", that sounds not very good as well.'

Bees shakes his head. 'Not very good, another one.' He says and sighs a deep and long sigh. 'Whether it's a double negative or a triple negative or whatever the right thing to call it may be is, you sure don't say "back in the day in the olden days".'

'How do you say it then?'

'You say, "back in the day", "long ago", "in the olden days", "in the past", "way back when" and so on,' he answers. 'Not how you said it.'

'I said basically everything you just said, so how wrong can it be?'

'That's the very point, sister,' says Bees. 'You're only supposed to say one.'

Clarafina puts one finger over her lips and thinks for a bit. 'I'll try and remember for next time,' she says.

'Do more than *try,* Clarafina,' says Bees. 'Make *sure* that you do, you are a Brungle and that means you have a standard to uphold so put more effort into doing so,' Bees 'barks' with pride. 'So, you were saying about the plank?'

Clarafina looks down at the plank she is holding, having completely forgotten about what they were busy with before they veered off into argument. 'Oh yes, the plank, I thought I should bring you this so you can save some time, just one hit with it should be enough.'

Bees takes the plank from Clarafina and runs the tips of his fingers over the top part of it. 'The nails?' Bees asks. 'Where they there when you found the plank or is it a touch you put there yourself?'

'Look at how rusty they are, brother,' says Clarafina. 'Obviously I did not put them there.'

Bees nods, with much exaggerating an effort. 'Very good, I was just testing you...' he says. 'I know you did not put them there, of course you didn't, you wouldn't have had the time to.

'Nice try, Bees, but I know that you weren't just testing me.'

Bees fills with strong dismay. 'Watch it, Clarafina,' he says. 'Don't get too comfortable with me, I might be your brother but I am still the man in this relationship and that counts for much more than being born on the same day.'

'Sorry.'

Bees nods. 'Thank you,' he says. 'And I forgive you.' He brings the plank closer to him. 'I wonder how old this is?' He murmurs.

'Probably older than me and you.'

'I know that.'

'Put together.'

Bees nods, 'Could be.' He turns to Clarafina, 'And you brought me this why you say?'

'To save you some time,' she says. 'You only have to hit her one time with this because it has nails obviously, that way you can get it over with quickly and Marana does not have to get as hurt were you to have to hit her many times with something else.'

Bees looks the plank over some more. 'I see where you are coming from but might she not get hurt even more than if I were to hit her many times with a plank that has no nails sticking out of it?' He asks. 'Sure, I only have to hit her once,

19

maybe twice, but because there are nails sticking out of this plank here, I think she might get hurt even more than with a normal plank.'

Clarafina looks at Bees with strenuous inquisitiveness. 'Why do you say that?'

'Because if I hit her with the plank that I have here, be that even once, she will surely bleed, but if I hit her with a plank without nails in it, and if I do so even more than once, she might only get a mild skin burn or something.'

Clarafina scratches the inside of her ear. 'I see what you mean,' she says somewhat disappointed with herself.

Bees moves his head noddingly along. 'A nice thought nonetheless sister.' he says. 'I'm sure Marana appreciates it.'

'I was more thinking that it will be good for you.'

'And right you were,' says Bees. 'It will be good for me, for sure it will, thank you, Clarafina.'

'My pleasure, brother.'

Bees rests the plank on his shoulder. 'How about we get to work then.' He says and positions himself behind Marana. 'Let's say a prayer before we begin…' He turns to the workers. 'Will everyone please close their eyes.' The workers and Clarafina and Bees, even Marana, closes their eyes. 'Dear Lord, we ask you tonight to let this beating be above all else a lesson to the sinner and not so much a punishment, may she, as well as her fellow brethren take away from this not anger and resentment but the knowledge that no one is above what you say is right and wrong, and most importantly that me and Clarafina is only doing what *You* want us to, Ahmen.'

Bees and Clarafina and Marana and the workers open their eyes. 'Now that that is over with, I want to say to those of you who get squeamish at the sight of blood that you may want to close your eyes,' Bees says. 'To those who are not of the kind I was just talking about, *you* may want to keep your eyes open because you are about to see something quite spectacular if I may, especially if you like the colour red.' Bees lifts the plank from off his shoulder. 'Choose quickly what you want to do because it's getting late.'

He leans forward and tears open the back of Marana's shirt before getting back to a standing position and holding the plank over his head. 'On the count of three then shall we…. One…' Out of nowhere Bees brings the plank down on Marana's back. She screams and bursts out in tears. After a couple of seconds, when to Bees it seems that Marana has in some way calmed down, even though she in no way has, her breathing having become so quick and successive following each other that she is almost unable to breath at all thus making it *seem* only to Bees that she is more quiet than from the moment she got hit with the plank. Bees puts his hand on Marana's head. 'That's a good Marana, calm down, it wasn't that bad now, was it?' He says with a drawn-out smirk on his face and lifts the plank from Marana's back, when he does so he is quite taken aback by how uncomfortable it makes him feel to feel the vibrations that the nails leaving her flesh makes as he does so and when he looks down, he feels even more uncomfortable when he sees about half a dozen holes in her back slowly 'sprouting' small amounts of blood.

Clarafina frowns. 'Dammit brother that went a bit more worse than I expected,' she says.

Bees shakes his head. '"Worse," Clarafina, just "worse",' says Bees. 'Not "more worse", I am tired of your dumb dictation embarrassing me, for both our sakes as well as the sake of the farm and business you should learn to speak proper,' Bees continues. 'And I say this with love, big sister.'

'You better not be calling me fat again.'

'There you go again, thinking I'm calling you fat when I'm not,' Bees says. 'It's because you can't speak properly that you make mistakes like this.'

'Oh, zip it already,' Clarafina 'chirps.'

'All I care about is if you're calling me fat, if you're not doing that, we don't have a problem.'

Bees nods. 'If you say so, big sister.'

Back in the house on the second floor, in the bedroom across from the top of the staircase, one of five bedrooms and one of four of the five of them which are the same size, the other being about twice as big as the latter four, a young boy is asleep in his bed. The boy is Klipp, he is 12 years old and Bees and Clarafina's nephew. His mother, Luinia, is Bees and Clarafina's older sister by eight years, the first child of Klipp's grandparents, Leena and Tember, on the Brungle side of the family.

Luinia left the Brungle farm at the age of 17, a couple of months after she met Klipp's father. His name was Kemmon, he was the only child of a moderately wealthy farmer family from a farming district half a dozen kilometres away from 'Golden Heart' who came there with his parents one day who were hoping to buy one of the farms in the district that was busy going bankrupt. While

Klipp's father's parents were talking to the owners of the farm they intended to buy, they allowed him to walk around a vicinity of town near the restaurant they were discussing the purchase of the farm at.

That same day, Luinia was in town with *her* parents and Bees and Clarafina to shop for groceries for the month and clothes for the coming year. When they had everything they needed, Luinia's parents told her that she has to take Bees and Clarafina for a walk around town so that they might be able to spend the rest of the afternoon alone having an early dinner at one of the fancier restaurants in town, like they did once a month when they came there to buy groceries.

Happy to oblige Luinia took Bees and Clarafina, who at that time was called Clarafinalia, her first name given to her at birth, she later shortened it to 'Clarafina' after her mother had passed away, who really loved the name 'Clarafinalia' because it was her grandmother's name who she loved dearly and who passed away when she was only eight years old, because she thought 'Clarafinalia' sounded too pretentious and 'Clara' sounded too common, to the town's ice cream bar, 'The Snow Globe,' for an afternoon treat.

This is where she met Kemmon. He was sitting at the table behind her and offered to buy Clarafina a bowl of ice cream because he saw that her and Bees were eating from the same bowl, this because Bees and Clarafina, as well Luinia, were not allowed ice cream or any other type of dessert or sweet for that matter because their father believed that denying them those things would make them more appreciative of things that cost money.

After declining his offer, Kemmon complimented Luinia on the dress she was wearing that day and that led to them starting a conversation and Kemmon joining them at their table and spending the next two hours buying Bees and Clarafina two bowls of ice cream each, so that he might get to know Luinia better. When Luinia had to take her brother and sister back to the restaurant to meet up with their parents, Kemmon went with and spent almost a quarter of an hour persuading Luinia's parents to allow him to come and visit her on the Brungle farm during the week that he is in Golden Heart with *his* parents.

For the next five days that Kemmon was there, he made his parents drive him to the Brungle farm in the mornings and leave him there until late in the afternoon so that he might be able to spend time with Luinia. During their five days together, Luinia and Kemmon talked much about how they would be able to continue their relationship once he left Golden Heart, exhausting many an option, Kemmon going as far as to ask Luinia's parents for her hand in marriage, a

22

request that was denied them immediately by Grandpa Brungle, they decided that when it came time for him to leave she would go with him, she would tell her parents that Kemmon would come and pick her up on his last night in Golden Heart so that she can go have dinner with him at a restaurant in town before he left to go back home the next day.

When the night came, she packed a suitcase filled with as much of her clothes as she was able to fit inside, all the money that she had in a jewellery box on her bedside table, which was a white, porcelain swan, as well as her favourite necklace which was the first thing that she had ever bought for herself with money she saved up from birthdays and various menial jobs done around the house. The last thing she did before she dropped her suitcase out of her bedroom window was to write her mother and Bees and Clarafina a letter each.

Before she went downstairs to meet Kemmon, she put both letters under Clarafina's pillow in her and Bees' bedroom, kissed them goodbye, hugged her mother and blew her father a kiss, before she walked out of the front door and down the porch steps, got into Kemmon's parents' car, waved her family a goodbye for whatever reason it may mean and asked Kemmon to stop the car just outside of the gate where he got out and walked to get Luinia's suitcase behind the house before putting the suitcase on the back seat and driving off into the night never to return to the farm again.

That same night when Luinia's mother put Bees and Clarafina to bed she found the letter that Luinia had left for her and her two younger children. The letter said that she loved the three of them very much but that the future she pictured for herself were she to stay on the farm paled in comparison to the future she would have, if she would go and live with Kemmon and his parents on their farm. She left no information on how her mother and brother and sister would be able to get into contact with her would they want to but wrote that she would do just that as soon as she was settled and when she thought that her overbearing father and grandfather might have come to terms with, as she herself put it into words, the betrayal that her leaving would have brought upon them.

After Bees and Clarafina had fallen asleep, Clarafina with much effort on her mother's part after she came to the realisation that she might only see her sister again when she is much older, Leema went to her bedroom and by Luinia's instructions burnt both letters so that her husband and father-in-law would never be able to read it.

Less than a year after Luinia left the Brungle farm, she and Kemmon got married on his parents' farm during a small ceremony of no more than 20 people and 18 years after that Klipp, their first and only child, was born. It took so long for them to have a child, because initially they planned on not having any children, during the early years of their marriage as well as for the remainder of their time together.

After 18 years of marriage though, Luinia fell pregnant, and how she felt after getting the news she would never have expected, mostly because she never thought about it, but at 36 years of age when she found out that she was pregnant she was happier than she was ever before in her life and eight months, three weeks and seven days after that Klipp, who a little more than a minute after he took his first breath was given the name Kedmin, was born.

Klipp grew up in conditions very different from the conditions his mother grew up in and led a very quiet, cared-for, busy and happy life. Things continued along those lines until he was 12 years old, when out for a picnic with his parents one afternoon on a mountain while on vacation somewhere Klipp saw them meet their end on the walk back down. After spending almost a week going from hospital to police station, waiting for someone to tell him where he would be spending the remainder of his young life, Bees and Clarafina, who Klipp had only heard of up to that point, came to pick him up to take him to the farm almost a week's drive from where they came.

Klipp cried for three days when he woke up in the hospital of the place him and his parents were on vacation in an orphan after another family who were up in the mountains found him unconscious next to the edge of the mountain. When he finally stopped crying one of the nurses asked him whether he wanted to see his parents' bodies, an offer he declined, thinking to himself that nothing good can come from it did he choose to do so also, when it came time to go to the funeral a month after the accident Klipp asked if he could stay behind on the farm while Bees and Clarafina attended the funeral.

Klipp opens his eyes and lays still and quiet in his bed for a while, wondering to himself if he had simply woken up from a break in his sleep cycle or if he did so from a scream, he thinks himself to have heard. Then he hears Clarafina yelling and gets out of bed and walks to one of two windows in his room that looks out over the lawn, to see if he might be able to see anything he just heard.

When he sticks his head out of the window, he realises that the spotlight is turned on, something that has only happened about three or four times since he came to the farm due to money constraints, and a feeling of unease rushes over him. In the distance by the cabin, he is able to make out with the help of the light from the spotlight, Bees and Clarafina standing over something while the workers stand behind them. He reaches for the handle of one of the drawers in a desk standing between the two windows and takes out a pair of binoculars he brought with him to the farm.

When he holds the binoculars to his eyes, he adjusts the focus thereof to get as clear a picture of what he is looking at as he can and sees that what he was unable to make out is Marana bent over a slab of rock with the shirt from her back torn open and blood gushing from various small holes in her back. Standing next to Marana is Clarafina who has her arms out and holding onto Bees who has the plank held halfway over his head.

'What are you doing, brother?' Clarafina asks.

Bees drops the plank down by his side. 'What does it look like I'm doing?' He pulls himself from Clarafina's grip.

'I'm not sure, that's why I'm asking.'

'I'm giving Marana what she deserves,' says Bees angrily. 'What other thing can I be doing besides that?'

'I was under the impression that she was only going to get hit once, that is why I brought you the plank.'

'Well then, you were wrong.'

Clarafina grabs a hold of her wine satchel. 'How many times do you plan on hitting her?'

'However, many times I feel that I want to.'

Clarafina shakes her head. 'Sorry, not going to happen, for my sake, for yours and for the sake of the farm,' she says. 'Marana is probably, no matter how old she is, she the best worker we have, if she dies, things here will do downhill fast. She is already sick to the point of stealing from us and punishing her more will surely send her to an early grave, and that we cannot have, so put down the plank, let the others deal with her and let's go have a drink so we can go to bed, please, so they can go to bed too, because they have to work in the morning.'

Bees looks at Clarafina suspiciously, 'What's to say you're just not making all this up to help Marana?'

Clarafina gestures to the farm around them. 'Everything you see here.'

Bees nods. 'Okay, enough it is then,' he says. 'But let me ever find out that you did this to help her...' Bees looks down at Marana. 'You will be lying here alongside her on that same day.'

Clarafina nods. 'Not a problem.'

Bees nods. 'Very well then my things,' he says. 'Lucky for you this is all you're going to get.' Bees steps to a side, 'Make sure you clean all this up before you go to bed and we'll see you back here tomorrow morning.' Bees drops the plank on the ground and makes his way to the house while Clarafina follows.

Chapter 2

It is the Thursday night after the night of the plank beatings and the night that looms between the farmhouse and the cabin is quiet, calm and comfortably cold, the only thing that pierces the night's quiet is the fast-paced creaking from various crickets that have come to find their way to the farm, crickets that have been making themselves known for so long now that their songs are as much a part of the farm's quiet than they are of the noise. Across the entirety of the lawn as well as the surrounding farm grounds lies a thick mist, almost knee high, moving slowly in and out of and around itself and that makes the farm look ghostly abandoned, especially under the light from the spotlight, as it looks almost never so often when a night like this one comes around.

The spotlight Bees and Clarafina decided to turn on nightly after the workers went to bed, to deter them from running away should they want to do so after the plank beatings because it was the first time since Bees and Clarafina took over the farm that blood was spilled on it due to punishment to break the darkness, the night will lend them if they decide to do so.

Inside of the cabin, the 12 workers and their five children are sitting on a carpet on the floor in the part of the cabin between the kitchen and the adults' sleeping quarters with Petrus reading to them from the Bible. 'What is being expressed here is the importance of the concept of faith and how easily it is and can be overlooked and misunderstood because of the circumstances in which it is 'born'. It is because of these circumstances that the concept is hard to apply to one's life, and at the same time, the same circumstances that allow for the true meaning of the concept to be grasped which in turn makes it so that it can be applied to one's life, in the manner in which it should.' Petrus closes the Bible.

The workers along with Petrus get up and those with children go to the children's sleeping quarters on the opposite end of the cabin to put their children to bed. There are five children along with Klipp who live on the farm, they are Mueno and Thomvul, ten and nine years old in that order, both boys, whose

27

parents are Kolos and Xhema, Gheska, also a boy, who is four years and the son of Varieda and Rommu and two girls, Finta and Scara who are both 12 years old, Finta being the daughter of Lavette and Koga and Scara, Petrus' daughter.

While the workers with children are busy putting them to bed, Marana comes over to Petrus, just as Scara is tucking herself into bed. 'Do you want me to fill the jug with wine while you say goodnight to my daughter?'

Petrus laughs. 'That will be nice, Marana, I'll tell her you say goodnight.'

'Make sure you do that,' says Marana before she goes to the kitchen and leaves Petrus to say goodnight to Scara. Petrus makes his way over to where Scara sleeps and kneels down next to her bed. 'Goodnight my angel, sleep tight.'

'Goodnight daddy,' says Scara. 'I will.'

Scara is Petrus and his late wife, Simla's only child, although they were never married, who was working on the farm already when he came to live there. She has hazel skin and thick, black curly hair down to her shoulders, brown eyes on an unusually round but pretty face and is quite short for her age, unlike Finta who is tall and petite and who's hair is in braids with skin quite a bit darker than Scara's and eyes green. Simla passed away in her sleep after spending almost four hours holding and talking to Scara after she was born, telling her entire life story up until that very moment when she gave her the name Scara.

Before she put Scara in her crib to get some rest, she said that if for some or other unkind and cruel reason she does not wake up again, seeing as she began to feel ill an hour or so after Scara was born that she is very much appreciative of the chance she had to hold and talk to her for as long as she did and even more than that, that she was able to give her the name Scara, a thing she had wanted to do ever since she was six years old and thought that all she wanted out of life was to have a husband who would love her to her dying day and with which she would be able to raise four children and that Petrus was more than she could ever have imagined just that.

Petrus kisses Scara goodnight before she pulls her blanket up to just under her chin, so much so that the top end of the blanket gets 'scrunched' almost four folds underneath it and he makes his way out of the cabin to the table outside in front of two windows in the side of the cabin where the children's' sleeping quarters are. Before Petrus walks out of the cabin, he bumps into Marana having stepped inside again.

'Where are you off to?' Petrus asks.

'I don't feel too good, I think I'm going to lay down.'

'Is it your back?'

Marana nods, 'A little bit.'

'Do you mind if I take a look?'

'Sure.' Marana turns around. When Petrus looks at the back of Marana's nightgown, he sees that blood and puss has started to seep through the bandages over her wound as well as her nightgown.

'How does it look?'

'Not too good,' says Petrus. 'How does it feel?'

'It's itchy, almost in a bubbly manner if I can put it that way.'

'Do you mind if I have a look at the wounds?'

'Sure.'

Petrus unties the back of Marana's nightgown and parts it to the sides before gently pulling off the bandages covering her wounds.

'What do you see?'

'It doesn't look like it's healing properly.'

'That explains a lot.'

'I wouldn't be that calm about it if I were you,' says Petrus. 'It seems to have gotten worse from yesterday.'

'What do you suppose we do?'

'I think I should take your temperature.'

'Okay, I have my medicine box by my bed.'

Petrus and Marana make their way over to Marana's bed where she takes a medicine box out from a small bedside stand by her bed and takes out from it a small cloth and a thermometer.

'How long does it usually take for this to work?'

'About half a minute.'

Marana nods and puts the thermometer under her tongue. After a while, Petrus motions at the thermometer. 'You can take it out now,' he says.

Marana takes the thermometer out from under her tongue. 'That was a lot quicker than you said it would be.' Marana gives the thermometer to Petrus.

'Your temperature is very high.' Petrus takes a closer look at the thermometer.

'What does it say?'

'A hundred and two degrees.'

'That's not very good.'

'I think we should put new bandages on the wound before you go to bed and then see what it looks like first thing in the morning, if it isn't better by then were going to have to ask for help from Bees and Clarafina.'

'Let's hope it's better by tomorrow then.'

'Where are the bandages?' Petrus asks.

'The bigger ones are in the bottom cupboard in the kitchen,' says Marana. 'Our side of the kitchen.'

Petrus makes his way to the kitchen and takes out a medicine box quite a bit bigger than the one they are currently using, from a cupboard on which the workers chop fruits and vegetables and also prepare meats along with other things and brings it over to Marana.

When the new bandage is covering the wound, Petrus puts the medicine box back in the cupboard and walks back over to Marana. 'If you have trouble falling asleep come find me,' he says, 'I have a couple of pills which might be able to help with that.'

Marana's eyes widen. 'Really?'

Petrus nods.

'Which you got where?'

'I got them from somewhere,' says Petrus. 'They're very old so their potency might have worn off a little but they still might do the trick.'

Marana nods. 'I'll be sure to do that, thank you.'

'You know where to find me.'

Marana walks to her bed and slowly positions herself on her stomach.

Petrus sits down at the table outside and picks up the vat of wine and fills his cup with it. While he is busy doing so three of the male workers, Kolos, Dwendo and Koga, take out pipes from their pockets carved by Petrus, from sticks of bamboo found in a small dam on a part of the farm a few feet higher than and right next to the ground on which the cabin and house is. They begin to stuff their pipes with tobacco from a large bag of it shared between the three of them, them and Petrus being the only of the workers who smoke, Petrus less frequently so, and light a match which they pass between the three of them to light the tobacco with. For a while, the workers sit and talk and drink and talk and drink some more.

Kolos and Dwendo are brothers and are 45 and 47 years old, they came to the farm the same time Petrus did when they were only seven and nine years old, originally Grandpa Brungle wanted workers at least ten years older than that but when he heard how old they were in comparison to their size and stature he immediately ordered them to be thrown into the trailer on the back of his truck. Both brothers stand at about six foot seven tall with no more than an inch of difference in height between the two of them, while Petrus stands four inches shorter than that and Lavette, the tallest of all the women, stands another shorter four inches than Petrus.

Lavette is 57 years old and came to the farm with Petrus the day they got taken from their home. She has a thick head of black frizzy hair that stands out in many directions and is starting to grey in certain areas and green eyes like her daughter and unlike her husband Koga, who has brown eyes, so dark that they appear almost black if looked at from certain conservative distances, and a piercing through the centre of her nose and lip.

Kolos finishes his cup of wine, the first out of all the workers to do so, as it happens almost every night that they drink around the table, which is four times a week. When it is not Kolos who finishes the first cup of wine it is always Koga, and every so often Dwendo, but mostly the race to finish the first cup is always between Kolos and Koga. Ever since Kolos decided one night to see how quickly he can drink a cup of wine, which happened the very first night that the workers were allowed alcohol on the farm, which was nine years after Petrus and Kolos and the rest of the workers who came there in the trailer on the back of Grandpa Brungle's truck, it became somewhat of a staple to see who between Kolos, Dwendo and Koga could finish their first cup of wine the quickest.

At first they drank as fast as they could and finished each of their cups in a matter of seconds but after a while they felt that by doing so they only wasted the wine that was given to them not very often and in amounts much smaller than they would have liked so they decided to try and pay as little attention as possible to the thought of the competition that had taken stance between them on the nights that they drank while still, and hopefully only when the first of the three of them—whoever that might be on whichever night it may—put down their cup, acknowledging it in as calm and unaware a manner as possible.

One time, Marana made a point of it to be the first one to finish her cup of wine, something she managed to do with more ease than she thought she would and also something that made her feel much more queasy than she was prepared to feel after undertaking this particular endeavour, and slammed her cup down in the centre of the table to make however strong a point of it that she could that she was finished.

To her surprise, no one noticed her doing so because at that point, the competition had fallen faint to a degree that only Marana still took notice of the first cup of wine to be put down on the table in the competitive and forceful manner that she grew accustomed to, a manner that had become very subdued from how it used to be between Kolos, Koga and Dwendo, but still different enough in comparison to the rest of the workers for her to take notice thereof.

Kolos is married to Xhema, a woman who came to the farm five years after him to fill a shortage of workers due to Grandpa Brungle's over-eager trigger finger. When Xhema arrived, just like Dwendo, she was only nine years old and was brought there as the only child in the second group of workers that were taken and brought to the farm with the idea of increasing the 'productivity' of Kolos and Dwendo by using Xhema as 'bait' by telling them that whichever one of them did the most work each week would get to spend an hour with her every Sunday; as a means of getting to know her and to hopefully win her affection if they so wanted.

Grandpa Brungle made it almost impossible for Kolos and Dwendo to have any contact with Xhema during the first six days of the week by threatening them with punishments as well as by placing various constraints on their daily lives to foster the need for company between them, beyond that which is normal in an attempt to make them want to work harder even than what they would have from solely having Xhema on the grounds.

During the first week that Xhema came to the farm, Kolos laid awake in bed for an hour every night until everyone fell asleep before sneaking out of the cabin to fill a bag in which the workers put their grapes from the baskets they filled while working in the vineyard, to make sure that he would have at least half a bag more grapes than Dwendo, every time they finished working. The first Sunday of the first week that Xhema lived on the farm, her and Kolos spent an hour together that afternoon having a picnic behind the cabin and when they were finished, she never spent another designated hour with either of them seeing as all she wanted to do after spending time with Kolos was to spend more time with him.

Over the coming weeks, Kolos and Xhema made many a plan on many different an occasion to see each other, other than the time they would be allowed to every Sunday, and every night after that when the rest of the workers were asleep, they snuck out of the cabin to see each other. Things continued along those lines for almost a decade until Grandpa Brungle passed away and Kolos and Xhema had their first child, a boy named Mueno, a year after which they had their second child, another boy named Thomvul.

After spending a couple of quiet minutes drinking, Nleeclo, a five foot four tall woman with grey braids down to the small of her back, a pot belly that barely hangs over a leather string tied around her hips to keep the decades old coat she is wearing from falling open, who is 60 years old, the oldest of all the women on the farm, with glasses of which the black rimming has been glued together so many times that it appears almost white, asks, 'Petrus, do you think because of how things are going backward with the farm that Bees and Clarafina are going to become more strict, like how Bees beat Marana with the plank the other night?'

Petrus puts down his cup of wine and thinks, then he turns to Nleeclo. 'It pains me to say that I think you are right Nleeclo,' he says. 'Things will probably start to get worse around here as time goes on for us.' He takes a hold of his cup of wine, made from a dark wood that has over all the years been stained seemingly a very dark red as the wine has slowly seeped through the cracks in the wood and moves it around in circles. 'I *can* say with surety though that it will never be as bad as it was with mister Clifford seeing as Miss Clarafina is here.'

'But Bees is the one that pulls the strings,' says Nleeclo. 'He doesn't listen to what Clarafina has to say about anything, and he definitely won't listen to her if she tells him anything along the lines of how he should go about disciplining us.'

'Having her around will help a lot in terms of keeping Bees calm, which in turn will make it easier for us to do so too,' says Petrus.

'But look at what happened with Marana? She got beat so bad that she fell ill?'

Petrus slowly drops his head. 'You might be right. Bees might be a bigger problem than I thought.'

'I think that Bees might turn out to be worse than mister Clifford was as time goes on, he is quite a bit younger than mister Clifford was still and if things keep going the way they are with the farm, he will probably just keep getting worse, in a couple of years' time he might have nothing better to do than kill us for his pure pleasure, not to mention hurt us in ways that he did Marana the other night just for the fun of it. He has always been like that, one to want to impose bad things, be they verbal or physical on others, especially our kind, he is a very sad man, Petrus, as you yourself said, you can see it in his eyes every day, and men like that, if they don't have the will to deal with what plagues them they turn to wanting… Needing to make others feel as they do, and that is how Bees has been ever since we've known him, and as of the other night what he is most probably going to continue to be, and worse and worse so, as time goes on.'

Petrus shakes his head. 'That is not a thought that I want to entertain.'

'Well, I cannot help but think around those lines after seeing what he did to Marana,' says Nleeclo. 'And if it wasn't for Miss Clarafina, he might have done even worse, mister Clifford, as bad as he was, never hurt us in the way that Bees did Marana, and that is something to think about.'

'How can you say that? Mister Clifford killed us without a shred of remorse?'

'I would rather be dead than go through what Bees was going to do to Marana the other night.'

'What do you mean what he was going to do?'

'Who knows how many times he would have hit her with that thing if Miss Clarafina didn't stop him.'

'Don't say that, Nleeclo,' Petrus responds.

'I have to, and what happened the other night might only be the start of what Bees might do or be able to do to us as time goes on, it might end up being torture after a while, and the way he was talking about what he did to Marana, if you take the time to think about it, it was like he was talking about drinking a bottle of brandy, I haven't seen him as excited as he was that night in all of the years that I've known him.'

'It *was* very disturbing.'

'That it was Petrus, and I strongly think that it's going to get a lot worse.'

Petrus looks at Nleeclo, his eyes set back far in his head. 'Why do you say that?'

'Because that's how he is, he is violent by nature, just like his grandfather, and he needs to be that way to appease whatever woes trouble him, be that whatever it may, most probably the state of the farm,' Nleeclo says. 'I began to think the other night that he is going to take every opportunity that from now on slowly but surely he'll be able to get to exact punishment on us in whatever way will make up for however bad he is feeling that day, I think with how things are with the farm at the moment, worse than they have ever been, he is going to need to indulge his violent tendencies more and more as time goes on, I'll even go as far as to say that if he doesn't he might become suicidal, because surely, he doesn't have much to live for seeing as how he is with us other than imposing his ill feelings on us in whatever way he deems fit on whatever occasion.'

'It's inevitable that things around here are going to get worse, Nleeclo, they always have, but we'll survive, we always have, as long as we keep Miss Clarafina as happy as we can that will hopefully help in keeping Bees so too,' says Petrus. 'Besides that, all we can do is hope for the best.'

Nleeclo nods. 'I surely hope you are right, Petrus.'

Monday afternoon after the workers had finished their work the sun had already begun its descent behind the mountain to turn the sky from a light blue to a muddy orange. A soft breeze accompanied the setting sun and moved the strands of wheat slowly from side to side, as if a quaint melody was being whistled up through the ground, which only they could hear.

On this particular night, the air is cold to the point of feeling like it almost pierces the skin when in contact with it and there is not a cloud in the sky which makes the presence of the air feel eerily out of place and almost unwelcome.

The workers are all in the cabin, busy preparing dinner for the night, a dinner that they look forward to from the moment they open their eyes every Monday morning before they start work right up to the time that they finish work on Friday because Friday nights is the only night a week they are allowed meat, red and white, very seldom white seeing as how hard it is to acquire white meat because of the distance of any part of the country to the ocean, which makes the Friday night dinner quite a bit more special than any of those before and after it.

Other than being given meat on Friday nights, the workers also get a ration of potatoes large enough to last almost three days if used sparingly on Wednesdays, potatoes which they hold off on eating until Friday night to make the dinner a bit more special.

On the opposite side of the farm, Bees and Clarafina have just started drinking for the night so that they might get as drunk as possible so that they might wake up as late and sleep as long as possible the following morning seeing as it is their day off and they have little to nothing to do with the workers then. Much like the workers do with the potatoes, Bees, unlike Clarafina, who only drinks red wine and the occasional beer or brandy or whiskey when an occasion might call for it, holds off on drinking any hard liquor during the week in order to better enjoy his time, come Friday.

35

Bees is sitting on the front porch on one of two unusually large rocking chairs, rocking chairs which usually stand under a small round wooden table there but one of which Bees moved closer to the set of steps that leads down from the porch to the driveway like he does most Friday nights so that he might be able to make use of more open space while drinking as well as to be able to put his feet up on the railing because he is very against the idea of making use of the table to do so.

In the living room, Clarafina is sitting by the fireplace in the wall adjacent to the garage on one of four couches, couches that no more than a half hour ago formed a barrier around the fireplace but which do so no more because much like Bees. Clarafina moved the smallest couch, one which seats only one person and which stands next to a couch which forms the part of the barrier closest to the window that looks out onto the porch to make it seemingly the same size as the opposing couch, in front of the fireplace to better 'wrap' herself in the warmth from the fire along with a blue plastic crate which held the last bottle of red wine a while ago turned upside down in front of the couch, so that she too might be able to put her feet up.

Other than having made a fire, Clarafina is also listening to her favourite record, a record that used to be her mother's favourite when Clarafina was younger and which soon after hearing it for the first time became Clarafina's favourite too as to help 'break' the Friday night quiet that looms a little bit heavier than any other night before it, unlike Bees who very much values the quiet time he gets to spend by himself and even though Clarafina is sitting but a few feet away from where Bees is he always tells her to keep the windows and door closed while she is in the living room listening to music, something which does not bother her very much because even before she is able to put on the record that Bees so enjoys complaining about.

He is already intoxicated to the point of talking or singing to himself and finds the music quite relaxing after yelling for Clarafina to turn up the volume on the record player one night after she opened the window a little to let out the smoke that gathers in the living room from using the fireplace for a certain period of time.

Back by the cabin, Petrus is making his way down the small hill that leads to the crop fields at the bottom of the farm. When he reaches the bottom of the hill, he walks over to the gate that cordons off the wheat field and takes out of his coat a set of keys which opens every lock and door on the entire farm. Petrus opens the lock and loosens the chain around the gate and steps inside before doing the opposite from the opposing side before putting the set of keys back in one of two pockets inside of his coat.

The workers managed to get a copy of this set of keys of which there is only one when Kolos, one Friday night almost four years ago, took the set of keys from off the railing while Bees was sleeping. Kolos' youngest son, Thomvul, fell ill one night with the flu and when his condition worsened over the coming 24 hours, Kolos and Petrus went to Bees to ask for medicine. Bees denied them the medicine and told them that it would do the boy good if he got over the cold himself by simply staying in bed and drinking lots of water and if it happened that he did not get better by doing so it meant that he was not of his father's loin and was not worthy to live and work on the farm.

Thomvul kept getting worse and the following night when Bees fell asleep after drinking on the porch, Kolos ran over to him and took the set of keys, with which he climbed up the back of the house and through the bathroom window to open the medicine cabinet to get the medicine his son needed, from off the railing. After giving Thomvul the medicine and putting the remainder thereof in the medicine cabinet in the cabin, Kolos, Dwendo and Koga went to the edge of the mountain to gather pieces of rock of a hard, clay-like substance which when put in water for about half an hour turns soft to a degree that it can be used like pottery clay.

The three of them brought back some of this rock and made small squares from it after soaking it in a bucket of water in which they then pressed each of the keys on the ring on which they 'reside' into the squares of clay and let them harden, while Dwendo ran the set of keys back over to house and put back down on the railing where Kolos found them.

When Bees and Clarafina took the workers into town one Sunday afternoon for their quarter yearly visit; Kolos and Dwendo took the imprints they made of the keys to the town locksmith to have copies made after which they hid the keys in a part of the cupboard underneath the kitchen sink where they remain to this day.

After Petrus had locked the gate behind him, he starts down the ground parting that separates each of the three fields of crop from each other to walk around the wheat field. As he begins his stroll, he reaches into his coat pocket and takes out a Bible with a brown leather binding over it, a Bible which first belonged to Petrus' great-great-grandfather and that was given to him *by his* grandmother a present after him and his three brothers, their father and two of his friends had built the church on the settling on which they, and much later Petrus, grew up on.

The binding around it was made by Petrus' grandmother in order to keep it from any further damage after she spotted a small tear on the front cover and today whenever someone removes the binding for whatever reason they always comment on how unusual it is to see in how much better of a condition the cover is to that of the binding. Most of the pages have started to turn a very light shade of brown and are stained here and there with small dark brown spots, as if very small droplets of coffee had been spilled on the pages over the years.

How these spots came to be there Petrus has no idea because neither Petrus nor his father or anyone that had the book before them drank coffee, nor did they eat or drink anything for that matter while reading from it thus, to appease his curiosity, Petrus told himself that the appearance of the small brown spots are simply what happens to a chemically whitened page over a certain period of time.

Other than the appearance of the Bible, the other most noticeable thing about it is the many notes and summaries scribbled over most of the empty spaces on most of the pages. When Petrus first got the Bible, most of the notes and scribbles were already there and from then on, until now only a very small percentage thereof are what he did himself. When Petrus began to read from the Bible, the notes and scribbles were what helped him better understand the passages and verses inside and what helped spark his interest in religion and made him, more so than his father and grandfather being it, want to become a priest.

Five minutes into his walk, which usually takes 30 to 40 minutes, Petrus hears a strong rustling of leaves near the edge of the field. After coming to a standstill and listening to hear if it might come again, when it does, Petrus closes his Bible and slowly and carefully parts the first row of strands of wheat and steps inside the field. As he does so, the rustling stops. Petrus stops too.

When the rustling starts up again, taking much care to make as little noise as possible and to not damage the strands of wheat while doing so, he keeps walking forward and when he reaches the area where he hears the commotion coming from the parts another row of wheat and when he looks past it, he sees an empty patch of soil on which Klipp is playing with a couple of his toy trucks on a 'bed' of various hills, ramps and ditches that he made there. When Petrus sees Klipp he breathes a sigh of relief, it is this sigh that catches Klipp's attention and he looks up to see where it might be coming from.

'Petrus?' Klipp says startled.

'Hello young man,' says Petrus. 'I did not think that when I set out to relieve my curiosity about the disturbance that peaked it, I would come across you.'

Klipp's eyes widen. 'Sorry.'

'That's okay,' says Petrus. 'It's probably one of the better things I could have come to find all things considered.'

Klipp smiles, 'Thank you.'

'What are you doing out here so late?'

'Just playing.'

'I can see that,' says Petrus. 'Do your aunt and uncle know that you're out here?'

'They know that I'm outside...' Klipp says. 'But they don't know that I'm here.'

'Are you allowed to be here?'

'I don't know.'

'How did you get in here?'

'I climbed over the gate.'

Petrus' eyes widen. 'It's a very high gate,' he says. 'Do you think it's safe to be doing that?'

'I used to climb up a tree at my old house all the time that was even higher than the gate.'

The day that Klipp came to the Brungle farm, after unpacking his belongings in his new room, Bees told him that it would be a good idea to explore the farm with him for an hour or two before they have dinner. As Klipp drove into the farm that day he sat in the back of his aunt and uncle's truck clutching his suitcase as if it were something that enabled him to breath. The first thing that caught his attention was the trees by the dam on the side of the farm where the cabin is, the first thing he noticed about them was the long and stringy leaves that hung about 15 to 20 meters long from the tree's branches covered from top to bottom in petals of a colour that Klipp had not yet seen.

Walking across the lawn from the house with Bees, Klipp looked over to where he saw the trees and looking at them for the second time the petals appeared a different colour to what they did when he first saw them. It was by the dam late that afternoon when Klipp first saw Petrus. The first thing he noticed about him was how tall he was. So tall was Petrus to Klipp that he appeared almost like an apparition to him, especially in the way that his long and slender body, dressed in a black coat that reaches down to just below his knees with a black hat around which is tied a brown leather string, tilted forward so the rim covers the top part of his eyes, and even more so because of his all black attire and how it made him appear almost shadow-like under the greying sky and made him look like the vigilante detective from Klipp's favourite TV show and which intrigued him in manners both uneasy and calming.

The other thing he noticed, other than his storied appearance, what was he was busy doing. When Klipp first saw him, he was standing next to a sawn-off tree stump with a piece of material in one hand and reaching into an open book out from half of which was cut a hole taking out if it a small rock.

What Petrus did after, surprised Klipp because it was something he thought he would never see happen in person in his lifetime. Petrus placed the rock in the centre of the piece of material and pressed the ends thereof together with his forefinger and thumb after which he brought it back over his shoulder and flung it forward to fling the rock from it toward a large bag filled with sand on top of an overturned crate.

Petrus keeps rocks in one of his two Bibles along with the piece of material because the workers on the Brungle farm, as well as the other farms in the district and those surrounding are not allowed to have on their person any object that resembled or could be used as a weapon, that being because of the way in which the farmers treated their workers made thoughts of escape and retaliation very common, thus the farmers went to the governing body of their particular district, a group of people which consisted of the five most prosperous families from each district that had ownership over the better part of the stores, restaurants and hotels in town, a group of which the last Brungle that was a part of.

It was Grandpa Brungle, to address the situation of the steadily increasing sense of rebellion amongst the workers which the governing bodies responded to by drawing up a petition which the farmers made their workers sign by means of threats of violence and even death which stated that were a weapon or object to be considered a weapon of any kind by whoever found it on the person of a worker may be put to death.

Petrus has been slinging rocks for as long as he can remember. He started doing so because his father told him how important it is for a person of colour, especially under the conditions in which they lived at the time and still live to this day, to be adept at using objects not conventionally considered a weapon to protect themselves. In all of his 72 years, the only things that Petrus had killed with his sling was four birds which ate the crops on the settling on which he grew up.

'Still be careful,' says Petrus. 'If you fall you could really hurt yourself.'

'I tie a rope around me and tie it to the gate in case something bad happens.' Klipp reaches behind him and holds up a rope.

Petrus laughs, 'Still be careful though.'

Klipp looks away for a moment and then back at Petrus and holds out his hand. 'I'm Klipp,' he says. 'Nice to meet you.'

Petrus shakes his hand. 'Petrus...' he says, 'And likewise.'

Klipp gets up and wipes the dirt from the back of his pants. 'What are you doing here?' He asks.

'I come here to walk around the field every now and then to read.'

'What do you read?'

'The Bible.'

'Really? What's that like?'

'Sometimes nice, sometimes not so nice.'

'Oh.'

'But the not so nice ones become nice after a while.'

'How?'

'If you're a nice enough person, you'll be able to interpret them the way in which they were intended and they'll become nice.'

'And if you're not?'

Petrus pauses. 'Then they stay not nice.'

'Oh.'

'But usually they become nice, you have to be a very bad person for them to stay not so.'

'Is it difficult to read the Bible?'

'If you don't find it difficult to read then "no".'

Klipp nods.

'Have you read the Bible before?'

Klipp shakes his head. 'No.'

'Can you read?'

'Not very good.'

'How old are you?'

'Twelve.'

'Would you like to learn?'

'Very much.'

'If you want to you can walk with me around here once or twice a week and I can teach you.'

'What days?'

'If you want to, we can start now?' Petrus asks. 'If you don't have to be back at the house any time soon?'

'I have to be back before it's dark.'

Petrus looks up at the sky, 'Looks like we have time then.'

'Okay, I'm going to leave my trucks here and get them when we come back.'

'Good, let's go then.'

Petrus and Klipp make their way through the strands of wheat and onto the pathway and begin walking down the width of the field. After walking quietly for a while, Klipp asks, 'How long have you been walking around here?'

'Almost twenty years now.'

'That's a very long time.'

'Not really when you get to be my age.'

'How old are you?'

'Half a century and ten years older than you are.'

'What does century mean?'

'It's another way of saying 100 years,' says Petrus. 'So, if I were to say that someone is a century old, I would be saying that they are 100 years old.'

'Why don't you just say they are 100 years old?'

'That is a good question, and one I do not have an answer to unfortunately.'

Klipp counts on his fingers. 'So, you are… 72 then?'

Petrus nods. 'And a couple of months, but 72 in general terms yes.'

'That must not be very nice.'

'It's not that bad, my life is pretty much the same as it was the day I came here, it only takes me a little bit longer to get things done than it did back then.'

'So, it just takes longer to do things?'

'For the most part.'

'That doesn't sound too bad.'

'It isn't.' Petrus turns to Klipp, 'What did you think it was like?'

'I don't know, not very nice.'

'It's a little easier than you might think, hopefully you'll get to be that age one day.'

Klipp shakes his head, 'I don't think I want to be that old.'

'Why do you say that?'

'It doesn't look very nice.'

Petrus laughs. 'It can't look that bad?'

'Not bad, just not nice.'

'You'll probably think different when you're that old.'

'Do you still think that girls look nice when they are as old as you are?'

'What do you mean?'

'If you thought that when you were twelve a girl was pretty and you married her do you still think she is pretty when she is as old as you are?'

'Not as pretty as she was when she was in her twenties but still pretty in many ways.'

'But do you think a pretty girl that is 20 is prettier than the girl that you married?'

'You do think that, yes.'

'That's not very nice.'

'Maybe…' says Petrus. 'But it's not as bad as you might think.'

'Why?'

'When you get to be my age things like how pretty a girl is matters a little bit less than it did when you were younger.'

'But do you still want to kiss a pretty girl that is 20?'

Petrus pauses, 'You do, yes.'

'How does that work?'

'When you are as old as I am and you see a pretty girl of 20 the idea of hugging and kissing her is much less than it was when you were that age because physically speaking, in most cases, the attraction that there needs to be between two people to want to do that is not there so it becomes of less importance to you.'

'But if you walk around with your wife and she sees a man that she likes and she wants to kiss him because you say you would want to kiss a pretty girl, also that is not really right?'

'Not in the way that you currently think about it.'

'How else can you think about it?'

'All I can say is that as you get older you start to think differently about things as to how you thought about them before,' says Petrus. 'The best thing to do is to not worry about it because at your age, the thing you are talking about very rarely happens, if it can happen at all that is.'

'I hope you are right about that.'

'Me too.'

After turning the corner and starting down the length of the field Klipp asks, 'What were you doing all the time when you didn't walk around the field?'

'Probably helping make dinner.'

'Why did you stop doing that?'

'About twenty years ago before the fence was here your uncle asked me to patrol the fields every day to make sure that everything is in order.'

'Did he only want you to walk *around* the cornfield?'

'Yes.'

'What if there was a mole in the middle of the field?'

'I think what he had in mind was to see if I would be able to hear anything should something, around the edges or in the middle, and also if it be the case to stop an animal from getting to the crops.'

'Did you ever see anything?'

Petrus shakes his head. 'No,' he says. 'After the fences were put up, I still kept walking so to speak, more so out of habit seeing as how accustomed to the quiet I became.' Petrus cups one hand over the side of his mouth. 'Your uncle does not know that I still walk here, so I would appreciate it if you did not mention it to him.'

Klipp shakes his head. 'Your secret is safe with me.'

'Thank you.'

'Because I know that you won't do anything wrong.'

Petrus laughs. 'Thanks again,' he says. 'Funny thing is, your uncle never told me to stop doing my rounds, I just assumed that he wanted me to.'

'That's good,' says Klipp. 'Maybe he didn't want you to stop walking then?'

'No, if that were the case, he would have given me a set of keys.'

Klipp thinks for a bit. 'How did you get in here then?'

'There is a copy of the set of keys that your uncle has in the cabin.'

'Why?'

'There came a day that we realised that it would be imperative to have a set of keys for the sake of our livelihood and survival.'

Klipp's eyes widen. 'Oh,' he says. 'If I could I would take the keys and give them to you too.'

Petrus laughs, surprisingly intrigued by the almost rebellious confidence with which Klipp responds. 'Thank your young man, I appreciate that,' he says. 'Almost more so than I am thankful that it would not be necessary for you to not have to do that.'

Petrus and Klipp walk quietly for a while. 'Petrus?'

'Yes?'

'Why do you think my uncle asked you to walk around the field if you were the oldest of all the workers?'

'I'm not sure,' says Petrus. 'I would like to think it has something to do with him trusting me enough to oversee something that is important to him.'

'Did you ask him if someone can walk with you?'

'I did.'

Klipp looks at Petrus. 'Did he say 'no'?'

'He said he preferred it if I would do it alone.'

'Aren't you very tired when you are finished?' Klipp asks. 'Shouldn't you get a break before the other workers because you are the oldest?'

'Maybe, but when I am done here, I get to go back to the cabin to have dinner, something which I never really enjoyed to help making,' says Petrus. 'And the rest of the workers don't get a break either because it takes quite a lot of effort and time to prepare it for so many people, I actually prefer it this way, 'every cloud' as they say.'

Klipp looks up at Petrus, 'What does that mean?'

'Every cloud?'

Klipp nods, 'Yes.'

'It means that for everything bad there is something good beyond it, the bad thing being the cloud and the good the silver lining.'

'That's very good.'

Petrus nods.

'So, the bad thing is that you must walk around here when you are finished working and the good thing is that you don't have to help make dinner?'

'Exactly.'

'I don't think every cloud has a silver lining.'

'How so?'

'I don't know, some things are just bad.'

'That might be true, but if you look long and hard enough you might find that every cloud does come to have one…' says Petrus. 'It's just a matter of having the patience to find it.'

'How do you do that?'

'Take the clouds in the sky for example, on days when the sun is out at least once a day every, or most of the clouds, have silver linings. If we are the sun and the bad things in our lives are the clouds; if we have the patience the sun will eventually shine its light on each cloud in such a way as for its silver lining to appear.'

'I see,' says Klipp. 'I can even say what the silver lining is with me, do you want to hear it?'

'Sure.'

'The cloud is my life here on the farm now…' Klipp says. 'Because I don't like it here very much, my parents are not here, my dog was not allowed to come with me, all my friends are not here and my uncle never lets me do anything that I want to and only talks to me when he wants me to do something for him, so that is definitely the cloud,' he says. 'But if it wasn't for the farm and my aunt and uncle, I would not have a place to live and I would be an orphan, I would also still have to go to school which is not very nice, so that is all the silver lining.'

'That is a very difficult silver lining to find for someone your age and in your position, you should be proud of yourself.'

'Thank you.'

Petrus puts his hand on Klipp's shoulder. 'And as your friend, I want you to know that.'

Not wanting to come across overenthusiastic and thank Petrus again, but at the same time wanting to continue along the lines of which the conversation is currently going Klipp gathers his thoughts with the hope of finding something to talk about which Petrus might find interesting. 'Petrus?' Klipp asks somewhat reluctantly.

'Yes.'

'Why do you always have your Bible with you?'

'I just like to read from it,' says Petrus. 'And every so often when I have something troublesome on my mind it comes in handy.'

'How?'

'If I have a question, I cannot seem to find an answer to or I have a problem of some sort I read from the Bible to help with that.'

'How many pages do you read?'

'No pages, you just read a passage.'

'What passage?'

'Whichever passage you open the book on.'

Klipp frowns. 'What you do is you hold the book closed in front of you and with your eyes closed keep in mind whatever question or problem you might have for a while, asking for an answer to the question or a solution to the problem, then you open the book at random and open your eyes and the first passage you see is the passage you have to read from to find help with what you need it with.'

'Does it always work?'

'That depends on the person, but to some extent it does.'

'I think I'm going to try it when I get back to my room.'

'Good, just be sure to not ask questions of a mostly material or superficial nature?'

Klipp nods. 'What do you mean?'

'If you want to know what or how many presents you are going to get for Christmas you shouldn't do it.'

'What if I want to know how old I will be when I can do what I want to and go away from here?'

'That you can ask, or better yet you can ask if you'll ever start to like it here.'

'Okay…' Klipp says. 'But I much more want to know the other one.'

'Ask both, and if you find an answer you like to the question, I proposed you ask you'll find an answer more important than any of the questions you might come to have for a long time to come.'

Klipp nods. 'I'll ask both.'

Petrus and Klipp turn the second corner and start up the width of the field. 'Why don't you and the other workers go to church on Sundays?'

'Because none of the churches allow black people to attend.'

'I thought it was something like that.'

'And it would also be very expensive for your aunt and uncle to take all of us there every Sunday with two trucks.'

'Why would they say that about people at a church?' Klipp asks. 'If a church is a good place why can some people not go there?'

'That's a good question, another one I do not have an answer to unfortunately,' says Petrus. 'But it doesn't matter much because every Sunday morning before breakfast we have our own church service right here behind the cabin.'

Klipp looks at Petrus wide-eyed. 'Really?'

Petrus nods. 'Yes.'

'Who does the service?'

'I do.'

'Because you're the oldest?'

'That, and because I used to be a priest at the church where I grew up.'

'What?'

Petrus nods. 'For six years before I came to live here.'

'Wow, how old were you when you started to become a priest?'

'I gave my first sermon when I was 26.'

'That's very old, do you have to be that old to be a priest?'

'Not necessarily, some people become priests at 23 or 24 but most do at around 25.'

'I thought you can become a priest when you're 18...' Klipp says. 'You finish school when you're sixteen so I thought you can become one after that almost.'

'Maybe in some places you can, but it took a little bit longer for me and the other people I know who were priests where I lived.'

'How old were you when you finished school?'

'17.'

'What did you do all the time after that until you were a priest?'

'Most people did different jobs around the area; some went away for a couple of years to go live and work in other parts of the country and the world while others stayed where we lived to start families and learn as much about the priesthood as they could before they became priests.'

'Did you like it?'

'Very much.'

'Why did you come live here then?'

'That's a long story and one I will tell you when we have more time.'

'We still have time left?'

'It's not the sun I am referring to…' Petrus points at the gate coming up a couple of yards in front of them. Klipp looks over to where Petrus is pointing. 'Oh.'

'I can tell you another time when we see each other again.'

'When do you think that will be?'

'When would you like it to be?'

'Tomorrow maybe?'

Petrus laughs, 'I don't usually walk on the weekends seeing as I'm busy with other things but I'll be back here again Monday night after work if you would like to join me then?'

'What day is it today?'

'Friday.'

Klipp counts on his fingers. 'Okay,' he says. 'I'll wait for you by the gate, what time?'

'Six o'clock.'

'I'll be here.'

'Very good…' says Petrus. 'See you soon then.'

'I won't ask so many questions again then.'

'I would actually prefer it that you do.'

Klipp nods excited. 'Okay…' he says. 'I'll think of good questions to ask then the weekend.'

'Looking forward to it.'

Petrus and Klipp reach the gate. 'Don't forget your trucks.'

'Oh,' Klipp says startled. 'Will you wait here while I go get them?'

'Sure.'

Klipp starts down the edge of the wheat field to the clearing where Petrus found him playing. A couple of steps there he yells and falls on the ground while grabbing his left foot. Petrus makes his way over to Klipp and bends down by his side. 'What happened?'

'I stepped in something.'

Petrus looks down at the ground and sees a sharp rock sticking out from it next to where Klipp is sitting. 'I think I see the culprit; do you mind if I take a look at your foot?'

'Sure.' Klipp holds his foot out to Petrus. Petrus takes a hold of his ankle and looks at the sole of his shoe and sees a fairly large cut in it. 'It went through the sole so the damage might be quite bad depending on how deep into your foot the edge of the rock went, do you think it's bleeding?'

Klipp nods, his eyes clenched closed. 'It feels like it is.'

'I think we should take a look at your foot to better see what we're dealing with.'

'Okay.' Klipp unties his shoelace, takes off his shoe and looks at the underside of his foot. He looks at Petrus. 'It's bleeding.' He holds his foot out to Petrus.

Petrus nods. 'I thought it would be.'

'What should we do?'

'I think you should take your sock off so we can tie something over the wound, I have a handkerchief we can use.'

'Okay.' Klipp tucks his thumbs into the top part of his sock and pulls it over his foot. Petrus takes the handkerchief out of his coat pocket and ties it around Klipp's foot at the bottom of his ankle to lessen the bleeding. 'Is that too tight?'

Klipp shakes his head, 'No.'

'I didn't put it over the cut for hygiene purposes but it should lessen the bleeding quite a bit until we get to the cabin.'

Klipp nods. 'Okay.'

'Does it still hurt a lot?'

'Not as much as it did a little bit ago.'

'Good, do you think you can manage to limp your way to the cabin?'

'I can try.'

'Why don't you try and get up and see.'

'Okay.' Klipp pushes himself off the ground and gets on his feet again, 'lightly' hopping on one leg to keep from having to put his wounded foot on the ground.

'Try putting a bit of pressure on the other foot and walking.'

Klipp puts his wounded foot gently on the ground and with the other pushes himself off it while at the same time stabilising himself with the other and moves forward.

'How was that?'

'Not bad.'

'Can you do it again?'

Klipp does the same thing and moves himself forward a little bit more.

'Good, now do you think you can do that all the way to the cabin?'

'I think so.'

'Good, let's go then.'

'What about my trucks?'

'I'll go fetch them.' Petrus walks through the strands of wheat to the small clearing where he found Klipp playing and picks up his trucks and makes his way back to Klipp. 'If you start to feel tired or dizzy in any way let me know, I can carry you the rest of the way.'

Klipp nods. 'Okay.'

'Off we go then.' Petrus and Klipp start toward the gate. Petrus takes his set of keys out of his coat pocket, opens the lock and removes the chain from around the gate. He pushes it open and waits for Klipp to walk out before closing the gate and putting the chain around it again and pushes the lock closed.

'I think this is as far as you should go for now, this hill is pretty steep.'

'I think I can do it; I can put my foot down a little bit so it doesn't hurt too much.'

Petrus nods. 'Okay then, give it a try.'

Klipp puts his wounded foot down on the ground at the bottom of the hill and pushes himself off the ground again with the other, this time with more force than before, and lands on the very bottom of the hill's rise.

'How was that?'

'Not too bad.'

'Do you think you can make it all the way up?'

'I think so.'

'Give it another try then; I'll walk with you.'

Klipp makes it up the hill a little bit higher and keeps doing so, each time with more effort and slower than the time before with Petrus walking by his side until he reaches the top of the hill. Klipp stops to catch his breath, Petrus does the same. 'Good, do you want to rest here for a bit or can you make it to the cabin now?'

'I can go now I think.'

'Let's go then.' Petrus and Klipp make their way to the cabin. Once they reach it, where the lawn meets the ground where the row of trees is planted, that separate the part of the farm on which the house and cabin is from the hill leading down to the crop fields, they make their way over to the table and benches outside of the cabin. Once there, Klipp sits down. Petrus puts his trucks down on the table next to him. 'If you don't know already young man, this is home.'

Klipp nods. 'Oh.'

'I'm going to go inside to get the medicine box.'

'Okay.'

Petrus goes inside the cabin. Soon after he opens the door the smell and heat from the steam that 'travelled' from the kitchen to him from the food cooking in their pots 'wraps' him in warmth and invigorates his sense of taste reminding him of the times that he too had special dinners with his parents before he came to the farm. Sitting there he finds himself unable to do so any longer and gets off the table and walks over to the cabin window on the left side of the cabin closest to the door and peers over the bottom of the window sill and into the cabin. The first thing he notices is the assembly line of people in the kitchen in the centre of the cabin.

In the very centre of the kitchen in the back, under two small open windows are two stoves, one of which is an old wood burning stove which used to be in the house when Grandpa Brungle was Klipp's age and the other an electric stove and oven combination which was also in the house until a year or two before Klipp came to the farm and was given to the workers when Clarafina won a set of five kitchen appliances.

One of which was a stove and oven pairing so expensive and modern in terms of model that if you were to look for it in the biggest of the two home appliance stores in town as well as those surrounding you would not be able to find it or anything very similar to it, thus there was no more need for the previous stove and oven pairing as well as place for it, and even more than that the new one did not fit aesthetically with the set of kitchen appliances that Clarafina won in a competition one night after seeing a toll free number across the television screen one Saturday night, while she was drinking and watching TV and decided to call it humorously in an attempt to convince herself that there is such a thing as luck, were she to win.

Next to that, on the side of the cabin into which Klipp is peering is a counter that consists of two parts that meet at a 90-degree angle. The first and smallest part is the length of either one of the stoves and the height thereof too and built into the back wall of the cabin next to the wood burning stove, the second is three times the length of the third but the same height and 'runs' along the entirety of the kitchen wall adjacent to the children's sleeping quarters.

On the opposing side of the kitchen is another counter a little bit longer than the one it opposes into which two sinks are built and on which is standing a kettle and two trays with various kitchen utensils. Underneath the counter are two, two door cupboards in which is kept various pots, pans and cooking and baking trays of different sizes, some of which are so old they were there the day Petrus came to the farm.

The second thing that catches his attention is the amount of people huddled together in the kitchen busy cooking and the way in which they stand together in groups in different parts of the kitchen, each group of people moving to and fro from one another as they work through their various duties in the process of preparing dinner.

Two of the women, Xhema and Varieda, along with their husbands Kolos and Rommu, are standing in front of the stoves watching over the food as it cooks in three different pots while the rest of the men, Koga, Dwendo, Jesta and Lumeo are standing over the counter with the sinks rinsing and peeling vegetables.

The two girls, Scara and Finta, along with Lavette an Nleeclo, are standing over the opposite counter, the shoulders of Scara barely 'peeking' out over the top of the counter, are busy cutting onions, tomatoes, potatoes, olives, avocados and another ingredients of which Klipp is not sure and throwing everything into two big glass bowls along with large handfuls of lettuce. Both Scara and Finta are smiling in a way, which to Klipp seems like they are having three hours of playtime which is allotted to him every day for the first five days of the week instead of being busy with what to Klipp is considered a chore back at the house. The three boys are standing around the dining table between the kitchen and the front door, cutting open oranges and squeezing the juice into two wooden jugs with the help of forks.

Klipp turns his head back to the two girls by the counter with Varieda and Nleeclo, one of the girls waves at him. Her hair is done in pigtails and she is wearing a white dress that consists of two parts, the first being the top part that sits around her very loosely almost like a T-shirt and comes down to just above her belly button and has short sleeves unlike Klipp would have thought to see when looking at the dress as a whole, the second being the skirt which is pulled up and over her belly button and reaches down in frills to just above her knees.

The most noticeable thing about the dress, other than its unique make, is the pictures of cupcakes, dolls and needle and thread pairings drawn on the skirt with black, purple and yellow marker. The pictures are faded to the degree that would imply that the dress should look the same but instead it looks as vibrant and new as Klipp would have expected it to look the very day the dress was bought or made seeing as how it looks so much different to any of the dresses Klipp had seen up until that point.

The girl is Scara and when Klipp realises that she is waving at him, the only thing he is able to do is wave back awkwardly while biting the bottom part of his lip to keep from smiling in a manner which he thinks would make him look uncomfortable.

At that moment he feels a hand on his shoulder and when he turns around, he sees Petrus standing behind him with the medicine box. 'There you are,' says Petrus as he leans over and peers through the window. 'The results are much different to what it looks.'

Klipp smiles. 'I think it looks nice.'

'Maybe one day if you are allowed you can join us.'

'That will be nice.'

'Good, we'll make a note of it.' Petrus holds the box out to Klipp. 'Here it is, everything we need to make you feel good as new.'

They make their way over to the table and benches and Klipp gets on the table. 'That's a big box, what's all in there?'

'Almost an entire hospital.'

'A hospital for only not so bad things.'

Petrus laughs. 'There are some things in here that could heal a broken bone too if it would come to that.'

'Have you had to use any of those things yet?'

'Luckily not.' Petrus opens the box. 'Let's take another look at the cut.'

Klipp lifts up his foot. 'Looks like the bleeding stopped.'

'Maybe we should leave it then and let a scab form, I heard somewhere that, that is what it is, just dry blood.'

'Right you are, but I think it's best to clean it in case of an infection, the blood that will form the scab then will speed up the healing process and cause the cut to heal better.'

Klipp nods. 'Okay.'

Petrus takes the handkerchief off Klipp's foot and puts it next to him on the bench. He opens the medicine box and takes out a roll of gauze, a couple of pieces of cotton and a solution of disinfectant. He opens the bottle of disinfectant and pours a couple of drops thereof on a piece of cotton and begins to clean the wound with it. 'Good thing we decided to clean it, looks like there was some dirt on there after all.'

'That's good.'

Petrus pours more disinfectant on another piece of cotton. 'Just to make sure that we get all of it.' After cleaning the wound for a second time, he pats it dry with a third piece of cotton and takes out of the medicine box a small bottle of cream and a flat piece of wood about the length of a pencil. 'This is to help with the healing.' He dips the piece of wood in the cream. 'And also, to relieve throbbing might there be any.'

'Did you get all of this from my uncle?'

'The roll of gauze and cotton balls yes, but the rest we made ourselves from various plants and even insects found around the area.'

'Really?'

Petrus nods. 'Yes,' he says and begins to apply the cream to the cut.

'Who makes it?'

'Nleeclo, the lady with the red T-shirt who was helping Finta and my daughter.

'Oh.'

'She was here even before I was.'

'How old is she?'

'65.'

'That's almost as old as you are.'

'Almost.' Petrus cuts off a length of gauze from the roll and begins to wrap it around Klipp's foot.

'How old were you when you came here?'

'38.'

'That's a lot of birthdays here.'

Petrus laughs. 'Quite a bit, but birthdays start to matter a little bit less when you are as old as I was when I came here.'

'What do you mean?'

'Just that it's not so much a festivity after a while.'

'Do you not have birthdays?'

'You have them, but not every year, and when you do there's more food than sweets and cake, maybe a little bit less people and it's not as much fun as the birthdays you've probably had so far.'

'That doesn't sound too bad.'

Petrus laughs. 'All done.'

'I didn't even know you started yet.'

'That's because I'm very good at treating wounds,' says Petrus. 'How does it feel?'

'Almost like I never stepped on a rock anywhere.'

Petrus laughs. 'That's good to hear.' He puts everything back in the box and closes the lid.

'Thank you, Petrus.'

'My pleasure, do you think you'll be able to make it all the way back to the house?'

'Yes.'

'Then you better get going.'

'Okay.' Klipp gets off the table and back on the ground. 'I'll see you Monday then.'

'Looking forward to it.'

'Have a nice night.'

'You too.'

Klipp starts back toward the house as Petrus makes his way back inside the cabin with the medicine box.

Chapter 3

It is the first Saturday of the first month of the year 1905 on the Brungle farm. The air is warm and dry but the sky is cloudy and grey which lends to the morning an eerily improper feeling. The only thing that offsets the day is a couple of birds sitting on the barb-wired fence along the top part of the farm 'chirping' a tune very different from the morning's atmosphere. On the front porch around the small wooden table on the rocking chairs, of which there was then four, is sitting Bees, he is sitting facing the living room because Grandpa Brungle likes to look out over the lawn when sitting there, the soles of his shoes barely touching the floor beneath them, something that makes him feel very uncomfortable whenever he sits at the table, his dark brown hair patted down so flat on his head that it looks to have been drawn on with a brown marker wearing the same outfit that he has to wear for the first five days of every week which consists of a cream-coloured button down shirt with a collar and short sleeves with his name stitched with black thread into the top front part of the pocket over the left side of his chest; with dark brown corduroy pants that goes down to just above his knees that are held up by a pair of multi-coloured suspenders with black leather dress shoes, of which he has two pairs, unlike his shirt and pants of which he has five pairs and like his suspenders of which he again has two pairs, one multi-coloured and the other black, over grey socks pulled up to just below his knees, the shoes look almost exactly like the day he got them because by order of Grandpa Brungle he has to polish them every day before he puts them on.

Something he can choose to do before he goes to bed at night or in the mornings before he gets dressed, in front of him lies a dark brown fedora, similar to the colour of the pants he is wearing, with a very light brown binding around it which used to have a feather sticking out from underneath it, a feather that much to Bees' dismay, because he liked to imagine that it was a feather that he took from an Indian chief while playing 'Cowboys and Indians' on the lawn, he was told to get rid of because Grandpa Brungle felt that it took away from the sophistication that a hat as such lent.

The hat is probably Bees' favourite thing to wear but he is only allowed to wear it on Sundays to church and on certain occasions during the weekend, this particular weekend day Bees was told by Grandpa Brungle that he had to put on his usual outfit with the choice of the adage of the fedora; as Grandpa Brungle had something important to do that day and wanted to Bees to look as presentable as possible.

On the weekends, Bees is allowed to wear whatever he wants to which usually consists of a camouflage T-shirt and long black denim pants with a pair of black sneakers with green details on the side which he got as a birthday present from his mother and grandmother much to the dismay of his father and Grandpa Brungle who felt that, especially Grandpa Brungle, sneakers made Bees look middle-class as well as ruined the material aesthetics that he wanted those who bore the Brungle name to have when they were together, but who succumbed to the pleas of his wife and his daughter-in-law, when they offered to forgo their activities of knitting and crocheting for a month, in return for Bees getting to keep the sneakers.

The only thing Bees had no say over concerning his clothing whichever day of the week it was, was having to wear either one of his two pairs of suspenders or a black leather belt which his mother bought him after he complained about the discomfort of the suspenders to keep his pants above his belly button where Grandpa Brungle preferred it to be instead of just above his hips where Bees preferred it, Bees always chooses to wear the belt besides the times that Grandpa Brungle on certain occasions demands of him to wear his suspenders.

This upsets Grandpa Brungle quite a bit, who is of the thinking that belts are for people of a low class, having known this Bees would have chosen to wear the suspenders despite the discomfort because for all of his young life he wanted nothing more than to impress his grandfather and to make him proud in whichever way he might have been able to, something which he unfortunately never felt that he was able to do and in turn something which Grandpa Brungle felt the same about, both cases due to the fact that Grandpa Brungle consciously tried to make it near impossible, through whichever means it may have been for Bees or anyone for that matter to be able to impress him.

Other than Bees, also sitting at the table is his only two uncles, and Grandpa Brungle's two favourite sons, Murkel and Vista. Murkel and Vista are 42 and 41 years old in that order, both are taller than six foot two and are built like rugby players, having played it provincially in high school and still enjoying playing it every now and then on the lawn with their friends. Much like their nephew Murkel and Vista have on brown leather dress shoes over black socks pulled up to just below their knees, black and brown suspenders, so because Grandpa Brungle thinks suspenders of any other colour than single of the darker bland kind are too immature a look for men the age Murkel and Vista are, though if they were to be of completely free thinking minds both would choose to wear suspenders of the same nature as Bees' multi-coloured one and even go a step further by choosing ones with pictures on them.

Their shirts are white with collars and long sleeves of which Murkel's is rolled up and Vista's left down with the buttons not done up, the manner of wearing their clothes, especially their shirts as they do is quite bothersome to Grandpa Brungle because he thinks it too casual a manner of dress to garner the kind of respect he deems important but is unable to have them wear it and other items of clothing otherwise, because both threatened to leave the farm and go off on their own if he did not give them the freedom to wear at least to an extent they deemed appropriate for their age what and how they wanted to because if it were up to Grandpa Brungle he would have them dress very similar every day.

Funnily enough, they unintentionally get dressed in almost the same thing every day, funnier than that even, because it is not to his exact liking, Grandpa Brungle fails to notice responsively the similarities in the dress of his two favourite sons which on most occasions were he able to so he would have thought to be more appealing even than what he himself had in mind. Other than the way they dress, the only other very noticeable difference between the two of them is the colour of their hair and the way in which they wear it. Murkel has blonde hair and wears it back while Vista has black hair and has it parted in the middle.

The most talked about thing about their hair, especially considering their last name and the opinions that the people of Golden Heart and the districts surrounding have on things as such is the length of their hair, which they have been wearing down to their shoulders since the age of 25, which is the age at which Grandpa Brungle believes a boy to become a man. The way they wear their hair is a luxury, a way of referring to having it Grandpa Brungle embedded in them for nine years since they were sixteen and seventeen and saw their first film with a restriction on age, a western in which the main characters were a band of five outlaw cowboys all with hair down to below their shoulders, that Grandpa

Brungle allowed them to have after they one day threatened to leave the house when he told them when they turned 25 that under no circumstances will any male with his last name that lives under his roof be allowed to have hair long enough to cover even the top part of the ears.

That same day they packed their belongings and told Grandpa Brungle that they were going to live in an apartment in town of a girl that Vista met during a party, before they were able to leave, they came to an agreement that if they were to work an extra hour on Mondays, Wednesdays and Fridays that they were allowed to wear their hair in whatever way they wanted to and still live in the house.

The last person sitting around the table with Bees, Murkel and Vista is Grandpa Brungle. Grandpa Brungle was born Clifford Capshaw Brungle on 16 February 1857 after his great-great-grandfather Capshaw Coyton Brungle and *his* father Coyton Clifford Brungle. At 16 years old after high school, Grandpa Brungle joined the army to fight what he thought to be 'a pointless war' as he himself referred to it before joining the army and at the start of his time there. Back then, unlike his father and grandfather, Grandpa Brungle detested all things government and the only reason that he joined was because after high school every white male deemed competent by the government was obligated to do so.

After signing up, he was stationed at a place about a week's drive away from the Brungle farm by the name of Culver's Crossing, one of eight bases set up by the army and the second closest to where the enemy was thought to be hiding, and remained there for four years, his first two years as a Private, his third as a Lieutenant and his fourth as a Colonel, rankings which after a year of being 'brainwashed', another one of the many terms he used when referring to certain aspects of the army, he was proud of to a degree very unsettling. After his first year, where the men who were stationed, there were infamous for their ferocious appetite for violence shared amongst them, Grandpa Brungle received the nickname 'Cutthroat Clifford.'

Before receiving the nickname, one by which he came to define himself over his remaining years there, he was called 'Kind Clifford', a nickname which everyone else at the base liked to make fun of him for, especially the instructors which gave it to him, and one which he came to greatly abhor because of it and so to a degree became the very reason he came to be called otherwise.

At first, Grandpa Brungle liked the original nickname he was given because despite his strict upbringing, an upbringing he loathed throughout his entire childhood, he was somewhat a kind and gentle man and prided himself on being so and for that reason was proud of the nickname, after a couple of months though he could take no more of the ridicule his fellow 'brothers', as the men stationed at the bases referred to themselves, exposed him to and after breaking down crying in his bed one night he decided that as some sort of experiment to himself he would fight back as a means of trying prove to himself that men like him are, and does not necessarily have to be weaker than those who are fuelled by anger and violence.

The following morning, Grandpa Brungle and the rest of the men that were stationed at Culver's Crossing were called to the base closest to where the enemy was thought to be hiding, a base called Razor's Edge, named after the excessively decorated general, Hegfort 'Razor' Meek, who had been living there for 15 years after his third year in the army, to help out the men already stationed there after receiving an anonymous tip that the opposing side was approaching with ill intent.

This no one at Culver's Crossing expected because the initial threat was thought to be much smaller than what the tip made it out to be and this made all of the men who were stationed there feel very uneasy because they were told that the manpower there would be enough to 'take care' of what the initial threat was thought to be, despite this, Grandpa Brungle and the rest of the men at Culver's Crossing had no choice but to make the drive from there to the much smaller and more derelict Razor's Edge eight hours away against all of their best plights.

When occasionally talking with whoever about his time in the army, Grandpa Brungle always talks about the day him and his 'brothers' left Culver's Crossing for Razor's Edge as the darkest day in his life but also that if it wasn't for that day, he would not have met the people he remained friends with till the day that he passed.

The three years he spent at Razor's Edge is something which Grandpa Brungle refuses to talk about, even with those who were there with him. Many years after he returned home; while drinking at the house one night Grandpa Brungle let slip that during his time at Razor's Edge, he killed more than fifty people, and not all of them by the bullet, the proudest of *them* being the three people he killed by hand.

After that night he began to talk about it more freely as the reactions he got pleased him very much. Since then whenever people heard the stories over the years, whoever it might have been, the thing that upset them most was not that he killed three people by most primal of means but how he smiled, almost with childlike naiveté, whenever he told them and whenever people talked about it after amongst each other they always commented on how they were and are unable to find words to express how they felt while listening to him only saying that it felt like they weren't talking with Grandpa Brungle but with someone or something else entirely.

One thing they did know for sure was that while they were talking with him about his time in the army, they felt uncomfortable to the degree that they were unable to move. The story Grandpa Brungle most liked to tell about his time at Culver's Crossing and Razor's Edge was how he came to get the nickname 'Cutthroat Clifford' after a while when telling the story—even prefacing it with the phrase 'from Kind Clifford to Cutthroat Clifford.'

The story begins one Friday night during the weekly base parties that all of the men stationed at whichever base they were threw for each another. These parties had more drugs and alcohol at them that Grandpa Brungle thought he would ever see and were in his own words 'as good as it got', so good that, as he always joked, 'you didn't even need a woman.'

Later in life, when Grandpa Brungle became a father, he came to detest narcotics of any kind for he felt that being synonymous with them in any way was demeaning to him and his family name and status and the like meant more to him than anything else and became his drug of choice as such after he came back to Golden Heart.

That being said, whenever Grandpa Brungle told the story of that night much later in his life, he laughed more than anyone had ever seen him do in a certain span of time and they could tell with ease that the time he spent with his fellow 'brothers' at Razor's Edge, especially the times drinking and doing drugs were some of, if not the fondest of all his memories. That Friday night, Grandpa Brungle and the rest of the 'brothers' had one of their weekly parties, parties where the last of them to stay awake were allowed to take whatever was left of the drink and drugs to with as he pleased, be it to consume right after or share with the 'brothers' the next night or the coming week.

On that night, the night that would become the catalyst for Grandpa Brungle's favourite story to tell, he was the last one to stay awake. After everyone had either falling asleep or passed out Grandpa Brungle decided to stay up and finish what was left over of the alcohol and drugs as quickly as possible with the intent to see if he would be able to make it back to his bunk after and wake up the following morning in his bed.

He gathered whatever he could find and laid everything out on a small fold out table which consisted of half a bottle of 'Blood Thinner,' a banned liquor made from distilling corn together with stale peaches found only in one very small part of the country's many, that is considered to be the most dangerous and derelict, six lines of cocaine and two small tabs of a hallucinogenic what after that night came to be his favourite drug and of which he never knew the name.

To begin, he downed the bottle of 'Blood Thinner' and leaned back in his chair to wait for the burning sensation in his throat and stomach to subside after giving himself one minute to consume all six lines of cocaine, which he remembers very vividly he finished in just under half of that. As the cocaine took effect Grandpa Brungle started to feel very lightheaded, though in a way uplifting and got down on the ground and did as many push-ups as he could.

What he remembers most about doing the push-ups is how quickly he did them in succession and for how long he kept doing them before he stopped which is ironic because up until that night Grandpa Brungle had never done so much as one push-up in his life.

When he stopped doing the push-ups, he stood back up, not because he had too because he was tired, but because he started to become bored with it and instead of how he thought there would be a burning sensation in his arms they were tingling almost cold as if lots of tiny snowflakes were rapidly falling on and melting into his arms. When asked how many push-ups he was able to do he could not remember.

When he got back in the chair, he leaned over the table and pressed the ends of his first two fingers onto the two tabs of the hallucinogenic drug and put them on his tongue and waited a couple of seconds for them to dissipate, he then sat back in his chair and closed his eyes, soon after which he got the idea to carve a knife out of a piece of wood so he got up and walked into the nearby woods to look for a suited piece of wood.

After no more than a couple of minutes, he got on his hands and knees and started to crawl through the woods in an attempt to become closer to nature in order to more easily find a right piece of wood. While he was on the ground, he heard indistinct whispers which he immediately thought to be the enemy because the rest of the 'brothers' were all asleep back at the base.

Once it dawned on him that he might have to engage in combat and intense rush came over him, like he was injected with a shot of adrenalin and he got up and ran back to the base where he locked the doors to the sleeping quarters and the mess hall in the event that his 'brothers' did wake up from whatever might transpire they would be safe, one time while telling the story, he added that he did so because he wanted to be sure that he would, were he to have to, engage in combat alone, and picked up two automatic assault rifles and slung them over his shoulders, a hunting knife with which he 'cut' the cocaine earlier and slid it into the sheath around his ankle along with a knife that was already inside and a grenade.

But added that him having the grenade might have just been his imagination because having looked at the area where he said to have fought off the enemy the following morning, it did not appear that an explosive had been used, and made his way into the woods where the story abruptly comes to an end because after catching sight of an enemy, he went blank and the last thing he remembers about the night was doing push-ups.

As the months went on, Grandpa Brungle started to remember more about the night, everything from doing the push-ups to getting into bed, and happily so because the events of that night, did he remember them or not, became the cornerstone by which he came to define his new self after returning home. When all of the 'brothers' were up the following morning having breakfast outside of the cabin, one of them commented on the blood smears on Grandpa Brungle after which the events of the night came flooding back to him and the rest of the brothers made their way about five minutes into the woods where they found twelve bodies laid out next to each other in a small clearing.

Upon closer inspection three of the bodies, unlike the rest, who were almost torn apart by the number of bullets in them, had their throats slit. When all of the 12 bodies were disposed of, the 'brothers' hoisted Grandpa Brungle onto their shoulders and cheered to his victory before giving, or as he likes to put it, 'bestowing' upon him the nickname 'Cut Throat Clifford' at which point the story of how he came to be called it and what is without a doubt the proudest day of his life comes to an end.

On his deathbed, he added that it was only so because at that point and three years into the army he was so far removed from the person he was before joining the army, having seen and done many things he never thought he would or even thought he would be able to, he had stopped thinking about or even forgotten about any life beyond his life in and after the army.

After Grandpa Brungle had passed, the people of Camel's Neck didn't talk much about or in the manner he wanted them to about his time in and stories from the army, what they did talk about, and still talk about to this day, was what he was like when he came back from the army, that was the man the people of Camel's Neck came to know as 'The Reaper' because of his excessively violent nature and short temper, as one of the few older ladies who live alone in town and don't attend church services for reasons of good character say when talking about Grandpa Brungle after he came back from the army.

'The boy whose eyes were once filled with life and love is now filled with nothing', a couple of times she even ended her popular phrase by looking into said person's eyes and with a poking finger saying 'dot... dot... dot...' The day that Grandpa Brungle came back from the army, his parents and grandparents could see right away that he was much different from how he was before he left, ironically enough Grandpa Brungle's father and grandfather was very much like him as he got older, tyrannic and self-proclaimed leaders who had little to no regard for anyone but themselves, especially those of black skin colour, but the sight of seeing Grandpa Brungle as he was the day he came back to the farm scared even them.

For the first two years back, he refused to speak to anyone, not even the friends he made in the army, this greatly upset his mother and grandmother who were of a nature much softer than their husbands, they tried everything they could in trying to get him to speak from therapy to begging to bribing to get so much as a glimmer of hope that he might speak to them again.

His grandmother was the first one to give up trying, as his grandfather convinced her that the effort to help regain his loss for words was a lost cause. Soon after that his father too stopped trying, not only that he gave up on him completely, going as far as to ignore him completely on the rare occasion that Grandpa Brungle did speak to him out of spite, for how he acted toward him.

With both Grandpa Brungle's grandparents and father out of the picture it left only his mother by his side, something which he greatly appreciated, more than he was able to put into words but sadly never had the chance to do even when the day came that he wanted to, he was so distraught by what he saw and went through while in the army that he had a very hard time making peace with what became of him and therefore found it very hard to believe that anyone, especially his mother and grandmother could or even wanted to love him again.

Thus was the reason he chose to not speak, to test the ones he wanted acknowledgement and love from, and although he knew it was selfish and therefore wrong to act in the manner his need to know if someone could still love and care for him overpowered every bit of selflessness and good nature he had left in him and he decided to see how far he could push his mother after the rest of his family went about their normal lives again, so that he might come to again believe, whenever that may be, that she loved him in the way that she did before he left for the army, something which if chosen to come by an answer of the nature of which Grandpa Brungle was after in a manner as immature and irrational as he did to appease whatever made him come to think the opposite, especially in conditions pertaining directly to what he wants to convince himself of, might never come to be.

When it was just his mother left by his side she decided to try everything that she could think of for at least a year from making him his favourite food every day, sitting by his bedside for hours on end talking to him to try and get him to do the same and inviting over friends that he made while in the army, friends which treated her with very little respect as well as friends that Grandpa Brungle secretly despised for most of his later life but was afraid to tell them because the thought of not having them in his life was more unsettling even than not having his family so.

For almost eight months, she carried on in this manner, feeling herself wither away more and more each day and decided after that she would spend the remainder of the year doing the same before taking measures more drastic with the help of Grandpa Brungle's father, this he heard her say in a prayer one night before she went to bed which was when Grandpa Brungle made the choice to continue to not speak until year end after which he would accept his situation for what it was and go to his mother to tell her that he acted in the manner in which he had been for so long because he needed to be sure that she cared for him.

When four months had passed Grandpa Brungle woke up one morning and knocked on his parents' bedroom door, in which his mother had been sleeping alone for almost two years by then and sat down beside her to wake her up in the manner that she had him soon after he came back from the army, only unlike he did every morning when his mother came into his bedroom she did not wake up. After about a minute or so of trying to get her to wake up, he sat quietly by her bedside for a couple of minutes before walking back to his bedroom to sleep for the remainder of the day until the following morning to wake up in the same manner he did for many months before then, only this time not by choice.

These are the four people sitting around the table on the front porch on the first Saturday of the first month of the year 1925. While Murkel and Vista are talking quietly amongst each other to appease the quiet around the table Grandpa Brungle is smoking from an ivory pipe which he had made for himself while Bees watches on all the while thinking to himself that when he is old enough, he too will get himself a pipe just like his grandfather's, maybe even bigger if he has the money, and smoke from it sitting in the same chair Grandpa Brungle is.

As the smoke from Grandpa Brungle's pipe makes its way over to Bees and he inhales it he starts to cough, and quite heavily for someone who no more than a couple of seconds ago wanted very eagerly to do one day, even right then if the chance presented itself, the very thing that caused him the uncomfortable reaction and gets out of his chair to better relieve his coughing. Wista holds out his hand and pats Bees on the back.

'Take it easy brother, let the boy cough it out as he might, it'll make it easier on his lungs when he starts to do the same one day,' says Murkel.

Wista looks at him with bother in his eyes. 'You take it easy...' he says. 'Who's to say he'll start doing it to begin with?'

Murkel laughs. 'He'll do it...' he says. 'You just wait, didn't you see how he was looking at dad just now, he'll do it right now if he could.'

Bees sits back down in his chair. 'Thank you, uncle Vista.'

Vista puts his hand on his shoulder. 'Not a problem young man...' he says. 'Just remember, right now if ever you find yourself wanting to smoke one of these someday.'

Bees nods. 'I will.'

Vista looks back at Murkel. 'Anyway brother, that's not the point I was trying to make, but it doesn't matter anyway seeing as you never listen to anyone.'

Murkel laughs. 'That's right, I don't, and there's nothing you can do about it.'

After the burning sensation in Bees' chest had subsided and he is looking eagerly on at Grandpa Brungle again Vista turns to Murkel and whispers. 'What do you think we should do about the situation brother; the workers are dropping

faster than the mosquitoes do when they fly into that electric thingy over there…'
He looks over at an electric mosquito catcher, plastered so thick with mosquitoes on the wire grid around it that little to none of the blue light that emanates from the fluorescent light in the centre of the contraption can be seen, hanging from the porch roof by the staircase. 'Pretty soon we'll have none left?'

'That's because pa treats them worse than that thing treats the mosquitoes when they fly into it,' says Murkel. 'Don't get me wrong, I'm all for having a good time, but my main goal is to make Munto and how are we supposed to do that if we don't have any dogs to do our work for us?'

Vista nods. 'What I was saying in the first place.'

'Don't look at me brother, there's the man you need to be talking to, I just follow orders.' Murkel and Vista look over at Grandpa Brungle from the corners of their eyes.

'Don't look at me you two…' he says. 'This is my farm, left to me by my father, left to my father by his father, and so on and so forth, and all the coloured specimens on these grounds are mine to do with as I please.'

Murkel and Vista nod. 'Okay pa…' says Murkel. 'Whatever you say, but fact remains that we still don't have enough workers and without that you will not have a working farm.'

'He's right, either you start treating them a little bit better or we'll have to start doing all of the work ourselves, and that is unlikely to happen.'

'Like dirt it won't, you two will work if I tell you to, and I will stand over you every step of the way to make sure that you do exactly as I tell you to.'

You're the boss,' says Murkel. 'But we are still short 12 workers and that is causing us quite a bit of discomfort, and you being the boss how do you want to go about solving this problem?'

Grandpa Brungle takes a long drag from his pipe and lets the smoke swirl around in his half open mouth watching remnants thereof slowly leave it before blowing it out in one big quickly dissipating grey cloud. 'There is a small community about half a day's drive from here, so small that very little people know of it.'

Vista nods. 'I know which one you are talking about, it's very small, a couple of houses here and there and a church by the entry way.'

Grandpa Brungle nods. 'That's the one…' he says. 'That worthless little place is the answer to your questions my sons.' Grandpa Brungle takes another drag from his pipe. 'Which I think to be my or one of my colleagues' property, to begin with.'

'Not to be a pest, pa, but I don't think the worthless little town you are referring to is your property, if it was you would know about it.'

'Quiet boy! When a man thinks something to be his he must claim it, by saying so however many times he sees fit or by claiming it physically, and I am going to do both.'

'How are you going to do that?' Vista asks.

'We are going to claim it by getting our rifles, getting in one of my trucks and drive over there *and tell* them that where they stand is our ground.'

'What if they don't bite?' Murkel asks.

'Then we kill them.'

Murkel nods. 'Say we shoot whoever refuses our proposal, what if the police find out?'

'Then we kill all of them, and I'll have you know that if that happens, we won't have to worry because the police around here and very far from here are basically my property too, they hate them even more than we do, you should see what they do to them in their cells, you will giggle at the things we do to them here if you see what they do to them over there.'

Vista's eyes widen. Grandpa Brungle laughs. 'Exactly.'

'Still…' says Murkel. 'If the police aren't going to be a problem what makes you think we can take people we know in no way shape or form for ourselves?'

Grandpa Brungle sits back in his chair. 'What is the colour of your skin, my boy?'

Murkel looks down at his arm resting on the armrest of his rocking chair and back up at Grandpa Brungle frowning. 'What do you mean?'

'Just what I said, what is the colour of your skin?'

'My skin is white, pa,' he says with an even bigger frown than a moment ago.

Grandpa Brungle nods. 'That is right, your skin is white, and in this world having white skin means that you have the power, the power to do what you want with who and what you want, especially if that be to something of the skin colour other than white,' he says. 'Because white skin symbolises right, it is a gift given to you from above, and that Murkel my boy is why we can drive wherever we want to and do whatever we want to with whoever we want to.' Grandpa Brungle takes another drag from his pipe. 'Now go upstairs and get our rifles, your brother will stay here so I can make sure that he fills the truck with enough petrol to make the trip there and back.'

On the second floor of the house, to the left of the top of the staircase, in the room which Grandpa Brungle made into his office the very day he came into possession of the farm and everything on it, the biggest room in the house, Murkel is standing in front of a steel safe about six foot high and four foot wide of which the steel panels from which it is made is a quarter of a foot thick staring at Grandpa Brungle's arsenal of guns.

The door to the safe is opened by a code which only Grandpa Brungle knows and changes often for reason that he adheres most to the moral to trust no one but oneself. The safe, which he had made custom with the Brungle family crest of an elephant standing on its hind legs roaring and ready to attack with a badge of thorny leafless branches around it to symbolise discipline and punishment above all else inscribed on the door.

To Grandpa Brungle the elephant was the king of the jungle because it was the biggest of all the animals, when asked once which animal was second to the elephant, he said the giraffe because of how tall it was, and to this day the elephant surrounded by the thorn branches remains the Brungle family crest.

No Brungle after Grandpa Brungle, knows what the old crest looks like seeing as he went to many lengths to have it disposed of in all the manners needed so that it would be near impossible to find out what it looked like before did anyone want to know. Over the last two decades, Murkel had been in Grandpa Brungle's office many a time and before then the last time he was in there, was when he was around Bees' age when Grandpa Brungle wanted to show him the rifle that would one day become his.

Always boasting to any and every one about his collection of guns Grandpa Brungle loved very few things more than talking at length about any of the guns he kept in his safe, how many of them there were, how much each of them cost, what and how many he killed with each did he do so and how he came to be the owner of each of them.

Most of the guns that Grandpa Brungle had collected over the years he had custom made for himself to exact specifications and what he stressed most about each one is that he spent far too much of his hard-earned money doing so but that it was and still is well worth because the worth of a man is determined solely by the number of guns, especially rifles that he has to his name. That being said,

Grandpa Brungle had 12 guns altogether, only three of which were not made custom.

The first four were handguns, two of which he bought from a gun and ammunition store in town and made minor changes to after and two which he had made from scratch by going to one of four factories, dispersed over 14 industrial districts that make up that part of the country that manufacture and supply firearms to various guns and ammunition stores around the country as well as for people who were willing to pay the amount of money to have a firearm made custom for them on small to single scale.

The two he bought from the shop in town are both made from aluminium, one silver and one black, and came with standard trimmings and fittings. After he bought them, he walked three blocks down the street to a firearm customising shop and asked for the handle of the silver handgun to be fitted with an ivory plate on either side inscribed with the phrase 'Cut Throat Clifford' in a font which to him represented power and status, while the handle of the black handgun was fitted also with an ivory plate, stained red, and inscribed also on both sides of the handle with the same phrase in the same font as the other.

The two that he had made for himself were cast respectively from silver and gold. The handle of the silver casted was fitted with two ivory plates with a picture of the family crest inscribed on both while one side of the barrel had the letters 'CCB' and his date of birth inscribed on it in small, simple font, the trigger, hammer and trimmings of the bottom part of the frame attached to the barrel are also of ivory.

Much like the silver handgun, the gold casted one is also fitted with an ivory plate, stained black, also with the family crest and Grandpa Brungle's initials and date of birth inscribed on it in the same font as the silver casted while the trigger, hammer and trimmings on the bottom part of the frame are all of black stained ivory. For both, he also had made silver and gold silencers because he liked the way it looked when attached to the guns.

Other than the four handguns, the fifth gun that Grandpa Brungle had in his safe was a 44. Magnum to which changes were made that it had been plated in gold, a set of ivory plates inscribed with the phrase 'Bad Dad' in a thick, stylistic flowing font painted with black ink in certain areas while the barrel of the gun and the cartridge is inscribed with a traditional floral pattern.

The 44. Magnum is the most expensive of all his guns and the one he is most fond of, especially because of how much it cost. Despite always talking about how humble he is and how important it is for a man to be humble, especially if you have money, Grandpa Brungle loved to show off what he had, especially his gun collection which are undoubtedly his most prized possession.

Next to the smaller of his guns sits two double barrel shotguns of which the barrels sit on top of each other. Both were custom made by going directly to the factory, the first being casted from gold and the second from steel with a matted black finish and are both of pump action. The handle, trigger and grip of the gold casted is of ivory with the handle again inscribed with the Brungle family crest while the frame aside from the two barrels are inscribed with a pattern of doves and roses intertwined with one another to symbolise peace and love.

The handle, trigger and grip of the steel casted are of oak which has been brushed over with varnish, the handle again inscribed with the Brungle family crest. The frame again aside from the barrels is inscribed similar to its counterpart with a pattern of fire and dragons to symbolise anger, punishment and power. On the top of the two barrels on both guns is inscribed 'Cut Throat Clifford' in small and simple font stretching about half the length of the barrel.

Along with the handguns, the Magnum and the shotguns are four rifles, all, like the shotguns made for Grandpa Brungle especially, each one somewhat different from the other, firstly in that they are all cast from a somewhat different material, the first three being more similar in that they are casted from less organic materials, the first from silver, the second from gold and the third from matted black steel.

Each one has a centre piece made from Tungsten, the strongest natural metal, of a dark silver colour which 'houses' most importantly the trigger and loading port while the barrels that sit inside the front of the frame are of steel, one of the strongest alloys, each plated three different ways to match their frames. The biggest difference between the three rifles is in the fittings and trimmings. That of the silver casted is a thick ivory plate, a degree of the size and shape of the frame of the rifle butt inscribed with the initials 'CC' in large and detailed font.

Like with most of the other guns the trigger and hammer are of ivory while the front part of the frame is inscribed with a traditional floral pattern similar to that on the barrel and cartridge of the 44. Magnum with very fine and detailed ivory trimmings placed inside certain lines of inscription throughout the pattern. The gold and steel casted have fittings and trimmings along with inscriptions where need be of the same material and in the same style and placing as that of the silver casted, differing only in colour, the gold casted' stained black with the silver's-stained red.

The last of the four rifles has a frame that is hand crafted from a very dark type of ironwood, a group of woods from around the world known for its hardness and durability, with no fittings and trimmings, only an inscription of the Brungle family crest on the rifle butt and a floral pattern inscribed on the front part of the rifle frame.

Underneath the 11 firearms, all slotted into a respective place from left to right in the order of the four handguns, the first two being those that are store-bought, the 44. Magnum, the two double barrel shotguns and the four rifles are many boxes of different types and makes of ammunition lined up under each of their respective owners.

Other than spending thousands on Munto on a safe made especially for his beloved firearms, Grandpa Brungle had names for each one of the 11 of the 12 guns inside of the female persuasion. The store-bought handguns were given a single name, 'Valerie Pudding,' to be viewed as a pair. The name comes from a folktale told around the country to young children by their parents and grandparents before they go to bed at night which has been so for many a decade before Grandpa Brungle was born.

The story is of a nine-year-old girl by the name of Valerie Greshman who lived with her parents and grandparents on a farm in a farming district by the name of Rainbow Ridge, one of four dozen situated along the edges of the country. One weekend while her parents and grandparents were away Valerie stayed behind with the workers who lived in a small cottage behind the house.

The night after her parents and grandparents left for the weekend, one of the workers' children, a girl by the name of Amanthina, fell ill with a fever after she had been bitten by a sort of critter which lived within the walls of the room in which the workers lived.

Finding the medicine cupboard to be void of anything to treat a fever and considering the condition the girl was in and so not having the luxury to wait 16 or so hours for her parents and grandparents to return from their weekend away Valerie decided to cook the little girl pudding, the only thing she knew how to by herself, to which she added vanilla pods due to reading somewhere that people use it, as luck would have it, to treat fevers.

She brought the pudding to the little girl and they kept feeding it to her with glasses of water every two hours to bring her temperature down and keep it stable until Valerie's parents and grandparents returned to the farm. The following morning the little girl awoke to feeling as she did before she fell ill with the fever. It was her who gave Valerie the name 'Valerie Pudding.'

The last two of the four handguns are called 'Hilda' and 'Harriet' respectively. They were given different names to distinguish them from the counterparts due to the fact that they were made specifically for Grandpa Brungle and were not store-bought. Each of the firearms following the handguns were given individual names as a means of setting them apart from the handguns, who were named to establish pairs, except for the two shotguns who were also named to establish a pair.

The 44. Magnum is named 'Margerie.' The two shotguns are called 'Sister Suzy' and 'Sister Sally.' Second to last, the first of the three rifles to be crafted not from wood were given two names each because rifles were by far Grandpa Brungle's favourite firearm, the silver casted 'Maggie Sue,' the gold casted 'Mary Lou' and the mated black steel casted 'Clara-Belle.'

'Lastly…' and in Grandpa Brungle's own words when he showed his collection of firearms to friends and family, 'But certainly not last,' is the rifle crafted from ironwood, and the only one of his firearms that carries a name of male persuasion, 'Sir William.'

So much did Grandpa Brungle love his collection of 12 firearms that his wife mentioned on one occasion to a friend of hers that she heard him talking to them many a time over the years while he was in the office drinking brandy and cleaning them.

The 12th firearm, leaned against the side of the safe separate from the others is an AK-47, the only automatic weapon that Grandpa Brungle owns, which he brought back with him from the army. How he came to have it in his possession after returning home from the army no one knows because he has no recollection of how he came to have it in his possession.

More so than not knowing how it came to be in his possession, Grandpa Brungle did not like keeping the AK-47 in the safe along with all the other guns for he felt that it took away from the theme of the collection but still could not find himself to keep it anywhere else in the house or outside for reasons strangely unbeknownst and sentimental to him.

He never named it like he did all the others and neither did he use it ever after bringing it back with him to the farm because he was of the thinking for it to be so beneath the man to hunt or kill anything besides what you do or have to during times of war with any weapon of the automatic nature.

This is the collection of guns that Grandpa Brungle kept in the safe in the office for all the years that he grew old on the farm after returning home from the army, a collection of guns, along with the safe in which they were kept, he had destroyed a couple of days after he found out that he was going to die from an illness he contracted from a bite of a certain type of critter like insect found only in the Southern half of the country mostly known for a very intricate pattern-like design on its wings which are about twice the size of the insect itself which is the size of the tip of an adult's little finger which causes the body's organs to slowly dry up within two to three weeks of being bitten. He had the safe and his collection of guns destroyed because he wanted no one but himself to have ever used them.

Looking at the guns in the safe brings back quite a few memories for Murkel; some he is fond of and some he would rather forget. One of the fonder memories is the first time he went hunting up in Camel's Neck Mountain with Grandpa Brungle when he was 13 years old. What he remembers most about the day was how excited he was because for the first time in a long time he was going to get to spend time alone with his father.

One Friday, when Grandpa Brungle came home from work, which consisted mostly of having drinks at different hotel bars and restaurants with other prominent figures in and around the district discussing various business ventures, he hooted the horn of his truck for Murkel to bring down their luggage as they discussed the night prior so that they may begin to make their way up the mountain before the sun sets.

Before Grandpa Brungle had pulled up in the driveway Murkel had already been waiting by the door with their luggage and was out the door with all of it before mere moments after Grandpa Brungle had tooted the horn. When all of the luggage was packed securely in the back of the truck and fastened with ropes to make sure that they stay in place during the drive over the rocky terrain Murkel got into the passenger seat with his father, something which Grandpa Brungle only allowed this one time seeing as it was a special occasion.

Because he believed that to sit up front in any vehicle is a right reserved only for those who know how to drive themselves and also because he did not want any of his children or grandchildren to sit up front because he thought it to be too dangerous, something he told them and others about only so he may seem a better person, but mostly he did not like having children under the age of 21 sitting next to him while driving.

After fastening their seatbelts, Grandpa Brungle turned the key and him and Murkel made the three or so hour drive up the mountain to begin the hunting trip that Murkel had been looking forward to for almost a year, reason being that Grandpa Brungle wanted to teach Murkel a lesson in appreciation and patience by having him wait as long as a year to do something, which Murkel had been pestering him to do since he was eight years old on the day that Grandpa Brungle had the safe and firearms delivered to the farm.

After an hour of driving around the district with small periodic conversations between the two of them they reached one of two sections of the mountain which allows you to drive onto and up it Grandpa Brungle told Murkel that if he did not manage to shoot a buck during the two days they spend up there he would be sent off to boarding school because at his age, to be considered a man, you have to shoot a buck during your first hunting trip, saying after that they can stay a day longer if need be to do so before telling Murkel that if he did not manage to shoot a buck, he would have to write him a letter saying why he thinks he could not do so in all the time they were up there and how he thinks he can do better be there a second chance and why he should get a second chance.

If the letter did not persuade Grandpa Brungle that he should get another chance at shooting his first but as to not get sent away to boarding school, he told Murkel that going to boarding school would be the best thing he could do for him in order to have him grow up and mature in the manner in which he and Grandpa Brungle would be satisfied with when he reaches the age of 25.

The idea of having to leave the farm and go to boarding school more than a week's drive away from the farm bothered Murkel very much and for the entire three days that him and Grandpa Brungle spent on the mountain he did not want to do anything but lay in his tent and sleep the time away, the thought of having to pick up a rifle that weighed almost as much as the animal that he was supposed to shoot with it that had no intention of harming him in any way bothered him more, even than it did having to go away to boarding school if he were to not do so and every bit of excitement he had built up over the year he spent waiting to go on the hunting trip 'melted' away as soon as he heard Grandpa Brungle mention it.

Unbeknownst to Murkel Grandpa Brungle had no intention of sending him off to boarding school were he not to shoot a buck and simply made mention thereof to encourage him to put as much effort into doing so as he could because of how much he thought it would mean to Murkel to do so. After an hour and a half of driving around Camel's Neck Mountain and another hour driving up its Grandpa Brungle and Murkel arrived at the same place Grandpa Brungle arrived at the same place that him and his father did when Grandpa Brungle went hunting for the first and a couple of times after that.

After turning off the truck and taking the keys out of the ignition, Grandpa Brungle goes to the back of the truck to get a fold out chair and a box filled with bottles of brandy and a couple of glasses and opens the chair and sits down and pours himself a glass while he waits for Murkel to unpack the truck and set up camp.

When Murkel had finished setting everything up to Grandpa Brungle's satisfaction he told him to fold out a chair and sit next to him and pour himself a glass of brandy. When Murkel heard Grandpa Brungle say so his heart began to 'race' for reasons both good and bad, bad because the idea of drinking a glass of brandy at so spontaneous a time and at what he thought to be, having been told so by his parents and Grandpa Brungle and his grandmother as well as to his own thinking, a very young age was quite unnerving to him but at the same time also something which, after having seen his father and grandfather's mood change for the better after having a glass or two themselves, he found to be equally, if not more intriguing.

When Murkel sat down Grandpa Brungle handed him a glass filled with brandy and told him that if he were to shoot a buck, and this upset him even more than the idea of having to go off to boarding school did he not do so, he would have to cut off the buck's testicles and eat both before he would be allowed to leave the mountain and go back to the farm.

For quite some time, Murkel pleaded with Grandpa Brungle not to have to eat the testicles but Grandpa Brungle would hear none of it, he told him that his father as well as himself and his father and his father before him had to do the same and all did so very quickly and easily and that if he did not do it he would have to pack up his things and go back to the farm and that he can forget about ever coming back because in getting to come back and hunt with your family for a second time the first time has to be successful.

He was also told that if he chose to not eat the testicles and go back to the farm, he may never again speak to Grandpa Brungle or any of the males in the family about anything that has to do with hunting and the like as well as any topic of conversation that is considered, by him or anyone he wants to speak to, to be mature and male. With that Murkel decided that he would ask Grandpa Brungle for as many glasses of brandy as he was allowed and that he would stay the night to try to persuade him to not have to eat the testicles as well as the following morning before they went hunting and that if it happened to no avail, he would purposely miss all of the very few shots he planned on taking the weekend.

After almost three hours and eight glasses of brandy between the two of them, three of which went to Murkel, both Murkel and Grandpa Brungle were quite intoxicated, Grandpa Brungle more so than Murkel, and before him even. The only difference in his demeanour which Murkel was aware of was that everything appeared somewhat hazy and that he laughed more easily at the things Grandpa Brungle said and that night him and Grandpa Brungle spent one of the most enjoyable nights together they would come to throughout their lives.

The following morning after a can of beans and two cups of coffee between them, Grandpa Brungle and Murkel made their way higher up the mountain onto a two- to three-mile-wide plateau which forms the very top of the mountain covered with bushes, small trees, ponds and a small river that runs along the entirety of the top of the mountain where most of the animals known to the people of the district make their shelter.

After spending almost three hours searching for the right buck, Grandpa Brungle was after a certain kind of meat which he heard from a colleague is the most expensive and sought-after in the land, they came across a herd of bucks drinking water from a small pond near the edge of the plateau which Grandpa Brungle thought to be those he was after, but found out later from the same colleague that told him about them that they were not after coming to the farm one evening to have some of the meat with Grandpa Brungle that his wife prepared for them.

Seeing this excited Murkel quite a bit and he thought to himself that an opportunity to shoot a buck standing from as up close as they were will probably not present itself again any time soon, the moment he held the scope of the rifle up to his eye Grandpa Brungle pushed the nose of the rifle down and whistled as loud as he could, to scare away the bucks, he did this because he thought that for

Murkel to shoot his first buck from a distance so close would defeat the purpose of their trip and he would not get from it what Grandpa Brungle wanted him to and that they should take more time to look for herds or bucks further away to make the experience more enjoyable as well as to make it last longer.

Almost half an hour after scaring away the first herd of bucks, Grandpa Brungle and Murkel came across another one standing by itself eating from small patches of grass growing out from between a couple of large rocks. Standing far enough away to make it near impossible to shoot it without making use of the telescope Grandpa Brungle told Murkel to hold the scope up to his eye and to make sure that the centre of the cross-air is three to four millimetres to the left of where he wants to shoot seeing as the scope is that much out of alignment.

How comfortable and calm Murkel looked when he steadied the cross-air over where he wanted it both impressed and agitated Grandpa Brungle seeing as the first time that he went hunting with his father it took him almost a dozen tries, after spending more than an hour trying to shoot a couple of plastic bottles placed on a rock about 100 meters away from where they were standing, to shoot his first of three bucks that he would come to shoot that weekend, and after Murkel pulled the trigger and watched the buck fall to the ground a sense of relief more than accomplishment 'washed' over him and he breathed a sigh of relief.

After leaving the buck where it fell, Grandpa Brungle and Murkel walked back to the campsite and got in the truck and drove back to where Murkel shot the buck and put it in the back of the truck to take back to the campsite again.

After they took the buck off the back of the truck and laid it down next to the fire pit that Murkel had built the night before Grandpa Brungle told him to make a fire while he sat by his tent with a glass of brandy. When Murkel had finished making the fire, he hoped that Grandpa Brungle would offer him a glass of brandy and that they would spend the remainder of the night like they did night before but when he turned around Grandpa Brungle was standing behind him with a large hunting knife and said, 'I hope you know what to do with this.'

After pleading with Grandpa Brungle for quite some time about not having to do what he wanted him to, Murkel agreed to eating one of the testicles in return for getting to come along when him and Vista went on their first hunting trip together and for as many glasses of brandy after he was finished as he could handle.

This was one of the fonder of his memories with Grandpa Brungle that sprung to mind when he stood in front of the safe. A memory he would forget if he were able to is the first time, and lucky for him the only time he saw his father kill one of the workers. This happened when he was around nine or ten years old when Grandpa Brungle accused one of the male workers of stealing something from the house and told all of the workers to stand in a line against the front of the cabin along with their children and proceeded to tell the accused worker that if he did not take the pistol and shoot himself, he would have to live the remainder of his years on the farm with his wife and two children getting 'lashed' once a week, both his children once and his wife three times, for the crime Grandpa Brungle had thought him to have committed.

After the accused worker and the rest of the workers stood in silence, all the while Grandpa Brungle taunted them to speak, he took his pistol and shot the worker in his head before giving the rest of the workers an hour to bury the body behind the cabin. What Murkel remembers most about that day is that when he ran to his mother in the kitchen to tell her what he saw Grandpa Brungle shouted after him, 'Where are you running to boy? This is the best part of the job.'

Murkel picked up at random one of the three of Grandpa Brungle's rifles which were casted and made his way down the passage to the room that him and Vista shared when they were kids, which now belongs to Bees and Clarafina, to get two rifles which were given to him and Vista on separate occasions when they were old enough and are kept in Bees and Clarafina's room because Murkel and Vista very rarely use it and because Bees likes to have it in his room.

When Murkel had all three rifles he made his way down the staircase, hoping that Grandpa Brungle and Vista would be waiting in the truck for him seeing as he would like to get the burdensome journey that lay ahead over with as quickly as possible.

Once outside, just like he had hoped for, Vista was busy putting the empty gas can back in its holder on the back of the truck while Grandpa Brungle was already sitting in the passenger seat smoking his pipe. When he sees Murkel by the porch steps he motions for him to get in the back of the truck, as it only has two seats, with the rifles and to put them in the gun rack he had installed on both of the trucks underneath the back window before they leave.

Once the rifles are securely in place, Murkel knocks on the window for Vista to start the truck and they make their way out of the driveway leaving a large cloud of dust behind them as always seems to be the case when Vista is driving.

After almost ten hours, with Murkel and Vista switching places halfway, they turned right into Porman's Passing and parked the truck right outside the church.

Grandpa Brungle's truck is the only vehicle there because the people of Porman's Passing, except for two of the older families that live there, do not own cars or vehicles of any kind, nor do most of them know how to drive as most everything they need to live off for long periods at a time is cultivated by them on the settling.

In the whole of Porman's Passing there are 52 houses, all very similar in that they are built from large slabs of rock and stone held together by a certain type of clay found around the area which when soaked in warm water for a couple of hours becomes like putty and dries very quickly and becomes harder and denser almost than the rocks and stones which it holds together when it does, ranging in size from the smallest one bedroom and one bathroom house to the largest three bedroom and two bathroom house of which all the bathrooms consist of a bathtub, shower, a toilet and a washbasin as well as a living or dining area in the bigger of the houses.

In the centre of the settling, for the people to make use of who's houses do not have their own, is a communal kitchen which consists of 12 self-built wood burning ovens and stoves, a ten meters long table in the centre of the kitchen, five sinks and wash areas, three fridges and various cupboards that hold various cookware, cutlery and baking trays and the like.

Whether Porman's Passing have running water and electricity is something that only the people that live there know, because anyone who dives past there at night for whatever reason, which happens very rarely because of how unsafe the area and others close surrounding is considered to be by people who do not live there or close by, cannot seem to recall seeing any light of any kind on the settling, largely due to the part that whenever anyone not familiar with the area does come to drive past there the only thing they had on their minds was getting away from there as fast as possible.

Other than the kitchen and the church the other communal building on the settling is the school building. It is as big as about three of the bigger family houses on the settling and consists of four classrooms in which the children spend five hours for the first five days of the week learn to read, write and do basic mathematics above other things which they might come to need would they choose to leave the settling when they are old enough to make a living.

The church is situated by the entrance and is entirely built from wood and the biggest structure on the settling able to comfortably house all of the 150 plus people that live there. Inside are two rows of benches starting from the back of the church where there is another door besides the entrance door while the part of the floor that forms the isle between the two rows of benches is a long rectangular carpet that covers the entire length of the isle.

In the front of the church directly opposing the isle is the lectern on which one of the always three priests stands when they give their sermons three times a week. The lectern was carved by an 82-year-old man by the name of Zamon who used to work as a carpenter and retired at the age of 72 to write a book he had been wanting to write for the last three years before retiring. Behind the lectern are two tables, each one about the width of about half of the width of the church building in front of a large collection of pillows strewn across the floor on which people kneel or sit to pray in front of candles stuck to the table which they make themselves.

The only times Petrus left Porman's Passing was about a dozen times between the ages of 9 and 23 when he went with his father and others from the settling to the nearest town a three-hour drive away by the name of Denmfort when they needed something they couldn't come by without money. As much as Petrus liked going to Denmfort to admire the stores and houses, not to mention the church, which is about four times the size of theirs and built much more extravagantly from the inside and out not once did he want more to live there than in Porman's Passing because everything the town had to offer in terms of food, drink, lodging, furniture, clothing, and when he was younger even toys, none of it compared to comfort with which he lived in Porman's Passing.

Petrus liked the manner in which him and his family and the rest of the families and people who lived there did so in terms of growing their own fruits and vegetables, raising their own cattle, gathering in the communal kitchen at night to cook as well as share food ever so often, how every Sunday night everyone met at the church to listen to his father or one of the two other priests give their respective sermons for that week and how him and the other children went to school five days a week and were able to choose to a certain degree what they wanted to learn about while the adults did various other things on the settling and surrounding areas.

The money which they used to buy things of the nature that could not come by through means their own, came from selling various fruits and vegetables, meats and baked goods at a flea market held once every quarter during the first weekend of every third month from nine o'clock in the morning till 12 noon after getting permission from a group of six woman who make up a governing body responsible for organising the flea market and various other fairs and the like around town during each year new.

They got permission to do so after agreeing to give a third of whatever they make to the women to be allowed to set up a stall on the grounds next to one of two churches in town so that they can use the money to pay for various necessities needed to have coming fairs and flea markets but mostly because the woman wanted them to do so that they could take for themselves what they wanted before anyone else as the food that came from Porman's Passing was a lot fresher than that from the various stores around town which is imported on a monthly basis.

Outside of the church, Murkel is standing on the back of the truck and hands Grandpa Brungle and Vista their rifles. Before Murkel is able to get back on the ground Grandpa Brungle reaches under the passenger seat and gives Murkel and Vista each a whip. 'In case you want to have some extra fun.' When Murkel is standing on solid ground, Grandpa Brungle winks at them. 'Follow the leader, boys.'

Murkel and Vista follow Grandpa Brungle to the church door. Grandpa Brungle steps inside, holds up his rifle and shoots at one of the windows. The people take cover in various respective ways. When the air inside the church is quiet Grandpa Brungle yells, 'Listen up, you nothings! Me and my two are here today to take a lucky few of you back to my farm to bless you with work to inspire your souls, should any of you at any point dare to do or say any different than what we ask of you will be shot.'

Grandpa Brungle cocks his rifle. 'No, one of your family members will be shot, if anyone here is that unlucky to be considered one on this filth that you call ground.' Grandpa Brungle turns to Petrus, lowers his rifle and uses one hand to pry open one of his eyelids.

'Am I seeing this right? Is that thing around your neck the same thing that the priest who preaches to me on Sunday mornings wears around his?' Petrus puts his hand on his collar.

Grandpa Brungle nods. 'That is the thing I am referring to.'

Petrus nods.

'Are you supposed to be a priest?'

Petrus nods again. Grandpa Brungle turns around and looks at Murkel and Vista with a sarcastic grin on his face. 'Are you seeing this my sons?'

Vista shakes his head. 'I can't believe it either, pa.'

'Well believe it Vista, this...' Grandpa Brungle turns and points at Petrus. 'Thing standing before you just nodded 'yes' to a question that he in no way possible should be able to nod 'yes' to...' Grandpa Brungle snickers. 'This man just told us that he is a priest.'

Grandpa Brungle rests his rifle on his shoulder. 'Well, call me Catherine, it looks like miracles really do happen, having said that, it's time for another one, all of you get up so I can take a look at you.' Petrus steps out from behind the lectern. As soon as he does so Grandpa Brungle holds up his rifle and shoots him in the knee. Petrus falls to the ground as the sound from the shot fired permeates the walls of the church sending shivers down the spines of the people of the sort, they never thought they would come to experience. Grandpa Brungle walks over to Petrus and stands over him with his rifle resting on his shoulder. 'If you move from where you are now, I'll shoot the other knee off too.' Murkel and Vista move closer to Grandpa Brungle.

'Keep an eye on this one, I have a bad feeling about him.' Vista nods and points his rifle at Petrus.

Grandpa Brungle turns around. 'Okay people, we are gathered here today because it has come to my attention that you lot serve no purpose around these parts, and seeing as all people must serve a purpose, because if they don't the world will not be able to function, me and my two behind me are here to help you with that, and that we are going to do by taking a couple of you back to my farm, one of the most prosperous around these parts I might add, so that you can there begin to serve a purpose.'

Grandpa Brungle holds his rifle over his chest. 'With that being said all of you get up so that we can take a look at you.' Grandpa Brungle stands watching as the workers sit quietly in their seats. 'And make haste, my time is money.'

The people stand up. Grandpa Brungle turns around. 'Murkel...' he says. 'Come help me with this, Vista you stay there and keep an eye on the bleeding one.'

Vista turns around upset. 'Why do I have to be the babysitter?'

Grandpa Brungle laughs. 'Because of the two of you, you are the baby, and if you bother me again with what you just asked me, I'll have you go sit in the car like one too.'

Vista turns around and points his rifle at Petrus with a vigour excessively renewed. Grandpa Brungle looks at Murkel. 'You take the left side I'll take the right.' Murkel makes his way over to the row of benches on the left side of the church. 'You are looking for strong, stocky and sturdy males who look like they will be able to give the two of you a workout, were you to get in a ruffle with them and who might be able to outrun bullets for a while do we ever decide to have some fun one day,' Murkel nods.

Grandpa Brungle starts his way up the row of benches. 'Also...' says Grandpa Brungle. 'And more so even than the strong males, you are looking for pretty girls, ones which look like they will be able to put up no fight at all are we to get in a ruffle with them too.'

Murkel stops and turns to Grandpa Brungle. 'Why will we need to do that?' Murkel asks.

'Is it just me or do you not have a bulge in the middle of your pants where your legs come together?'

Murkel frowns. Grandpa Brungle nods suggestively. 'Well, is it just me?'

'I don't understand?' Murkel asks.

Grandpa Brungle rests his rifle on his shoulder. 'I am asking my son if you have a set of balls on you?'

Murkel nods.

'Is that a yes?'

'Of course.'

Grandpa Brungle nods. 'Well then how can you ask me a question like what you just asked me?'

Murkel frowns. 'What question?'

'The question where you asked me why we would have to take women back to the farm with us?'

Murkel nods. 'I still want to know the answer to that?'

'In that case...' says Grandpa Brungle. 'So, we can have something to look at while we look at the bunch of them, to show that we are not sexist, to ensure that the males have more of a reason to get up in the morning besides only work, and also, if we manage to find ones pretty enough by our standards, to have a special kind of fun with.'

Murkel nods disconcertingly. 'Whatever you want pa.'

Grandpa Brungle nods. 'Very good, Murkel...' he says. 'Also, make sure that they are not over the age of thirty, that way they'll last for quite some time.'

'Not a problem.'

Grandpa Brungle nods. 'On you go then.' After a while, Grandpa Brungle stops in front of two boys, almost as tall as he is and quite a bit more muscular. 'Who might you be?' He asks one of the boys with his hair in dreadlocks down to his jaw. The boy drops his head. Grandpa Brungle grabs a hold of the boy by his chin with his thumb and forefinger and lifts up his face. 'I asked you what your name is, boy.'

The boy clears his throat. 'Kolos,' he says.

Grandpa Brungle laughs. 'You know what I like most about you people, other than what you were built for, of course...' he says. 'Is your names, they never seem to fall short of great amusement and laughter...' Grandpa Brungle points to his mouth. 'As you can see, I would even go as far as to say it takes away from the ill feelings I have toward you, and that is saying a lot.' Grandpa Brungle puts his hand on Kolos' shoulder. 'Well then, Kolos, how old are you?'

'Eight.'

Grandpa Brungle nods surprised. 'Eight years old,' he says. 'That is quite a bit younger than I thought, are you sure you are only eight years old? You're not just saying that you are because you think it'll make it so you don't have to go to the farm being so young?'

Kolos shakes his head.

Grandpa Brungle nods. 'Okay then,' he says and takes his hand off Kolos' shoulder. 'And who might this be standing next to you?'

The boy standing next to Kolos, about the same height and size as him, looks up at Grandpa Brungle. 'Dwendo.'

Grandpa Brungle nods. 'Another winner,' says Grandpa Brungle. 'Dwendo, Kolos and Dwendo, are the two of you related by any chance?'

Kolos and Dwendo nod.

Grandpa Brungle does too. 'I thought as much,' he says. 'Looking at the two of you I would have thought if you weren't twins, you were at least brothers.' Grandpa Brungle pauses. 'Are you twins?' Grandpa Brungle holds up his hand. 'Wait, don't answer that, rather tell me how old you are, Dwendo.'

'Ten.'

'Brothers it is, then,' says Grandpa Brungle. 'Before we go any further, can one of you tell me how I could have come to the conclusion that you were not twins considering all the similarities between you by asking just this one's age?' Grandpa Brungle puts his hand on Dwendo's shoulder and looks the boys over for a while. 'Well, can you?'

Kolos and Dwendo shakes their heads.

'Never mind,' says Grandpa Brungle. 'Considering how big you are for your age you two will do fine even though you might not have much up here.' He taps Kolos on the head. 'Now get out of here and go and stand at the front of the church, by the priest with the broken knee.' Kolos and Dwendo's mother grabs a hold of them. 'Now, now madam…' says Grandpa Brungle. 'If you don't let go of your sons, you will be forcing me to have them watch as I shoot you.' Grandpa Brungle looks at Kolos and Dwendo's mother with eager anger. She squeezes their shoulders tighter.

Grandpa Brungle sees this. 'I'm not saying that you're definitely going to have to say goodbye to them when this is all over, there's still a lot of people ahead of me, I'm just saying that they are strong contenders for what I have in mind for what I want to take to the farm with me and therefore they have to go stand over there before you force me to shoot you,' says Grandpa Brungle.

'So let go of them madam, so they can go stand where they need to, or if you don't want to do that, I can shoot them to solve the problem.' Kolos and Dwendo's mother let's go of them and Grandpa Brungle steps aside to let them out of the isle, to go stand at the front of the church.

When twelve people, along with Petrus who is sitting on the floor, is standing at the front of the church with Murkel and Vista Grandpa Brungle joins them. He stands in front of the line of people and looks them over. Grandpa Brungle nods. 'This will do fine,' he says. 'With you lot, I might be able to ease more of my needs even than what I had in mind coming here.' Grandpa Brungle steps in front of a young girl and pinches her cheek. 'Thank you very much darling.'

Grandpa Brungle turns around. 'To those of you who are still here and think yourself to be lucky…' he says. 'Try not to look for comfort in that luck because we might be back sooner than you think to pick up another dozen of you, we do things a little differently at my farm.' Grandpa Brungle rests his rifle on his shoulder. 'And to those of you who are close to the parents of these two fine young boys behind me…' Grandpa Brungle turns to Kolos and Dwendo and then back to the people still standing by the benches.

'You can thank me when we see each other again, any parents who refuse to give their children the chance of getting to come and work on a farm as prosperous as my own and leaving behind whatever you call this little kraal you live on are not parents to begin with.' Grandpa Brungle turns around. 'Half of them should have been in the trailer by now, you two,' he says to Murkel and Vista. 'Get a move on.'

Murkel and Vista take the workers outside to put them in the trailer on the back of the truck. Grandpa Brungle turns around again. 'And Vista, bring me the can of gasoline when you're finished.'

Vista nods. Murkel turns around. 'What do you need that for?'

'I want to make these guys a drink.' Grandpa Brungle says sarcastically. 'Just make sure your brother brings me the can when all of those are in the trailer, and when that is so you come back here to get the priest.'

Murkel and Vista walk out of the church with the workers in tow. Grandpa Brungle turns back around. 'If any of you are scared of fire, I suggest you leave now, because you are going to get very close to it very soon,' he says. 'And out the back please, I don't want any of you making trouble of what is going on outside.' The people inside the church stand still and quiet. 'Or if you feel like dying feel free to stay right where you are, I would prefer it that way actually.' Murkel and Vista come back inside the church, Vista holding a can of gasoline.

Grandpa Brungle looks at Murkel who is staring at him blankly. 'The priest please boy, we are almost done here.'

Murkel goes over to Petrus and helps him up and walks him outside to the trailer.

Grandpa Brungle turns to Vista. 'Empty that out starting from where you are now to the back door and in between the isles every now and then,' he says. 'And if anyone gets in your way, they are a part of the floor.'

Vista nods and begins to pour gasoline out on the floor while the remaining people hastily make their way out from between the lines of benches and out of the back door. When Vista is finished pouring what was inside the can of gasoline out on the majority of the church floor and walks over to Grandpa Brungle. 'Now what?' He asks.

'Now you take the box of matches from out of my shirt pocket, strike one and drop it on the floor right by your feet.'

Vista nods. 'Which pocket is the matches?'

'Right.'

Vista takes the box of matches from Grandpa Brungle's shirt pocket, lights one and drops it on the floor. Grandpa Brungle takes the box of matches from him and puts it back in his shirt pocket and makes his way out of the church. 'Don't take too long my boy.'

Vista turns around startled as Grandpa Brungle walks out of the church and after looking back as the last of the gasoline catches fire he jogs after him.

During the drive back to the farm, Murkel decided to leave the farm the following morning and that same night shortly after midnight he packed his belongings and took an old shoebox filled with enough money to live comfortably on his own for about a year, that he had been saving ever since he was 12 years old and saw his father kill one of the workers for the first time, climbed out of his bedroom window and walked to the back of the house to the garage where him and Murkel's truck stood parked and drove for 24 hours before stopping at the nearest town to get himself a room at a motel to rest before deciding where he would go to start his new life.

The following morning, Grandpa Brungle's wife brought to him one of two letters left by Murkel explaining that he had left the farm to go and live on his own and had been wanting to do so for quite some time and they should not try to find him because he did not know where he was going to go and that did he arrive wherever he decided he wanted to stay he is going to change his name in the event that Grandpa Brungle decides to try and find him, the other letter Murkel wrote only to his mother and said that he will let her know by phone how he is doing and where he is staying as soon as he is settled there.

Later that day, Grandpa Brungle called his lawyer and had Murkel's name removed from his will before going into his office and taking Murkel's rifle from the safe and driving it up the mountain to where him and Murkel set up camp during their first hunting trip and buried his rifle in the ground under the fire pit which was still somewhat intact, after almost thirty years of last being there.

After two years of being away and speaking to his mother on the phone about once a month, Murkel came back to the farm during a time when it was only her who was there and spent a couple of hours with her talking about what his and her life had been like since he left and how content he was with his new over more cups of coffee than they ever thought they would come to drink during a span of time as short as drinking a cup of tea or coffee.

Chapter 4

It is two o'clock in the very early morning of Monday after Marana was beaten by Bees with the plank. Unlike many other very early mornings on the farm, it is quite a bit quieter than anyone is able to remember, so quiet that if you are completely still and breathing very softly in the cabin you are able to hear the electrical current surge through the wire grid around the bug zapper hanging from the roof over the porch. As usual, every light in the house is turned off except for the spotlight on the roof. Before it was installed, Bees was not able to see the cabin at night and after starting to wake up of night terrors three or so years ago after getting them periodically since he was a teenager; after seeing his father beat one of the workers with a whip and having nothing to do but stare at the workers cabin while waiting to want to go back to sleep in hopes of trying to catch one of the workers trying to escape, Bees had the spotlight installed with the intent to deter the workers from running away do they want to and so easing his night terrors.

Inside the cabin Petrus, Lumeo, Xhema and Nleeclo and Varieda are standing around Marana who is lying on her stomach on her bed in a white nightgown with her back exposed shivering with a cold sweat. 'Are you in pain at all?' Petrus asks Marana.

'No, just very tired.'

'Do you think if we stay awake with you, you'll be able to stay awake through the night? As soon as the sun comes up, we'll go over to the house and demand that Bees takes us into town or has a doctor come here.'

Lumeo nods. 'We already talked about it, if Bees refuses, we're going to take one of the trucks and take you there ourselves, we'll come back as criminals but at least we'll know that you'll be okay.'

Marana laughs. 'Thank you, but I'm sure that won't be necessary, I'm just very tired.'

The day Petrus came to the farm Marana, along with five other workers, stood waiting for him and the rest of the workers from Porman's Passing by the edge of the lawn by the driveway with black jumpsuits for each of the new workers. Marana had been living on the farm with her mother and grandmother along with a man by the name of Jesta and a woman Nleeclo, who when Marana was born was 22 and 12 years old, along with two other workers and Lumeo, who was 15 at the time and was taken from his home and brought to the farm along with Marana's mother and grandmother in 1896 when he was only six years old, by Grandpa Brungle and his father, Grandfather Brungle, as he was known to grand- and great grandchildren, and a foreman who lived and worked on the farm for Grandpa Brungle's father, who was in his late thirties and brought to the farm to fill another shortage of workers.

Grandfather Brungle was born on 21 August 1810 as Clifford Cormeinus Brungle. Not much is known about him other than he was the first of all the Brungle men who when he came to be the owner of the farm stopped paying the workers, giving them three meals a day as their only form of compensation, as well as who gave the workers black jumpsuits to wear to make them feel more like captives rather than workers and most importantly so that it will attract the heat from the sun to them during the day while they were working.

The day that his father, Lanton Clifford Brungle, passed away and Grandfather Brungle became the sole owner of the Brungle family farm and fortune at 18 years of age, his mother died when he was two years old and he was raised by his father as an only child, something which bothered him all throughout his life because of how lonely it was, mostly due to the fact that he did not go to school because his father was of the thinking that school was only for children less fortunate whose parents did not have anything to leave their children when they died, was the day that things began to change for the worse on the Brungle farm.

Rumours started to spread throughout the district that Grandfather Brungle's father had been murdered, and by Grandfather Brungle himself as a means of seizing the Brungle family farm and fortune for himself before he turned 21, which was the age at which he should have rightfully come into possession thereof. No one knew for sure whether it was in fact Grandfather Brungle who killed his father because there was never a wake held for him and his body was never seen by anyone other than Grandfather Brungle, who told those who asked that his father shot himself on accident while cleaning his gun and that it was his wish to be buried as soon as possible after he passed in an area of the mountain opposite the farm where he liked most to hunt.

When Grandfather Brungle was maybe ten or nine years old his father used to have get-togethers for anyone from the Camel's Neck district or those surrounding who wanted to make the drive through to Camel's Neck to 'trim the fat off their lives' as he used to say when he referred to them. These get-togethers quickly became well known for reasons both bad and good and increasing amounts of people showed up to them as time went on. Lanton Brungle began to have the get-togethers a year or so after his wife passed away and he decided to spend the remainder of his life as a bachelor so that he may have them.

When he told his friends and colleagues about it, they saw it as the perfect opportunity to indulge, having never thought that something of the nature of which their friend was talking would ever come their way living where they did. Grandfather Brungle was a very handsome man and was known around the district as 'Camel's Neck Casanova,' something which bothered his wife quite a bit and caused her to have suspicions that he was cheating on her throughout their marriage.

Soon after Grandfather Brungle was born his wife told him that she had suspicions that he had been sleeping around for the better part of their marriage and that it drove her to have an affair with another man. When he told her this the first thought that sprung to his mind was not one of jealousy or anger but that the boy, he was holding might not be his own because for the most part he needed a son to take over the Brungle family farm and fortune after he passed, so he decided that no matter if the child is his own or not, he would raise it as his own.

As Grandfather Brungle started to come of age the sinister side he became known for in his later years began to rear its head and people started to talk about how different he was to his father and rumours started to flourish that Grandfather Brungle might not be his father's own, something which his father never paid any attention to because he knew that petty gossip was the driving force in the lives of most people in the district because of the banality in which their lives are stooped living so secluded.

The first of the many get-togethers that Lanton Brungle would come to host at the house happened five years after his wife died and consisted of only him and four of his closest friends, all divorced, which he knew would say nothing about it mostly playing card games for money and drinking copious amounts of alcohol while flirting with the women who served drinks and food and helped with the card games.

During the get-togethers Grandfather Brungle very much enjoyed walking around the house and watching the adults go about their night, something which his father and his friends did not mind because they thought that it would be good for him to be exposed to their doings when they thought it to be age appropriate. On most nights Grandfather Brungle had a camera with him and took picture of all that he thought to be worthwhile.

One day Grandfather Brungle's father got a call from his accountant, who was also a regular at the gatherings, and told him that he was using the family money much quicker than what they first talked about when they started to have the get-togethers. The following day Lanton Brungle called the four of his friends that he invited to the first get-together and told them to spread the word that he would no longer be hosting them.

A couple of months after the last get-together Grandfather Brungle went into town with his father and spent a couple of hours walking around town as he usually does when his father has to be there for business or has errands to run and besides visiting the bookstore and reading the backs of as many books as he could in one hour, going to the most popular clothing store in town, where he likes to walk around and look at girls who are out shopping with their mothers and going to 'The Snow Globe' after to have a bowl of vanilla ice cream he went to a small greeting cards and gifts store close to the bar where his father was having drinks and discussing business and bought a photo album into which he put the photos taken from the various get-togethers to put away under his bed.

Ten years after putting the photo album away under his bed, Grandfather Brungle became the owner of the farm and the family fortune. A couple of weeks later Grandfather Brungle was sitting on the front porch drinking and thinking of ways to expand his wealth but unlike his father, he had very little experience in communicating and socialising with people, due to the fact that he did not go to school, something which he was very upset with his father for, although completely unfounded because many a time did his father offer to send him to school instead of having a tutor come to the house to home school him but he always declined because of how far from the farm the school was and he did not want to be a boarder.

Two years on, Grandfather Brungle found that the family bank account was quickly diminishing, something which worried him more than he thought it would as he had no worthwhile ideas and ways with which to continue to make money the way his father did and thus decided to go a route more sinister. He went into the office and picked up the telephone and proceeded to call as many of his father's friends as he could, some of the most prominent figures in and around the district, and went on to remind them of how he used to walk around the house with his camera taking pictures while they were enjoying their time there and threatened to show the pictures to their families, those who had families at the time, as well as business partners if they did not agree to demands he had.

That day, he called six people and each one agreed to every one of his demands for as long as he kept the photos out of the wrong hands after they came to the house to make sure that he did have in his possession the photos he was referring to. After the phone calls, which Grandfather Brungle was quite nervous about because if the men he called did not respond in the manner in which he wanted them to or if he went to their families with the pictures and they responded similarly things could have gone awry for him in very many detrimental manners both monetarily and physically speaking, most aspects of his life flourished in ways he could not have imagined, so much so that through the friends of his father he managed even to bribe certain people very high up in the police force as well as a few members of government which brought much elation to his life and which he wore as a badge of pride for better the part thereof but also caused him great grief and nuisance beyond it.

This is how the Brungle family, as it came to be after Grandfather Brungle came to be in possession of the name and espoused his values onto it, became the most feared family in the Camel's Neck district and those surrounding and Grandfather Brungle, until his first son was born, came to be known as the 'baddest' Brungle of them all.

The morning that Petrus, along with 11 others from Porman's Passing, arrived on the farm was when him and Marana first met. Marana remembers this very clearly because Petrus was the only one of the twelve workers sitting on the floor of the trailer bleeding and holding onto his knee. Once the truck was parked, after the long drive back in the early morning cold, on the driveway between the porch and the edge of the lawn Grandpa Brungle, Murkel and Vista got out of the truck and walked to the back trailer and let out the new workers.

When all of the new workers are standing in front of the old workers holding a black jumpsuit each facing Grandpa Brungle on the edge of the lawn while

Murkel and Vista sit on the porch awaiting orders from Grandpa Brungle may it come, he pats his shirt pocket and takes out a box of matches and a small bag of tobacco and stuffs the 'butt' of his pipe with two pinches thereof. 'Before we begin, I want the new twelve of you to take the jumpsuits being held out to you behind you and put them on.' Grandpa Brungle puts the bag of tobacco back in his shirt pocket. 'Not over the clothes you are wearing now, those you take off first, then you put on the jumpsuit.'

The workers, new and old, stand still and quiet. Before he is able to light the tobacco Grandpa Brungle places the box of matches in his hand in which he is holding his pipe and looks the workers over with a sly smile. 'I feel that I have asked something of the lot of you which makes you feel uncomfortable, am I right in saying that?'

The workers remain as they are. Grandpa Brungle's entire body tenses up. 'I said, "am I right in saying that!"' The workers answer him in a cascade of nods.

'Very good.' Grandpa Brungle bites down on the end of his pipe, strikes a match and lights the tobacco. 'Very good, to tell you the truth I did not expect to hear what you just admitted to because to my knowledge all animals on this earth walk around with no clothes on all the time, in front of each other and anyone or anything else for that matter too.'

He looks back at Murkel and Vista on the porch steps from the corner of his eye. 'Isn't that right, my boys?'

Murkel and Vista nod. 'Right, pa,' says Vista. 'Looks like we have a shy group of animals here today.'

Grandpa Brungle nods. 'Right you are, my boy, it looks like we have,' he says. 'Maybe we should give the papers a call, looks like we have quite a story on our hands.'

'I was thinking the same thing, pa,' says Vista.

'I feel obliged to tell you that if you think that there is any chance that you will not have to take off the clothes that you are wearing and put on what I had made for you, you are sorely mistaken,' he says. 'I will not hesitate in the least to leave each and every one of you standing out here without so much as a speck of clothing on, until you do what I ask of you or until you die of starvation.' Grandpa Brungle begins to pace up and down the driveway in front of the workers smoking from his pipe. 'Now, you all have two choices, do as I ask of you and take off your clothes and get dressed in the jumpsuits or do not and face the consequences of not doing so...'

Grandpa Brungle stops and stands still. 'Consequences that is if all of you are not standing naked in front of me within five minutes you will be tied to a tree in just that way,' he says.

'Also, if that happens to whoever it may that or those persons will be there as playthings for whatever type of fun, I feel like on whichever day I might come across whoever might be there.' He bites down on the end of his pipe. 'Having said that, ladies, know that I am very harsh a judge when it comes to the female form.' He takes a couple of steps back. 'Your time starts now.'

Petrus and three other male workers begin to take off their clothes. Grandpa Brungle smiles and makes his way over to Petrus and stands in front of him. Petrus looks up at him from under his eyelids. Grandpa Brungle takes a drag from his pipe.

'Ah, the one-legged wonder...' he says. 'I thought that you would be one to not take off his clothes...' He looks down at Petrus' knee, with a piece of material from one of the other workers' shirts who came to the farm with him tied around it. 'Because of your injury of course...' he says. 'How is it going with that, by the way?'

'Better,' says Petrus.

Grandpa Brungle nods. 'Happy to hear it...' he says. 'And what might your name be?'

'Petrus, sir.'

'Petrus, huh?' That sounds like a name from the language most of you black folks speak, even some white people have names like that these days, the worthless ones that is.' Grandpa Brungle laughs. 'The only thing worse than a black person with a name like yours and that speaks the language you speak is a white person with a name like that...' He taps Petrus on the shin of his injured leg with the front of his shoe. 'That being said, taking into account the colour of your skin, you should consider yourself lucky.'

When all twelve of the workers are standing undressed in their underwear, the women with their arms and hands covering as much as possible. Grandpa Brungle's eyes move toward Lavette, a girl that he took somewhat of a liking to back at Porman's Passing and walks toward her. When he is standing in front of her, she looks down.

'Very good young lady, I knew you were something special when I laid eyes on you back at that dirty little zoo you lot call home.' Grandpa Brungle brushes her cheek with his finger and she begins to cry. 'That's its little missy...' Grandpa Brungle says with a quiet, hoarse voice. 'I like it better when they cry.'

Lavette wipes the tears from her face. 'Now, why aren't you doing as I asked of you?' Grandpa Brungle slaps Lavette on her bum.

She lets out a quick, sharp moan and begins to snicker somewhat uncontrollably, so much so that the woman standing next to her takes her hand. Grandpa Brungle sees this and slaps the woman on her arm. 'Let go of her, touching is not allowed, only I am allowed to touch.'

The woman lets go of Lavette's hand. 'That's better,' says Grandpa Brungle and takes a step toward the woman next to Lavette, moves her arm away from her chest and puts his hand on her breast. 'Because you consoled her, I have to console you in my own special way so that you may never want to console her...' Grandpa Brungle puts his other hand on Lavette's stomach. 'Again.' Grandpa Brungle takes his hand off Lavette's stomach and reaches behind the woman standing next to her and puts his hand on her bum.

Murkel sees this and closes his eyes and decides to wait until Grandpa Brungle leaves the woman be, but upon opening his eyes again he gets up, grabs his rifle leaned against the porch, walks up to his father and presses the nose of the rifle against the back of his head. 'If you don't stop what you are doing, I will be forced to shoot you pa.'

Grandpa Brungle lets go of the woman and turns around. Looking down the length of the barrel he smiles sly and sinister, a smile that Murkel had seen many a time before growing up, one that scared him, even made him proud in certain situations, but mostly one that he thought would never be directed at him. Murkel takes a step back and lowers his rifle.

'Wise choice, my son,' says Grandpa Brungle and takes a drag from his pipe. 'Wise choice indeed, for I do not think you would have liked what you would have forced me to do to you, were you to keep that thing pointed at me for any longer than you did.'

Murkel nods. Grandpa Brungle winks at him and turns around and slaps the woman on her bum. 'Now, put on your jumpsuits so we can get on with the day, we have already wasted enough time due to the sensitive natures of the ladies here.'

When all 12 of the new workers are dressed in their jumpsuits, Grandpa Brungle claps his hands together. 'Good, this is what each of you, along with those behind you, will wear every day while you are working, if I see you wearing anything other than what you have on now you will not eat the following day, is that clear and understood?'

The workers nod. Grandpa Brungle walks onto the porch and grabs the railing with both hands. 'Now, before I let you leave to go get acquainted with the rest of you, I have to tell you that from this moment onward you will all, those of you who do not know this already of course, address me as 'Leader', nothing more, nothing less, only 'Leader',' he says. 'You will answer me 'yes Leader', 'no Leader', you will ask 'may I go to the bathroom Leader', 'may I have a glass of water 'Leader'...' He holds up his finger.

'To which I will always reply 'no'...' He puts his hand back on the railing. 'But you may ask nonetheless, if you ask it in the manner in which I just told you to.' Grandpa Brungle holds his arms put to the side. 'So!' He yells. 'People of Porman's Passing, know that I am very much looking forward to our time together and I hope that you feel the same.'

He holds his pipe up to his mouth. 'Now please follow my sons to your new home, there they will tell you what you can come to expect come tomorrow morning.' Grandpa Brungle turns around and as quickly as he showed up in the church in Porman's Passing a little more than twelve hours ago he disappears into the house to go and pour himself a drink.

When Grandpa Brungle is inside the house, Murkel and Vista get up and walk the 18 workers across the lawn, Petrus with his arms around two of the other workers to the cabin in a line so orderly it would be hard to think that two-thirds are doing so for the first time. When they reach the cabin Vista tells the workers to line up in front of the cabin. 'Before I leave you be, I have just a few more things to tell you,' says Vista.

'Tomorrow morning at seven o'clock, you will all be lined up here as you are now so that you can be told what to expect for the coming day, this you will do every day for the first five days out of the week along with me and my brother here, except for the days that my father has something to tell you, is that clear?'

The workers nod.

'Good,' says Vista. 'As for food, you will be given a certain amount thereof at the beginning of each week which has to last you until the beginning of the next week, under no circumstances will you be given anything more than what you will be given tomorrow morning.' Vista puts his hands in his pockets. 'That being said, after work each day as well as during the weekends, you are allowed to go up the mountain to hunt for whatever food you might come to find.' Vista clasps his hands together.

'That's about it, if you have any questions be only a little bit hesitant to come and find me or my brother or my father...' says Vista. 'Actually, just come and find me or my brother, better than you leave my father out of that part, for your safety.' Vista nods. 'And you can call me Vista because that is my name...' Vista points to Murkel next to him. 'This is Murkel, and the old man with the pipe is Clifford, any questions?'

The workers shake their heads.

'Great, enjoy the rest of your day.'

Murkel turns around and starts back toward the house, for the first time in a long time with Vista not by his side, one of his fondest memories being when him and Vista walked back to the house with their friends after playing a game of rugby.

'If any of you plan on running away, please do not...' says Vista. 'We know these parts better than we know the back of our hands and we will not stop looking for you until we find you, be that dead or alive.' Vista salutes the workers. 'Good day to you all.' Vista turns around and quickly makes his way over to Murkel, unaware that when he will be saying goodnight to his brother in a couple of hours it will be the last time he will say anything to him at all.

When Murkel and Vista are halfway across the lawn, Marana and her mother, Thimti, and grandmother, Grandma Gartha, walk over to Petrus and the two men holding him up while a couple of the workers go inside the cabin and others stay outside to get acquainted with each other. Grandma Gartha puts her arm around Petrus. 'Hello young man, my name is Gartha, what is yours?'

'Hello madam, Petrus.'

'Nice to meet you Petrus, I see you've hurt your knee, how is that by the way?'

Petrus looks down at his knee. 'Not bad.'

Grandma Gartha nods. 'That's good to hear.' She looks at the men standing next to him. 'You gentlemen can leave. We've got it from here.' The men let go of Petrus and make their way inside the cabin.

'Do you think you have enough strength to make it over there to the table?' Grandma Gartha points to the table in front of the cabin. Petrus nods.

'Very well then.' Grandma Gartha looks at Marana. 'Be so kind as to go get the medicine box from the cupboard dear?'

Marana makes her way into the cabin.

'On three then…' says Grandma Gartha. 'My daughter and I will help you over there.'

Petrus, Grandma Garth and Thimti make their way over to the table and Petrus sits down on one of the benches and rests his injured leg over the length thereof just as Marana comes running out of the cabin with the medicine box and puts it down on the table.

'Are you in any pain?' Grandma Gartha asks.

Petrus shakes his head.

'Good.' Grandma Gartha opens the medicine box and takes out a pair of scissors. 'I'm going to have to cut off the bottom half of your pant leg if that's okay with you?'

Petrus nods.

'To get a better look at the wound…' Grandma Gartha begins to cut the pant leg. 'And also, to get it away from the wound so that it doesn't cause an infection.'

'It's fine.'

When the bottom half of Petrus' pant leg is off, Grandma Gartha puts the scissors back in the medicine box and puts the pant leg off to the side on the table. 'Do you mind if I take a closer look at it?'

Petrus nods.

Grandma Gartha looks over the wound. 'The bullet went right through. you can consider yourself lucky.'

Petrus smiles.

'After we get it cleaned and dressed, you should be good as new in no more than a week.'

'That's very good to hear.'

'Now comes the easy part.' Grandma Gartha reaches into the medicine box and takes cotton swabs, disinfectant, a roll of gauze and a clear jar of white salve and begins to clean the wound with a cotton swab. For the remainder of the time that Grandma Gartha spent dressing Petrus' wound along with Thimti and Marana, they talked so much that when they got up to go inside the cabin, they found that Grandma Gartha had dressed the wound twice.

Afterward they went inside the cabin and Murtha brought over a cold cloth to put over Petrus' head as he lay down on a bed that Grandma Gartha and the other workers that were already at the farm prepared for him and the rest of the workers from Porman's Passing, while everyone else made dinner which they had outside for the remainder of the day and into the night around the table while everyone got to know each other.

Grandma Gartha was 79 years old the day that Petrus and the other workers from Porman's Passing came to the Brungle farm, although no one would think her to be that old because of her youthful appearance and bubbly personality and the manner in which she carries herself and interacts with others. She has fair, light brown skin with very few wrinkles except for those that appeared under her eyes a couple of years before her 75th birthday and hands that looked like the hands of a woman easily fifteen to twenty years younger than her.

Other than her youthful appearance the thing that stands out most about her is how unusually short and petite she is, when asked one time by Marana how tall she is she said that she does not know but that she is not tall enough to get into the passenger seat of Grandpa Brungle's truck by herself and short enough to walk under one of the taller deer found on Camel's Neck Mountain. She has dark brown eyes and hair that is almost completely grey down to the small of her back which when she isn't wearing it on top of her head in the style of a beehive, isn't that long, considering her height.

How Grandma Gartha came to live on the farm no worker that lived there 15 or so years after she came to knows, whenever someone asks about it the only answer anyone is able to give is that she had already been there when they got there and the only thing she says when someone asks her about it is that she was always meant to be there and that the Brungle farm was the only place that she was ever able to call home.

A little more than 170 years ago in 1735, Grandma Gartha's great-great-grandmother lived with her husband and their parents and other members of their family as well as a couple of other families besides theirs on the land and that surrounding the land on which the Brungle farm is. Back then Golden Heart, as it was not yet known as, had very few farms, maybe two dozen at the most, spread out very thinly over it while the rest of the land and that surrounding had people from different tribes of people of colour living on it for many decades before farms sprang up over the land. Grandma Gartha's great-great-grandmother, Balentha, was 28 years old when she fell pregnant with her first child, a daughter by the name Ona, three years before Grandfather Brungle's great grandfather, Boss Brungle, claimed the land along with the help of members of government in 1732 when he was 22 years old.

Within a year, he turned it into a scaled down version of the Brungle farm, almost 75 years later in 1807, Grandma Gartha was born on the by then very prosperous Brungle farm.

In the house at the time was living only Grandfather Brungle, who at the time was nine years old, and his father and Grandfather. Grandma Gartha always said that she was brought up by stories from the Bible and that she was raised as much by the writers thereof as she was by her mother and grandmother, every morning and night before she went to bed her mother read to her while her grandmother, when she wasn't reading to her herself, sat by and listened. Those times Grandma Gartha looked very much forward to because she had a great affection for the stories from the Bible and ever since she was very young felt that there was an aspect of life that was inexplicable, a part that had a delicate balance between the believable and the unbelievable, a part which the stories from the Bible gave life.

Along with learning from the Bible as her mother and grandmother read stories from it to her until she was old enough to read herself, a time she very much looked forward to ever since her mother and grandmother started to read to her, she was also taught, by her grandmother mostly, various things about nature and all that grows in it.

She learned many things about different types of flowers, plants and bushes and what each of them has to offer in terms of general usage, nutrition and most importantly healing ability, she learned how to make different creams, oils and ointments from various different combinations of greenery, some intended to be used as soon as they get plucked, due to the quickly decaying nature of the minerals and vitamins that they bare, she learned to be kind toward all living things, be they edible or not, but most importantly she learned that a loving heart is the most important healer all, something which she only came to understand as it should be much later in life.

When Grandma Gartha was 17 years old, both her parents were shot and killed, back then there was serious tension between the English speaking white farmers and the farmers that spoke the language that most of the people of colour spoke as the English speaking farmers wanted to secure more land for themselves in order to be in possession of all the land that is the Camel's Neck district and that surrounding until they would come to be in rule over the entire country. This was done with little to no regard for the lives and wellbeing of the opposition or anyone that stood in their way no matter what colour by killing them off in ways that were equally empathetic as they were violent.

This fight for land lasted almost three years until not one of the English farmer's opposition was thought to be left alive or in possession of any land in and around the district.

One morning, almost two years into the dispute for land, Boss Brungle along with five of his accomplices loaded all of his workers except for Grandma Gartha and her grandmother and four other children who lived on the farm with them into the back of his truck and drove three hours to one of the neighbouring farms to claim to land for himself. Four days went by before they returned to the farm and when the last worker got out of the back of the truck Grandma Gartha realised that her parents were not there.

Her first thought was, as she began to squeeze her grandmother's hand was that her parents, along with the other workers that were taken along and was too amiss when they returned, stayed behind on whatever farm Boss Brungle took them to for work.

As Grandma Gartha began to squeeze her grandmother's hand to the point of her grandmother having to forcibly remove her grandchild's hand from hers Boss Brungle began to tell them that Grandma Gartha's parents and the other workers that were amiss did not make it back as they were killed during the siege and the picture of her most dreaded thought was 'painted' more clearly in her mind than she ever thought it would be.

When Boss Brungle and his accomplices went into the house and Grandma Gartha's future with the two people she loved most in the world settled in on her, she did not start to cry as she thought she would but simply took her grandmother's hand and started back to the cabin.

When inside her and her grandmother sat down on her bed and after Grandma Gartha, sensing that something was bothering her grandmother, asked her what the matter was she told her the real reason why her parents were taken away so abruptly, she also said that her parents made her promise not to tell her why they were being taken away because it would cause her too much worry because they would have no choice what to do what Boss Brungle wanted them to and although it made her very sad hearing why her parents had to go away it made it easier for her to accept what happened.

When the remaining workers could not handle the workload by themselves anymore and work on the farm started to fall behind schedule, Boss Brungle brought in a new group of workers, among them was a young man in his late twenties by the name of Tynum, who was taller and more muscular than any man she had ever thought she would come to see living where she did with long hair in dreadlocks down to his shoulders which she liked very much about him because back then hair like that was very much a rarity and she felt that it said about him that he was an individual and not afraid to express himself.

The next day Tynum was forced to cut his hair but by then the bullet was already through the church roof having spent the remainder of the day since meeting talking with him by the dam by a fire that Tynum had made for them over which they cooked and had for dinner two birds that Tynum had shot and killed with a slingshot and the following day they told everyone that they would like to be thought of as a couple.

The relationship 'blossomed' for two months before Tynum and Grandma Gartha decided to marry and a small ceremony was held for the occasion one night behind the cabin with all of the workers in attendance where Grandma Gartha and Tynum said vows to each other before everyone drank together through the night until the sun came up the next morning.

As one would come to expect the workers were all very happy for Grandma Gartha and Tynum except for one of the older male workers, a man by the name of Dampo, for him the union between the two of them had an adverse effect as he had his eye on Grandma Gartha for quite some time before Tynum came to the farm but never had the courage to do or say anything to her about it. The following evening the workers found Dampo's body hanging by his neck from a tree behind the cabin, with a note saying that it was the fault of Tynum and Grandma Gartha that he took his life because the thought of living with her living with another man was too much to live with.

What Dampo wrote in the note upset Grandma Gartha to the point where she started to blame herself for his death, this made Tynum very angry because he knew that Dampo did what he did with the sole intention to cause Grandma Gartha discomfort, so much so that two weeks after Dampo was buried she had completely lost her appetite, had trouble sleeping and very little energy to do work, feeling faint for most of the time during the hours she had to work while sitting in whatever shade she could find with her head resting on her knees.

Although it was upsetting for Tynum and the rest of the workers to see Grandma Gartha as she was after Dampo's death it did not bother them in the sense that they knew she blamed herself for some reason for Dampo's death and simply needed time to work through whatever she was feeling and they were prepared to give her as much time as she needed.

Tynum, on the other hand, although he was willing to give her the time she needed to work through her grief, had a very hard time seeing her the way she was and one night when they were lying in bed, Tynum told her that she could only hold herself responsible for Dampo's death did she know how he felt about her. Grandma Gartha then kissed Tynum goodnight and they went to sleep when the following morning Tynum awoke to find her in somewhat better spirits than she was the night before, and when they stepped out of the cabin they spent the remainder of their life together like they intended, when they decided to get married and after ten years they had their first and only child, a daughter named Murtha. They waited so long because they felt having a child to be one of life's most altering things and they wanted to devote as much time to themselves as possible to be able to devote all of their time to their child once they have it.

After baby Murtha was born, Grandma Gartha got two years off from work to raise her, back then the law stated that any woman of colour that works on a farm must get at least a year to two years off from work to raise a child until the parents and the owner of the farm felt that the child was fit enough to be taken along by the parents during work hours or cared for by whoever responsible while the child's parents had to work, a law which angered Boss Brungle for all of his time as owner and overseer of the Brungle farm because his dislike for black children was stronger even than it was for black adults as when a black child smiled at him it made him feel more uncomfortable than he was able to bear.

For many years after Murtha was born, Boss Brungle tried to have the law abolished by means of bribery, blackmail or both, even threats of violence were a popular choice for many months, despite all of his attempts the law stands to this day. During the first year after Murtha's birth, Grandma Gartha spent as much time with her as possible, reading to her twice day for a half hour, teaching her to walk outside on the lawn and when she was able to do so, playing games with her and taking her for walks around the farm as well as taking her to the house once a week so that she may play with Boss Brungle and his wife's daughter who was born only a couple of months after Murtha while the two grownups had tea together.

After just over a year, young Murtha was able to walk and articulate herself so well that she was able to be around the other workers without them having to worry about her safety and she started to accompany her parents three days out of each week to lend a helping hand however she could and much to everyone's surprise, after only a couple of weeks she took to farm work better than most of the grownups did when they first got to the farm and much like things were after her second birthday, they stayed for many years until Murtha turned 18 and got married and after two years had a daughter of her own she gave the name Marana, who her and her husband raised much like Grandma Gartha did Murtha.

Those were the makings of what led Grandma Gartha, Murtha and young Marana to dress Petrus' wound the day he came to the farm and what led Grandma Gartha to meet the young man that she wound come to see as her own very soon after they met.

After dinner, Grandma Gartha comes over to Petrus. When she sits down next to him, he opens his eyes, she smiles. 'How are you feeling?'

'It's quite cold in here.'

Grandma Gartha laughs. 'That's your temperature talking…' She takes the cloth from Petrus' forehead and pats it down.

'This is as dry as a desert floor which isn't helping your situation much.' Grandma Garth turns around and calls to Marana. Marana makes her way over there. 'Deary?'

'Yes grandma?'

'Would you please run this down with cold water and bring it back to me with a glass of water too? Water of the same temperature as the cloth, Petrus is in grave need of it.'

Marana nods. 'Sure, I'll be right back.'

Marana walks to the kitchen and takes a glass out from the cupboard and fills it with cold water before running the cloth under it too and wringing it out and bringing it back to Grandma Gartha. 'Here you go.'

'Thank you dear.' Grandma Gartha takes the cloth and glass of water from Marana. 'Are you able to bring your head up a bit, so you can drink some of this water, it might even be more important than the cloth?' Grandma Gartha asks Petrus.

Petrus nods and lifts his head up a little, Grandma Gartha gives him the glass of water and he finishes it in one go.

Grandma Gartha laughs. 'That was quick, goes to show how much you needed that glass of water.' She takes the glass from Petrus and puts it down on the bedside table next to his bed.

'Do you need anything else?' Marana asks Grandma Gartha.

Grandma Gartha shakes her head. 'No thank you dear, this will do fine.' Grandma Gartha folds the cloth over length wise twice and puts it gently on Petrus' forehead.

'Okay grandma, goodnight.'

'Goodnight, dear, sleep tight, I'll see you bright and early in the morning.'

'You too grandma, love you.' Marana leans over next to Grandma Gartha and hugs her; Grandma Gartha puts her hands on her arms and squeezes them. 'You too dear.'

Marana lets go of Grandma Gartha. 'Goodnight mister,' she says to Petrus.

Petrus turns his head a little to the side and looks at Marana out from under the bottom of the folded cloth that somewhat covers the top part of his eyes. 'Goodnight young lady, see you in the morning.'

Marana waves Petrus goodbye and makes her way to her bed.

'Do you feel a little bit better?'

Petrus nods. 'Yes, thank you.'

'Great, maybe two or three more glasses of cold water throughout the night and you'll be feeling hopefully almost right as a rowboat in the morning.'

Petrus smiles. 'Thank you for the bandages...' he says. 'And the water and the cloth, the cloth is really very nice.'

Grandma Gartha smiles. 'Not a problem dear,' she says and gets up. 'You sleep well.'

Petrus nods. 'I will, you too.'

'I always do,' she says with a smile. 'My name is Gartha just so you know.'

'I know, you told me earlier.'

Grandma Gartha laughs. 'Silly me, I completely forgot.'

'That's okay, I did not, how can you such a pretty name.'

'Why thank you, young man, that's very nice of you to say.'

'Not a problem, very pleased to meet you.'

'Likewise,' says Grandma Gartha. 'See you in the morning.'

'Likewise.' Petrus closes his eyes and falls almost immediately asleep as Grandma Gartha turns around to go and kiss Marana goodnight. As always Grandma Gartha is the last of the workers to go to bed, not because she is quite a bit older than the rest of the workers and it takes somewhat longer for her to do so but because she prefers it to be that way, seeing everyone she has come to love during her time living on the farm with their covers pulled over them gives her a sense of peace that she is almost unable to fall asleep without if she is not the last one to do so.

The following morning, Petrus felt much better than he did the night before and although he still could not walk properly, he got out of bed and put on his jumpsuit and got ready for the day's work the lay ahead while the rest of the workers did the same. Looking around for Grandma Gartha, he was unable to find her. Seeing as how busy it was inside the cabin with everyone coming up to him to introduce themselves and ask how he was doing.

Once outside with the rest of the workers waiting in line for Grandpa Brungle or Vista to inform them of what they will have to do in the day, Petrus walks up to Grandma Gartha. When she sees Petrus, her eyes widen. 'Petrus, what are you doing out here?'

'Same as you are.'

'But your leg?'

Petrus looks down at his leg. 'I still have trouble walking but it is quite a bit better than it was last night so I thought I would get dressed and see if Mr Brungle wants me to work.'

Grandma Gartha nods. 'A wise choice, if there is one thing that might get you a day off from work it is not expecting one today.'

Petrus laughs. 'My thoughts as well, Mr Brungle does not seem to have much sympathy when it comes to these things.'

Grandma Gartha nods. 'About that, you are not mistaken.'

'Mostly I wanted to come out here to thank you and your daughter and granddaughter for helping me yesterday, if it wasn't for you, I don't know what would have happened.'

Grandma Gartha smiles. 'Pleasure, happy to have helped, after work I think we should take another look at your knee to see how it is coming along.'

Petrus nods. 'That will be nice, thank you.'

'Not a problem.'

Petrus looks up. 'It's quite dark out for it being so late in the morning, where I come from its quite a bit sunnier at this time.'

Grandma Gartha tilts her head upward. 'Really?' She puts her hand over her eyes. 'Today is actually cheerfully bright considering what the days here look like on average.'

Just then Vista comes walking across the lawn with his rifle and a pair of crutches and stands in front of the workers. 'Good morning, worker bees...' Vista cups the butt of his rifle with his hand and places the nose thereof on the ground and rests on it as a cane of sorts. 'Happy to see that you all made it out here this morning...' Vista turns to Petrus. 'Especially happy to see you here, priest.'

Petrus nods. 'Thank you.'

'May I enquire what your name is?'

'Petrus, sir.'

'Very well, Petrus, as you can see my father sent along a pair of crutches for you to work with today, so if you thought that you were not going to have to work today let me be the first to tell you that you were wrong.' Vista lifts up his rifle and walks over to Petrus and gives him the pair of crutches.

Petrus takes them from him. 'Thank you, sir.'

'Not a problem priest, and you can call me Vista, I'm too young to be referred to as sir.'

Petrus nods.

'Good.' Vista takes a step back and rests his rifle on his shoulder. 'Now will you all be gracious enough to follow me down to the vineyard, today you will be picking grapes.'

The workers follow Vista off the lawn and down the hill to the vineyard in the line in which they are standing.

Petrus very much enjoyed his first day of work, he found that the workers where more at ease with their life on the farm, however that may be, and that they were relaxed in a way different when they were labouring than when they were not and that in a way they spoke more openly and freely and also about different things than when they were dressed in more casual clothing and in and around the cabin, also, and mostly so, due to the fact that Vista left them alone for the entire day while he went to go get drunk, like he did every time it was his turn to keep watch over the workers, somewhere not too far off from where the vineyard is, only to return a couple of minutes before the end of the work day falling over his own feet.

So it went every time Vista had to watch over the workers, he would walk them to where they needed to be and then go about his day with a bottle of wine or brandy a couple of yards away from where the workers where and return always no more than five minutes before the workers were done with work for the day, something that Petrus and the workers that came with him from Porman's Passing, as well as the workers who had been on the farm when Petrus got there, being quite used to it by then, found very funny considering how drunk he was every time he came back to walk them to the cabin.

The days when Grandpa Brungle watched over them were a lot worse, those days were filled mostly with yelling and screaming, even the occasional lashing of a whip he carried with him when he kept watch over the workers, the lashing of the whip which he was never able to do as well as he wanted to and which upset him quite a bit when the 'clang' from the tip of the whip tearing through the air did not sound as loud as he wanted it to.

One time he grabbed one of the male workers who he felt was slacking by the back of his jumpsuit by his lower back and yanked it upward so hard that it caused the man to bleed. No more painful than that, as well as the whip lashings, the times it did come into contact with skin, but quite a bit more absurd was the time that Grandpa Brungle told a male worker to get down on his hands and knees and sat down on the man's back with his legs on either side of him and made him carry him around in that manner.

As well as with his whip around the man's neck for certain periods of time for the remainder of the work day, while the man did whatever he could in terms of work for the day considering how he was made to do it.

During work, Petrus spent most of his time talking with Grandma Gartha about stories from the Bible, their meanings and how they might come to be applied to one's life in many a manner, Petrus' knowledge of the Bible was something that impressed Grandma Gartha quite a bit and made him take a special liking to him, when she found out that he was the priest at the church back at Porman's Passing she asked him if he would like to lead a small church service of sorts behind the cabin on Sunday mornings. To this, Petrus agreed, thinking that by doing so might make him feel like he was still at Porman's Passing rather than living on the farm.

The first Sunday after Petrus came to the farm, him and the other male workers walked up onto the mountain an hour before dawn while the women and children were still asleep to hunt for a deer which they cooked over a fire in a small fire pit built by some of the male workers after they came back to the cabin. After Petrus lead the first of many church services they would come to have and still have to this day and had to eat along with potatoes and a salad and wine and orange juice for children, as well as some of the adults who do not drink before they spent the remainder of the afternoon sleeping, playing outside on the lawn with the children or doing various other activities of leisure until they had to gather together again to make dinner.

In addition to bonding over stories from the Bible, Grandma Gartha also taught Petrus everything she knew about medicine and the healing arts. Every couple of days after work, Petrus and Grandma Gartha walked around the outskirts of the farm and up on the mountain looking for various roots, plants, flowers and even the occasional insect with which to make different salves, creams and ointments, sometimes spending so much time doing so that they only came back to the cabin after the sun had set while Grandma Gartha talked with Petrus, about how to make the various healing concoctions that her mother and grandmother taught her to make.

During his first month on the farm, Petrus became very close with Grandma Gartha and most of their time were spent telling stories from and about their lives before they came to live on the farm. When Petrus told Grandma Gartha about Porman's Passing and how things looked and worked over there she was very intrigued, not knowing much about life besides her own on the farm, to her the idea of cooking in a communal kitchen and over and in gas stoves and ovens with meat from animals self-raised and vegetables self-grown was as archaic as the piece of paper on which the recipe for one of the first ointments she learned to make from her grandmother when she was a child, which learned to make it from the same piece of paper from *her* grandmother.

The idea of going to church inside of a building was something she only read about in books and working unsupervised and in clothing not uniform was something which she had never even thought of.

The stories that Grandma Gartha told Petrus all came from a time before so much as a brick was laid on the ground on which the Brungle farm is standing, in those stories people slept in huts and lived outside of them for all of the time they did not sleep in them, had no running water and electricity, the people bathed in rivers and had only the bush as their bathroom, they cooked only over something and never inside or on it, didn't know what ice cream was and had no idea of people of skin colour different to their own. Grandma Gartha's stories did come from a much different time and Murtha and Marana and herself were now very much accustomed to a way of living similar to that which Petrus was describing at Porman's Passing. Hearing about the freedom and sophistication with which the people at Porman's Passing lived was something which they only thought possible under the employment of white families and folk.

Lumeo, Nleeclo and Varieda are sitting on pillows around Marana's bed who is still lying on her stomach on her bed. Petrus and Xhema come over from the kitchen with a tray holding a jug filled with water and an empty glass and pillow and a cold soaked cloth. Petrus puts the tray down on Marana's bedside table and fills the glass with water while Xhema kneels down next to Marana, tucks her hand gently under her chin and lifts up her head and takes her pillow out from under her before replacing it with the new one she brought over. Petrus picks up the jar and glass and fills it with water and sits down next to Marana as Xhema puts the cold soaked cloth on the back of her neck. 'Are you still feeling feverish?'

'I'm not sure.'

'Do you think you can sit up to take a drink of water?' Petrus asks. 'If anything, it will help you stay awake, and if you feel like falling asleep, we'll stay awake with you until tomorrow and see who out of the six of us can drink the most water, we might even be lucky enough that you'll need to get up a couple of times to use the bathroom.'

'With how much I'm sweating you're going to fall asleep from having to constantly fill the jug long before I have to use the bathroom.'

Petrus laughs. 'That's why there's four other people sitting here with us.'

After two hours and nine glasses of water between Marana and her five friends only Petrus and Xhema remained by her bedside, Xhema asleep next to Marana with her head on the bed. Petrus looks at his watch. 'Just two more hours to go until sunrise, then we'll get you the help you need.'

Petrus pours the remainder of the water in the jug into a glass. When he wants to give it to Marana, he sees that she is asleep, quickly he puts the glass of water down on the table next to her bed and puts his hand on her shoulder and shakes her. When she doesn't wake up, he shakes her again, this time a little bit more intensely, still she stays asleep. Petrus takes the cloth from the back of Marana's neck, pours what little water is left in the jug on it, wraps it around his hand and dabs her on the forehead with it, she opens her eyes.

Petrus breathes a sigh of relief. 'Thought I lost you for a moment.'

'Lucky for the both of us it looks like you didn't.'

Petrus nods. 'Sun will be up in two hours or so.'

'That's good news.'

'How are you feeling?'

'The same as I felt a while ago.'

'Could have been worse.'

Marana reaches under her chest and grabs a hold of her necklace which she has been wearing around her neck ever since she was ten years old—of a small gold cross she found on the mountain one Sunday morning, when her and a couple of the other children went with a few of the workers to look for a deer or a buck lying next to a bunch of fig trees at the very top of the mountain and pulls it over her head.

'What are you doing?'

She opens Petrus' hand and places the necklace on the inside of his palm. 'Give this to Scara, tell her that I came across it at a time in my life when I was in need of an answer to something important, tell her that if she ever finds herself in need of something, she should go up the mountain to the group of fig trees almost at the very top and sit under them and close her eyes and contemplate a question she wants answered, while holding the necklace in her hand.'

Petrus fights back the tears.

'Tell her that if a clear answer doesn't come to her within a week of going there, she should take it that her thoughts on whatever she was contemplating at the time were right to begin with.'

Petrus rests his chin on his chest to give himself a moment to cry. After a couple of seconds, he wipes the tears from his cheeks and looks back up at Marana. Just as he is about to thank her, he realises that her hand weighs a bit heavier in his than it did a while ago and takes the necklace from her and places his first two fingers on the inside of her wrist and feels it without pulse, he bows his head to pray.

Chapter 5

It is a little after ten o'clock Friday night on the farm. Outside the spotlight that lays its light across the entirety of the lawn somewhat offsets the cold weather as the view from the living room window appears to show daylight still looming there. Bees and Clarafina are sitting on two plastic crates turned upside down which used to hold two dozen bottles of Clarafina's favourite red wine, mostly due to how cheap they are, in front of the fireplace on opposite sides of a fairly large sawn-off tree stump, about knee height, acting as a table playing cards.

Both Bees and Clarafina are wearing think leather jackets, Bees' black and Clarafina's light brown, about two sizes too big for them lined with fur on the inside and have blankets wrapped around them for added warmth besides that which is coming from the fireplace. Besides the deck of cards, the table holds a half empty bottle of brandy and two glasses each holding amounts of the liquor much different than the other, an empty can, which many a week ago was filled with beans and had printed paper wrapping around it, acts as an ashtray in which Bees empties tobacco from his pipe and Clarafina drops the ashes from the cigar she is smoking.

Ever since Bees first saw Grandpa Brungle smoke from his pipe, he wanted to do the same as soon as he was old enough to do so and the day, he turned 18 he went into town and bought himself a pipe as close to Grandpa Brungle's fist sized ivory pipe with patterned details carved into the butt of the pipe. Initially Bees had his sights set on Grandpa Brungle's original pipe and pestered him quite often as he was coming into adulthood about maybe getting the pipe from him when he passes, something which never came to pass seeing as a week or so before he passed he called Vista and Tarsa, Bees and Clarafina's father, along with young Bees into his office where he had his pipe laid out on the front of his desk sitting in its stand and proceeded to tell them the story of how he was given the pipe by his father when he turned 18, to whom the pipe was given by *his* father, who had it made for himself when the first tobacco shop opened in town who told the both of them to pass on the pipe just as they did to their son, or would they have more than one, to the son they thought to be most deserving thereof.

He then went on to say that neither Vista nor Tarsa, and in his own words, 'especially not the bastard Murkel,' he felt to be deserving thereof and for that reason he wanted to be buried therewith. To this day, no one knows what happened to the pipe Grandpa Brungle smoked so often from.

In the back corner of the living room, in the corner of the room against the wall adjacent to the garage, is standing an old gramophone playing a record of a soundtrack to Clarafina and her mother, Doriuna's, favourite film, and which today still remains to be Clarafina's favourite, which happens to be a musical, from when Clarafina was much younger.

The record is from a film which Clarafina and her mother used to watch once a week or so when Tarsa, Vista and Grandpa Brungle was away from the house for business reasons while together they talked of a life away from the farm closer to the city about a week's drive away from Golden Heart.

Doriuna and Clarafina watched the film only during the times when the adult Brungle men were away from the house because unlike her mother her father, as well as Grandpa Brungle, was not at all fond of them watching the film due to the fact that the leading man in the film was quite well known at the time and considered to be one of the more attractive of the celebrated men in the country and both Tarsa and Grandpa Brungle felt that their wife and daughter-in-law watching the film took away from as well as diminished the attention and time that had to be directed toward them, so much they detested them watching the film that twice, when they caught them watching it Tarsa beat Doriuna in front of Clarafina, and also Bees the second time he caught them watching it, which happened just over a month of catching them watching it the first time, to the point of her lying unconscious on the living room floor, until Bees ran over a glass of water and poured it out over his mother's face to have her wake up.

Another time, Tarsa gave both Doriuna and Clarafina, to an extent, a beating after they made mention of the film while they were having dinner, it was then, at 13 years old, after he helped his mother and sister to their bedrooms, that Bees decided to kill his father. About a week after deciding that he would kill his father, the easiest choice he had ever to make he once told someone who was sitting next to him at a restaurant bar in town after having drunk there for a couple of hours, Bees went into his parents' bathroom and from the medicine cabinet mounted against the wall above the wash basin took a bottle of the strongest sleeping pills he knew of and ground up as many as he was able to take without having it look as if the bottle had been meddled with and put it in his father's food when no one was around before they had dinner that night.

After dinner when his father went up to his bedroom, where he had been sleeping alone by then for quite some time after beating Doriuna for the first time after catching her and Clarafina watching the musical in the living room, Bees took a pocket knife from under his pillow which he took from the drawer from a small bedside table next to his father's side of the bed a couple of hours before dinner when his father was helping his grandfather with something behind the house, a piece of very strong tape which he would put over his father's mouth and a rope which he cut into fours and sat on his bed and waited to hear his father begin to snore.

When he first heard the snoring come from his parent's bedroom, he got up and without any hesitation walked there and carefully opened the door and stepping inside before closing and locking the door behind him and walked over to his father's bedside and began to tie his hands and feet to the bedposts on either side of the bed.

After tying his father to the bed, Bees stood by its side and pondered going through with what he wanted to for quite some time and the thought of untying his father and going back to his room and forgetting that he ever wanted to do what he set out to do that night crossed his mind a couple of times before the picture of his sister knelt down by his mother's side on the kitchen floor clutching at her lifeless body burdened him and he took the knife out of his pocket, exposed the blade and ran it across his father's wrist before he stood by and waited for him to bleed out completely before untying him, wiped the pocket knife with his shirt and put it in his father's hand before removing the tape from over his mouth and untying him and quickly walked out of the room and back to his own and got into bed and fell asleep.

The following morning Grandpa Brungle knocked on Tarsa's door as he was late to meet him outside on the porch and after waiting outside of his bedroom door without a response for about a minute he went inside and came across his son's body. After standing staring blankly and of empty mind at Tarsa for a while he went inside the bathroom and took a towel from the cupboard under the wash basin and put it over Tarsa's body before going downstairs to tell the rest of his family that he came across his body and that he is no longer with them.

116

To hear what they heard Grandpa Brungle tell them that morning none of the other Brungles in the house ever expected to hear, be whatever may be, none also suspected Tarsa's death to be anything other than what Bees made it appear to be, nor did they question it in any way as Tarsa's passing did nothing but better the spirits in the house, even Grandpa Brungle, who was upset by his passing only to the point of realising that his death might come to mean the start of the demise of the Brungle family farm and fortune.

The living room used to be filled with quite a bit more than that which is currently standing therein, along with it was a piano that stood next to the gramophone to fill up an empty space which Grandpa Brungle did not want to fill with a table of the gambling kind as suggested by his three sons nor a space to paint as suggested by his daughter-in-law and granddaughter which he then filled with the piano he bought from a colleague who had to get rid of it during the remodelling of one of his two restaurants in town when he found one day that the space had become somewhat of a play area for Bees and Clarafina on the off chance that there were no adults there.

Along with the piano, there were also a couple more pieces of furniture and four paintings against the walls opposing the living room entrance and the wall facing the porch which gave the living room its cosy feeling which made it easily, amongst all of the members of the Brungle family except for Grandpa Brungle and Tarsa and also somewhat Vista, to whom their favourite room was the office, the room in the house they were excited to spend time in came the time to do so.

A little more than five years after coming into possession of the farm, Bees and Clarafina had to start selling various items in and around the house to make money to keep the quickly decaying farm from being taken from them after they came into debt due to being ill informed about Grandpa Brungle's ways of doing business. The day that Clarafina came home to find the piano sold was one of her worst because other than drinking wine and smoking cigars, the thing she loved most to do was play the piano, mostly due to the fact that as a little girl she spent countless hours on the piano stool next to her mother watching her play hoping that she too might one day come to play just like her.

A couple of weeks after Clarafina started to sit with her mother while she played the piano, she asked if she could teach her, her mother agreed because living in the house with her husband and his brother and father being able to do things such as play piano came with much hassle if not under the guise of having to teach her daughter to play.

Clarafina took to playing very quickly, partly because she really enjoyed it but mostly because she wanted to start playing to impress her mother, and besides being naturally gifted as told to her by her mother, who had known how about the instrument as well as music in general, Clarafina spent countless hours with and even more so without her mother practicing until she was able to play her favourite song of mother's without hesitation from beginning to end, going so far as to cover the piano cover with her blanket and pillows from the living room couches to dampen the sound so that she may practice without bothering anyone else in the house.

After six months of playing, she had written her own piece of music, five minutes in duration, the thing in her life which she was most proud of and to this day still is, as she would admit only to herself because since before she started to play her and Bees were taught by their father and grandfather that for a person, especially a male, to do anything other than hard labour to make money during your lifetime makes you foolish and worthless.

Still Clarafina used every chance she could get when her father, uncle and grandfather were out of the house to practice and play piano and over the years, more so after Grandpa Brungle passed, she wrote many pieces of music which she practiced until she was able to play them to perfection and intended to take to a couple of the more expensive restaurants and hotels in town at which piano players where a regular occurrence to ask whether she might be able to play her own as well as music of their choice as an occupation.

Unfortunately, she was never able to do that because of the piano's untimely departure. What bothered her even more than not being able to take her music to restaurants and hotels where she might be able to get a job was that she was no longer able to play as a means of relaxing because the only times that she truly felt at ease having grown up in the Brungle household and thought of herself as something more than the granddaughter of Clifford Brungle was when she was playing piano.

For quite some time after the piano was sold, Clarafina made an effort to get it back, the same piano that stood in the living room and which she learned to play on growing up, but after learning that it might not be possible due to the manner in which and to who Bees sold it, she gave up on the idea to get back the original piano she started to plead with Bees to get a pre-owned one from an antiques store in town, an idea she gave up on the moment Bees told her that in order for it to happen, she would have to give up smoking cigars and drinking as much red wine as she does until she had enough money saved to buy herself one.

In the dim light of the living room fireplace, Clarafina puts her hand of cards down on the table between her and Bees. 'I win,' she softly yells. 'This hand, and more of your money.'

Bees leans over the table to have a better look at Clarafina's hand of cards. 'How much do you owe me now?'

Bees looks at her blankly. 'I don't owe you anything,' he answers. 'You live in my house, that's payment enough.'

Clarafina sits back on the crate and laughs. 'Nice.' She holds her hand out to Bees. 'Pay up, brother.'

Bees looks around the sitting room and back at Clarafina. 'Is there someone else in the room here with us which I am not aware of that just told you a joke Clarafina?' Bees asks. 'Because you can't be laughing at me because I did not make a joke.'

Clarafina looks at Bees with wide eyes. Bees nods. Clarafina lifts up her pant leg and from a sheath strapped around her shin she pulls a hunting knife, grabs Bees by his collar and pulls him toward her holding the knife to his throat. 'This is my house just as much as it is yours, brother, and you will give me everything you owe me or I will give you another slit to breath out of.'

Clarafina lets go of Bees and they sit back on the crates staring blankly at each other. Bees starts to laugh, almost falling off the crate as he does, Clarafina starts to laugh with him to ease the uncomfortable feeling that him laughing arouses in her. As their laughter dies down, Bees reaches into his pocket and pulls out a bunch of crumpled up notes and puts them down on the table. 'There you go, sister.'

Clarafina reaches over the table and picks up the money and starts to count it. 'Thanks so much, brother.' She puts the money in her pocket on the inside of her jacket. 'And just so you know, the next time you talk to me how you just did I won't hesitate to do what I said I would.'

Down the stairs, Klipp is making his way to the bottom floor as quietly as possible to not make known his presence to his aunt and uncle. When he reaches the bottom of the stairs, he presses his body against the railing and moves around it and onto the floor so that there may be no chance of Bees and Clarafina spotting him, when he is safely standing on the floor away from the line of sight that the view from the living room through the doorway to the foyer gives, he tiptoes his way into the kitchen.

Once inside he opens the fridge door. Inside are two six packs of beer, four packets of red wine, one-half full packet of white wine and two bottles of brandy along with three cartons of eggs, a loaf of bread, a slab of cheese and a pot of leftover curry from two nights ago. After looking over the contents of the fridge for a while, Klipp closes the door and makes his way out of the kitchen and onto the porch taking much care when passing the living room doorway to not get noticed by crawling on his hands and knees across the doorway and out the front door.

Clarafina sits upright on the crate and looks at Bees with wide, flaring eyes. 'Did you hear that?'

'Hear what?'

Clarafina points to the door. 'That.'

'It was probably just the wind.'

Clarafina shakes her head. 'Wind doesn't cause floorboards to creak like ours just did.'

'Then maybe it was an animal or something.'

Clarafina lifts up her pant leg. 'Are you saying there is an animal in this house?'

'No, I'm saying that an animal might have caused what you heard.'

'In that case, let's go have a look.'

Bees picks up his glass of brandy. 'You go, I've been sitting here for too long to get up this quickly.'

'Have it your way then.' Clarafina takes the knife out of its sheath and gets up. 'Stay alert, in case I might need assistance.' She turns around and slowly starts toward the door.

Bees nods, 'Okay detective.'

'Don't mind if I do.'

Halfway across the edge of the lawn Klipp stops running and rests his hands on his knees to catch his breath. As Clarafina takes her last step onto the driveway Klipp gets up and starts toward the cabin again. When he reaches the cabin, he peers through the door and sees that all of the workers, except for those sitting awake in their beds reading or knitting, are asleep and he makes his way around the cabin to the back windows by the kitchen and pokes his head through.

On the kitchen counter is a bread bin, a half-eaten bowl of salad and three bowls, one filled with different fruits while the other two holds tomatoes, balls of lettuce and onions in one and potatoes in the other. Klipp reaches into the bowl with the fruit and takes out a peach and makes his way around the remainder of the cabin to an area by the side of the cabin next to the row of trees that sits along the top part of the piece of ground that leads down to the fields of crop. When Klipp walks around the edge of the cabin, he hears a soft voice greeting him, 'Hello.'

So startled is he by the interruption of quiet that he stops dead in his tracks and puts his hands up in the air. When he looks to his left, he sees Scara sitting under a blanket under a tree with a book in her lap.

'Hello,' says Klipp.

Scara laughs. 'Why do you have your hands up?'

Klipp looks to either side of him. 'Oh.' He mumbles as he realises what position he is standing in and puts his down quicker even than he put them up. 'I don't know,' he says.

'Maybe it's because of the peach you have in your hand?'

Klipp looks down at the peach he is holding and back up at Scara with worry.

'Which if I'm correct, you took from the fruit bowl by the kitchen window.' Scara looks at Klipp with awaiting eyes.

'I'm sorry, there was so much fruit in the bowl that I didn't even know that I was taking one, there was nothing in the fridge in the house.'

'Nothing?'

'Not nothing, but only stuff for my aunt and uncle.'

Scara nods. 'I see.'

'I can put it back?'

That's fine, as far as I know everything on this farm belongs to you anyway.'

'To my aunt and uncle.'

'In that case, everything belongs to them, but if you really are their last remaining relative which I am told then it might as well belong to you too, at the very least in a couple of years, everything except for me and the other children and workers.'

Klipp's eyes widen.

Scara laughs. 'Just kidding.'

Klipp smiles and shrugs off the comment.

'I should probably apologise for being out so late...' says Scara. 'Please don't tell your aunt and uncle I am out here so late.'

'Never.'

Scara smiles. 'Thank you.'

Klipp and Scara stand staring blankly at each other for a while. Klipp uses the point of his shoe to draw a line in the dirt, he looks up at Scara. 'Do you come out here so late every night?'

Scara shakes her head. 'No, only weekends.'

Klipp nods. 'Why only then?'

'Excuse me saying so, but that is I've come to learn when your aunt and uncle like to drink most often and the most so it's quite a bit safer to be out here then.' Scara closes the book. 'How often do you come out here?'

'Not a lot, maybe one or two times a week when I can't sleep.

'That's quite a lot actually, I've never seen you around here?'

'This is the first time I'm here by the cabin.'

Scara nods. 'Oh, why can't you sleep?'

'My aunt and uncle make a lot of noise sometimes when they stay up late so I can't sleep.'

'I see, ever tried closing your door?'

Klipp nods. 'It doesn't really help, and they don't like it when I do that.'

'That's not very nice.'

Klipp shrugs. 'It's okay.'

Scara positions herself somewhat more upright under her blanket. 'I come out here for something of the same, although it's not as bad as why you have to.'

'Why do you come here?'

She holds up her book.

Klipp nods. 'Wow.'

'I can read inside, but it's a little bit better here, and when it comes to my favourite thing the little bit better here makes quite a big difference.'

'That's nice.'

'More so lucky I would say.'

'That is a little bit better.'

'Do you want to join me?' Scara holds up her book. 'I have another one here, if you want it?'

The thought of getting to sit next to the pretty girl who waved at him a week or two ago is overwhelming to Klipp in a way he had not yet experienced, especially because it was Scara who made the suggestion, and the last thing he feels himself wanting to do is sit next to her, out of worry of what might or might not happen does he do so.

Being unable to come up with anything to say which might excuse him from having to sit next to her so unexpectedly; he reluctantly makes his way over to there and sits down next to her under the blanket. 'It's a little small but it's probably better than standing in the breezy weather.'

'It's a lot better than that.'

Scara picks up an orange lying next to her and holds it out to Klipp. Klipp holds out the peach he has in his hand. Scara laughs. 'The stolen peach, I forgot.'

Klipp laughs. 'This is a nice blanket,' he says as he looks down at it. 'Where did you get it?'

'Thank you, I knitted it myself.'

Klipp looks at her with wide eyes. 'Really?'

Scara nods. 'Took me two whole days.'

'Is that long?'

'How do you mean?'

'To knit a blanket like this, is it a long time?'

'I'm not sure, I don't think so, the women tell me that I'm a pretty fast knitter so I don't think so.'

'Did you knit the pictures too?'

'Yep.'

'Wow.' Klipp looks over the pictures on the blanket. 'Do you knit the pictures like the rest of the blanket?'

'Sort of, it's a little harder and takes a little bit more time to knit the pictures than the rest of the blanket.

'How?'

'Well, you have to use different coloured wools and you have to switch to and fro from them a lot and quite fast than what you have to knitting the other part of the blanket.'

Klipp frowns.

Scara holds up a piece of the blanket with a picture of a rose on it. 'You see here.'

Klipp takes a closer look at the blanket.

'The blanket is made up of rows of lines of knits...' She holds her finger over the petals of the rose. 'The petals of the rose are of different lengths of lines on top or under each other depending on how you knit while the stem, leaves and lining is the same only with different colours.'

'Sounds like it's very hard to do.'

'Not really, it gets easier the more you do it.'

'It looks very nice.'

'Thank you.'

'Have you made anything else from knitting?'

'Many things.'

'Like what?'

'Sweaters, dresses, scarves, pairs of gloves and a couple of other smaller things.'

'Do you only make things from wool?'

'No, I've made lots of things from different kinds of materials and yarn as well.'

'What's yarn?'

'It's the thing you use to stitch pieces of material together.'

'Oh.' Klipp nods. 'Any leather jackets?'

Scara shakes her head. 'No, we can't afford leather, would be nice though if we could.'

Klipp nods.

'Are you particularly fond of leather jackets?'

'My dad gave me one just before he died, it's my favourite.'

Scara's gaze falls somewhat. 'I heard about that.'

'The jacket?'

Scara laughs. 'No, that your parents died.'

Klipp smiles. 'Oh, yes, that's why I came here actually.'

'I know, I heard that too,' she says. 'Very sorry to, just so you know.'

'That's okay and thank you.'

They sit quietly for a while.

'I lost my mom too not long before you came here.'

'I didn't know that; how did it happen?'

'She died of heart failure soon after I was born.'

Klipp goes quiet. 'Sorry to hear that.'

'That's okay, she's comes around here ever so often.'

Klipp looks at Scara blankly. 'What?'

Scara laughs. 'I don't mean that she comes and sits next to me and reads to me, I mean sometimes I can feel her almost, or hear her say things to me.'

'Can you hear her voice?'

'Not like I hear yours and mine, more like things come to mind that only she would know about and want to talk with me about.'

'Oh, that's never happened to me.'

'Maybe it will, or maybe it doesn't need to.'

Klipp nods. 'Maybe,' Klipp fiddles on the edge of the blanket. 'I'm sorry to hear about Marana too.'

Scara nods. 'That was almost as bad as hearing the news about my mom, I didn't know you could lose two moms until I heard Marana died.'

Klipp laughs faint. 'I'm sure she's very happy that you said that.'

'I hope so.'

Klipp lets go of the edge of the blanket he has been fiddling with. 'Do you have a leather jacket that you didn't make?'

'No, wish I did, I really like looking at the ones that the girls wear in the magazines that your aunt gives to us when she is finished reading them.'

'Is there one that you like the most?'

'A red one, I have the picture in a box under my bed where I keep all my favourite things.'

'What does it look like?'

'It's red with lots of gold buttons and zippers and some other small details of leather too, most people will think it's a couple of sizes too small but I think it looks really nice like that, I already started saving so I can buy a piece of red leather when I have enough money to make one just like it, maybe even a little different.'

'How long do you think it will be before you have enough?'

'Hopefully I'll have enough by the time I turn 16.'

'How old are you now?'

'12, you?'

'Also 12.'

'Snap.'

Klipp laughs. 'I can save some of the pocket money I get for a while and then give it to you on your next birthday if you want?'

'I can't let you do that.'

'There's nothing I want to buy with it, and my uncle said that if I don't spend it before the end of the year, he's going to take it back.'

'Why don't you just tell him that you bought something with it and put the money away?'

'I have to show him what I buy with it.'

'Oh.'

Klipp thinks for a bit. 'Maybe I can buy something and tell my uncle that it cost a lot more than it did and give the rest of the money to you?'

'You don't have to do that, it's your money, use it to buy something you want, there must be something?'

Klipp shakes his head. 'Not really, so maybe the money is to buy you the piece of leather with?'

Scara looks at Klipp blankly.

'And maybe you can make me something with the leather too, if there's any left?'

'Is there really nothing you want to buy?'

'No.'

'And your uncle really said that he's going to take the money if you don't spend it before the end of the year?'

Klipp nods.

'Then I guess you have to buy me the leather?'

'Okay.'

'Thank you, that's very nice of you.'

'Pleasure, thank you for letting me buy you the leather so my uncle can't take the money.'

Scara laughs. 'Pleasure.'

They sit quietly for a while, Klipp nibbling on his peach.

'How about it then? Do you want to read with me?'

Klipp swallows struggling. 'What book is it?'

'It's a book with a lot of short stories in it.'

'What's the stories about?'

'Lots of different things.'

'How long are the stories?'

'About ten to 20 pages.'

'Don't you rather want to read by yourself?'

Scara shakes her head. 'No.'

Klipp groans softly. 'Okay, that will be nice.'

'Great.' Scara picks up the book next to her and gives it to Klipp.

'What story is the best?'

'That depends on who you're asking?'

'What story is your favourite?'

'Haven't read the book yet so I wouldn't know.'

Klipp looks at Scara with wide eyes. 'Really?'

She nods.

'Is there any ghost stories?'

'I'm not sure.'

Klipp looks down at the book. 'Are there pictures?'

'Yep.'

'I'm just going to look at the pictures and then choose one from that.'

'How I would have done it too.'

'Okay.' Klipp opens the book and begins to look over the pictures while Scara removes the bookmark from hers and begins to read where she left off.

'Found one,' says Klipp.

Scara turns her head. 'What?'

Klipp holds up the book. 'A ghost story.'

Scara takes a closer look at the page. 'I'll have to notify my dad about this one.'

Klipp looks at the picture again. 'Maybe I should read another story?'

'Why?'

'Because this one might not be very nice.'

Scara laughs. 'I was only joking.'

Klipp laughs. 'Oh.' Klipp turns a page. 'Maybe I should just look at the pictures for a while, I like that a little bit more than reading anyway.'

Klipp turns to Scara, reading seemingly unaware of his presence before looking back down at the pictures in the book in his lap drifting slowly into a similar state.

Chapter 6

It is just after five in the afternoon and the workers are making their way up the hill having just finished with work. As the first of the workers are about to make their way into the cabin, they hear a whistle being blown, they stop and turn toward the house and see Bees standing on the porch with his thumbs tucked under a pair of suspenders, he waves at them to come over to him. When the workers reach the edge of the lawn, Bees tells them to form a line along the width of it.

With his pipe in his hand, Bees walks down the porch steps and over to the workers, he bites down on the end of his pipe and smokes from it as the last of the tobacco burns out, he then steps in front of Kolos, turns his pipe upside down to empty it of as much of the tobacco as possible and holds it out in front of Kolos. 'I want you to use your finger, whichever one that may be, to scrape the inside of the butt of my pipe here to clean it before we go any further, I don't feel like getting my hands dirty.'

After some hesitation, Kolos takes the pipe from Bees.

'Dig, Kolos, I want to see that pipe clean soon.'

Kolos scrapes the butt of the pipe clean with his forefinger and holds it out in front of Bees. Bees takes the pipe from him and looks into the butt of the pipe, he nods. 'Not bad, Kolos, I don't think I could have done a better job myself.' Bees looks back up at Kolos. 'And I shouldn't have been able to anyway.' Bees takes a step back. 'That being said, there are three things a person can notice about a man's nails, one is whether they are bruised or broken in any way, two is how clean they are and the third, and most important in my opinion, is how long they are.'

Bees tucks his thumbs under his suspender straps again. 'What I noticed about your nails, Kolos, was how long they are, so long in fact that I had to look twice to make sure that what I thought I saw was what I actually saw because in all of my 49 years, I have never seen nails as long as yours on any man, not even one of colour I might add. The thing about a man's nails, is that you should not be able to see any white edges at the end of the nails, and if you do they should be no longer than a millimetre, if the edges are longer than a millimetre, it does not only look unpleasant it shows a lack of respect for yourself as well as for your fellow man, not mention woman, but more importantly is shows the man to be lazy, and the lazier the man the longer the edge of the nail.' Bees takes a bag of tobacco out of his shirt pocket and begins to stuff the butt of his pipe with it.

'It is for this reason that I am upset as I am, Kolos, not only because it makes me feel uneasy to have to look at nails as long as yours on a man but mostly because it upsets me to know that I have someone like that working for me on my farm, someone with such blatant disregard for basic human etiquette as yourself, and because you are my property, it makes me look bad having you work for me, because the way you choose to present yourself is a reflection on me.'

Bees puts the bag of tobacco back in his shirt pocket. 'Long story short, my puppet, I was after a way to remedy seeing how long your nails was made me feel and having you scrape the butt of my pipe clean was that remedy.' Bees bites down on the end of his pipe again, strikes a match and holds it to the tobacco in the pipe butt and pulls on the end of the pipe. After blowing the smoke from his mouth, he flicks the match away from him and tucks the thumb of his free hand under his suspender strap.

'Don't let me catch you with nails that long again, Kolos, I will be forced to take measures more drastic if I catch you like that again.' Bees holds his pipe up to his mouth. 'I will check in with you tomorrow about the nails.'

Kolos nods.

Bees claps his hands together. 'The reason I called you over here is because I have some exciting news to share with you, and that is that as of last night we have two new additions to the farm.' Bees takes a whistle out of his pants pocket and blows. Out of the front door and onto the porch Clarafina comes walking holding two leashes, one in each hand, around the necks of two dogs.

'On the one side, we have 'Cof' and on the other we have 'Fin'.' Bees says.

Clarafina makes her way down the porch steps with the dogs and stands next to Bees.

'Or is it the other way around, I'm not sure, at this point it doesn't even really matter.' Bees takes a step back next to one of the dogs. 'The reason you can think of these two being here you can think of there being more of me, they came from an associate of mine's, a man that goes by the name Mr Frappounne, farm late last night, his grandfather was the first farmer around these parts from that country where success means wearing a suit and tie to bed and people the colour of you lot are only to be found in sewers, a place where not even the likes of the two standing beside my sister here can be found to urinate in would there be no other place to do so.'

Bees claps his hands together. 'That being said, for 'Cof' and 'Fin' being here there are two reasons, one is that my sister and I have been looking for two just like them without having to pay for quite some time now and two, and by far my favourite, is because they were going to be put down in a day or so for killing too much of Mr Frappounne's sheep, a thing that I felt to be unfair to put down dogs of such a violent nature and for that reason 'Cof' and 'Fin' are not to be thought of as pets to play with but as two sets of teeth here to enforce rule as well as to lend a certain amount of class to the farm by enforcing said rule.'

Bees nods. 'And with that I have to leave you to go to the bathroom.' He turns around and makes his way inside the house.

'Something my brother did not tell you is that my two little babies here only eat raw meat, none of that stiff in the can, only meat that is dripping blood like you find in the window of the meat store in town and so a couple of you, whoever it is, have to go up the mountain one time a week after work to look for an animal which they can eat, which you have to cut up and make look like the meat from the meat store, do you think that is something you can do?'

The workers nod.

'Very good, because thing is you have no choice in the matter, my things.'

Just then Bees comes back out of the house holding a small white rabbit, Clarafina turns to him. 'Whatever may this be?'

'Not now, Clarafina.'

Clarafina nods.

'Another thing you might want to know about 'Cof' and 'Fin' here is that they eat only raw meat...'

Clarafina leans over to Bees and whispers. 'Already told them that.'

Bees nods. 'Glad you took the initiative on that.'

'Thank you,' Clarafina leans in to pet the rabbit but Bees pulls it away from her before she is able to do so. 'This thing is not for playing with.'

'What is it for then?'

'You'll see in a minute.' Bees walks over to the workers and parts the line they are standing in and puts the rabbit down on the ground. 'As you can see the animal in front of me isn't moving much, which makes what I wanted to show you much less exciting.' Bees smokes from his pipe. 'At least you know that it feels comfortable around the likes of you which is good.' Bees tells Clarafina to bring the dogs to him. 'To figure out what is going to happen next should not be very hard at all.'

Bees takes the ends of the leashes from Clarafina. As the dogs approach, the rabbit it begins to hop away from them. 'That's it, little one, now you're thinking, run as far and as fast as you can.' Bees yanks on the leashes to get the dogs agitated. 'If any of you are thinking about covering your eyes for what is going to happen next do not, it is important that you see what is going to happen so that any idea of what you might have of 'Cof' and 'Fin' here being playthings of any kind be killed, as hopefully they will kill the rabbit.'

Clarafina steps closer to Bees. 'Brother?'

Bees turns around. 'Don't worry, Clarafina, I injected it with something so that it won't feel anything.'

'You're lying?'

'No, I'm not, and even if I was there's nothing you can do about it.' Bees waves her back with his hand. 'Now go stand behind me so we can get on with it.'

Clarafina takes a couple of steps back.

'Now, on the count of...' Bees pulls at the leashes a couple of times before letting them go to have the dogs run after the rabbit. Looking ahead in the direction of where the dogs are running, Bees sees the rabbit disappear into the bushes at the side of the lawn. 'Cof' and 'Fin' come to a standstill by the bushes and begin to sniff around them in search of the rabbit, poking their heads in and out of the bushes accordingly. After a while of rummaging through the bushes, they come trotting back to Bees with their mouths hanging open.

Bees picks up the end of their leashes. 'That was disappointing.' He gives the leashes back to Clarafina. 'Now that that's over, it's time to tick off the final topic of discussion for the day, and that is that Mr Frappounne will be joining us on the farm over the weekend for a bit of dog fighting, which we will be watching from the porch, unfortunately you will not be allowed to join us on the porch but I am sure, having gotten to know Mr Frappounne's kind nature over the phone the other day, he won't mind you watching from the cabin, he might even be gracious enough to have you come ringside of the ring in which the dogs will be fighting and watch the fight from up close.' Bees taps the butt of his pipe against his leg to empty it out. 'And with that, my puppets, I bid you a good night until tomorrow.'

A little after one o'clock the afternoon on the following Saturday, the workers and the children are enjoying the added freedom that the weekend brings. On the other side of the farm down the driveway are coming three vehicles, in front is Mr Frappounne and his driver in a black limousine of a shorter than average kind, behind them his two associates in a vehicle of much the same proportions and white while behind *them,* in one of the many trucks that Mr Frappounne has to his name, two of his employees responsible for the transport of the materials of which the ring is made as well as six dogs, two each belonging to Mr Frappounne and his two associates.

Bees and Clarafina, along with 'Cof' and 'Fin,' are waiting for their guests by the bottom of the steps by the driveway. When all three cars are parked and switched off Mr Frappounne's driver as well as the driver of the car his associates are in get out of the respective vehicles to open the door for them. His driver opening the door for him is something that Mr Frappounne has him do solely for the purpose of impressing friends, associates, and even more so *potential* associates, upon first meet, as well as to help establish an upper hand of sorts, he actually prefers to get out of the car himself; as it takes quite a bit longer to have his driver open his door for him but having people see him get out of the car in the manner in which he does means more to him than the comfort it costs as well as have had many a time the intended impact on the people he intended it to have on.

When Bees sees Mr Frappounne's driver open the door for him he turns to Clarafina. 'You know what they say about men who let people open doors for them?'

Clarafina turns to Bees. 'No, what do they say?'

'I have no idea, but it definitely isn't good,' he says chuckling.

Having not yet met or spoken to him the first thing that Clarafina notices about Mr Frappounne is his extravagant sense of dress, getting out of the car he is wearing a tailored suit jacket made from purple suede over a white button down shirt with embroidering on the chest pocket, the cuffs on the shirt sleeves sticking out from under the jacket sleeves as well as the excessively big collar sticking out from the lapel of the jacket, the shirt tucked into black cotton pants held up by a brown leather belt with gold trimming over black, pointy leather boots and a brown hat with a big, black fur coat slung over his arm.

When Mr Frappounne, known to most in the district in which he lives and some surrounding as 'Friendly Frappounne,' woke up this particular morning he was happy about the cold and gloomy weather as it was good reason to wear his fur coat, his most beloved item of clothing, which he rarely gets chance to and saw it as good luck that he was able to do so today.

Much like Bees and Clarafina, Mr Frappounne, whose first name is Fransauw, grew up in one of the districts neighbouring Golden Heart, a district which Bees always felt was better than Golden Heart seeing as it was the district closest to town. He lived in a house with his parents and father's grandparents in a very big single-storey house built entirely from red brick.

The architect who built the house intended it to be three stories high but Mr Frappounne's grandfather, Fransauw Frappounne, was afraid of heights and instructed the architect to divide the second and third floors into four equal parts and build them, as even in proportion to the first floor around it to make a single storey.

The house is said to be the biggest in all of the seven districts that surround the town of Golden Heart and make up the district of the same name. The thing that sets the Frappounne farm apart from all of the other farms in the district besides the size of the main house is the lake on the property, besides rivers, lakes are the thing that lends the most prestige to farms in the district and although many of the farms do have lakes the lake on the Frappounne farm is the biggest and also one of the very few that sustains certain aquatic life because of how close it is to a fresh water spring that runs throughout a large part of the country dedicated to farming.

Stepping out of the car behind Mr Frappounne's is Mr Trewton and Mr Gulthro, two of his more liked associates, both of whom breed dogs for a living.

When Bees and Clarafina step down the porch steps, Mr Frappounne is the first to extend his hand. 'Hello friend,' says Mr Frappounne. 'Thank you kindly for inviting me and the two gentlemen beside me over to yours on this fine day.'

'Excuse me for asking, but what about this day is fine, there is not so much as a spot of sun in the sky?'

Mr Frappounne looks at Bees somewhat agitated. 'As they say Mr Brungle, every cloud has its silver lining…' Mr Frappounne motions toward the sky. 'And as you can see there are many of them in the sky today so we should be in for a belter of a time...' Mr Frappounne turns back to Bees. 'On top of that we are going to be watching a few rounds of dog fighting and there are few things better than that wouldn't you agree?'

'I would if I could,' says Bees. 'I'm just here to win some money.'

Mr Frappounne nods. 'Either way, Mr Brungle, today will be a day to remember.'

'I hope you are right sir, looking at the dogs you have with you it might not be so much for me,' Bees says with a sly smile, very sure that either one of the two dogs that were given to him by Mr Frappounne will be able to take down any other having spent the entire previous day hosing them down with water and yelling obscenities in their faces while tied to a pole behind the house to enrage them.

Clarafina Mr Frappounne greets by kissing her on her hand. 'Mrs Brungle, I presume? A pleasure to finally meet you.'

Clarafina smiles, blood rushing to her cheeks, having not yet been greeted by a man in so romantic a manner. 'Pleasure to meet you too.'

While Clarafina stares bewildered at the top of her hand Mr Frappounne turns to Bees. 'Mr Brungle, where do you want my men to start setting up the ring?'

'On the topic of names, you can call me Bees.'

Mr Frappounne nods. 'Very well then, Bees, where do you prefer the ring to be?'

Bees points out in front of him. 'A couple of steps away from the edge of the lawn here.'

Mr Frappounne snaps his fingers and the two men who work for him unpack the back of the truck and begin to walk the pieces of the ring over to the edge of the lawn.

Mr Frappounne puts his hand on Bees' shoulder. 'And you can call me Fransauw, Mr Frappounne is much too formal for a time like this.'

Bees nods. 'Not a problem Fransauw, now how does some brandy sound?'

'Whiskey will be better, if you have it?'

'Coming right up.' Bees turns around and makes his way up the porch steps. Before going inside, he turns to Mr Frappounne and his associates and points to the table and chairs next to him. 'Feel free to find your seats, gentlemen.' Bees steps inside the house.

Mr Trewton and Mr Gulthro make their way up the porch steps and take their seats by a table, facing the lawn, that Bees and two of the male workers brought out to the porch from the garage the night before after work, one of a couple of tables that stood in the house during the get-togethers that Lanton Brungle used to have after his wife passed.

'Can I take your coat, Mr Frappounne?'

Mr Frappounne obliges and gives his coat to Clarafina, who struggles to hold it up. 'And you too can call me Fransauw.' Mr Frappounne takes Clarafina's hand and kisses the top of it again.

Clarafina smiles, 'I wasn't sure that you said it toward me also?'

Mr Frappounne lets go of her hand. 'Even more so than your brother.'

'Thank you.'

'Not a problem…' says Mr Frappounne. 'Now where do you want me to sit madam?'

'Follow me.' Clarafina turns around and walks Mr Frappounne up the porch steps and waits for him to take his seat next to Mr Gulthro and Mr Trewton. 'Where do you want me to put this coat of yours?'

'Wherever it is safest Mrs Clarafina.'

Clarafina nods. 'Not a problem, I'll go put this away in the office and bring some snacks out for you.'

'That will be wonderful, Mrs Clarafina.'

On her way to the kitchen, she bumps into Bees holding a box with two bottles of whiskey, a bottle of brandy and a couple of glasses. 'Quite the character, that Mr Frappounne?'

Bees leans into Clarafina. 'That might be the person that gets us out of the trouble we are in Clarafina, let him be all the character that he needs to be.' Bees looks over Clarafina's shoulder to make sure that there is no one by the door. 'And it's Fransauw, not Mr Frappounne.'

'Frans… Frap… who gives a hooter, is the man even a real farmer, did you see the way he is dressed?'

'The man has more money than we can dream of, if he wants to use your T-shirt to urinate on because he is too lazy to get up and go to the bathroom you give it to him, today has to go exactly like he wants it to.'

'Don't worry about a thing, brother, I have him right here on my palm, he kissed my hand twice already, and called me 'madam'.'

'I'm sure he calls all woman that, Clarafina.'

'But does he kiss their hand twice?'

'I'm pretty sure he does that too, now hurry up with the food.'

Outside on the porch Bees puts the box on the table and takes out a bottle of brandy and whiskey and puts them down on the table. 'Brandy for the brawlers and whiskey for the wise man,' he says as he takes out four glasses and puts the box away under the table.

'Would you like me to pour a drink for you, gentlemen, or do you prefer to do it yourself?'

'I prefer to do it myself,' says Mr Gulthro as he quickly reaches for the bottle of whiskey and the glass and pours himself some.

'As would I, Mr Brungle.'

Bees nods. 'Very well then, pour away.' He turns to Mr Frappounne. 'Fransauw?'

'I don't know about these two but I think it would be rude of me to decline an offer as kind as yours, Mr Brungle.'

'Coming right up.' Bees takes the bottle of whiskey from Mr Trewton and fills a third glass a third of the way full.

'Any chance of you bringing me a couple of ice cubes my friend?'

'Unfortunately, that will not be a problem Fransauw sir, the freezer is broken.'

'Some cold water maybe?'

'Not a problem.' Bees turns around and holds his hand over the side of his mouth. 'Clarafina!' He yells.

'Yes!'

'Bring out a glass of cold water with the food when you're finished!'

'Okay!'

Bees turns back to Mr Frappounne. 'Coming right up.'

'Thank you.' Mr Frappounne pulls out a chair for Bees. 'Why don't you sit down? So, we can get to know each other better.'

'Don't mind if I do.' Bees sits down next to Mr Frappounne. Mr Gulthro and Mr Trewton take out single cigar holders from their jacket pockets hung over the back of their chairs and with a pair of cigar cutters each begin to prepare them to smoke. Seeing this Bees takes his pipe from his pocket and begins to stuff it with tobacco.

'I was going to wait until we've had a couple of drinks in us but as you all are already there...' Mr Frappounne takes a three-cylinder, gold cigar holder out of his jacket pocket and takes a white dyed cigar from one of the cylinders. Mr Frappounne sees Bees admiring the cigar. 'Some of the finest cigars that money can buy in this county.'

'Looks like it.'

'And the finest of cigars deserve the finest of housing.' Mr Frappounne holds up the cigar holder. 'Solid gold, not the plated stuff.'

'I wouldn't know.'

Mr Frappounne holds the cigar holder out to Bees. 'You can feel it if you like?'

'Don't mind if I do.' Bees takes it from him and feels for the weight thereof. 'It is quite heavy.'

'Found the little wonder on vacation where I went to go buy these a couple of years back.' Mr Frappounne holds up the cigar. 'One costs more than three of those.'

Bees gives back the cigar holder to Mr Frappounne and takes the cigar from him almost unknowingly. 'Are the leaves really this colour?'

Mr Frappounne shakes his head. 'No, they make it the colour with a certain type of dye, also very expensive, not to mention rare, which adds to the flavour of the leaves.'

'Reminds me of the pipe that my grandfather used to smoke from.' Bees gives the cigar back to Mr Frappounne.

'How so?'

'It was the same colour, and also very big for being a pipe, he had it made especially for him, it was maybe the nicest pipe I have ever seen.'

'Where is it now?'

'Still with my grandfather.'

Mr Frappounne's eyes widen. 'Your grandfather is still alive?'

Bees shakes his head. 'No, died when I was very young, he wanted the pipe to be buried with him but when he died no one knew how or where he did so we couldn't find the pipe.'

'That's unfortunate.'

Bees nods.

'What did it look like?'

'It was made from ivory in the shape of an elephant's head and the handle was of some type of wood and the mouthpiece also of gold.'

'I would have liked to see it, could have given some idea of the type of man he was, aesthetically speaking that is.'

'It did suit him a little bit.'

'The pipe you have now looks quite good too, did you have it made for you also?'

Bees nods. 'When I turned 18, still as good as the day that I got it.'

'I more collect these things than smoke from them.'

'I do too actually.'

Just then Clarafina walks onto the porch with a large silver tray, probably the most expensive thing they have in the house, with two plates of food, a glass of cold water and a box of toothpicks on it. 'Here we go gentlemen,' she says as she puts the tray on the table.

The excitement with which Mr Trewton and Mr Gulthro look at the food on two plates quickly turn to disappointment when they see what it is. On the first plate is a variety of finger foods of small, pickled onions, cherry tomatoes, olives and pickles while the second looks somewhat more appealing than the first because of the contents thereof being a variety of crackers arranged around the plate edge with another so of cheeses in the centre but quickly becomes the anti as the amount of cheese pales in comparison to the number of crackers.

Clarafina puts the plates of food along with the box of toothpicks on the table. 'So, you don't get your hands dirty,' she says and puts the glass of water in front of Mr Frappounne. 'The cold water you asked for.'

'Thank you much, fair lady.'

'Thank you much, fair sir.' She picks up the tray.

'I think I'll stick with the whiskey and the cigar for now, my appetite hasn't gotten the better of me just yet,' says Mr Frappounne.

Mr Gulthro raises his glass, as does Mr Trewton. 'Likewise,' says Mr Gulthro.

'Is there something wrong with the food?' Clarafina asks.

Mr Frappounne shakes his head. 'Not at all, we're just used to food of this sort coming at a later time than what you just brought it.'

'Great, let me know if you need anything else.'

Bees picks a toothpick out of the box and pricks a pickled onion with it. Clarafina takes the tray back to the kitchen.

Bees turns to Mr Frappounne. 'Did you ever meet my grandfather?'

Mr Frappounne nods. 'He came to the house once when I was much younger, for business of some kind with my own grandfather.'

'Did you speak to him at all?'

'I did not get the chance to, nor do I think he wanted to speak to me.'

Bees nods. 'Did he have the pipe with him at all the day he came to your farm?'

'I'm not sure, I doubt I would even have been able to remember did he have it with him, being that young at the time I surely would not have known what I was looking at had I seen it.'

'With how that pipe looked, you would have remembered.'

'You might be right, on that subject, what I very clearly remember is how impressed I was with his sense of dress, especially with how neat and calculated almost a manner in which his outfit was put together, seeing him that day was very much the inspiration for how I dress today.'

'He was always very particular about the way he dressed yes, even those around him had to do so a certain way.'

Mr Frappounne nods. 'I have to say that I agree with your grandfather on that, a man should not be judged by the company he keeps but by the way he dresses.'

'Agreed.'

Mr Frappounne holds his cigar up to his mouth. 'Another thing I remember about your grandfather is that one day I asked my own about him after seeing him at the house for the first time and he said that even those closest to and who are much like him quiver when they hear stories about him and said that I am better off not knowing anything concerning him.'

Bees sits quietly for a while as memories of his grandfather come rushing back to him in an instant. 'I might have to agree with your grandfather on that one.'

Mr Frappounne laughs. 'After 57 years around these parts and a story or two about your grandfather now to my name, I too can agree with you.'

Mr Frappounne puts his cigar in his mouth, strikes a match and holds it to the end of the cigar, Bees does the same with his pipe.

Clarafina comes back out with her satchel filled with wine and pulls out a chair and moves it a couple of inches away from where Bees is sitting so that she may drink somewhat alone, sits down, removes the cork from out her satchel and sits back in her chair.

'Looks like your men are almost done setting up the ring...' Bees turns to Mr Frappounne. 'What time do you want to start the dog fighting?'

'In an hour or so maybe, it is a thing that is better appreciated when somewhat intoxicated, that reminds me.' Mr Frappounne takes his cigar holder out of his jacket pocket, puts it down on the table and places his cigar thereon so the front of it may not rest upon any surface, leans over to Mr Gulthro and whispers something to him. Mr Gulthro reaches to the side of him into his jacket pocket and takes out a glass tube filled with a white powdery substance and gives it to Mr Frappounne. Bees looks at the tube with wide eyes. 'Please tell me that is some kind of medicine for the dogs?'

Clarafina leans over Bees to look at what it is that Mr Frappounne is holding. 'Please tell me that is not some type of medicine for the dogs?'

'It is indeed not something for the dogs, Miss Clarafina.'

'For who is it then?'

'It is for whoever wants it.'

'What is it?' Clarafina asks.

'It is what you both probably think it is.'

Clarafina gets out of her chair and stands by the edge of the table in front of Bees, she claps her hands together and looks closer at the tube that Mr Frappounne is holding. 'I can't believe I'm actually looking at what you're holding there.'

'That still depends on if what I'm holding is what I'm actually holding.'

Bees looks at Clarafina agitated. 'Why are you so excited, Clarafina?'

Clarafina looks at Bees the same. 'Why are you not, brother?'

'Because what Mr Frappounne has there is illegal, not to mention that it can kill you.'

Clarafina waves away Bees' comment. 'Quiet, if he has it, cannot be that bad.'

Mr Frappounne turns to Bees. 'Do you not like this, Mr Brungle?'

'Not particularly fond of it, no.'

'That I can understand, do you mind though if me and Mr Trewton and Mr Gulthro make use of this here? We'll be discreet, you won't even notice.'

'Go ahead.'

'Thank you, Mr Brungle.' Mr Frappounne looks at Clarafina. 'And yes Miss Clarafina, this is indeed 'the superintendent's sugar'.'

Clarafina frowns. 'What?'

'"The rich man's bath salt", "the dove's ashes", "the queen's cake mix".'

'I don't follow.'

'This is what you think it is, Miss Clarafina.'

'Oh...' Clarafina says surprised. 'I know.'

'My mistake then...' says Mr Frappounne. 'Will you be joining us?'

'If my brother here isn't going to be too much of a 'nilly' about it.' Clarafina looks at Bees.

'Our grandfather used to call it 'fool's flour'.'

Clarafina looks at Bees blankly. 'What's it going to be, brother?'

'You're an adult, Clarafina, you can choose for yourself.'

'I know I am, but you can also be very nasty sometimes, that's why I'm asking.'

'Go ahead.'

'Thank you.'

'Don't thank me.'

'Thank you not then.'

Mr Frappounne turns to Bees. 'Do you think you can bring us a mirror on which to prepare this?'

'There might be something like that somewhere.'

'Thank you, if not a flat piece of glass or a dinner plate will do fine too.'

Bees gets up. 'Not a problem.' He walks into the house. Clarafina sits down next to Mr Frappounne. 'How much of this is in there?'

'Quite a bit.'

'Enough to last the whole day?'

'Just about.'

'That's very good news.'

Mr Frappounne puts the tube down on the table. 'Have you tried any of this before?'

'No, but I hear very good things.'

'Then you should be careful, too much of this at one time can knock you out for a couple of hours at least.'

'Is this very strong?'

'Of the strongest.'

'What makes it like that?'

'You'll have to see for yourself.'

141

Bees walks up to them and puts a small mirror down on the table in front of Mr Frappounne. 'Hope you didn't wait too long.'

Mr Frappounne shakes his head. 'Not at all Mr Brungle, thank you kindly.'

'Not a problem.' Bees turns to Clarafina. 'Get out of my chair please Clarafina.'

Clarafina looks up at Bees agitated.

'Seeing as your sister will be joining myself and Mr Gulthro and Mr Trewton here, I think it best that she sit where she is sitting now, that would make it the easiest for everyone.'

Bees nods. 'Very well.' He pulls Clarafina's chair over to him and sits down next to her by the edge of the table.

'How are we going to do this?'

'We'll divide a bit of what's in here...' Mr Frappounne holds up the tube. 'into smaller portions on here...' he moves the mirror closer to him. 'And then we're all set.'

'Mirror-mirror on the table.' Clarafina says and laughs.

Mr Gulthro looks over at her. 'We thank you for the festivities for us you enable.'

Mr Frappounne laughs. 'Very good, Mr Gulthro, I quite enjoyed that.'

'Not a bother Fransauw.'

'Now...' Mr Frappounne holds his finger over his mouth. 'Let me think, 'cable', 'label', 'stable'.' He lifts his hand from his mouth. 'Who the most tolerant you will label?' Mr Frappounne looks around the table.

'Very good...' says Mr Trewton. 'An inch better than my friend here's if I may.'

Mr Gulthro looks at Mr Trewton and nods. 'You may.'

'I like yours better too,' says Clarafina.

Mr Frappounne nods. 'Thank you m'lady.' He looks over at Mr Trewton. 'Mr Trewton, how about yourself?'

Mr Trewton grabs a hold of his chin, then shakes his head. 'Nothing at the moment.'

'Very well...' Mr Frappounne places his finger over his mouth again. 'I love you more than a horse hates a stable.'

They laugh.

'Very good Fransauw...' says Clarafina. 'Did you have some of this before you got here?'

Mr Frappounne laughs. 'No Miss Clarafina, I do not partake of this in small or confined spaces, I like to be out in the open when flying with the white canary.'

'Sounds about right.'

Mr Frappounne turns to Bees. 'Maybe you should harden yourself to the ideas of your grandfather and join us Mr Brungle, you might like it, most of the people I do business with partake in this activity if you will, it clears your mind and tightens up your thinking, so it's good for business, these days, no deal is made without it.'

'I would rather not Mr Frappounne sir.'

'Not a problem,' says Mr Frappounne. He tosses the tube to Clarafina who barely catches it with both hands. She looks up at Mr Frappounne distraught. 'Why would you throw this? Like that?'

'Not to worry, the tube is plastic.'

Clarafina laughs. 'Oh, that's funny…' She holds the tube up to her eye. 'Are you sure you didn't have any of this before you got here?'

Mr Frappounne shakes his head. 'I can assure you I did not Miss Clarafina.'

'Okay.'

Mr Frappounne reaches into his jacket pocket and takes out of his wallet a business card. Bees gets up from his chair. 'Excuse me, I have to use the bathroom.'

'As you would, Mr Brungle, you know where to find us.'

Bees disappears through the front door to the bathroom. Clarafina gets out of her chair and sits down on the chair Bees did opposite from Mr Frappounne by the edge of the table. 'Do you mind if I sit here, it's better leaning over this way.'

Mr Frappounne nods. 'Sure.'

'Thank you.' Clarafina leans over to Mr Frappounne. 'What's up his bum?' She motions to the door with her head.

Mr Frappounne laughs. 'Probably some of that food you brought out a while ago.'

'No, I mean what's up his bum in that…'

'I know what you mean Miss Clarafina.' Mr Frappounne shakes his head. 'I have not the faintest, I can only speculate as they say it is only the unhappy stiffs who choose to not partake in what we are about to.'

Clarafina smiles a sceptical smile as Mr Frappounne begins to divide the heap of white powder into lines with the business card. 'Someone once said that it's also only the very happy ones that choose to not partake.'

Mr Frappounne shakes his head. 'That's only something the unhappy stiffs say to make themselves look good.'

Clarafina sits quietly for a while. 'Where did you get this from?' She asks.

'I got it from an associate of mine, who got it from one of his.'

Clarafina nods. 'Do those associates also like dog fighting like you do?'

'They do not.'

'When did you start doing it?'

'A couple of years ago, where I got this from.' Mr Frappounne points to the tube Clarafina is holding.

'What is so great about it? Wouldn't you rather keep the dogs to play with or to protect you or something?'

'There is a lot of money to be made from it and many important people do it to make more, and much more, of what there is to be made from it.'

'How much money do you mean?'

'On average about three of your farm's worth.'

'How much is that?'

'What is your farm worth?'

'I don't know.'

'On average if a dog has a good couple of rounds, which mostly is about three non-consecutively over a period of three or four hours, maybe 300 000 Munto or more.'

'Wow…' Clarafina sits upright in her chair. 'You can probably buy ten of these farms with all of that money.'

'Let's hope not.'

Mr Frappounne reaches for the tube Clarafina is holding. 'May I?'

Clarafina gives him the tube. He heaps a small amount thereof on the face of the mirror and begins to divide it into lines.

'You might as well start emptying your wallets now gentlemen, my brother was up the whole night last night getting those dogs as worked up as possible.'

Mr Frappounne puts his hand over his jacket pocket. 'I'm afraid my wallet is staying just as it is now, I gave you and your brother my two weakest dogs and I did not come here to watch the two I have now, lose to the two I gave you.'

Unable to come up with an amicable response Clarafina opens her wine satchel and drinks from it.

'What do you have their Miss Clarafina?'

Clarafina looks at her satchel. 'Red wine.' She holds the satchel in front of Mr Frappounne. 'Would you like to try some, we make it ourselves, or we used to before we started to have money problems.'

'That is one of the reasons why I am here I understand.'

'That is one of them yes.'

'Does the wine have a name?' Asks Mr Frappounne. 'Or *did* it when you were making it?'

Clarafina nods. 'It's called 'Brungle Brew'.'

Mr Frappounne looks at Clarafina with wide eyes. "Come again?"

'Brungle Brew.'

'You know that you brew beer and not wine, why for a thousand wine barrels would you name your brand of wine that?'

'Because it sounds so nice, it has that thing where both words start with the same letters, 'altercation' or something.'

'I think you mean 'alliteration'.'

'Something like that.'

Mr Frappounne sits in mild bewilderment while dividing the remainder of what is left on the mirror into lines.

Clarafina sits back in her chair 'running' the name over in her mind. 'Brungle Brew...' She whispers a couple of times before saying out loud. 'I like it.'

Just then Bees comes back from the bathroom and sits down by the table.

'Welcome back Mr Brungle...' Mr Frappounne turns to Bees. 'Much lighter are we I hope?'

Bees nods. 'Quite a bit.' He looks over at the two men that work for Mr Frappounne almost finished setting up the ring. 'Looks like your men is almost finished over there, how long do you think till we get to see the dogs in action?'

'Soon my friend, now that you've said it, we should get to the fun part quickly so that we can get to the better part the same way.'

'Well said, Mr Frappounne.'

'Thank you, I used to be quite the wordsmith when I was younger, for a while I even wanted to become a writer.'

Bees looks at Mr Frappounne wide-eyed. 'Really?'

Mr Frappounne nods. 'Kid you not.'

'Did you write any books?'

Mr Frappounne shakes his head. 'No.'

'How so?'

'Too many ideas, there was so many of them I was never able to finish one.' Mr Frappounne takes his wallet out of his jacket pocket. 'Come to think of it, I didn't start any either.'

Bees nods. Mr Frappounne puts his business card back in his wallet and takes three 100 Munto bills from it before putting it back in his jacket pocket. 'Lucky for me I was a much better businessman than I was a writer.' Mr Frappounne gives Mr Gulthro, Mr Trewton and Clarafina each a bill and Mr Gulthro and Mr Trewton begin to roll up theirs. Clarafina looks at Mr Frappounne inquisitively. 'What is the money for?'

'To consume the product, of course?'

Clarafina nods. 'Oh.'

Mr Frappounne looks at her out from squinting eyes. 'Did you really not know that?'

Clarafina shakes her head. 'No.'

Mr Frappounne nods. 'Oh.'

'How is the money going to help with *that*?'

Mr Frappounne frowns. 'I was not aware that you know this little about the product, are you sure you want to partake?'

'If you can say for sure that I'm not going to fall dead of a heart attack then yes.'

Mr Frappounne nods. 'If you consume very little thereof at first then you should be fine.'

'Then I am too.'

'Very well, do as Mr Gulthro is doing with his bill then.'

Clarafina begins to roll up her 100 Munto bill.

Bees turns to Mr Frappounne. 'Why do you use 100 Munto bills? Why not 50 or 20?'

Because I only carry 100 Munto or more bills with me, when you have as much money as I do there is no reason to carry bills of a value less than 100.' Mr Frappounne slides the mirror away from him. 'Having said that, lady and gentlemen, as you can see, I have divided the product into a dozen equal lines, three for each of us, that should be enough for the first time around.' Mr Frappounne turns to Clarafina. 'You should do only half of a line to begin with, maybe even less than that and give it a minute or two and let us know what you feel.'

Clarafina nods. 'Not a problem.'

Mr Frappounne slides the mirror over to Clarafina. 'There you go, miss.'

'Thank you, sir.' Clarafina breathes a couple of quick, short breaths and rolls her shoulders before holding the rolled-up 100 Munto bill under her nostril and above the first of the 12 neatly divided lines on the mirror and pushes closed her other nostril with her free hand and to clear her lungs she blows out through the bill and turns all 12 of the neatly divided lines into a very expensive cloud of white dust. When the realisation of what has happened settled on her she looks at Mr Frappounne with heavy eyes while Mr Gulthro and Mr Trewton lean over the table in disbelief and Bees smiles sly on the inside.

Clarafina puts her hand over her nose, her other hand still holding the rolled-up 100 Munto bill under it.

'Easy mistake to make.' Mr Frappounne slides the mirror over to him and wipes it with his jacket sleeve, reaches into his jacket pocket and takes out the tube and begins to make another 12 lines on the mirror face. When the face of the mirror is covered once again with four sets of three lines each, he slides the mirror over to Clarafina again.

Bees leans over to Mr Frappounne. 'Those two don't say much, do they?'

Mr Frappounne turns to Bees. 'Excuse me?'

'Your associates, they haven't said a word since they got here.'

'That's because they are mute Mr Brungle.'

Bees frowns. 'What?'

'They are mute, they cannot speak.'

Bees positions himself upright in his chair. 'What do you mean they cannot speak? Do their mouths not work like other people's or do they just have nothing to talk about.'

'I'm not quite sure how it works, Mr Brungle all I know is that for some reason they cannot speak.'

'How do you talk to them then?'

'We write on pieces of paper.'

Bees looks over at Mr Gulthro and Trewton out of the corner of his eye. Mr Gulthro sees him and Bees quickly looks away.

'Mr Brungle?' Mr Trewton asks.

'Yes, Mr Trewton?'

'In case you believe what Fransauw just told you let me be the first to say that it is not true, me and my partner are not mute, we are simply quiet people who enjoy the silence that life is kind enough to offer us.'

'Right indeed…' says Mr Gulthro. 'And beyond that we believe that it is not polite to initiate a conversation when you are guests in another's home, that is a privilege reserved for the host, or hosts, if you were a guest at one of our homes we, as well as you for that matter, would have spoken many a sentence thus far into the visit, and quite frankly it upsets me, and I'm sure Mr Trewton as well, that you would believe us to be such a thing as mute.'

'I'm sorry that you feel that way Mr Gulthro and Mr Trewton…' Bees says. 'In no way was it my intention to have you think what you are about what I was told.'

'Thank you for the apology, Mr Brungle…' says Mr Trewton. 'But you should have been much more a sceptic when you were told that about us.'

'I don't know what else to say but that I am sorry gentlemen.'

'Your apology will settle after a while, Mr Brungle, thank you,' says Mr Gulthro.

'I just think it is very upsetting that men such as yourselves would feel the way that you do about being thought of as people like mute people, especially after my brother was told so by your comrade Mr Frappounne, if you say that my brother should have not believed him you are saying not good things about Mr Frappounne and that is not good.'

Mr Frappounne claps. 'I must say that after hearing what I just did I am very much looking forward to doing business with you and your sister Mr Brungle.'

Bees puts his hands behind his head and leans back in his chair. 'Call me Bees, Mr Frappounne. Mr Brungle is much too formal for a time like this.'

Mr Frappounne nods. 'Bees it is then,' he says. 'And call me Fransauw, for reason the same.'

'Not a problem.'

'Great, and with that…' Mr Frappounne looks down at the mirror and sees that by clapping his hands most of the second set of lines disappeared under him, he shakes his head. 'Did not see that coming.'

Bees and Clarafina take a closer look at the mirror, as does Mr Gulthro and Mr Trewton. 'What is the matter?'

'More loss of the sugar fairy.'

'There is still some left,' says Clarafina.

'It does not look as inviting as it should, and in all my years of doing business the most important thing I've learned is that more than the quality of a product the most important thing is how it is presented, and that is why I must do this.' He picks up the mirror and throws the remainder of what is on it away over his shoulder before covering it with another 12 lines and again sliding it in front of Clarafina. 'Would you like to do the honours?'

'Don't mind if I do.' Clarafina picks the 100 Munto bill up again and begins to roll it cylindrically. 'Now I just have to remember what happened the first couple of times, this stuff has blown away so many times that I don't know what I want to be doing anymore.'

Mr Frappounne laughs. 'Remember to blow the air out of your lungs before you hold the bill to your nose and breath in.'

Clarafina nods. 'That is right.' She holds the back end of the bill to her nose and positions the front over the first line of cocaine.

'Just half at first, to see how your body takes to it.'

'Sure.' Clarafina presses one side of her nose closed and breathes in the entire line through the rolled-up bill unintentionally. After it has been consumed, she sits still in her chair staring off into a distance and grabs a hold of the arm rests of her chair.

Mr Frappounne and Mr Gulthro and Trewton look at her with excited concern. 'Miss Clarafina?'

'Yes?'

'Are you okay?' Mr Trewton asks.

Clarafina sits quietly for a while. 'I'm not sure.'

'How do you feel?' Mr Frappounne asks.

'I'm not sure,' she answers still sitting stiff.

'Do you know whether you are awake?' Mr Gulthro asks.

Clarafina looks at Mr Frappounne out from the corner of her eyes somewhat agitated. 'Of course, I do.'

Mr Frappounne nods. 'Then you're probably fine, and if that is the case then you are feeling just as you should.'

Clarafina nods. 'That is good news.'

Almost an hour later, the five of them are sitting snugly watching, ever so often with a pair of binoculars to their eyes, Bees and Clarafina passing the one pair that they have to and fro between them, the third fight of the day. The men that work for Mr Frappounne are sitting at the opposite end of the porch on two crates drinking beer and smoking cigarettes.

When the third fight comes to an end with one of the dogs jumping over the top of the ring and running back to the side of the farmhouse where they, the five dogs that remain alive, are tied with leashes unusually long to a metal pole sticking out from the ground and wait for when they are needed to fight again Mr Frappounne tells his two workers to get the remaining dog from out of the ring and take him back to where the others are.

Next to the dogs is a large steel bin out of which the hind legs of 'Fin' is sticking who met his end, much to the surprise and more so the dismay of Bees who thought for sure that 'Fin' would stand the better chance of beating whoever he was up against being the more muscular of the two. After tying both dogs to the pole one of the workers calls over to Mr Frappounne and asks him which of the two remaining dogs they should put in the ring next. Mr Frappounne turns to Bees. 'What do you think my friend?'

'I think we should give the dogs a break for a while, that way they will be not so tired when they fight again and we can have the fun last a little bit longer.'

'A great idea, Mr Brungle.' Mr Frappounne tells his workers to go about the remainder of the day as they want to for an hour or two to give the dogs time to rest. 'Ms Clarafina?'

'Yes?'

'Would you like some more of what you have off the mirror?'

Clarafina nods. 'That will nice.'

'Great…' Mr Frappounne slides the mirror over to Mr Gulthro. 'Mr Gulthro, do you mind?'

'Of course not.'

Mr Frappounne gives the tube to Mr Gulthro and he begins to make another 12 lines. As he is doing so, he picks his nose, Clarafina looks over at him and sees and laughs before turning to Mr Frappounne, leaning over the table and saying in a soft voice. 'What do you call a man that picks his nose?'

Mr Frappounne looks at her somewhat distraught. 'Someone that picks his nose.'

Clarafina nods. 'Yes.'

Mr Frappounne stares blankly at her. 'And?'

'What do you call him?'

'I just told you.'

Clarafina sits upright somewhat. 'Told me what?'

'A man that picks his nose?' He answers suggestively.

'I know, what do you call him?'

'What do you call a man that picks his nose?'

Clarafina nods. 'Yes.'

Mr Frappounne frowns. 'You call him a man that picks his nose?'

Clarafina shakes her head. 'No…' Clarafina smiles. 'Do you want to know what you call him?'

Mr Frappounne nods. 'Most definitely.'

'You call him a gold digger.' Clarafina gently slams her palms down on the table. 'How good was that?'

Mr Frappounne nods. 'Quite good, where did you hear this?'

'Just made it up now.'

Mr Frappounne laughs. 'That's quite funny, Ms Clarafina.'

'Thank you.' She sits back in her chair. 'Because normally people only call women gold diggers, but when a man…' Clarafina leans over the table again and puts her hand over the side of her mouth. 'Does what Mr Gulthro just…' She sits back in her chair again. 'You can call him a gold digger too.'

Mr Frappounne nods. 'That makes it even funnier.'

'I know.'

Mr Frappounne looks over at Mr Gulthro. 'Mr Gulthro, how far are you over there?'

'About halfway.'

Mr Frappounne nods, 'Great.' He picks up his pair of binoculars and holds it over his eyes. After a while he puts the binoculars down and turns to Bees. 'Mr Brungle?'

'Yes.'

'What is the name of that tall fellow there by the cabin? The one standing next to the other tall one with the long hair?'

'Do they look similar?'

Mr Frappounne picks up the binoculars and looks over at the cabin again and nods. 'They do.'

'Then it's Dwendo, the one with the long hair is Kolos, or black and the beast as we call them over here.'

Mr Frappounne laughs. 'I can see why.' He puts the binoculars back down on the table. 'They quite frighten me those two.'

Bees nods. 'As they should.'

'Why do you say that?'

'Just look at the size of them.'

Mr Frappounne nods. 'Why don't you get the one with the short hair over here so we can see up close just how frightening he is?'

'Why would you want to do that?'

Mr Frappounne leans over to Bees and whispers something to him.

Bees looks at him perturbed. 'Really?'

Mr Frappounne nods. 'Could be a lot of fun.'

Bees thinks for a bit. 'Let's get him over here then.' He looks at Mr Frappounne. 'Can you get one of your workers to go get him?'

'Sure.' Mr Frappounne calls over his workers, they stand behind the porch railing. 'Can one of you go over to the cabin where the workers are and get the tall, very dark one to come over here.'

'Which one of us do you want to go?' Asks one of the workers.

'Whichever one of you wants to.'

They nod. One of them takes a coin out of his pocket, tosses it into the air and catches it with his hand closed, when he opens his hand, the worker standing opposite him drops his head and begins to 'slump' his way to the cabin.

'And do not take your time please,' says Mr Frappounne.

The worker begins to walk faster.

Mr Frappounne turns to the worker still standing by the porch. 'Why don't you join him, in case the big guy decides to give him trouble.'

The worker nods and catches up with the other.

When Mr Frappounne's workers return with Dwendo behind them Bees calls Dwendo over to the porch. Dwendo stands behind the railing. 'Welcome to the porch, Dwendo, I hope this is the first time you have been here.'

Dwendo nods.

'Good...' Bees says. 'You might be wondering why we brought you up here and that would be because Mr Frappounne came up with the wonderful idea to have you get into the ring over there with one of the dogs to see how you would hold up.'

'Two dogs, Mr Brungle, looking at the size of him one dog might not be enough.'

Bees nods. 'Two dogs it is then.' Bees rubs his hands together. 'Now take off your clothes to just your underpants and get in the ring, Dwendo.'

Dwendo turns around and makes his way to the ring. Mr Frappounne yells after him. 'Would you like something to lighten you up before you step into the ring Mr Dwendo?' Mr Frappounne asks.

Dwendo stops and turns around.

'I'm sure his kind don't know what you are referring to Mr Frappounne,' says Bees.

Mr Frappounne nods. 'Very well then.'

Bees looks over at Dwendo. 'On you go, Dwendo.'

Dwendo nods and keeps toward the ring. When Dwendo is standing by the ring Bees yells over to him. 'I want you to know, Dwendo that you being by far the bigger and stronger of the two animals you are going to be fighting now you most probably will walk away from there with a few scratches at the most, so if you are worried about your wellbeing at all do not, we will not put you in the way of harm of that kind.'

Dwendo nods.

'Very well then…' says Mr Frappounne. 'I will not wish you luck because you will not need it.'

Dwendo nods.

'In you go, then,' says Bees.

Dwendo climbs over the railings and into the ring. Once inside over brings one of Mr Frappounne's workers two dogs.

Bees leans over to Mr Frappounne. 'I can't believe I haven't thought of this before.'

Mr Frappounne nods. 'Don't mention it.'

After Mr Frappounne's worker had walked the dogs inside the ring he stands firm holding onto the leashes across from Dwendo.

Mr Frappounne looks over at Mr Trewton. 'Mr Trewton, will you?'

Mr Trewton nods and from a bag next to him he takes a whistle.

'On the sound of the whistle,' yells Mr Frappounne.

Mr Trewton blows the whistle and the worker lets go of the leashes…

Chapter 7

Friday night after the weekend that Mr Frappounne and his two associates came to the farm most of the workers are getting ready for bed while the rest go about their various doings as they would every other Friday night, in the children's side of the cabin Finta, Mueno and Thomvul are sat across from Mueno's bed on the floor playing a board game, Gheska is lying in his bed drawing on a piece of paper while Scara is in the kitchen filling a small canteen filled with ground coffee with hot water from the kettle.

When the canteen is filled to just below the edge, she fastens the lid on top and shakes the canteen a couple of times to have the coffee mix with the water before removing the lid to let the foam that formed on top of the coffee dissipate and takes from the cupboard under the sink a coffee cup.

After putting the lid back on the canteen, she walks to her bed and picks up a book written by one of her favourite authors when he was sixteen years old, comprised of 12 short stories of how water in different forms and situations can come to save or change people's lives within the context of topics such poverty, loss, injustice and love amongst others, written in a manner which she enjoys reading about being almost the same age, and her wool blanket and makes her way out of the cabin to where she always sits and reads.

Once there she lays her blanket on the ground under the tree, tucks her dress under her bottom and sits down and puts one end of the blanket over her and pours herself some coffee, waiting for it to cool down, she opens the book in her lap and begins to skim through it as the steam coming from the coffee warms the side of her leg through the blanket next to the cup of coffee.

After one cup of coffee and one short story, read twice over, she sees Klipp standing by the corner of the cabin and smiles.

'Hello,' says Klipp.

'What are you doing here?'

'Same thing I was last time.'

'In that case, care to join me?'

'That will be nice.'

'Hurry up, I'm quite warm under the blanket already.'

'That is why I brought this.' Klipp lifts up one side of the jacket he is wearing to reveal a sweater underneath.

'What is that?'

'My jacket is going to be my blanket.'

Scara smiles. 'How nice of you.'

'Thank you.'

'Take all the time you need then.'

Klipp makes his way over to her, takes off his jacket and sits down next to her with the jacket over his lap.

'What have you been doing since you were here last?'

'Just schoolwork most of the time.'

'Learn anything interesting?'

'Not really.'

'I find that hard to believe.'

'I don't really like schoolwork.'

Scara laughs. 'That I can believe.'

'What have you been doing?'

'Mostly reading and doing work around the farm with the other kids, and some schoolwork too.'

'Did *you* learn anything interesting?'

Scara thinks for a bit. 'Not really.'

They sit quietly for a while. 'Do you want some coffee, it's still warm?'

'I don't really like warm coffee.'

'What other kind of coffee is there?'

'I like coffee when it is cold.'

'I've never heard of anyone drinking coffee that is cold.'

'Really?'

Scara nods.

'It's very nice.'

'Do you make it different than warm coffee?'

'A little bit.'

'How do you make it?'

'You make it like warm coffee but you put in more sugar after and also ice to cool it down, then you put it in the fridge for a while and then you drink it.'

'Never had coffee that I didn't drink right after I made it.'

'You make more of it than warm coffee because you can drink more of it, and it tastes a little bit different than warm coffee too, I can bring you some if I see you again.'

'That will be nice.'

Scara pours herself another cup of coffee. 'I only have one cup with me.'

'That's okay.'

'I can go inside and get you another one?'

'That's fine, I had dinner before I came here so I'm not really hungry.'

Scara nods. 'Okay.' She puts the lid on the canteen. 'Have you been reading at all since you were last here?'

'School books?'

'No, just normal books?'

'A little bit, I'm not really good at reading.'

'You seemed to be quite good at it the last time you were here.'

'I didn't really read, I just looked at the pictures.'

'Oh.'

Klipp sits quietly for a while. 'I don't really know how to read very good.'

'Oh.'

'But it would be very nice to.'

'Lucky for you I hear that I am quite good at it, I can teach you if you want?'

'How long will that take?'

'Not very long…' Scara holds up the book in her lap. 'This one here is not very difficult, the guy that wrote it did so when he was 16.'

Klipp's eyes widen. 'Really.'

'Yes, why?'

'I thought you had to be a lot older to write books.'

'You can write a book no matter how old you are.'

'Maybe.'

'So…' Scara places her hands over the cover of the book. 'Do you want me to teach you?'

Almost two hours later Klipp looks up at Scara. 'That was not bad?'

'It was very good.'

'It's a little easier than I thought it would be.'

'You weren't that bad to begin with.'

'I think it's just because you're a good teacher.'

'Hopefully that helped a little bit.'

'That was a nice story about the man who was scared of water and then became a swim teacher.'

Scara nods. 'I like the one where the young boy has a cold and his mother gives him lots of glasses of warm water because they don't have money for medicine.'

'That one is nice too.'

'Are all the stories about water?'

'Yes.'

'Do you have other books like this?'

'Books with short stories?'

Klipp nods.

'One or two.'

'I like these ones.'

'I do too, it seems like there's a lesson to be learned from most of them more than longer ones.'

'There was a girl in my school who was a swimmer, she was very good, she even beat the boys.'

'I didn't know that girl was allowed to swim with boys?'

'They weren't, she was just so good that they had to let her swim with the boys because she swam so far past all the other girls, her mom was a swim teacher.'

'That's probably why she was so good.'

'I think so.'

'Did you do swimming when you were at school?'

Klipp shakes his head. 'No.'

'Did you play any sports?'

'I played rugby.'

'I don't know much about that, what position did you play?'

'The guy next to the guy that takes the ball out of the scrum.'

'What's that?'

'A scrum?'

Scara nods.

'It's when the guys that play the front part of the team lock their arms over each other and push like that against the other teams' scrum and so that the guy from their team that has to get the ball can get it before the guy from the other team can, then the guy with the ball throws it to me and I throw it to the guy next to me?'

'Did you like it?'

'A lot.'

'Did you play any other sports?'

'No.'

'You?'

'I've never been to school.'

Klipp laughs. 'Oh, sorry, it's not that nice.'

'I can't imagine that.'

'If you like to read and write it's probably quite nice.'

'That I can imagine.'

'Have you ever written anything?'

Scara shakes her head.

'Why?'

'I don't know, it's just not something I want to do.'

'Oh, I thought you definitely would want to looking at how much you read.'

Scara laughs. 'That I can also imagine.'

'You? Now that you read so well?'

Klipp thinks for a bit and shakes his head. 'No, it doesn't look like fun, I like drawing, I do that a lot.'

'Really?'

Klipp nods.

'What do you draw?'

'Lots of things.'

'Like what?'

'Monsters most of the time, and cars and airplanes and other things like that.'

'What kind of monsters?'

'Monsters you see in the movies, sometimes different ones I try to draw myself but they never look as nice as the ones in the movies.'

'Do they look scary?'

'Not really, you have to be pretty good to make them scary, I'm not that good yet.'

'How long have you been drawing for?'

'Maybe when I was ten, I got a colouring book for Christmas one time and then drew pictures from there.'

'How many pictures have you drawn?'

'I don't know, lots.'

'More than a hundred?'

'Maybe not that much, maybe almost a hundred if you count the ones I threw away.'

'Where are they?'

'In a box under my bed.'

'Do you think I can see them some time?'

'If you want.'

'Can you bring them with next time you come here?'

'If you want me to come here again?'

'Of course, I do, even without the pictures.'

Klipp smiles. 'Okay, I'll bring them with.'

'You can bring other pictures besides the ones of monsters, that will be nice to see too.'

'Okay, I'll bring the ones of cars and airplanes with.'

'Do you have a lot of those?'

'Maybe as much as I have the monsters, I really like drawing cars too, maybe even more than monsters.'

'Is it hard to draw those ones?'

Klipp nods. 'Yes, I'm not very good at that yet.'

'I'm sure you will be if you keep drawing them?'

'I know, the ones I drew when I started is not as good as the ones draw now.'

'Do you still have the old ones?'

'No, I threw them away.'

'Oh, would have liked to see them.'

'I don't think so, they were not very good.'

'Oh.'

'Maybe one day I can draw pictures like the ones in the book I looked at last time I was here.'

'That would be nice, if you want, I can go get the book and you can take it with you to draw from until you come back next time.'

'That will be nice.'

'I can go get the book now if you want?'

'Okay.'

Scara takes the blanket off her and gets up. 'Just make sure your aunt or uncle doesn't see it, it's one of my favourite books.'

'I won't.'

'I'll be right back.'

'Okay.'

Scara makes her way around the cabin and inside. After playing with his fingers for a while Klipp picks up a twig lying close by and begins to draw something in the sand. When Scara sits back down, she looks over at the picture that Klipp drew in the ground. 'What's that?'

'It's a monster that's hands and mouth is hearts.'

Scara laughs. 'That's nice, because he's a nice monster.'

'Yes.'

'Did you draw this one as a picture already?'

Klipp shakes his head. 'No.'

'Maybe you can and bring it with next time you come?'

'Okay, how must I draw it?'

'It will be nice if you can draw it with colour?'

'Okay, that will be nice.'

'I can bake you a cake to say thank you?'

'That's okay, you don't have to do that.'

'I want to, it's Mueno's birthday in a couple of days and me and Finta are going to bake him a cake, I can make you a smaller one?'

'If it's not a lot of work?'

'Not at all, I like to bake so it will be nice to bake one for you, I can make it look like a monster maybe?'

'That will be nice.'

'Great, when I see you next Friday, I'll give you the cake and you can give me the picture?'

'Okay.'

Scara gives Klipp the book she got from the cabin. 'Take good care of it.'

'I will.'

Klipp opens the book and begins to look the pictures over. 'Do you think the people that draw these pictures get money to do it?'

'I think so.'

'So, they do it for work?'

'Yes.'

'What is the work called?'

'I think it's called being an illustrator.'

'Wow.'

'Maybe you can do that one day?'

'That will be nice, what do you want to be when you grow up?'

'A teacher.'

'What do you want to teach?'

'Anything not too hard,' she says giggling.

Klipp laughs.

'Maybe music or art or something along those lines, homemaking or making garments of sort.'

'You will probably be good at all of those, I thought you were going to say that you want to make clothes that you make yourself?'

'A fashion designer?'

Klipp nods. 'Yes.'

'That is what I would like to do, teaching is what I want to do.'

'What is the difference?'

'What I would *like* to do is what I want to do more than anything else, what I *want* to do is what I have to do because I can't do what *I like* to do.'

Klipp nods. 'Oh, it probably costs a lot of money to make clothes.'

'It does.'

Klipp turns to her. 'Do you think you might never be able to do it?'

'I don't know.'

'Maybe you can ask my aunt for money, if she likes the things you make, she can give you money to make more and then you can sell it in the shops and you can give my aunt back the money.'

'I think that might be too much of a stretch.'

'She could, if the clothes you make is good?'

'Maybe.'

'Or I could do something along those lines by taking the clothes to stores in town and see if they can help me out.'

'How much clothes will you have to take?'

'Probably just one of each garment I make.'

'If they like it then they give you money to make more?'

Scara nods. 'Yep.'

'That's nice, then you can just make a couple of your best things?'

'Exactly.'

'Or you can draw them what you want to make or tell them what you want to and what you want it to look like with pictures or something?'

'That's a good idea actually.'

'If the clothes look like the white dress with the pictures on the bottom you wore a couple of nights ago in the cabin, then people will definitely like your clothes.'

'Was that the night you were peeking through the cabin window?'

Klipp nods. 'Yes, you waved at me.'

'I remember that.'

'That was a very nice dress.'

'Thank you, I'll keep that in mind.'

'How much did it cost to make that?'

'Nothing, everything I needed to make it we had here and a couple of other things too from the garage.'

Klipp nods. 'There is a lot of things in there, I went there one time to look for something but walked out when I saw how much stuff was in there.'

Scara laughs. 'It would be nice to see what all is in there some time.'

They sit quietly for a while, Klipp picking up the twig next to him and scribbling something in the ground again, Klipp looks up at Scara. 'Maybe if you can't get money to make clothes now, you can use some from being a teacher to make clothes, it's going to take a bit longer but you can still do it then?'

'I plan on doing that too, thing is it might be harder to get a teaching job than I would like to think.'

'Why?'

'Because of the colour of my skin.'

'Oh, I didn't think about that, there must be some black teachers at the schools?'

'I'm not sure, I hope so.'

'If not, you should go somewhere else, I'm sure there will be better schools further away from here?'

'If there's nothing around here, I'll definitely do that.'

'Maybe with the money I give you won't even have to go somewhere else, maybe you won't even have to here.'

162

Scara laughs. 'That will be especially nice.'

'Maybe you won't even have a choice to go somewhere else.'

'What do you mean?'

'With how things are going with the farm my aunt and uncle will not even be able to live here much longer because they'll probably have to sell it so they can have money.'

'Are they having trouble with money?'

'I think so.'

'Why do you say that?'

'Lots of stuff around the house they have been selling.'

'I did not know that.'

'My uncle also told my aunt one night to not buy so much wine because they don't have money to pay the electricity.'

'Are they trying to do anything about it?'

'I don't know, I think that's why the three people came here last weekend, so that my uncle can talk with them about money.'

'Do you know how it went?'

Klipp shakes his head. 'No.'

Scara sits quietly for a while. 'That would be quite a thing if we will have to move from here.'

'Can't be too bad.'

'How so?'

'It can't be very nice to live here, especially with my uncle.'

'Do you think someone will buy the farm from them and let them stay on?'

'I don't know, I'll ask my uncle, maybe that's why the man that was here with his two friends was here?'

Scara nods. 'Maybe.' She sits looking up at the sky thinking how frightfully big the universe must be seeing as how many stars in the sky it looks to her there might be while Klipp is doing the same only thinking about what she might be thinking at that moment. As Scara's thoughts on the size of the universe begin to fade away, hers too drifts toward that of what Klipp might be thinking and after a while she turns to him and asks, 'Can I have your arm please?'

Chapter 8

Bees and Clarafina are running down the stairs, Clarafina behind Bees trying to catch up with him. When they reach the bottom of the stairs they race to the kitchen and once they are inside, they stop running and walk over to the cupboards above the sinks. Bees gets on the counter wherein the sinks are and opens a cupboard door and takes out a cake pan.

Outside by the driveway, Grandpa Brungle, Murkel and Visa are getting out of one of Grandpa Brungle's two trucks, with a detail on either side of the truck in black ink that reads 'WMP.' As Murkel and Vista go about their way Grandpa Brungle goes inside the house, by the door he hears commotion coming from the kitchen, he yells out for Bees and Clarafina. At the sound of his voice, the cake pans falls on the floor and he makes his way toward the kitchen. By the kitchen door, he sees Bees and Clarafina knelt on the floor with a roll of paper towels by their side fervently wiping cake batter off the floor. He yells out to them again. They look up and see him standing by the door and stop what they are doing, he walks over to them and kneels down next to them. 'What is going on here?'

Neither Bees nor Clarafina is able to get a word out, Grandpa Brungle laughs, staring at them with purposely piercing eyes. On the rare occasion that Bees and Clarafina talk about that day, both say that they saw Grandpa Brungle's eyes look at both of them in different directions at the same time.

'I cannot say that leaving the two of you without my supervision I expected anything different to what I am seeing.' Grandpa Brungle looks to and fro between them. 'Now which one of you is going to tell me what this stuff is and why it is on my floor?'

Bees and Clarafina stare blankly at him.

'I've got all day.'

'We were going to bake you a cake,' says Clarafina.

Grandpa Brungle laughs. 'The cake part I believe, the baking it for me part not so much.'

'We were really going to bake it for you,' says Bees.

Grandpa Brungle rubs Bees' head. 'Now that you have seconded what your sister here said why don't you make me believe it.' He taps the glass face of his watch with his finger. 'You have one minute.'

Trembling, Bees tries to think of something to say.

'I don't have all day boy.'

Bees looks at Grandpa Brungle blankly. 'We weren't going to bake the cake for you,' he says hurriedly.

Grandpa Brungle smiles. 'Now there is something I can respect, good for you for telling the truth, for that you will be rewarded.' He puts his hand on Bees' shoulder. 'However, for lying to me in the first place, the punishment you will get will be far greater than the leniency you will be offered for coming clean after doing so and you will be punished greatly still.' He turns to Clarafina. 'And so will you, young lady.' He gets up and tucks his thumbs under his suspender straps.

'Here's how the rest of the day is going to go, the two of you are going to use your hands to scoop up however much of that dung you can and put in the cake pan how you planned before putting it in the oven to bake, then you are going to decorate it however you please, I would prefer it if you did not decorate it at all but it is your cake, so do as you want with it after cleaning this place to make it look better than it did before you stepped foot in here this morning.' He reaches for the stove and turns on one of the plates. 'Before that can happen though, you must be punished for the mess you made here and that...' He holds his hand over the pan. 'Almost ready,' he says and moves away his hand. 'Is going to happen in just a moment.'

As quickly as possible Bees gets up and runs out the kitchen door and to the front, Clarafina decides to do the same but is not able to get away before Grandpa Brungle grabs a hold of her by the straps of her own set of suspenders. By the front door Bees turns around to see if Clarafina is behind him, when he does so, much to his horror he sees that she is still in the kitchen trying to get away from Grandpa Brungle and thinking to himself that it would be better if only one of them gets punished, instead of both he decides to make a run for it and leave Clarafina behind, when he sets foot on the driveway he sees something that upsets him quite a bit more than the thought of Clarafina getting punished by Grandpa Brungle and freezes up.

In front of him, attached to the back of Grandpa Brungle's truck is the trailer which whenever he sees in the garage thinks to himself what might it be used for being as big as it is, even more so than being surprised by seeing the trailer out of the garage for the first time is the workers sitting, standing and lying spread out over the floor thereof.

Bees waves at the workers, without a moment's hesitation they wave back at him and right there he decides that it is his duty to get the workers out of the trailer by any means no matter what the consequences. He reaches for a holster he keeps on his belt and takes out a knife that he keeps on his person during all times of the day except for at night when he sleeps with it under his pillow. With the knife in his hand, he makes his way to the back of the trailer, folds open the blade on his pocketknife and begins to fiddle around inside the lock with it.

In the kitchen, Grandpa Brungle is holding onto Clarafina by her arm, squeezing it so hard while he is doing so that it might as well be the punishment itself. He holds the palm of his hand over the stove plate and immediately shakes off the burning sensation after doing so. 'Just right.' He looks down at Clarafina. 'Before we go any further, I have to tell you that I take no pleasure in doing what I am about to but that I have to in order for you to know to not do it again, do you understand that?'

Clarafina nods.

'Good, now give me your hand.'

Clarafina shakes her head.

'Give me your hand.'

Again, Clarafina shakes her head.

'If you don't give me your hand, young lady, I am going to have to burn another part of your body that you will like a lot less me doing so than the hand I am asking you to give me.'

Clarafina tries to run away but again is unable to do so as Grandpa Brungle is still holding onto her arm. 'That's a very silly thing you tried to do young lady, now I am going to have to punish you doubly.' Grandpa Brungle grabs both of Clarafina's wrists and presses the palms of her hands down on the stove plate.

Outside Bees hears Clarafina scream and he turns around and runs down the hill to the vineyard where he sat until sundown hoping that Grandpa Brungle might forget about what happened earlier in the day. When he came back to the house, he found Grandpa Brungle and Clarafina waiting for him sitting by the

166

kitchen table, Grandpa Brungle made her sit with him there until Bees came back to the house so that Bees could be dealt his punishment in front of her.

When Bees sat down with them by the table Grandpa Brungle told them to put the cake in the oven and sat with them in complete quiet until the cake had finished baking after which he cut the cake into two equal pieces and sat by and watched them eat their respective pieces. After the first couple of bites, Bees puked on the kitchen floor, after cleaning up the mess he sat back down and ate the remainder of his piece of cake with as much determination as he has ever done anything in his life.

By the table across from him, Clarafina finished eating her piece of cake before Bees had even finished cleaning his puke off the kitchen floor. When they were finished with their pieces of cake, Clarafina went up to her bedroom while Bees stayed behind and washed the dishes forced to listen to Grandpa Brungle's stories of how his father punished him when he was Bees' age.

Chapter 9

It is ten o'clock Friday night and like most other nights on the farm, it is quiet to a degree almost unsettling. One of only two lights 'eating' up electricity is the spotlight on top of the roof, when Klipp was told by Bees when he was asked to give him a quarter of his savings when he first came to the farm had to be installed after the house had been broken into and many valuables were stolen, of course there was no break in and nothing was stolen, nor has there ever been a house broken into or a robbery of any kind in the entire recorded history of Golden Heart, the reason that when Bees was 13 years old the police station was demolished.

He still remembers the day very vividly, when Grandpa Brungle took him into town to see it get demolished first because he was of the thinking that it is better to see history in the making rather than to learn about it in school and Bees remembers how excited he was to miss his first day of school where he would not have to do so while staying in bed.

Shortly after the police station was demolished a gun and ammunition store opened up in its place by the name of 'The Golden Bullet,' a name which the owners of the other four guns and ammunition stores in town very much envied as well as berated themselves for, for not having thought of a name for their stores likened to that of the town. 'The Golden Bullet' was the first of the five stores to use silver and gold to cast firearms and ammunition as well as that paid much attention to smaller details concerning their product in the form of making engravings in their bullets and firearms as well as making that to customers' specifications, different to what the average store offered.

Ever since the store opened its doors there has been somewhat of a divide between the people, especially the men, of Golden Heart, a divide born not from a dislike for each other but from the gun and ammunition store they decided to support, this happened gradually about a year or so after 'The Golden Bullet' opened its doors and eased its way into the lives of the people of Golden Heart without them taking note thereof, going as far even as the farmer's wives embroidering their husbands' shirts with the names of the respective stores they chose to support and buy from.

The restaurants and bars also started to cater to clients based on their choice of store and although anyone was allowed to dine and drink wherever they wanted to each chose to stick to the places that somehow became allotted to them because of the more relaxed atmosphere that each the places would offer certain clients in different ways.

On nights when families went to go eat out, the men brought with them at least a pistol and a couple of personalised bullets they might have gotten new that quarter to show off and compare amongst each other, spending their time waiting for their food mostly bad mouthing the stores which they did not support and those that they did, spending many an hour, sometimes so long that their families had already finished their food when they got back to the dining table from the bar, comparing guns and their specifications to see which is better until they met again.

Things continued along those lines for almost three decades and guns as well as bullets became more talked about by the men of Golden Heart than any other topic that had ever been a part of their conversation up until that point, because more than being farmers the men of Golden Heart considered themselves to be collectors and connoisseurs of guns as well as ammunition after 'The Golden Bullet' opened its doors and prided themselves mostly on the size and quality of their collection of guns and ammunition.

The second of the two lights turned on in the house is the living room light where Clarafina is sitting by herself drinking red wine and playing cards while Bees is already in his bed sleeping having had too much to drink as usual which every time it happens to Clarafina is quite funny because Bees had the spotlight installed to better his chances of catching the workers trying to run away or causing trouble on the farm at night.

One night when Bees was sitting on the porch, drinking and looking out over the lawn after a day's work, which consisted primarily of berating the workers while having a beer every now and then to line his stomach so that come sundown he might be able to more safely drink stronger liquor, he began to think of what his reasoning might have been for installing the spotlight and how doing so made him think it will increase his chances of catching the workers doing something he did not approve of or even increase the chances of them doing something of the manner might they be afraid of dark and him getting to berate and scold them for it he was unable to think of a reason good enough that made him think it was necessary to do so.

In Klipp's room the lights are turned off, not because he chose to have it so but because since the spotlight was installed, to conserve electricity, he was not allowed to turn on any of the lights in his room during any time of the day, which to him was quite funny because out of all of the rooms in the house his room had the most lights in it, a lamp each on small bedside tables on either side of his bed, a smaller lamp on a desk across from his bed, a light in the roof as well as a switch above the headboard of his bed which turns on a small light bulb directly above the switch of which the bulb is no longer working and which Klipp found a suitable replacement for in the garage but was told by Bees he was not allowed to install because he has to sleep with his lamp turned on beside his bed after drinking due to night terrors.

What makes Bees' rule more preposterous even is the fact that Klipp is the only one out of the three of them to always turn off every light after walking out of a room as well as sometimes not even turning one on unless necessary, when Klipp is in need of a light, he is either allowed to sit in the living room with Bees and Clarafina while they are there for whatever reason or he is allowed the light of one candle every two days in his room.

Since the previous Friday, for the fifth night in a row, Klipp spent most of his time reading by his desk from sundown to early into the morning, going as far as to use two candles a day to do so after finding a couple of dozen of boxes of them in the garage, from the home-schooling books that he got from Clarafina so that he might be able to become better thereat to improve his vocabulary and understanding and knowledge of things because despite his uncle telling him that he does not need an education because everything he will ever need is on the farm; Klipp very much wants to go to university to get a degree in something other than agriculture someday, something he has not yet told Bees as well as won't, as it might only lessen his chances of getting to do so he did tell Clarafina one night while they were having a cup of coffee after cleaning the kitchen and she expressed to him how proud she is of him wanting to do so because she never did.

After hearing about Klipp wanting to go to university she gave him, because Bees refuses to pay for schooling for Klipp, a chest full of books for home-schooling, a book on every subject from grades 1 through to 12 which, that if Klipp finishes them all, puts him on the same level as the average high school graduate. Altogether there were 38 books to study as well as 38 smaller counterparts in which there are questions on every chapter in each book, better than having the textbooks was the fact that in each of them was underlined and highlighted what the important parts are along with various notes here and there to help better understand what is written in them.

The Saturday after reading with Scara behind the cabin, Klipp spent almost 12 hours reading through the first one as many times as he could moving to and fro from his desk and his bed and even sometimes the carpet on the floor next to his bed until he was able to read the first book with as much ease as doing so for almost half a day allowed him.

When the clock struck nine on Friday night, Klipp was almost halfway done with the third of the home-schooling books that he started reading the week before the first of the crickets that usually do so, whether they were the same crickets every time Klipp always wondered, began to chirp as the darkest part of what is the night set. Another thing he wondered about when he heard the crickets starting to chirp was whether they also began to do so because that was the time, every Friday night, around which Bees fell asleep after spending a couple of hours drinking, which usually is on one of the rocking chairs on the porch for an hour or two before he waddles his way up the stairs to his bedroom does he find himself lucky enough to do so.

After putting the book back in the chest under his bed, Klipp puts on his leather jacket, grabs the book that Scara lent him a week earlier, the picture he drew for her and a canteen full of cold coffee with lots of sugar and some cinnamon powder and climbs out of the window and down the drainpipe to the back of the house and makes his way across the edge of the lawn away from the light of the spotlight to the cabin, where he would hopefully find Scara sitting where she did a week prior.

Upon reaching the cabin, he had the thought of peering through the window to the children's' sleeping quarters to see whether she might not be in her bed sleeping but held back from doing so as he felt that he did not want to take away from the excitement sooner than he had to getting to see her.

When Klipp turns the corner by the edge of the cabin, he sees Scara sitting almost exactly where she was the last time with the same blanket pulled somewhat the same over her lap with the same canteen, which Klipp assumed was filled with coffee like the time before, and a coffee mug next to her but reading from a different book than she was last time.

'Hello,' says Klipp.

Scara looks up and smiles. 'Hey, funny seeing you here?'

Klipp frowns. 'I thought last time…'

Scara laughs. 'Just kidding…' She closes the book. 'Come sit down.'

Klipp sits down next to her, takes off his jacket and puts it over his lap. 'Here.' He gives her the book she lent him.

She takes the book from him. 'Did you like it?'

'Didn't read it, just looked at the pictures.'

'I guess what we were talking about last time that's pretty much the same thing.'

Klipp laughs. 'I did read a lot from my schoolbooks.'

'Really? Why?'

'I think I'm going to start reading from them every day now because if I want to get a job one day, I will have to be able to read and know the things that school kids know and the school books are what they read.'

'Seems like the last time you were here rubbed off on you?'

Klipp laughs. 'A little bit.'

'What books did you read?'

'Mostly a book that says how the country started and the people that were there when it happened and so.'

'History.'

Klipp nods. 'Yes.'

'Did you like it?'

'Yes.'

'So, are you now going to keep reading all the schoolbooks until you've read them all?'

Klipp nods. 'As much as I can.'

'How many books are there.'

'Maybe 40.'

Scara's eyes widen. 'You're going to be reading for quite a while then?'

'Maybe, but there's still a lot of time left until I'm as old as kids when they finish high school.'

'True.'

Scara looks over at the canteen next to Klipp. 'Is there cold coffee in there by any chance?'

Klipp nods and picks up the canteen. 'And lots of sugar and some cinnamon.'

'Can't wait to try it.'

'Do you have a place I can pour it in?'

She picks up her mug next to her and holds it out in front of Klipp. 'This.'

Klipp takes the lid off and pours some coffee into Scara's mug.

'That there's no steam coming from it is somewhat strange...' She holds her hand over the mug. 'I'll try it anyway because you made it.' She holds the mug up to her mouth and takes a drink and swallows. 'It's really good, like a very runny kind of chocolate milkshakes almost, with cinnamon.'

'Never thought of it that way.'

Scara nods. 'Maybe next time you make it you should put ice cream in it.'

'There's no ice cream at the house.'

Scara takes another drink. 'If there ever is.'

'I'll try and remember that.'

'If you ever do, bring me some too if you can.'

'I'll remember that probably more than I will the ice cream.'

Scara takes another sip of coffee and puts her mug down next to her. 'Did you have a hard time getting out of the house?'

'I heard my uncle go into his bedroom a while before and my aunt was already asleep in the living room, but I climbed out of the window just to be safe.'

'How is climbing out of a window being safe?'

'Less chance of my uncle or aunt seeing me go outside.'

'More chance of breaking an arm or a leg too.'

'I'd rather break an arm or a leg than have my uncle find out I tried to sneak out of the house so late.'

'The little I do know of your uncle I would say that you have a point.' Scara picks up her coffee mug. 'This is a lot nicer than I expected it would be'

Klipp pours himself some and takes a drink. Scara looks at him. 'That's a really big sip.'

'I'm very thirsty.'

'I still drink mine like I do warm coffee.'

'That's maybe because you want to warm yourself up?'

'Maybe.'

'I've never really drank anything to warm myself.'

'Not even warm milk?'

Klipp shakes his head.

'Maybe you've just never been very cold?'

'Maybe, I like the cold a lot more than I like warm.'

'Really?'

Klipp nods. 'It's harder to make yourself cold on a hot day than to make yourself warm on a cold day.'

'How so?'

'If it's a hot day and you sit under a tree you can still be hot, to get as cold as you want you have to have a pool or you have to use a hosepipe to spray yourself with water, if it's a cold day you can sit under a blanket or just put on something warm.'

'Maybe.'

'You can also be less stinky on a cold day than a hot one.'

Scara laughs. 'That one's definitely true.'

'Can I ask you something?'

'Sure.'

'I read in the book I've been reading that long ago girls got married when they were just a little bit older than me, and you and that the guys they married were maybe two times as old as we are, do you think that really did happen?'

'I'm pretty sure.'

'How can that be?'

'I don't know, it's just the way things were back then I guess.'

'But it's wrong, so why did it happen?'

Scara looks at Klipp. 'Why is it wrong?'

'Because the girl is so young.'

'If she wants to get married no matter what age she is to whoever regardless of what their age might be how can it be wrong?'

'I don't know, it just is.'

'What makes you so iffy about it?'

'What if the girl has to kiss the guy?'

'Then it is because she wants to.'

174

'How can she want to kiss a guy that old?'

'Are you a bit upset that girls you think should be chasing after you are doing so after older guys?'

'No.'

'Then why are you so upset?'

'I don't know, I just didn't think that you would want to do something like that.'

'I'm not saying I want to, but if Catin Gates was standing here right now and asked me to kiss him why would I say 'no'?'

'I don't know, you don't have to because he's a movie star.'

'But he's still twice my age?'

'It's just a bit different then.'

'Not really.'

They sit quietly for a while.

'I don't know.'

'Sorry to disappoint you.'

'You didn't.'

Scara positions herself differently under her blanket. 'Let me ask you this…'

Klipp nods. 'Okay.'

'Do you think Renu Hearten is pretty?'

'Yes.'

'If she asked you to kiss her, would you?'

'Yes.' Klipp answers somewhat more confidently than before.

'Why is it so bad if I want to kiss Catin Gates then?'

'I don't know, because you're a girl and it's just a bit different for girls.'

'That's not very nice.'

'I know, but that's how it is.' Klipp picks up the canteen. 'I think I should go back to the house.'

Scara's eyes widen. 'Why?'

'It's just not nice being here now.'

'If we talk about something else it might be again?'

'I don't think that is going to work.'

'At least stay for a little while so we can try and talk about what caused all this?'

Klipp gets up. 'I don't think that is going to make a difference, this is just how I feel.'

Before Scara is able to talk a sharp light 'stings' their eyes and they slam their eyelids closed. Once their sight had gone back to normal and they opened their eyes, they see Clarafina standing by the edge of the cabin. 'What in the name of the utmost wrong are you doing here, nephew?'

'Reading, auntie Clarafina.'

'In the dark?'

'We can see quite good in the moonlight.'

'Do you expect me to believe that? I can barely make out who is who between the two of you and I'm shining a flashlight on you.'

Klipp and Scara stare blankly at Clarafina. Clarafina tilts the flashlight forward onto the book in Scara's lap. 'What are you reading?'

The sudden movement of the light gives Scara such a fright that she grabs a hold of Klipp's hand without knowing that she does so. Clarafina shines the light from the flashlight onto their hands. 'Let go of my nephew's hand missy, this is not the kind of world where things like this can happen.'

Without any hesitation, and again not aware that she is doing so Scara let's go of Klipp's hand, his hand still held out somewhat to his side in awe that he was just holding hands with her.

'What are you thinking, holding the hand of the nephew of the man that your father works for?'

Scara shakes her head. 'Sorry, I didn't know I was.'

'Like donkey droppings you didn't.' Clarafina shines the flashlight over the both of them. 'You should be glad that I am so shocked at what I'm seeing here so I'm not more angry about it.'

Klipp nods. 'We are auntie Clarafina, she was teaching me to read.'

Clarafina frowns. 'She...' She shines the flashlight onto Scara. 'Was teaching you to read, do you even know what a book is missy?'

Scara nods her head.

'She reads very good, auntie Clarafina, maybe even better than you.'

'Take that back now...' Clarafina says and brings her satchel forward over her shoulder and brings it up to her mouth. 'And let me know when you have so I can continue to address the situation here.' She takes a drink, puts the cork back in the satchel mouth and moves it back over her shoulder, she taps her shoe on the ground. 'Is it gone, nephew?'

Klipp nods. 'Yes, auntie Clarafina.'

'Good, and even if by some act of the impossible the little girl next to you was able to read better than me the fact that you, nephew, are able to believe that shows only how very grey you are up here.'

Klipp nods. 'Yes, auntie Clarafina.'

'Good, now get your things and follow me back to the house.'

Early the next morning Bees, Clarafina and Klipp, who had not said a word for almost 15 minutes as per Bees' instructions to do so to think of an excuse good enough as to why he went to the cabin the night before knowing that it might upset him and Clarafina, are sitting by the kitchen table. After he finished eating Bees turns to Klipp. 'I have a suspicion that you did not do what I asked of you for the last quarter of an hour, so I'm going to have to ask you to sit still for another 15 minutes until I'm satisfied that you did as I asked of you.'

Klipp nods. Almost ten minutes later, Bees slams his fist down on the table sending a shiver so strong up Klipp's spine that all the shivers he felt up to then made it seem that the shiver he just felt was the first one he ever did and Clarafina, who had fallen asleep almost as soon as they sat down on the table falling off her chair. Bees and Klipp look down at Clarafina on the floor squeezing the bottom of her back. 'What was that for?' Bees asks.

'I should ask you the same thing?'

'You're the one on the floor so you first.'

'Get away from me,' she pushes Bees to the side and gets up and sits back down.

Bees turns to Klipp. 'Why you are sitting here is because I hear you have yourself a little girlfriend?'

Klipp sits quietly.

'Okay...' Bees nods. 'Now I have to ask, are you blind nephew?'

'What kind of a question is that?' Clarafina asks.

'Quiet Clarafina, let the boy answer the question, the answer might be more surprising than you and I can know.'

Clarafina nods.

'So, nephew, are you?'

'Excuse me uncle?'

'The question was whether you are blind nephew?'

'I don't understand?'

177

Bees leans in to Klipp. 'Let's try this again, 'Are you blind?' 'do you need glasses?' 'do your eyes work?'...' Bees holds up five fingers. 'How many fingers am I holding up?'

Klipp frowns. 'Five, uncle Bees.'

'That was not the question, the question was whether you are blind?' Bees asks overly agitated.

'No, uncle Bees.'

Bees nods, calmer. 'Spiritually blind you are definitely, spiritually blind you are blinder than a batch of bats, spiritually your eyes have been picked out by crows...' Bees gets up and walks to the fridge. 'And after what happened last night, the things didn't even leave you your eyelids.' He opens the fridge and takes a bottle of brandy from it and brings that and a mug to drink it from over to the table and sits down.

'Let's not use language so harsh in front of the boy brother, we shouldn't be the ones to expose him to things as such.'

'Come again, your choice of words was so... nice that I didn't hear a word of what you said.'

'I'm saying we shouldn't talk so angrily with the boy; our father taught us better than that.'

Bees opens the bottle of brandy and pours some into the mug. 'Our father didn't teach us a thing Clarafina, not a thing, the man was colder than a tombstone in a blizzard.' Bees drinks a couple of mouthfuls of brandy. 'Are you aware of the relationship that Brungles have with people of colour, nephew?'

Klipp shakes his head.

'I would have guessed; the relationship nephew is that we do not like them very much.'

'I know, uncle Bees.'

'If you know then what in the name of all things upside down were you doing socialising with some of that colour, and a woman of that colour?'

'We are friends uncle Bees.'

'Do you expect me to believe that?'

Klipp shakes his head. 'No.'

'Then why did you say it?'

'Because it's true.'

Bees takes another drink of brandy and finishes what is in the mug. 'You nephew are a liar; I can smell those and you smell bad.' He picks up the bottle of brandy and pours himself and mug full. 'Let me also say, that being friends with someone of that colour and more importantly sex makes matters a lot worse, just being friends with her means you are not using her for what she was intended to be used, especially because she is the colour she is.'

'Actually nephew...' Clarafina turns to Bees. 'Do you mind if I say something here boet?'

Bees nods. 'I would love to hear a woman's opinion on this.'

Clarafina turns away from him agitated. 'There is a point to what your uncle is saying, but the point is very demeaning to women.'

'Where did you get that from, Clarafina?'

'What?'

'"Demeaning"?'

'From a magazine.'

Bees nods. 'Oh, are you sure you're using it right?'

'Yes.'

'How can you be?'

'The sentence I got it from in the magazine says that's how to use it, that's why 'mean' is in it.' Clarafina turns to Klipp. 'Anyway nephew, it's not nice to think of your situation like your uncle says it is, using her for what your uncle says is just as bad as being her friend, that's why it's better to stay away from her completely, does that make sense?'

Klipp nods.

'Dare I say it myself nephew...' Bees picks up the mug of brandy. 'Your aunt here is right, it's better to stay away from her altogether, that way you take out the risk factor.'

'What risk factor?'

'If the boy were to be bad enough to kiss her, he would become sick.'

'Sick how?'

'Sick like with the flu or a cold of some sort, maybe even measles for all we know.'

'I think you have what you're talking about now, that's why you are talking about it.'

Bees gets up and makes his way over to one of two large steel sinks in a pantry attached to the kitchen by an open door that leads outside, positions himself over one of them, unzips his pants and urinates inside of it.

Clarafina hears this and turns around. 'What are you doing?'

'What does it look like I'm doing?'

'Something that you shouldn't be.'

'Why?'

'Because of where you're doing it.'

'People urinate on the ground and against walls all the time and people don't think a thing about it, I would say going where I am is a step *up* from the last two.' Bees zips up his pants. 'How do you like those yellow apples?' He sits back down at the table. 'Don't ever try what I just did, it takes years of experience to be able to do that.'

Klipp nods.

'Now, on the topic of the wrong you committed just a few hours ago I am not going to punish you like you wrongfully might have thought I would I am going to teach you a lesson, one that you will be able to carry with you throughout the remainder of your life and hopefully, if you carry the lesson with you and understand it in the way that it is supposed to be you will thank me for one day, would you like to know what that lesson is?'

Klipp nods.

'Before I tell you, I need you to tell me what you did wrong.'

Klipp stares at Bees blankly.

'Go on.'

'I don't know uncle Bees.'

'Give it a try.'

Klipp thinks for a bit. 'I was out of the house too late?'

'Close, but not quite.' Bees takes another sip of brandy. 'Try again.'

'I don't know.'

'Didn't expect anything more.' Bees finishes what is left of the brandy and puts the mug back down on the table. 'What I wanted you to get at was that if we allow what happened last night to happen regularly this whole operation will crumble, soon we'll have Petrus knocking on our door asking if we want to share a glass of wine with the rest of him, and if that happens all is lost, we might as well burn this place to the ground because the chain of command will have been broken, and where two kinds of people as different from each other in authority as us and Petrus and the rest of the workers is concerned the chain of command is everything, and if that gets broken, so does everything that follows so it might as well be put down.' Bees leans over the table. 'Having said that nephew, I have decided to send you to boarding school.'

Klipp goes still.

Clarafina turns to Bees. 'Excuse me brother, don't you think I should have a say in this?'

'No.'

'Why not?'

'Can you give me a reason as to why?'

'I can give you a couple, I was the one that caught him and the little missy behind the cabin, he is my nephew just as much as he is yours, I am the older of the two of us and also what school is going to take him if he hasn't been to one in almost a year?'

'You make a good point, sister, but the point falls flat when you take into consideration who our grandfather is, one mention of his name to the admissions people and our nephew here will be the first to be accepted.'

'What about money?'

'That won't be a problem either if we mention our grandfather's name.' Bees fills the mug with some more brandy. 'Another reason, and most importantly why I want to send the boy to school is because it is no secret that things around here have not been going very well, why that is I think is because unlike our grandfather and his three sons we do not have an education to our name and were we to have one, things might have turned out quite a bit different than how they are now.'

Although Bees was not right about how him and Clarafina not having educations affected them doing business he was right that it did so in the manner as Grandpa Brungle knew how much his associates and colleagues valued education and in certain circles, the personal work bonds that it established and he did not send them to school because he felt that they would have everything they need to lead successful and fulfilled lives having the farm and also because he did not want to pay school fees but mostly because he did not want there to be any chance of there being any one better Brungle than he thought himself to be. 'That's why I want to send our nephew to school so that he may have the education we never did so that he can help us get the farm back to the way it should be.'

Clarafina sits upright in her chair. 'News I did not think I would ever hear, or that I want to seeing as how much I like having our nephew around.' She turns to Klipp. 'Not that you would have had any choice in the matter to begin with nephew but it looks like you're going to boarding school.'

Bees claps his hands together. 'So, it's settled, laddie here is going to go to school like all the other boys.' He gets up. 'Hope you are excited nephew; many kids would kill for a chance like this.' At the door he stops and turns. 'Hope you have a nice day.'

When Bees is out of the kitchen, Clarafina leans over the table. 'Don't worry nephew, this might not turn out as bad as you think it will, when you get to wherever you're going to go you might actually start to like it, it's only because the news was sprung on you so fast that you feel upset, when you wake up tomorrow morning you might like the idea of going to school.'

Klipp nods.

'I know the thought of having to go to school is not very nice especially if it's far away but if your uncle and I did like you are going to now we might not be in the situation we are in at the moment, other than getting to say to our friends some Sunday nights that we do not have to get up early for school the following morning, like they did it didn't even happen that much really because we had to get up even earlier than they did sometimes to do work on the farm.' Clarafina sits upright in her chair. 'I hope that helps, because that's all I've got.'

Unbeknownst to Clarafina it did help, and quite a bit more than Klipp could have thought, many a time when he was feeling down after first coming to the farm it was her that made him feel better and helped him more easily get through those times as well as made him feel better when he felt not so when he first got to boarding school.

'It's okay, auntie Clarafina, I might maybe like it like you say.'

Clarafina smiles. 'That's the spirit nephew, that alone shows that you will be better than okay.'

Klipp gets up and gives her a hug, 'Do you think it's okay if I go lie down?'

'Sure, you can do whatever you want to today, just as long as you don't run away.'

Klipp laughs. 'Do you know when I will have to go?'

Clarafina shakes her head. 'Not a clue, you'll have to ask your uncle about that one.'

'Okay.' Klipp walks out of the kitchen he will step foot in only once before leaving the farm and makes his way to the front door to see if Bees is outside on the porch. When he pokes his head outside the door Bees is sitting on his rocking chair with his feet up on the railing with a glass of brandy in one hand and a pipe in the other. When Bees hears the light creaking of the floorboards he turns around and when he sees Klipp, he smiles with a content that Klipp had not yet seen since coming to the farm and one that instead of upsetting him like it should have made him feel elated with the idea of getting to be away from him for as long a period of time as he might be.

'Hello, nephew?'

'Hello, uncle Bees.'

'What can I do for you?'

'I was just wondering when I will have to go away?'

Bees takes his feet of the railing. 'Funny you should ask, I just got off the phone with your future principal and he said that there will be a place waiting for you as soon as you get there.'

Klipp nods.

'The school is four days' drive away so we will have to leave first thing in the early morning tomorrow to make it there as soon as possible.'

So soon Klipp nods after the shock of what Bees just told him settles on him it masks the dismay that fills him almost completely disappear.

'The news seems to have settled on you better than I would have thought,' Bees says surprised.

Klipp nods. 'Thank you, uncle Bees, if you don't mind can I go lie down for a bit?'

Bees nods. 'Sure nephew, go right ahead.'

Klipp nods.

'And make sure that you have everything packed that you want to take with you before you go to bed.'

Klipp nods. 'Yes, uncle Bees.'

'Good.' Just as Bees is about to turn back around, he stops and points a finger at Klipp. 'And if I catch you anywhere near the cabin before we leave, I will not only punish you, but your little girlfriend too, do you understand?'

Klipp nods. 'Yes, uncle Bees.'

Bees smiles. 'Good, off you go then.'

When Klipp woke up after going to lay down and falling asleep the sun had just set and after he rubbed the sleep from his eyes, he lays two suitcases out on his bed and packs them with all of his clothes, as well as other belongings he wants to take with him. When both suitcases are packed, he zips them closed and puts them on the floor next to his bed and tip toes down the passage to Bees and

Clarafina's bedrooms to see whether he might be lucky enough to find them both asleep.

Very recently, Bees started to make a point of it to get himself into his bed before falling asleep anywhere else besides there from drinking too much which used to be most regularly the rocking chair on the porch as well as on one of the couches in the living room in front of the TV, a couple of times, Clarafina, and sometimes Klipp, found him asleep in the back of his truck with his head on a bag of wheat, the strangest place they found him asleep, which happened only once, was the workers cabin, which when Clarafina asked him what he was doing there, he had no idea.

As luck, as well as a couple of concerted efforts on Bees' part would have it, Klipp found him asleep in his bed. Once downstairs on his way out, Klipp finds Clarafina asleep too on the couch in the living room in front of the fireplace with a blanket wrapped around her. Once outside, he makes his way down the steps and over to the edge of the lawn where he walks along the length thereof to the cabin. Once there, Klipp sees Petrus and the rest of the adult workers sitting around the table drinking red wine and chatting away.

Not wanting to bother Petrus or any of the other workers with the news he carefully makes his way around the cabin to where Scara would hopefully be sitting and when he turns the corner, he sees her sitting just as she was when he saw her both times before.

'Hello,' says Klipp.

Scara looks up. 'Hey, didn't think I would be seeing you again so soon?'

'Me neither.'

'Come sit, there probably is much to talk about.'

Klipp makes his way over to her and sits down next to her.

'No jacket this time?'

Klipp shakes his head. 'Had to pack it.'

'What do you mean 'pack it'?'

'After last night my uncle is sending me to boarding school.'

Scara sits upright with surprise. 'What?'

Klipp nods.

'When are you leaving?'

'Early tomorrow morning.'

'Really?'

Klipp nods.

'Why so soon?'

'I don't know, he called someone he knows at the school and he said there is a place for me and that I have to be there as soon as possible.'

They sit lingering for a while. 'How far away is it?'

'Four days' drive.'

'That's very far, are you coming back here at all while you're away?'

'I don't think so.'

'How long are you going to be away?'

'Until I am finished with university.'

'That's ten years maybe?'

Klipp nods.

'We haven't even been alive for that long almost?'

Klipp laughs.

'So, I'm not going to be able to see or talk to you for ten years?'

'Not talk to me like we are now but we can write letters to each other.'

'How will we do that?'

'My uncle got me something a while ago that had to come through the post office and he had to open a post-box for me because he already had so many for himself, I'm going to send you as many letters as I can to that post-box while I'm away, he probably doesn't even know about it anymore.'

'And if he does?'

'If he finds them, he'll probably just throw them away.'

'Then he'll just keep doing that and I won't get any of your letters?'

'You always go to town when him and my aunt does so when you do just go to the post office and get the letters before he does.'

'What if I can't?'

'Go there as soon as you get there with a letter for me that says if he found the letters or not as well as a new post-box number where I can send other letters too if my uncle still knows about this one, you can write down a new number on the letter there, and if he finds them before you do, post your letter to me so I'll know that he did, you can ask the post office person what address the letters I sent you me came from.'

'Okay.'

'I'll write as much letters as I can for three years and if I hear nothing back from you until then, I'll stop writing for a year and after that year I'll write for another year and if I still don't hear anything back from you, I'll start writing you again a year before I come back.'

Scara gets up. 'I'm going inside the cabin to get you something.'

'Okay.'

Scara makes her way inside the cabin, while she is away Klipp thinks to himself that it is going to be quite hard to write to her does he get to where he is going and he does not like it, what will the name of the first friend that he supposedly makes be, what will the far above average test score be that he gets for the first test that he writes on his favourite subject, just as he begins to think about what the girl's name will be that starts to pine after him after a couple of weeks.

Scara comes back around the corner of the cabin and sits down next to him and holds out her hand. 'Do you want to know what's inside?'

'Sure.'

'You'll have to guess then.'

'How many guesses do I get?'

'Three.'

'Okay, a ring?'

Scara opens her hand. 'How did you know?'

'I saw it in a small wooden bowl next to your bed one time and you never wear it so I thought that it might that?'

'That's quite clever.'

'Thank you, you don't have very many things so maybe not so clever.'

Scara nods. 'Maybe not, anyway...' She holds the ring out to him; he takes it from her.

'Is it real gold?'

Scara nods. 'It is.'

'Why are you giving it to me?'

'So, you can remember me.'

Klipp nods. 'Then I probably shouldn't take it with me at all.'

Scara laughs. 'How nice.'

'What finger do I put it on?'

'Anyone.'

Klipp puts the ring on his first finger and holds his hand out in front of him. 'It looks very nice.'

'Sure, it does, I have very good taste.'

Klipp laughs. 'I can see that.'

Scara pulls her blanket back over her lap. 'Wear it whenever you want, just don't lose it or don't sell it for money, definitely do not sell it for money.'

'I won't.'

They sit quietly for a while, Klipp looks over at her with somewhat wide eyes. 'Before I come back to the farm, I'll get lots of little pictures drawn on it or cut into it at some place.'

'Why?'

'As a present for you, hopefully by then I'll be very good at drawing so it will look like a ring I bought at a shop.'

'That will be very nice.'

'I hope so,' Klipp says somewhat proud of himself. 'What do you want me to put on it?'

'You're going to have to come up with that yourself.'

Klipp nods and looks again at the ring on his finger. 'Where did you get this from?'

'It was my mom's, she left it for me before she died, her first boyfriend gave it to her.'

'Your dad?'

Scara shakes her head. 'No, someone else.'

'Who was he?'

'His name was Tadao, he died before I was born.'

'How did he die?'

'He got shot by one of the farmhands that worked for the family that he did.'

'Why did he shoot him?'

'The man who's farm it was thought that his wife was making eyes at him and he told his farmhand to shoot him.'

Klipp shakes his head. 'Was he?'

'Was he what?'

'Did your mom's boyfriend and the lady do things?'

'No, and he probably wouldn't have either even if she were making eyes at him.'

'Sorry to hear that.'

'That's okay.'

'How did your mom and him meet?'

'They met while they were both wandering up in the mountains.'

'Camel's Neck?'

Scara shakes her head. 'No, but one close by, very far from where we are now but close in terms of the mountains.'

Klipp nods. 'Where they working there when they met?'

'No, they were just walking around, Tadao potentially saved my mom from being eaten by a lion.'

'Really?'

Scara nods.

'How did he do that?'

'My mom was sitting under a tree reading when out of the corner of her eye she saw a lion approaching, her first thought was to run away but after seeing the size of the lion she thought that her best chance of survival was to stay put as she was and hope the lion would go away, but he didn't. When the lion was about the toss of a stone's length away from her, she heard a loud yell coming from somewhere behind the lion, her and the lion looked to see where the yell came from and saw Tadao standing a couple of feet behind the lion with a rock in his hand. When the lion saw Tadao, he turned around and kept toward my mother until Tadao ran over and stood in front of the lion with the rock held up over his head…'

'Then what happened?'

'My mom said that they stood staring at each other for a while until the lion turned around and walked away.'

'Really?'

Scara nods.

'Wow.' Klipp sits upright having fallen into a somewhat slump listening to Scara tell the story. 'Should lions just run away like that?'

'I don't know.'

'I wonder why this one ran away?'

'My mom said that lions sense an overwhelming sense of pride from us because we are able to walk on two limbs and we are on top of the food chain and that the sense of pride that comes from it, as well as other things outweighs the appreciation we should have for it, this angers the lion sometimes to the point of having very little regard for human life, but when we show bravery or something similar of the kind that Tadao did, especially when it concerns the protection of another of the other kind, the lion sees that as a letting go of the pride which in turn causes them to let go of theirs.'

'Wow, that's quite nice.'

Scara nods.

'What time is it?'

Scara looks at her watch. 'Almost two o'clock.'

Klipp's eyes widen. 'Really?'

Scara nods.

'I didn't think it would be that late already?'

'What time do you have to leave?'

'I don't know, my uncle told me that I have to be packed and ready to leave before the sun comes up.'

'That's maybe four hours at the most.'

Klipp nods.

'You should get going then.'

'Probably.'

'I guess this is goodbye then?'

'Almost.' Klipp reaches into his pocket and pulls out a piece of paper.

'What's this?'

'It's the key for the post-box I'm going to send the letters to, and the piece of paper is the picture of the monster with the heart hands and mouth.'

Scara takes the piece of paper from him and presses it tightly between the palms of her hands. 'I'm not going to look at it until I'm back inside the cabin.'

'Okay, I'm probably going to go back to the house then.'

'I'll walk with you.'

They get up and gather their things and make their way to the edge of the cabin where they say goodbye and Scara goes back inside the cabin and Klipp starts the walk back across the lawn to the house longer than he had ever to before.

Chapter 10

Saturday afternoon, three months after Klipp left the farm for boarding school, things are much the same as they were before, Bees' greatest form of pleasure is the mistreatment of the workers, Clarafina's her wine satchel and the workers' each other. Scara had only been to town once since Klipp left and is yet to receive a letter from him. On this particular afternoon the energy of everyone, especially the workers are very upbeat, them because of the warm weather there had not been for almost a month, Clarafina because she is almost halfway through a crate of red wine that she bought about two weeks ago and Bees, who is just pulling up in the driveway because of who is sitting in the back of the truck with him.

Bees gets out of the truck and walks to the back where two men, both tall and lanky with fair skin, maybe about half the age of Bees, wearing dungarees, one of denim with black boots and a straw hat that looks to be about three generations older than him and the other one of light brown corduroy over a white vest with black boots and a trucker cap.

After the men, who Bees picked up in town sitting in an alley behind one of the guns and ammunition stores to bring back to the farm as farmhands, unloaded the truck they go to stand with Bees by the porch. 'Now that that's over and done with welcome to the farm.' Bees points behind him, 'It might not look like much now but I can assure you that not too long ago it was one of the most sought-after farms in all of Golden Heart.'

'What happened?' The farmhand with the trucker cap asks.

Bees looks at him with uncomfortable surprise, regretting right then that he had brought the man back with him due to the ease and manner with which he interrupted him, thinking to himself that he might be the type of person who would stab him in the back, maybe even literally, for a case of beer. 'Forgive me for asking this late in the conversation, but what is your name?'

The man shakes his head, grabbing onto his hat while doing so to keep it from falling from his head. 'No two worries about its sir, the name is Swenton, Swenton Tucket.'

'Well Swe...'

The man next to Swenton interrupts. 'And mine is Cadd sir, 'Cadd' with two d's.'

Just as Bees is about to start talking again Cadd interrupts again. 'I don't know what my last name is sir, I did have one but I cannot remember what it is ever since the day I came back from the hospital after someone found me with a needle sticking out of my arm behind the gun store.'

Wanting more than anything to take the men back to town and drop them off where he found them the thought of what they might do to him were he to do so scared him to the point of convincing himself that he would lose the farm would he do so, so he continues to address them with whatever authority he thinks he might still have to let the conversation play out as best possible before he plans on spending the remainder of the day thinking of a safe way to tell them to leave. Bees nods somewhat uncomfortable. 'Nice to meet you both.'

'The wise is like sir,' says Cadd laughing. 'The man I was lying next to in hospital said that to me one time and I thought it was very good.'

Swenton nods.

'Then when I met Swenton here I said it to him and we've been saying it ever since when we can.'

Swenton nods. 'The wise is like here too sir.'

Bees nods, more uncomfortable than before. 'Very good, nice to meet you.'

Swenton and Cadd nod.

'Are the two of you related by any chance?'

Swenton and Cadd look at each other. 'No sir, why do you ask?' Asks Cadd.

'No reason, just wondering.' Bees positions himself more firm on the ground. 'The first and most important thing I have to tell you about life here, is that you must at all times address me as 'boss,' never anything else, even when you are not working.'

Swenton and Cadd look at each other frowning.

'I know this might seem funny to you but because I found you on the streets without food or shelter and brought you back here to give you that and more to work for me, I would say that is only a fair trade?'

'Yes boss.' They say in unison.'

Bees nods. 'On the subject of where you will be sleeping…'

'Don't worry about that boss…' Swenton interjects. 'Wherever we lay our heads is where we sleep.'

'But a real place to sleep will be nicer,' says Cadd.

'Then a real place to sleep is what you will get.'

Swenton and Cadd nod.

'Also…' begins Bees. 'I must tell you to not interrupt me in the manners you have so far when I am talking to you, especially in front of the workers, if they see you treating me as your equal, which I not am, it will cause a commotion among them that will not be good for me or you.'

Swenton tips his hat forward.

'Not a problem sir,' says Cadd.

'As to where you will be sleeping there is a small room at the back of the house next to the garage with two beds and a separate bathroom as well as a small kitchen area with a stove and oven, a sink, a microwave and fridge as well as a fairly new couch in front of a small table with a TV set on top next to the two beds, do you think you'll be able to manage there?'

Cadd tips his hat forward. 'Sounds better than the best hotel in town sir.'

'Very good, also, a certain amount food will be given to you once a week that you will have to make yourself, you are never to step foot in the house unless you are invited in or given permission to do so, you are free to roam the farm as you please, but will have to be in your room with the lights out and the TV off before ten every night of the week, on the weekends you have to be so before 12 at the latest, is that understood?'

Swenton and Cadd nod.

'If you want to stay up after ten during the week you can but you have to do so with the lights and TV off.'

'No problem, sir,' says Cadd.

'Very good, before I leave you for the day follow me to the cabin so I can introduce you to the workers that you will be overseeing.'

'Not a problem sir,' says Swenton.

When they reach the front part of the grass in front of the cabin that has been stepped on quite a bit more than that before its Bees holds two fingers to his mouth and whistles. The workers who are close enough to give their attention line up in front of him. 'Those of you who are standing here now turn around

192

and gather all of the rest of you and your children and come back here as soon as possible.' Bees claps his hands together. 'As quick as you can people.'

When all of the workers and their children are standing in front of Bees, he grabs a hold of his suspender straps and rests himself thereon. 'I want to introduce you all to your new bosses...' Bees gestures toward Swenton and Cadd. 'This is Swenton and Cadd...'

Before Bees is able to talk further Cadd taps him on the shoulder, Bees turns around. 'Yes Cadd?'

'That is a good one sir, we call you boss and they call us boss.'

'Do you remember what I told you about interrupting me?'

Cadd nods. 'Yes sir.'

'Then why did you do it now, and in front of the workers?'

'I did not sir, I just said something to you.'

'Very well, if you feel like saying something to me from now on wait until I have stopped talking.'

Cadd nods. 'No problems about its sir.'

'Thank you.' Bees turns back around, 'As I was saying the two new gentlemen standing next to me are going to be your bosses when Ms Clarafina and I are not around, they will be with you the entire day, to make sure that you do as you are supposed to before walking you back to the cabin. If at any time you want something you ask them, if they can't provide it, they will come to Clarafina and I to ask for help, is that understood?'

The workers nod.

'Also, if you fail to adhere by these rules in any way, they are allowed to rectify the situation in any whatever they see fit.' Bees takes a step back, 'Be sure to be here for tomorrow morning at seven o'clock sharp.'

The workers nod.

'Enjoy the rest of your day.' Before Bees makes his way to the house, he stops in front of Swenton and Cadd. 'That is all for today gentlemen, meet me on the porch steps tomorrow morning at half past six.'

Swenton nods.

'Not a problem sir,' says Cadd.

'See you in the morning then.' Bees starts toward the house. Swenton and Cadd take a stand in front of the workers. 'You can get back to what you were doing, we'll be around if you need us,' says Swenton.

'Whatever you might need you call on us,' says Cadd. 'My name is Cadd and the man standing next to me is Swenton.'

Swenton nods. 'You can call us boss.'

Cadd nods. 'If you call out the word' boss' both of us will come running.'

Swenton and Cadd nod. 'You can consider us friends,' says Swenton. 'Only friends who are better than you and who you work for.'

Cadd points to Swenton with his thumb. 'What he said.'

Swenton nods. 'See you all tomorrow morning.'

Cadd nods. 'What he said.'

They wave the workers goodbye and make their way back to the house.

Two hours later, Swenton and Cadd are still sitting on the porch steps having gone through almost two packs of cigarettes while trying to come up with jokes about their new life on the farm. Swenton drops his cigarette on the ground and gets up. 'I'm have to use the toilet.'

'Go well, my friend.'

'Don't smoke all of those while I'm gone.'

'Don't take as long as you usually do and I won't.'

'Leave a couple out for me so you don't.'

'Don't take too long and I can keep them fresh in the packet for you.'

Swenton walks down the porch steps and around the house to the room they stay in. After a while of looking out over the lawn Cadd's gaze settles on Lavette busy washing clothes on a scrubbing board inside of a large tin bucket close to the side of the cabin next to the rise of ground that separates the lawn from the dam.

Staring at her for a while he gets up and makes his way over there, reaching the cabin he passes Lavette and waves at her from afar before walking around the cabin and poking his head through the windows and coming around the other side and walking up to her knelt down on the ground with her back to him. After staring at her washing for a while, he grabs her around the waist with one hand and puts his other over her mouth before pulling her up toward him and dragging her to the back of the cabin behind a bush out of sight from anywhere on the farm. Swenton tightens his grip around her waist and over her mouth before putting his mouth to her ear. 'Make a sound and I will kill you right here.'

Lavette nods.

'Good, I'll be quick says Swenton, I promise.' He takes his hand away from over her mouth and she breathes in deep to scream but he manages to get his hand over her mouth again before she does so. 'Now you're really going to get it.' He pushes her up against the rise in ground and reaches under her dress and grabs a hold of her underwear, before he is able to pull it down, Nleeclo sees them and when the realisation of what is happening settles on her she runs over to them and jumps on Swenton's back, he reaches behind him and throws Nleeclo off him before kicking her in the stomach. Lavette screams just before Swenton reaches around her and puts his hand over her mouth again.

Having heard Lavette scream, Kolos and Dwendo come running around the cabin and grab a hold of Swenton to get him off Lavette and throws him on the ground and beat him until he is barely breathing. Just as Dwendo and Kolos are about to pull Swenton up off the ground to continue beating him Bees and Clarafina step in front of them, Bees holds a rifle out in front of Dwendo and fires off a shot that grazes his ear.

When they hear the shot, they let go of Swenton who falls on the ground and stand facing Bees with their hands up, drops of blood from the wound on Dwendo's ear slowly dripping down the side of his face and neck, before Bees hits Kolos over the head with the back of his rifle.

When Kolos regains consciousness again, he is lying face down on the lawn a couple of steps away from the cabin next to Dwendo inside of a circle of stones with their hands tied behind their back. When they look up, they see Swenton and Cadd standing over them shirtless with the top of their jumpsuits pulled down to just above their waist and Bees and Clarafina standing beside them. Bees turns around to the rest of the workers standing spread out around the cabin. 'Gather round people, the show is about to begin.'

The workers stay where they are.

'Have it your way.' Bees turns back around and looks down at Kolos and Dwendo. 'As you might know just a moment ago blood was spilled on the farm, forced by the fists of two men to run from the brow of another and because of that the scales of fairness weighs much heavier on one side than it does on the other and must be moved back in place and for that to happen the blood of the two men who spilled the blood of the other's blood must be spilled, having said that, Dwendo and Kolos, please tell us why you did what you did today?'

Dwendo looks up at Bees. 'The man was forcing himself on Lavette boss.'

'Did he manage to do so, Dwendo?'

'No boss.'

'If that is the case Dwendo the man you hurt did not deserve to be hurt, am I right?'

'No boss.'

Bees laughs. 'Please explain to me why you say that is?'

'If we didn't stop him, he would have done it.'

'How do you know that?'

'Why else would he do it?'

'Maybe just to play around with her a little.'

'If someone were to do that to boss' wife what would boss do?'

'That all depends on whether she was asking for it or not, and was Lavette?' Dwendo shakes his head. 'No.'

'Then I would kill him, but the thing you are forgetting Dwendo is that you and your brother next to you assaulted a man that is your superior, and also for something he did not specifically do and therefore you must be punished more than Swenton.' Bees takes a step toward Kolos and Dwendo.

'Now I ask you, will you rather want to be punished less and Swenton be punished not at all or want to be punished as you should and also get to see Swenton get punished under the terms of him taking his crime maybe 40 percent of the full 100 and the two of you taking yours about 80 percent, then Swenton being the first to commit his crime and his crime being worse than yours we can take away 30 percent of yours, which will make it that you have 50 and he has 70, but because he is your superior you have to take half of his and put it to yours which makes it...'

Bees counts his fingers, 'That Swenton has 35 percent punishment and you have 85.' He rests his rifle on his shoulder. 'What's it going to be you two?' Bees taps his foot on the ground. 'Before you answer that, if it were up to me, I would say that you should take Swenton's punishment from yours so you can be punished only 50 percent.'

'What will that be?' Swenton asks.

Bees turns to him. 'I would say that you and Cadd should get in the circle with Kolos and Dwendo and fight them with their hands tied behind their backs.'

The fight between them lasted no more than eight minutes and consisted of Kolos and Dwendo dodging the blows that Swenton and Cadd continuously tried to land on them before Swenton and Cadd gave up from exhaustion without ever laying a hand on either Kolos or Dwendo.

A week or so after Bees brought Swenton and Cadd to the farm he started thinking of ways which might help with the money problems they were having because he had more time on his hands now that he had two more people helping out as well as wanting to do so with the hope that an idea might present itself with which he might be able to tell Swenton and Cadd that their help is no longer needed on the farm.

Bees sat at the table on the porch for the better part of the day for almost three days and came up with six ideas altogether, the first was to buy the workers equipment with which to exercise so that they, to his thinking even more so the female workers than the male workers, might become stronger and fitter so they might be able to do more work within their given work hours to increase productivity. Unfortunately, he never found out whether the idea would have worked seeing as he did not have enough money to buy gym equipment with.

Another idea was to start making brandy and wine so that him and Clarafina might not have to buy their own, another which fell through when he realised that after putting the idea together in more detail doing so would take too much time. After 'rummaging' through all six ideas, Bees had no choice but to go with the idea he, at first, thought to be the least helpful and call Klipp to see if he might have any ideas and also to tell him to keep thinking of ways in which him and Clarafina might be able to improve things on and concerning the farm.

Another thing to happen with the intent to excuse the company of Swenton and Cadd was that Clarafina spent a month without drinking red wine so that she may buy herself the cheapest piano from one of two second hand goods stores in town which she planned to practice on until she was just as good or better than she was before the piano she played on as a child was sold so that she might be able to find a job playing in one of the many restaurants in town, after acquiring the piano she even went to her cupboard and picked a dress which she would wear, when going into town and looking for a job seeing as how fearful she was of not having enough money to buy food even due to the continuously decaying state of the farm and she would not only be able to help with matters concerning the farm but also be able to live in her own apartment, away from Swenton and Cadd who she very much detested.

In order to save money and so have more to give to Bees to use for the farm as well as have more for herself she planned on asking the managers at the restaurants at which she wanted to apply for work at that if she, who unlike most other piano players in town that played mostly the same compositions as each other, played her own if she might be able to drink at the bar as well as have a meal for free if she did so.

After three months of practicing and writing almost six of her own compositions during the time, which to even Bees' standards were quite good, Clarafina never did make the move to town as she did not want to leave Bees alone without her helping hand and also because not long before she planned on making her into town to look for work; Bees managed to persuade one of his grandfather's old colleagues to lend him a fairly large sum of money.

During the three months which Clarafina spent practicing piano, Scara, along with the rest of the workers, went into town for the second time after Klipp left to amongst other things see if there might be a letter from Klipp at the post office.

Upon arriving in town, after the workers had finished their errands, Scara and Petrus and the rest of the workers and children went to 'The Snow Globe' like they did usually when they were there and when she was finished with her bowl of ice cream, she said that she needed to use the bathroom during which while she was away, she went to the post office with the key for the post-box that Klipp left her before he did and found six letters.

Back at the farm after hiding the letters under the many layers of clothing she wore that day with the intention to do so before she left the post office Scara put away the letters and key in a box under her bed telling not even Petrus about them.

Every three months when Scara went into town after finding the first pile of letters, while at the ice cream parlour she waited till whoever she was sitting with finished their bowl of ice cream halfway; when she excused herself to go to the bathroom. She walked as quickly as she can to the post office for the letters that were usually waiting there for her.

With the first six letters, she decided that she would read one a week so that the wait for those coming might be a little bit more exciting. The first letter that Klipp wrote said that he was very much enjoying his time at boarding school, so much so that even though he didn't think she would asked her not to mention anything to anyone about it as news thereof might make his uncle want to bring him back to the farm, another thing she learned was that the school Klipp was attending was in a small town next to the country's capitol, Litchwith, by the name of Wioden Kettle, the second smallest of the towns surrounding Litchwith, of which there are eight, but with the biggest primary school, Kettle Primary, out of all eight towns and the five schools, all of which is boarding, that make up the city's schooling district.

The primary reason that Kettle Primary was one of the more popular schools is because unlike three out of the five it was one where the children had to wear uniforms and there were many a rule concerning scholar appearance. He also wrote that seeing as the school does not allow casual dress, he has to take off his ring while attending class but put it away safely in a lock box under his bed and wears it as often as he gets the chance to.

Klipp also wrote that the school is an all-boys school but that they get together with girls from an all-girls boarding school in the town hall once a month for a supervised dance. On his first day of school during the second lunch break he met two boys who were sitting together under a tree who became his two best friends. The first is Gulmon Mijo, who is two years older than Klipp and the other boy, he has short black hair and brown eyes and is about a head taller than Klipp and the other boy whose name is Yutro Trouy.

He is the same age and height as Klipp, he is black and has thick, black curly hair cut into a style which makes it look like he has a fringe parted upward with hair gel, dark brown eyes and stubble over the bottom part of his face, something which he likes quite a bit because it looks like he has half a beard, something which very little boys at the school have. Klipp says that there are not very many boys of colour at the school, maybe a dozen or so, but out of the 400 or so boys that attend the school Youtro has maybe the most money to his family name out of everyone.

Youtro spent the first six years of his life quite poor on one of the most prosperous farms in the country, his father was the foreman on the farm and had a very close bond with the owner of the farm and was like a son to him seeing as he had no children of his own and when he passed away, he left the farm to Youtro's father as he had no relatives to leave it to and his wife too passed away a couple of months prior to him from a snakebite.

After the owner of the farm passed away, Youtro's father ran the farm much like he was taught by the previous owner and as time went on expanded it in ways quite different from that which the owner would have because other than being a very hard worker Youtro's father was also very smart and had a very good mind for business and because of who he worked for had the opportunity

199

to meet and do business with many very wealthy white farmers in and around the country who liked the idea of doing business with a man of colour.

Nowadays, Youtro's father and uncle run the farm together and live with their families on it. There primary source of income is breeding and farming with crocodiles, the hide of which they sell to various manufacturers of leather products around the country, while after crocodiles their second biggest source of income is farming with salt, not the salt Klipp writes that most people are used to but a purer kind, salt that is unrefined and light pink in colour unlike the refined salt that they are used to that gets washed with chemicals before it gets packaged and therefore turns white.

Klipp says that many decades ago, the first people that farmed with salt on a large scale washed it not only to clean it but also because they thought it would look more appealing next to pepper, he says that white salt is cleaner than pink salt but because of the chemicals they use to wash it pink salt is more potent in taste and less of it is needed to acquire the same taste intensity that more white salt would yield and also that the very thing they wash off the salt with the chemicals might be what makes it healthier than its counterpart.

Unlike Youtro's family who farm with few but specific and rare commodities Gulmon's farms with small amounts of many things, which Gulmon knows very little about and when asked about what he wants to do one day, unlike Youtro who wants nothing more than to take over the family farm with two of his cousins, his answer is always that he wants to do as little as possible while making as much money as he can.

Klipp writes that he is not sure what he wants to do when he graduates from high school, but that he enjoys art class more than he thought he would and that his art teacher regularly comments on the quality of his work.

The last thing he mentioned was that his favourite thing about Litchwith is the small beach town about four hours' drive away and that one weekend out of every month whoever wants to from his as well as the girl's school go to spend a weekend there under the supervision of a couple of teachers. The first time he went he tried surfing, an activity where you stand on a varnished piece of wood cut and sanded into the shape of a long, flat rectangular plank with rounded edges and a piece of foam on the inside, so that it may float called a surfboard with someone expectedly standing on it.

After manoeuvring the surfboard while lying on top of it on your stomach into a wave until it is strong enough to carry the person without any effort on his or her part and so giving the person time to push themselves upward off the top of the surfboard onto their feet so they may float along the 'face' of the wave as it pushes them forward for a certain period of time until the wave loses all of its power. Klipp says that he took to surfing quite quickly and that other than spending time in his room drawing and painting, surfing is what he likes to do most.

The letter that Klipp got from Scara mentioned only the arrival of the two new farmhands and how the shorter of the two, Cadd, always whistles at her when they walk by each other, she says that she somewhat understands why men would sometimes want to whistle at someone of the opposite sex and has seen it happen a few times when she was in town but when Cadd does it makes her feel like a thousand cockroaches are running up and over her body at the same time.

She also wrote that one time he exposed himself to her explaining that he always wears a cream-coloured dungaree of which the pant legs used to be long but he cut short after a while to 'sit' just below his backside and that one day while they were working when he came back from having used the bathroom and he lifted up one of his pant legs and exposed himself to her, she says that the worst thing about it was that he didn't look at her at all while doing so.

Along with that she also mentioned that she became quite fearful that he wanted to force himself on her so she decided one day when her and the other workers went into town she would try to get a bottle of pepper spray for herself, she took as much money as she could, from a small wooden box in which she keeps all her savings from under her bed and went into the security store in town where the owner, which happened to be a woman, told her that she did not have enough money.

When she told her about Cadd and asked whether she might have the bottle for as much as she had with her, to which the woman replied by putting on the counter a 'busy' sign and going into the storeroom. She said that before she left, she took a bottle for herself without feeling bad in the least and that luckily, she is yet to find reason to use it.

Chapter 11

Five years after Scara received the first six letters from Klipp—which she kept in a cardboard box under her bed, the same box now holds 76 letters, after writing to her almost once a week for the first year. Klipp wrote that due to not having much new to tell her every week he would rather write to her once a month so each letter might be a little more interesting than if he were to write once a week, in turn Scara wrote that she will still be sending only one letter every second or third month seeing as she was then and still is living on one of the most unsuccessful farms in all of Golden Heart.

With all of the 76 letters that she had gotten from Klipp since after his first year away from the farm the most interesting thing she learned was that he had begun to surf in competitions held four times a year on the small beach of the beach town, which is now about half the drive it used to be away from his new school, he visited once a month while he was still attending Kettle Primary along with four other boys from his high school, Litchwith High, another all-boys boarding school in the centre of the town where he attended primary school, where they compete against boys from other all-boys boarding schools in and around the city and although Youtro and Gulmon do not accompany him there anymore, they still remain best friends.

On the occasional weekend that he doesn't have to stay in and study, he goes surfing with one of the judges from the competition, Milno, who he does not know his last name having asked him once and being told that he *too* does not know it and never has having grown up an orphan and going from home to home ever since he can remember until he was old enough to get a job to make money to live on his own.

He is in his early twenties and is better at surfing that Klipp thinks anyone in the surf magazines to be, he says that they have become quite close and that he has become like an older brother or even father to him, although one much more mischievous in his older and wiser ways than you would expect a father to be.

He is a couple of inches taller than Klipp and has long black hair down to almost the small of his back, very rarely has anything covering the top part of his body, wears three rings with emblems of whatever kind embedded on the 'faces' of the rings on one hand and has a ring, much like a small, hooped earring, pierced through the centre of his nose. The most unusual thing about his appearance other than his hair and the jewellery he has on and through his body is that covering the entire left side of his chest and well as his left arm are small pictures of many kinds of a black ink of sort that sits close to each other so that they appear a whole.

The pictures are called inkies and are drawn or technically speaking pierced, in very quick and successive outward movements, into the skin on or over whichever part of the body whoever is getting them chooses it to be, with a small machine of sorts that comprises of a motorised rotary mechanism that forces the points of a group of small needles that sit very close together at the bottom of the machine through which a special kind of ink of many different colours moves as the needles are propelled forward incrementally.

Once the inkie is on the skin, it takes one to two months for the skin under which the inkie is to heal and form a new protective layer that protects it from minor skin damage such as scrapes, cuts and the like and is there permanently or until the person with the inkie chooses to have it removed with treatment, three to four thereof once a month, of a small infrared light that burns off the first top couple of layers of skin until the inkie is gone. Klipp writes that it took almost two years for Milno to have his chest and arm covered with inkies and that he plans on getting the other side of his chest and right arm covered in the coming year or two as well.

Milno makes his living from running a small restaurant situated on the beach that doubles as a beach bar with a surf shop attached to it, Milno got the money to open the restaurant from his father who owned a construction company who passed away a couple of years before him and Klipp met and left him a large sum of money when he sold the company a couple of months prior to his death, Milno used a small portion of the money to get the inkies and buy the plot of land on which the restaurant and surf shop was built; as well as a car before putting away the remainder of the money in two large steel safes built into the back of the surf shop of which a part has been made to be an apartment of sorts where Milno lives, because he does not trust that banks care for their clients' money as they are supposed to.

The restaurant is called 'Banana Board' and is quite well known around the town of Coral and Shell for the food, especially the range of burgers, the most popular being the 'Banana Burger,' as well as a beer that Milno brews himself in his apartment and plans to brand whenever he has the money to do so.

Klipp also mentioned that he has become quite fond of painting and spends most of his time doing that and since graduating from primary school over the last two years has done just over thirty paintings, a couple of which Milno said that he could hang in the surf shop, until he finished high school to see if they would sell. His high school art teacher told him during the last semester of his second year to enter his examination painting into a competition where first place prize is 500 Munto, Klipp came in third place for which he won two arms full of art supplies.

Over the last year, he has been living in a single room which used to belong to the floor monitor which traded it to Klipp for three of his paintings, he saw the paintings in Klipp's room while doing room checks and asked him how much he wanted for it, Klipp said the painting is not for sale but that he will paint him something else and he can offer him whatever he thinks it to be worth, the floor monitor proposed that Klipp paint him three paintings in exchange for his room as the space in which Klipp was painting in *his* was very cramp and he had mentioned to him a couple of times that he was looking for a single room so the floor monitor said that he will give him his room, in exchange for three paintings which he wanted to decorate the apartment he was moving into after graduating.

Klipp started painting as soon as he got settled in his new room, the first painting he did was of a coffin overflowing with comically large gumballs, the coffin was brown with gold trimmings and the lid was being held open by a skeleton leaning forward over the coffin wanting to get in. Klipp did the painting because the floor monitor wanted something uplifting and sombre with heavily contrasting colours and the coffin filled with gumballs was the first thing that came to mind.

The second and third was much the same style and subject and was of a skeleton dressed in a black suit jacket and pants over a white long sleeved collar shirt with a black bow tie that was sitting on a chair in front of the coffin with the lid closed and a white table cloth over it, eating a steak and potatoes dinner with a glass of red wine while the third was of the skeleton lying with his hands folded over his chest inside the coffin under a blanket.

During the first five years that Klipp was away, Scara wrote him 36 letters in total; out of which two things stood out, the first being that Bees had a business partner by the name Mr Triffon who had been driving around Camel's Neck in search of a farm with a small to medium sized vineyard and that the Brungle farm suited his needs perfectly as he wanted to increase production of his brand of wine and because the Brungle farm was the last farm he was visiting that day he is willing to pay Bees a substantial amount of money, much more than the farm is worth as he does not feel like driving around the district a second time to have another look at the other farms.

Bees told him that he could not sell the farm as he would have nowhere to live would he do so but Mr Triffon would not have it as, a couple of months before he came to the farm he sent a friend of his over to audit the farm under the guise of a prospective buyer who wanted to buy the farm for business purposes and used the estimate to convince Bees that the farm is worth much less than it actually is telling him various fibs about the condition of the farm as well as others in the district, to try and convince him to sell the farm for the price he wanted.

By the end of the day, Mr Triffon had told Bees that he had gotten word of the farm's deteriorating state and because he was in urgent need of a farm with a vineyard the size of theirs, he would offer him a sum of money worth the amount of one of the three bigger farms in the district making it look as if Bees as selling the farm for a substantial profit.

After Bees kept declining Mr Triffon's offer, he asked Bees whether he might be able to make use of the vineyard in exchange for having ten of his best workers work for him free of charge on top of paying to build another cabin in which his workers will stay which Bees may use as he pleases, after Mr Triffon leaves besides paying for food for his workers and anything else they might come to need all besides given him 5 percent of whatever he makes with his brand of wine which was not in the least more than he was getting from Bees, but because of his desperate need for a steady income, Bees had no choice but to agree to the terms of Mr Triffon.

The other change along with going into business with Mr Triffon is his workers that now live there, among them is a boy named Trehun, he is two years older than Scara has hair in the style of dreadlocks down to his shoulders and quite tall for his age, when Bees first saw him, he told him to cut his hair but at the request of Mr Triffon from Bees to leave his workers as they are and in whatever manner they are Bees left him be.

Two days after being on the farm Trehun knocked on Scara's cabin door and asked her whether she wanted to accompany him on a walk around the farm, she agreed because of the manner in which he asked her, she wrote that he asked her with the words 'You will come with me for a walk around the farm?' and proceeded to explain that he asked her in the form of an order with the tone of a question and over the coming weeks, Trehun and Scara walked around various places on the farm many a time and came to know each other quite well and said that he reminds her somewhat of him in the sense that he very inquisitive.

She also wrote that her and Trehun had begun to go on dates of sort in town whenever they go there, which is now once a month instead of only once a quarter, with the rest of the workers under the supervision of Swenton and Cadd to buy food and other necessities they might need for the coming month, of which for Swenton and Cadd would be four cases of beer each they buy with money she presumes they pickpocket from various unsuspecting passers-by around town.

Besides that, she writes that Swenton and Trehun had become quite fond of each other seeing as they exercise together every second day and also that she doesn't quite understand why that is, seeing as how different they are but that if she had to give a reason it would be because Swenton enjoys the idea of having a black friend while Trehun enjoys laughing at him trying to be funny all the time.

She has not told Trehun about Swenton trying to force himself on Lavette because she doesn't want the chance of anything to potentially change the dynamic between the two for the worse for fear of it disturbing the added peaceful 'air' that them becoming friendly had brought over the relationship that Swenton and Cadd have with the rest of the workers because she very much enjoys going into town with Trehun ever so often.

Other than the dates they go on in town, they also spend every Saturday night behind the cabin having dinner and a glass of red wine, Trehun very much enjoys cooking and cooks most of the meals for the workers and likes to get her opinion on new and unique dishes he tries to come up with and so cooking them for her on Saturday nights.

When Klipp found out about Trehun and the time that him and Scara spend together, he laid awake in bed that night for quite a while pondering the idea of her telling him she would rather have him stop writing her so she may spend her time better so with Trehun before falling asleep and waking up the following morning with the idea of writing her a letter every two weeks with which he would take out on dates in strictly the conversational sense.

In them, he would suggest to her what to cook and have to drink alongside the dish accompanied by a dialogue of sorts where he would write what he would have said to her where he there beginning with a simple 'How are you?' down to 'Have a nice night, see you in two weeks' while alongside each line he would write her; what he thinks she would say to him as well as why he thought she would say so while also saying in the letter to take a radio outside with her to listen to a particular station which he too would be listening too while she was having dinner from eight o'clock every first Saturday night after she picked up the letter to at least midnight.

A couple of times, Klipp even called into the radio station he told Scara to listen whichever night and dedicated a song to her.

After reading the first letter from Klipp in which he proposed the date, Scara told Trehun that they can still have diner together behind the cabin but only as friends to which Trehun responded, he would rather stop seeing her in that manner altogether and within a week was cooking for a girl who lived with him in his cabin.

Chapter 12

It has been nine years since Klipp left the farm, six years since he left primary school and a year since he graduated from high school. He is currently studying art at a quite prestigious university about an 18 hour drive from Litchwith, it is not affiliated with the primary and high schools he attended and not the university Grandpa Brungle attended either so that Bees might not be able to keep tabs on him while he was there, it is though one of the three universities that Klipp wanted to attend after reading about the art programs they offered and because many well-known artists around the country went there, one of them being Klipp's favourite.

Because this was not the university that Bees could have gotten Klipp into through affiliation, to study there he needed to get in with a scholarship, which lucky for him his high school art teacher was good friends with the dean of admissions and knew the tastes and preferences of the board of admissions and helped steered him in the right direction to be a strong candidate for one of the three scholarships offered by the program, each of which had different requirements, at very least the one Klipp's art teacher told him he would be best suited for.

One year after Klipp graduated high school, he sent to the board of admissions at the university a painting that his art teacher told him to with feelings of hope that he will land one of the three scholarship positions. At first, he was quite averse to sending into the university, one of the paintings he had done up to that point because he did not much like the idea of giving away anything of what he had done in that regard, even struggling with the idea of having to *sell* any of his paintings, and wanted at first to paint something new for the scholarship position but forewent the idea after his art teacher told him to be sure to send a painting he did during his fourth year of high school.

After graduating high school, Klipp and Gulmon spent a month on Youtro's family farm while spending another driving around the country and staying at various motels to do so in order to see parts of the country which they had not yet before. Klipp had to get on a bus and set off for university without Youtro or Gulmon by his side in a setting as such for the first time in a long time, this because Youtro did had no intentions of attending university, nor did he ever because more than studying agriculture he wanted to spend the time he would have at university with his father so he may teach him the workings of their farm.

Gulmon on the other hand, did not yet know what he wanted to do and asked Youtro if he wanted to work for him on the farm for a year for pay before he would take the money from working on the farm, as well as what was left over of money his parents gave him after graduation and travel around the world as far as he can in search of inspiration for what he might want to come to do one day.

Having a room to himself and more space than he ever thought possible for his art supplies Klipp quickly settled into life at university and spent his free time painting and working at an art gallery a couple of blocks away from the university. After being there for almost a year and a half, he found a notice stuck to his door saying that he has been evicted from the programme for poor attendance and had to vacate his room and the premises before two weeks after receiving the notice and so packed his things and walked a couple of blocks from the university to a motel a 20-minute walk away from the gallery.

When he got to the motel, he paid for a room three months in advance and get settled in it before cleaning out the mini fridge in an attempt to get drunk for the first time in his life as well as paint while being so, so he picked up a brush and spent four hours painting what he thought would be his masterpiece. When he woke up the following morning, he found lying next to him on the bed, a painting that was three times the size of those that hung in his room and looked like it belonged outside under the motel staircase above the ice machine instead of in his room even.

After six months at the hotel, Klipp asked the owner of the gallery, a woman by the name of Roca, if she would allow him to hang up a couple of his paintings to which she replied that they were too different a style than those which filled the gallery so he asked if he could work one of his fellow employees' shift for free in return to hang his paintings up on a small space in one of the corners of the gallery and that if after six months they were still gathering dust, he would take them down and continue to work for her as he did before, she agreed and

Klipp spent many an hour a day without pay but thought the arrangement to be in his favour as he was able to spend most of his time there painting.

The first of his paintings sold within a month to man whose son was in a folk band that were quite well known around the city and was of a microphone with hair of green, red and blue wiring holding the head of man with a black cable coming from his neck singing into it. When the man asked Klipp what he wanted for the painting he told him to pay him whatever he thought the painting to be worth, the man gave him 100 Munto and from then on Klipp sold most of his paintings of that size for 100 Munto.

The second painting he sold to someone who had just finished studying and was moving into his own apartment and wanted paintings different from how his apartment was decorated, it was of a female zombie lying on a hospital bed with her feet up and a doctor sitting at the foot of the bed in between two nurses ready to catch the child the woman is giving birth to.

Both the doctor and the nurses as well as everything in the room is painted shades of black with a couple of red crosses strategically placed over the room to form a cross themselves while the female zombie was painted green, brown, red and purple and trimmings of black and white to give her a more lively feel than her surroundings, the guy liked the painting so much, that he offered Klipp 200 Munto for it and went on to buy seven paintings from him altogether while Klipp worked at the gallery.

The last painting that Klipp did for him a couple of months before he left was of a zombie dressed in a black suit, the guy said that it represented how he felt and that he wanted a painting that had some sort of meaning to it.

The third customer to buy a painting happened shortly after he finished it and was bought by a girl who was close with the guy who bought paintings for his apartment and was of a cupcake made up of many smaller cupcakes with frosting of many different colours and bases of chocolate, vanilla, caramel and red velvet, among them was one that was painted with a purple base and white frosting which he put there solely with the intention of having someone find it.

The fourth, fifth and sixth sales went to the son of a banker and consisted of three different paintings of similar style, they were of three different colours being white, grey and red, the first was of a 100 Munto bill with the face of a homeless person on it, the second a 50 Munto bill with no picture on it and the third a ten Munto bill with the face of a businessman on it.

The last four paintings that Klipp sold while working at the gallery went to a friend of Roca's who was a painter himself and wanted something much different to what he is known for and was bought with the intention to paint over each of them small details with black and white paint.

Around the time he sold his last four paintings he was nearing the end of his second year in the city and was beginning to think how he might differently come to spend his last year in the city when he got a call from Milno. Klipp hadn't seen or heard from him for quite some time after leaving for university and was pleasantly surprised when he got the call from him saying that he wanted to close 'Banana Board' for a while and come to the city to visit, when Klipp told him about his living situation he suggested that he come to the city for a week, before Klipp come back with him to Coral and Shell to work for him at Banana Board would he want to in exchange for food and lodging and a place to hang up some of his paintings in the surf shop until he has to go back to the farm.

A couple of days after speaking with Milno, he arrived at the hotel on a motorbike to which a side car and trailer is attached and they spent a week riding around the city with it before Klipp packed his belongings in the trailer, said goodbye to Roca and him and Milno set off on the six-hour drive to Coral and Shell.

Once they arrived in Coral and Shell, they spent a couple of hours at a lonely bar hidden somewhere off the side of the road, where they ate many different kinds of seafood tacos and drank many a glass of the 'lightest' beer that Klipp thought he might ever come to taste before heading to Milno's house where they unpacked their belongings and slept for the remainder of the day. Later that night, when they woke up Klipp moved his things into the garage with an inflatable mattress and a small living room area with a couch and a TV where he would sleep and paint.

The following morning, Klipp put on a yellow shirt with blue outlines of a banana and the name of the restaurant and bar on the back. When Klipp first set foot in the restaurant the most marked thing about it is the thick layer of sand over the entire floor of the restaurant and large clay pots with small palm trees sticking out of it placed randomly over the floor, wooden table and chair sets as dining areas, the bar at the back of the restaurant and a jukebox in the centre with surfboards sticking out of the sand and various other ornaments such as a mannequin on a bicycle amongst other things.

'Banana Board' is open from ten o'clock in the morning to two o'clock in the early morning, Klipp works the last of two eight hour shifts along with three other people. The first being a chef by the name of Kawetcha, a seven-foot-tall man from the island of Salndi who came there when he was 26 to open his own restaurant that is open 24 hours and serves only Salndion food as well as have a small area at the side of the restaurant where you would be able to order food while still sitting in your car.

Salndi is a mass of land that sits somewhere in the ocean many waves away from any countries adjacent to each other, because of its position it is referred to as 'the lonesome land' and therefore considered to be an island and not a country, although some experts have argued that it is too large a mass of land to be considered an island most people talk about it so, others again agree with the experts because the island is home to three of the biggest mountain ranges of that which is known on which reptiles are found to grow to be the size of sheep and said to be the last living incarnations of dinosaurs.

In the centre of the island is a volcano most known for never having erupted, around which is a circle of sand around which is a mass of water around which is another circle of sand that leads to land mass which leads into the ocean.

The better part of the island is covered predominantly by two types greenery, the first being a bush found only on the island, it can grow to be half the length of a palm tree and sprouts flowers of purple and lime green by the name of Qerolia which translates to different twins, in the centre of each flower is ball made of small white crystals that stick together much like pollen and is about the size of a marble, the crystals have a sweet taste and is used over the island as a substitute for sugar because of its healthy qualities.

Unlike the ball in the centre of the flower that has a somewhat chewy texture, the petals thereof dissipate in one's mouth and has the same sweet taste as the crystals only less intense.

The most marked thing about them is that when one is picked another of the opposing colour of the two colours in which they come grows back in its place within a week, if you pick a green flower a purple flower grows back in its place, if you pick a purple flower a green flower grows back in its place.

Other than being a substitute for sugar the primary usage of the flowers is that their petals are used to make frosting with, the frosting comes in the two colours which the petals are and tastes quite a bit different from any other frosting as well as somewhat different from each other, it is found in only five countries around the world, Salndi being one of them, the other being the four richest countries in the world and has quickly become one of the most expensive and sought-after delicacies in the world. So sought-after it is that the four countries besides Salndi pay other countries large sums of money for the right to exclusively have and sell it and the majority of Salndi's income come from the export of the frosting. Each batch is processed, made and packaged in Salndi due to the quickly deteriorating quality of the flower after being picked, the flowers cannot be put in water to be kept fresh for longer as they have no stems.

Another thing which the crystals of the flower are used for, although it is more so a myth than it is even a rumour, is that when set alight the fumes therefrom can be inhaled for intoxicating effect, this is not done very often as the stories surrounding the practice go many years back when Salndian people sprinkled small amounts of the crystals onto the surface of a small, flat rock while passing it around and inhaling the fumes from the burning crystals, it is even said that one is able to see one's future when intoxicated from inhaling the fumes, when asked about the practice on occasion not a single person is able to say whether it is true as they have not yet tried it or know of anyone who has.

The second type of greenery found on the island, other than palm trees, grass and various types of small plants, is a type of palm tree called 'Yummuy' trees, a palm tree not so much because of how it looks but because of what it bears, they are about twice the length of average palm trees, from the trunk, which is a very light brown colour, grows light green to yellow coloured leaves about the length of the quarter of the height of the tree that the Salndian people use to cook fish with as well as coconuts; of which the shells are a very dark charcoal with milk more light pink than white and more sour in taste than normal coconut milk and because of the abundance of palm and Yummuy trees the Salndian people cook only with coconut oil and every bit of food that is prepared is done so with it.

Along with the frosting another export which constitutes most of the countries income that of a crustation namely the 'Salndi Sea Snapper,' it looks similar to a crab in that it has a somewhat round body and six legs, three on either side of its body, it is black and blue in colour and about three times the size and twice the density in meat than the average crab, it is what makes the island's national dish of 'Seekrap,' the 'Salndi Sea Snapper' in which many holes are poked with a skewer and put in a pot filled with three cups water, one cup of coconut milk and an array of 12 different flavouring leaves found around the island; cooked at a low temperature to ensure that the meat cooks evenly and becomes as soft as it can possibly be, as well as to allow the flavours from the leaves to retain its original potency and to penetrate the meat in a consistent and uniform manner as to solidify its flavour on the inside of the meat.

The dish is served looking much as it did while still crawling around on the ocean floor only having turned orange after having been cooked while the excess liquid in which it was cooked is poured in a separate bowl to which flour to thicken the mixture is added so that it may be used as a dipping sauce for the meat along with a side of corn with butter and salt and a small amount of the Qerolia crystals to be had as either a starter or dessert.

There are 15 hotels on the island that grew tall over the last decade or so with permission and request from the Salndian people as their economy grew stronger. Along with the hotels, 30 to 40 percent of the houses on the island too are of brick while the rest are of bamboo much like they were many decades ago when people first started to populate the island, Kawetcha told Milno and Klipp that this ratio will probably stay as is for many years to come as most of the Salndian people still choose to live in houses built from bamboo because it is healthier for the environment.

Other than the houses and hotels, other buildings on the island are four hospitals, six libraries, one shopping mall, a small museum and various kinds of small to medium size stores 'strewn' over the island, the majority being bakeries, grocery stores and surf shops and various clothing stores and the occasional boutique.

As for the Salndian people, who make up just over 60 percent of all the people that live on the island, all of which, men and women alike, have hair either as white as the sand on the island or hair as dark as the coconuts that grow on the Yummuy trees, black lashes, eyebrows and facial hair if they are male, green or brown eyes and light brown skin.

As for Kawetcha and his goal to open a restaurant away from his birth country: the reason he chose to do so was because with all the money he had saved up till his 26th birthday he did not have enough to open the restaurant he would have and how he would have liked to and not wanting to settle for anything less, he did some research and found that he would get the most Munto in exchange for a single Salndian currency, Hjanas, which is 13 Munto for one

Hjana, he decided to pack his bags and make his way to Famurantia with the hope of opening the restaurant he always wanted to.

When he got there, he realised that even though he had much more Munto than he had Hjana, the prices for most things was on paper almost the same amount more than the Hjana is the Munto and that equated to everything being the same price if not more than it did his own country and decided it best to work as a chef or any other job a restaurant has to offer, until he had enough money saved to open his own restaurant the way he wants to, after spending a week sleeping on various beachside benches around town and eating what he caught he came across Banana Board.

Which reminded him of many of the small eateries and take away restaurants from his own country, late one night in search of a bench to sleep on he went inside to ask if they might be in need of a chef, the restaurant had only been open for just under a month at that time and all of the food was made by Milno himself with the help of two waiters, after talking with Kawetcha for half an hour Milno gave him the job as chef and they spent the remainder of the night coming up with new dishes to add to the menu.

Other than Kawetcha and occasionally Milno three other people work at Banana Board, two of which are girls who have been best friends ever since they met in kindergarten and are married to guys who are quite a bit older than them, one being a police officer and the other the owner of a pet store, who had been working there since it opened and the other a guy two years younger than Klipp who was busy with his last year of high school and worked there as often as he could to make money to spend a year abroad after graduating.

During the year that Klipp stayed with Milno, he only went surfing maybe a dozen times at the most, not because he didn't want to but because he did not so much have time to do so seeing as he worked in the restaurant and wanted to spend as much time as he could painting and wanted to finish at least a painting every two weeks, as promised Milno made space for Klipp in the surf shop to hang up a couple of them to see whether they would sell.

They did, only very slowly, the people of Coral and Shell didn't find the paintings very appealing and most said that looking at them made them feel uneasy and during the course of the year only two of his paintings were sold, both to the same person, a lady known around town for having too many cats who bought the first painting from him for much less than it cost him to paint it of a cat riding a broomstick before buying the second painting for a bit more than the she did the first which too, at her request, was of a cat, only a different kind of cat, riding a broomstick.

Six or so months into his stay with Milno, him and Klipp, more so Milno, started a business together, the idea came to Klipp one night after him and Milno had a couple of drinks after work and he went to his room and decided to paint his surfboard to give to Milno, as a thank you for letting him stay and work for him for the year, to start, he painted the entire board with a coating of very thin white paint and waited for it to dry so that what he paints over it can be more easily seen.

After spending the two hours it took for the paint to dry, thinking of something to paint over it he settled on an idea he came up with two minutes into waiting for the paint to dry. After choosing the three primary colours to give what he planned on painting on the board an infantile look he began to paint a picture of a family, which consisted of a boy and a girl holding their parents hands standing in between them—the boy holding his father's hand with a surfboard in the other and the girl holding her mother's hand with a small bucket and spade set in the other, on a beach holding hands with two palm trees on either side beside the family, in the style a child might draw the picture on a piece of paper with crayons.

When he was finished, he put the surfboard outside for the paint to dry as he did with his paintings as theft was a great rarity in that part of the country because of how heavily the crime is punished and the following day Klipp gave Milno the surfboard and leaned it against one of the palm trees in the restaurant. Other than lending to the decorative aspect of the restaurant, it gave Milno the idea to start making a brand of surfboards with designs that him and Klipp came up with as well as designs that customers themselves did or explained to Milno and Klipp to do before him and Klipp spent the next two days working on ideas for the company.

The following day, Milno gave Klipp five surfboards of which the last layer of coating has yet to be applied and told him to paint on them whatever he wanted to however big he wanted to while he thought about names for the company and ways to market it and the brand and later that day, about an hour or so before midnight when Klipp had just finished painting the last surfboard and Milno had decided on a name for the company and ways in which to market it; as well as came up with the idea to trademark it in the manner of if any surfboard comes standard with a design bigger or more flamboyant or detailed than the average board up until that point Milno and the company would get a percentage of the selling price. The company was to be called 'Mr Crayon's' after the picture that Klipp painted on the surfboard he gave to Milno and became the company's logo and every Mr Crayon's board from that point forward, was to have a smaller version of the picture somewhere on each board.

Milno's first order of business was to spend the entirety of the following week on the beach and in the water as much as possible surfing and sitting on the beach with the boards sticking out from the sand while they took a break from surfing and had a drink in an attempt to market the boards and so the company and to this day whenever someone asks him about it was the best way to market the company out of all the other methods that were made use of.

During the first two months after the company was established, 16 orders for Mr Crayon's surfboards were placed and Milno and Klipp got straight to work, staying up for hours on end, working on designs for the surfboards as well as painting them on them, almost every person that surfed that came across a Mr Crayon's surfboard wanted one and for the remainder of Klipp's time there him and Milno spent working on surfboards for various customers, so often orders came in for the surfboards that Milno had to employ two surfboard shapers to help with the workload and within the coming months, orders for Mr Crayon's surfboards came in from all over the country, both to surf with and well as to use for decorative purposes.

Two years into the venture a couple of other companies started to make surfboards with designs of many kinds on them as well, the designs were of ink and quite a bit more 'structured' and precise due to their choice of medium than the designs for Mr Crayon's, of which all was of oil paints but that regardless thereof came very close to the precise nature in detail and neatness of the companies' designs that were done with ink on a larger scale, which kept a more natural look than the others that people seemed to appreciate. Up until a week before Klipp left to go back to the farm he painted altogether 36 surfboards and made 1750 Munto doing so.

The last three days that Klipp spent in Coral and Shell Milno closed the restaurant and him, Klipp and Kawetcha spent the first of the three days paddling three hours away to a beach by the name of Bubble Beach where the waves are known for being well suited for beginners, Milno wanted to take Kawetcha there because since three months after starting to work at Banana Board he hadn't yet been in the water, due to how busy he was and the waves there was much better suited to his, as well as Klipp's at that point, skill level. It took a while longer than three hours to get there because of Kwetcha's big stature but not *very* much longer due to the unusually nimble manner in which he moves for someone his size.

Once they reached the shore they walked over to a part of the beach with many makeshift fireplaces made of various kinds of stones and rocks and unpacked from the waterproof backpack Milno had strapped to his back six bottles of water, six burger buns and patties, a block of cheese, three tomatoes, a packet of lettuce and a box of matches and after cooking, preparing and consuming everything that was inside the backpack they spent the remainder of the night stoking the fire, while Milno and Klipp listened to Kawetcha tell ghost stories from his country which were told to him by his parents and grandparents which Klipp very much enjoyed and Milno had heard quite a few times before but nonetheless still enjoyed mostly due to that they were the only three people on the beach that night.

The following morning, they hitch hiked back to Coral and Shell because their arms were too tired to make the journey back by water. Once there Kawetcha went to Klipp's room to rest while Milno and Klipp walked 20 minutes to a shop at the edge of town called 'Perma Brush' where Milno got all of his 'inkies'. The inside of the shop was decorated in the style of a haunted mansion, with the walls painted black and a chandelier hanging from the ceiling with imitation spider webs over it and red and white candles placed throughout various corners and spaces along with a gramophone that was playing on repeat a thirteen-minute composition by one of the most famous composers of the classical era by the name of 'Krampurini' named '13'.

It comprises of three notes played at different tempos in different sequences interchangeably within three structures all different from one another and is rumoured that whoever listens to it 13 consecutive times will be haunted by the ghost of the composer, when Klipp asked the owner of the store whether he had listened to the composition 13 times after each other, he said that he had, and quite a bit more than 13 times so and is yet to see the ghost of 'Krampurini' as well as any other ghost in the shop or anywhere else.

After almost three hours Milno had the whole of his right chest covered with a picture of an abandoned cabin in the woods. When they got back to the house Kawetcha was awake and waiting to hear what was on the agenda for the second day of the three day excursion, when Milno told him what he had planned he felt almost embarrassed that in all of his 14 years as a chef he had not yet thought of it himself and the three of them spent the next seven hours cooking every dish on the menu of 'Banana Board' and laid them out on the table along with six jugs of water and spent the almost five hours after that eating until their spoons spoiled.

After sleeping until just before sunrise when Kawetcha packed his bags and got on a bus to go home for a couple of days, before Klipp and Milno spent another couple of hours sleeping before getting showered and dressed so that they may go to a place by the name of 'Lady Lethila' later the night Milno knocked on Klipp's door and found him lying on his bed in a pair of black sneakers, a black pants and a white-collar shirt with long sleeves. Although he was dressed quite a bit more 'smart' than usual, Milno told him that was still too casual for where they are going and gave him a suit jacket to put on and told him to meet him outside in 290 minutes, where a car will be waiting to take them to where they are going.

To get there took three-quarters of an hour, half of which Klipp spent trying to get Milno to tell him where it is they are going, a request to which Milno had no reply, when they pulled up outside of the building Milno paid the driver and told him to be back to pick them up at two' o clock before the driver sped off to continue with his rounds for the night. By the door, Milno and Klipp were greeted by two very tall and stocky black men who asked to see their identification documents as well as wanted 150 Munto from each of them before they would be allowed to go inside.

On the inside, the building looked much bigger than it did from the outside. Klipp later learned from the owner of the establishment that it was his intention to have it be so as a way of making it feel to people that they were stepping into somewhere much greater than themselves, it consisted of four separate rooms, the first being a dining room where customers have dinner and drinks, the second is a bar room, the third a dimly lit room referred to as the waiting room with a small stage built against the back of the room while the fourth room spans the entire square footage of the building and 'sits' on a floor below the ground floor.

Each of the three rooms on the ground floor is decorated in much the same style, the dining room is the brightest of the three, the floor is of white marble with the 'Lady Lethila' logo, a silhouette of a woman wearing stockings and lingerie and a corset under a suit jacket that comes down to just below her chest and a top hat leaning on a cane, of red marble in the centre of each tile, the walls are painted light brown and has four rows of four paintings against each of the four walls that comprise the restaurant. Each painting is a solid colour of shades of warm arranged randomly around the room, the chairs are of a dark type of wood while the seats are of black velvet and the backrest of only the wood that the chair is made of, later the owner said that it was his intention to have it so as it would deter people from leaning back in their chairs and have them sit upright while they were there to lend a more tasteful atmosphere to the room and the establishment as a whole.

The tables were of the same wood as the chairs with white table cloths over them and a lantern in the centre of the table so people might better be able to see the table while dining as the lights in the room is very dim.

The floor of the bar is covered with dark red suede carpeting and the walls painted a light shade of black with eight lamps with gold fittings and sand blasted lamp shades over the bulbs mounted two next to each other in the centre of each wall, on one side of the room against the wall is a 12 foot long bar made from the same wood as the chairs in the dining room with 12 bar stools that stretch the entire length of the bar of black coated steel with the seats covered in black suede.

The remainder of the room consists of six tables, again from the same wood as chairs in the dining room and the bar, with four couches around them covered with sections of black and purple suede, on each of the tables are the same lanterns as in the dining room which customers can choose to make use of or not considering how dark they like their area to be along with a jukebox in the corner of the room by the bar that plays only instrumental music.

The third room, referred to as the show room, is the smallest out of the three ground floor rooms of which the interior is a cross between that of the dining room and the bar room, the floor is covered with black suede carpeting and the walls painted a dark red with eight lamps mounted against the walls in the same style and manner as that of the bar room along with six tables of the same wood as the others, though without table cloths and lanterns over and on them with a six foot high lantern in the centre of the room to give light to it with a small stage built against the wall opposing the bar.

Walking into the dining room, Milno and Klipp sat down at an open table along with four other pairings of people, shortly after they settled into their seats a waitress dressed in the same manner as the lady of which the logo of the establishment is came over to them and put down on the table two menus and asked if they would like anything to drink and they ordered a double whiskey on the rocks and a beer before the waitress gave them time to look over the menu.

On it, for 'starters' and 'main course,' there were only three dishes, mussel soup, fried snails with a honey and mustard dressing and a plate of toothpick fries for starters and a steak served only medium rare with a side of baby potatoes, steamed fish of which Klipp is unable to pronounce the name with a side salad and chicken livers cooked in a peri-peri and lime reduction with a side of croutons for the main course while for dessert they had a chocolate, caramel and vanilla cheesecake served with apricot jam and cream, the drinks are either a bottle or glass of red or white wine, a glass of either whiskey, brandy or cognac or a bottle of sparkling or still water.

A short while after looking over the menu the waitress comes back to the table with their drinks and takes a small notebook and pen out from the back of her corset and asks whether they are ready to order.

'Is this the entire menu?' Klipp asks.

The waitress nods. 'Short and savoury… ish.'

Kipp laughs. 'Is that something you were told to say?'

'No, it's just something I say sometimes.'

'I'll have the chicken livers please?'

The waitress looks over at Milno, 'And for you?'

'The steak please?'

The waitress writes down their orders. 'Will you be having dessert?'

Klipp shakes his head.

'No thank you,' says Milno.

The waitress nods and puts her pen back inside of her notebook.

'Actually, I'll have the cheesecake, if that's okay?'

'Of course.' She writes down the order and puts the notebook and pen inside of it back in her corset.

After 45 minutes or so, the waitress brings over their food and after another hour or so she came back to settle their bill, Milno said that they will be staying until two and asked if she would open a tab for them which they will settle before they leave which she did before they left to go to the bar room which is in the centre of the three rooms on the ground floor of the building next to which is also the show room, the entrance is decorated much different to the rest of the building in that the floor and walls are of varnished concrete to give it a colder and more unwelcome feel than the three rooms to which it leads.

Walking into the bar, Milno stops Klipp before he makes his way over to one of the tables and couches. 'Neither the couches nor any one of the bar stools in here will know the print of your bum tonight because the drinks we are going to order here, we are going to take with us next door as soon as we get them…' Milno points to a wooden door at the opposite end of the room. 'What are you having?'

'Whatever you are.'

Milno nods. 'Be right back.' When he comes back with their drinks, they make their way to the stage room and sit down by an open table in front of the stage, after a while a woman wearing a white silk nightgown over white stockings comes walking onto the stage, she has fair skin almost as white as her gown, red hair and green eyes and is dragging a chair behind her, she sets the chair down in the centre of the stage and begins to seductively dance around it.

As music begins to play in the background while sliding her nightgown off her shoulders and lays it over the back of the chair, under her nightgown she is wearing a white one piece lingerie outfit and white silk gloves and her stockings come up to just below her knees, for the duration of the five minutes that the song lasts she skips, hops, twirls around and straddles the chair in a way that to Milno and Klipp makes it feel as if they were watching a 50 minute film instead of a five minute long piece of choreography until the song comes to an end and she slips her nightgown back over herself and drags the chair back with her through and behind the curtain at the back of the stage.

'How was that?' Milno asks.

Klipp turns to Milno somewhat dazed. 'Good.'

'Only good?'

'It was very good.'

Milno laughs. 'That's better.'

Klipp looks back over at the stage. 'I wonder what her name is?'

'We should find out.'

'How are we going to do that?'

'After being up there, they come down here and talk to you if you buy them drinks.'

'Only if you buy them drinks?'

Milno nods. 'Only if you buy them drinks.'

'That's nice.'

'Do they just talk to you?'

'Yep.'

'For how long?'

'However long they want to, or for however long you can keep them talking to you by making their time worth their while.'

Klipp takes a drink of whiskey. 'Do they do other things besides talk to you?'

'Not sure, if they do you probably have to pay them a lot of drinks worth of money to find out.'

Klipp nods.

'If the girl that was just up there comes down here, you should ask if we can buy her a drink.'

'Okay.'

'And ask her right when she walks past us otherwise somewhere else might get to her first.'

'Why don't you ask her?'

'I'll ask her.'

Klipp looks at Milno suspiciously. 'I think I should ask her.'

'Do that.'

Just then the woman steps down from the stage and walks by them.

'Excuse me miss?'

The woman stops and turns to Klipp, 'Yes?'

'Would it be okay if we buy you drinks?'

'Sure.'

The woman pulls out a chair and sits down with them.

Klipp holds his hand out to her, 'Klipp, nice to meet you.'

'That's a funny name.'

Klipp smiles, 'I've been told that.'

'Does it mean anything?'

Klipp shakes his head, 'No, just a funny name from where I come from.'

'And where would that be?'

'A place where there are lots of farms a long way away from here.'

'Can't say that I know it.'

'Can't say that you should.'

She laughs. 'And you are?' Milno holds his hand out to her before she is able hers to him. 'Milno.' They shake hands.

'Nice to meet you, Milno.'

'Likewise, and you are?'

'Around here, they call me Lady Lethila.'

'Does whoever call all the girls that work here that?'

The woman nods.

'Is there any chance we might be able to get your name when you are not around here?'

'If you give me 100 Munto.'

Milno reaches into his pocket and puts a 100 Munto bill down on the table. 'Just because I wouldn't feel comfortable calling you Lady Lethila the entire night.'

The woman picks up the money and puts it in the front of her brassiere. 'Just because I wouldn't want you to call me that the entire night.'

Milno laughs.

'Auburn.'

'That's a very nice name.'

'I hear.'

Milno gets up. 'How about I go get us some drinks? What are you having?'

'Beer please.'

'Me too.'

'Four beers and two whiskeys it is, I'll be right back.' He makes his way to the bar.

'Did your parents give you that name?' Klipp asks.

Auburn nods. 'Yep.'

'Now I know for sure it's your name.'

Auburn laughs. 'That was quite good, you?'

Klipp nods. 'Yep.'

They sit quietly for a while.

'So Klipp, do you have a lady in your life?'

Klipp shakes his head. 'No.'

'How so?'

'Haven't met the right lady yet.'

'I see.'

'Or I have, I just haven't seen her in almost 12 years.'

'What?'

Klipp nods.

'Haven't heard that one before.'

Klipp laughs.

'Why is that?'

'I used to live on a farm with my aunt and uncle and her dad worked for them on the farm, just when we started to become friends, I had to go away to boarding school.'

'And the closest school was so far away that you weren't able to see her for 12 years?'

'A little bit.'

'That's… I don't know what that is.'

Klipp nods. 'I think he also wanted me to go away for that long so I can grow up or something.'

Auburn nods. 'Have you talked to her at all since leaving?'

'With letters every now and then.'

'That's okay.'

Klipp nods.

'What's her name?'

'Scara.'

'That's a pretty name.'

'Very.'

'Is she as pretty as her name?'

'Prettier.'

Auburn laughs. 'She must be very pretty then.'

'Prettier than you even maybe.'

She bats her eyelashes. 'I'll take that as a compliment.'

Klipp nods. Milno comes back to the table with a tray of drinks and puts it down on the table. 'Here we go.' Auburn and Klipp take their drinks from the tray.

'That was quick.'

Milno nods. 'I told the barman that we are having drinks with you and it was like he waved a magic wand and the drinks just appeared.' Milno sits back down.

Auburn laughs.

'Hope me being away didn't cause you too much grief?'

'I didn't even know that you were gone up until just now.'

Klipp laughs. Milno picks up his glass of whiskey and holds it out in front of him. 'To getting to know the lady behind Lady Lethila.'

'That's nice.'

Milno nods. 'Thank you.'

They each take a sip of their drinks. 'So, what do you guys do for a living?'
Asks Auburn.

'I have a restaurant.'

'Really, that's nice.'

Milno nods. 'It's also a bar too and there's a surf shop attached to it as well.'

'It gets better.' Auburn turns to Klipp, 'You?'

'Studied art for a while and worked at an art gallery for a little bit too after
that.'

'I myself quite like art.'

'I also started a surfboard company not too long ago; he helped a little but
mostly it was me.'

'What's the company?'

'Mr Crayon's.'

Auburn's eyes widen. 'I know it.'

Milno nods. 'Wouldn't have thought any different.'

Auburn laughs.

'How do you know it?' Klipp asks.

'A friend of mine bought one of the…'

'Surfboards?' Milno adds.

'That's the word I was looking for… Yes, he bought himself one a while
ago, had a really nice picture on it.'

'What was the picture?'

'It was a picture of a dolphin with his fin around the board, I thought that
was quite funny, they all look really nice, I've seen a couple around here.'

'Thanks.'

'That's quite thing that?'

'What?' Milno asks.

'Surfing.'

Milno nods. 'Have you tried it?'

Auburn shakes her head. 'Don't plan to either.'

'How so?'

'Not really one for doing anything in the water besides cooling off in it after
lying in the sun for a while.'

'What do you do?' Klipp asks.

'I run a daycare.'

'Why do you work here then?'

'You make a lot more money working here than you do running a daycare.'

'What would you be doing if you weren't working here?'

'Not sure really, art teacher maybe, children's book illustrator.'

'Do you like painting or drawing?'

'I do, but I don't have much time these days to do so, so I haven't in a while, used to draw a lot in my spare time before I started working here.'

'Anything you might be able to show us?'

'Right now?'

'If you have anything here?'

'Do you think I have anything here?'

'Do you have a handbag here?'

Auburn nods.

'Then you might have something here.'

Auburn laughs. 'I don't have anything in it of what you want to see though.'

Milno nods. 'Too bad.'

Klipp finishes his beer. 'I have to use the bathroom.' Klipp gets up.

'Take more time than you need please.'

Klipp laughs. 'I'll see what I can do.' Auburn waves him goodbye as he makes his way to the bathroom.

Milno takes a sip of whiskey. 'Do you think I can see some of the things we were talking about just now?'

'Everything is at my house.'

'I would hope so.'

Auburn laughs. 'Do you really want to see them or do you just want to come to my house?'

'Both.'

'Which one do you want to do more.'

'Both equally.'

'Do you come here often?'

'A couple of times a year.'

'If you give me 50 Munto I'll bring you one next time you're here.'

'How will you know when that is?'

'You can tell me.'

'That would be like a date then, I might as well just come to your house to get it?'

'I'd rather give it to you here.'

'Why?'

'I'd feel safer.'

'Okay…' Milno reaches into his pocket and takes out a 50 Munto bill and gives it to her, she puts it in the front of her brassiere. 'Thank you.'

'Maybe at the end of the night you can invite me over to get it, there's an empty spot on my wall that's really been hurting my eyes lately.'

Auburn laughs. 'What about Klipp?'

'Tomorrow night then.'

'Maybe.'

'If you do, I'll buy ten of the ones you like the least.'

'If you do that you only have to pay for nine.'

'So, I should definitely come over then?'

'I'll let you know.'

'On the topic of pictures…' Milno rolls up one of his sleeves. 'Do you know what this is?

'Of course, I have one too.'

'Really?'

Auburn nods, she turns around and pulls down the top part of her lingerie to reveal an inkie underneath it.

'What is it?'

'A butterfly that's wings are two parts of a painting.'

'Wow, now I feel bad about everything that I have.'

Auburn laughs.

'Did you come up with the idea yourself?'

'Yep.'

'What is the painting of?'

'It's the house in which I grew up on the farm of the man my parents worked for, the idea came from one of my drawings.'

'Was the painting on the wings also your house?'

Auburn shakes her head. 'No.'

'What was it?'

'I can't really remember.'

'That's okay, I'll just see it when I come to your house.'

Auburn laughs. 'It's probably around there somewhere.'

'How big is it?'

'The inkie?'

Milno nods.

'About a third of my back.'

'That must have hurt?'

'A little bit when he went to get the first part of it done, the second time was a lot better, the time when they finished it, I actually fell asleep for a while.'

'That's the best thing I've ever heard.'

Auburn laughs. 'It was woman who did mine so that might have something to do with it.'

'Not the best thing I've ever heard but still probably true.'

'I've never seen someone with as much as you.'

'Neither have I.'

'Any particular reason you have so many?'

'I just like the way it looks.'

'Do any of them mean anything special to you?'

'A couple, have you ever thought about getting another one?'

'I have, but I want to get them on places where I would have to put cover up on them when I'm working.'

'Oh, if you didn't though, would you get more?'

'I would, but I don't think I should.'

'Why not?'

'There can't be a man out there who likes girl with that many inkies?'

Milno nods. 'If a man you really like doesn't mind, would you get more?'

Auburn looks down at her arm. 'I think so.'

'Then you should do it.'

'What if I meet a nice man and he doesn't like me because of it?'

'The that's not the right nice man for you.'

'What if I get them and I meet the man of my dreams and he doesn't like how they look?'

'If you don't get them, you might never meet the man of your dreams.'

Auburn nods. 'Something to think about.'

'If you were to get more how many would you get?'

'Probably as much as you have.'

'Thank you for the compliment.'

Auburn laughs.

'What would you get?'

'I would get a children's story down my arm with words and pictures.'

'Wow, that is now the first best thing I've ever heard.'

Auburn laughs.

'Do you know what the story will be?'

'My mom used to tell me a story when I was a little girl of two fairies who lived in a village where the people that lived there only ate sweets and other sweet things that they made themselves and made a lot of with not much effort and thought put into what they were making because of how nice it was which they ate so quickly and so much of that it, left them feeling uneasy and disappointed when they were finished eating which upset the fairies very much.

'They then baked a cupcake with special ingredients that they procured themselves and baked with lots of care and effort, these cupcakes were the best sweet thing that the people of the village had ever tasted and after eating one or two of them they were satisfied beyond what they were after eating what they themselves made and were left feeling mote satisfied.'

'That's a beautiful story.'

'It is, it's probably my favourite story even now.'

'It will definitely make a very nice inkie.'

'And it will have some meaning to me.'

'If there are any clouds in the story, you should make them of pink and blue candy floss.'

Auburn laughs. 'I'll be sure to do that.'

'Hey.'

Milno and Auburn startle.

'You scared me,' says Auburn.

'Sorry, didn't mean to.'

'That's okay.'

Klipp sits back down.

'You really did take your time.'

'My pleasure.' Klipp turns to Auburn, 'Are there children allowed here?'

'Why do you ask?'

'I'm think I saw one in the bathroom.'

Auburn nods. 'You probably did then.'

'So, there is?'

'For 250 Munto you can bring your kids if you want.'

'Do people bring their kids?' Milno asks.

'Sometimes.'

'What do they do here?'

'They sit with their parents while they do whatever they do.'

'Do they cause a lot of racket?'

'Sometimes, but for every customer that complains about another customer's kid, the customer with the kid has to pay the owner 250 Munto, for each kid they have with them if they have more than one with them, even if only one of however many kids they have with them caused the commotion, the owner isn't too fond of kids but he makes a lot of money by having them here, one time, he told one of the girls that he made more money from complaint fees the entire night than he did the from the dining room.'

'Speaking of kids...' Milno says. 'Do have you any?'

Auburn nods. 'A daughter.'

'How old?'

'Six'

'Does she have red hair too?'

'She does, a shade or two darker than mine but yes.'

'What's her name?' Milno asks.

'Ruby.'

Milno laughs. 'I'm not too sure now what the first best thing I've heard you say tonight is, you're really good with that.'

Auburn laughs. 'Thank you.'

Milno takes a drink of whiskey. 'Speaking of jobs, does your daughter know that you work here?'

'We weren't talking about jobs.'

'I know, needed a segway instead of just asking you.'

Auburn laughs. 'Nice, no she does not.'

'Do you plan on telling her?'

'When she turns ten or twelve maybe.'

'What will you tell her.'

'I don't know, I'll probably say that it's quite hard for a woman to make money these days and that men have been whistling at her ever since she grew breasts and that she is really fond of dancing and does not care much to do so wearing lingerie in front of strangers. I was quite lucky to get the job because it pays three times more than what a regular job does for half the time you have to work there and so I get to spend more time with her.'

'I hope I get to see what she is going to be like one day.'

'I'll tell her you said so.'

'Thanks, maybe I'll even get to tell her myself sometime soon.'

Auburn laughs. 'Maybe.'

Milno looks at Auburn's empty glass. 'More drinks, seeing as you didn't take your time at all with the last two.'

'Would have been rude of me if I did.'

Milno laughs.

'You asking me too?' Klipp holds up his two empty glasses.

'Don't need to, would have gotten another two either way.'

Klipp laughs. 'Thanks.'

'I'll have another two as well please.'

'Coming right up,' Milno picks the tray up off the table and makes his way over to the bar.

'How long have you been working here for?'

'Almost three years now.'

'Is that long?'

'Not really, some girls have been working here for three times that long.'

'Do you have to take off your clothes sometimes?'

'On the floor below.'

'What happens there?'

'Same as what happens here, only with less clothing.'

'Do you have to pay to go to the bottom floor.'

Auburn nods. '500 Munto, you also have to give the girls money while they're dancing, and you can't give anything less than a 20 Munto bill.'

'Do they just dance there?'

'Yep.'

'How much does that cost?'

'How much would you say it should if I were to be the girl down there with you?'

Klipp thinks for a bit. '2000 Munto.'

Auburn laughs. 'Close, but it's 1500 Munto for half an hour.'

'What are the guys like that go down there?'

'Some of them really nice, a lot like you and Milno.'

Klipp nods.

'What did you think they were like?'

'I don't know, just not nice guys.'

'Sometimes, but we don't talk about those ones.'

After they finished the third round of drinks that Milno brought back to the table he bought 36 shots of fruit liquor with which they played a drinking game involving Auburn's inkies before going to the bottom floor where Milno and Klipp spent the better of an hour trying to convince Auburn to go on stage after which Klipp fell asleep and Milno asked Auburn questions on where she would most like to live one day, what her dream house would look like, if she wanted more kids, what the name of her bakery would be were she to have one and spending the last hour or so before closing time telling her how pretty he thinks she is, in as many ways as he was able to come up without having them all sound the same.

Chapter 13

When Klipp steps out of the bus that brought him all the way from a bus stop close to Milno's house to Golden Heart, the bus stop there that as of four years ago has become as well a taxi rank in the centre of town, the heat from the sun that stings Klipp's skin is quite a bit sharper that he expected it to be seeing as how warm and stuffy it was inside the bus, he picks up his belongings and sits down with them in a spot of shade by the edge of the bus station.

Looking around, he sees that most things look much the same as it did before he left other than a couple of smaller stores which underwent minor changes aesthetically on the outside, one of them being 'The Snow Globe' which is now painted light shades of pink and blue instead of white as it used to be, after a couple of minutes and the sweat drops on his forehead disappearing—Klipp makes his way over to the ticket desk and asks the clerk how far 53 Munto will get him.

15 minutes later, Klipp is sitting in the back of a taxi talking to the driver on his way back to the farm about everything he got up to since leaving Golden Heart to a couple of nights ago that he spent with Milno and Auburn in Lady Lethila, likewise Klipp found out about the driver, how he came to study in the country on a scholarship and how even with that and how he had the third best marks in his graduating class, how hard it was to find a well-paying job and how he does carpentry in his spare time making small houses for pets in the form of famous buildings around the world.

So well has it been going that, that some people buy three at a time, for one pet even, also asking him to make playhouses for their children to very large and flamboyant specifications and so soon he will stop driving taxis and focus full time on carpentry as his primary source of income.

Standing by the gate with his things, Klipp sees Bees and Clarafina playing a game of cricket on the lawn with the workers and decides it best to run his belongings up to his room from the back of the house before going to greet them in the case that Bees might want him to get rid of any of his paintings, leaving his suitcase and art supplies behind to first take his paintings inside. He walks around the side of the house and through the back door by the kitchen and up to his room and puts his paintings away under his bed in three separate stacks before walking back down the stairs and out of the house to get the remainder of his belongings to do with the same.

Walking onto the porch to make his way toward greeting Bees and Clarafina; he stops in his tracks when he sees that the three wooden poles that is supposed to make up wickets used to play the game with is one of the male workers with his hands tied and made to stand on his knees with the rest of the workers spread out over the lawn doing the part of the fieldwork.

Making his way across the lawn, Clarafina is the first to see him, at first, she is unable to make out who it is that is approaching her but after remembering the call her and Bees got from Klipp a week before, saying that he will be back on the farm at around the time it is she throws the cricket ball over her shoulder. 'Nephew?' She yells. 'You actually came back.'

Unlike Clarafina, who might as well be floating her way over to Klipp on a cloud, the excitement that Bees feels for seeing his nephew pales heavily in comparison to that which Clarafina feels having laid in bed the previous night thinking that having another grown male presence in the house other than himself might impede on the way he prefers to go about his daily doings, more so than he would like. As Klipp walks up to them, Clarafina steps out in front of him and puts her arms around him. 'Welcome back, so glad to have you here.'

Klipp puts his arms around Clarafina and hugs her. 'Glad to be back, auntie Clarafina.'

After letting go of her nephew, Clarafina turns to Bees, standing quite uneasy in the presence of his nephew after all the years that he was away, Clarafina slaps Bees over the head. 'Why don't you see if you can look less excited to see your own flesh and blood for the first time in ten years, brother?'

'Maybe you should calm down instead of poking at me, Clarafina.'

Clarafina shakes her head. 'No, the difference in the levels of our excitement is far too big.' Clarafina pushes Bees in front of Klipp. 'Now give our nephew a hug so we can get on with the game.'

'Welcome home, nephew, it is good to have you back.'

'Thank you, uncle Bees, it is good to be back.'

'And it is good to see the two of you back together.' Clarafina pats Bees and Klipp on their backs, 'How are you doing, my boy?'

'Very good.'

'Happy to hear it, I have much to ask you, nephew.'

'I have much to tell you.'

'Great, but before we get there, we have a game of cricket to finish if you care to join us?' Clarafina turns around, 'As you might be able to tell me and your uncle here are quite the bit outnumbered but because this is not your average game of cricket with not your average players, it is okay, we actually prefer it that way.' She turns back around. 'Still, it will be nice if you can join us.'

Klipp looks over at Mueno knelt on the grass. 'I would rather go inside and sit down and have a drink with you and talk about what has been going on?'

Clarafina smiles. 'The best news I've heard since you've been away, we can make a drinking game out of it, see which one of us is the last to fall asleep.'

'Sounds great,' says Klipp.

Clarafina turns to Bees. 'How about it?'

'If we must.'

'That we have to.' Clarafina puts her hand on Klipp's shoulder, 'I have never been more proud of, you nephew,' she says, the idea of having a drink with someone other than Bees for the first time in 12 years making her feel as excited as she has ever, she cups her hands over the sides of her mouth. 'Okay people, me and Bees are going to go inside to have a drink to welcome back our nephew, you can untie your friend there and go about your day doing whatever you do around here during the weekend, before you do make sure you take the bat and ball inside the cabin and put it away in a safe place and fluff up the patch of grass, like how it was before Mueno messed it up, very good then, on you go!' Clarafina turns to Klipp, 'Shall we?'

After a couple of hours at the kitchen table, Bees fell asleep and after being woken by Clarafina went upstairs to his bedroom to go to sleep. Klipp and Clarafina stayed up quite a bit later talking about Clarafina's love for playing the piano and how she wanted to get a job playing at a restaurant in town as well as Klipp's time at school and studying art at university as well as his job at the art gallery they got to know each other quite a bit better and found that through their mutual love for most things—the arts that they have quite a few things in common and enjoy each other's company more than they thought they would,

Klipp finding even that him and Bees can somewhat warm up to each other now that he is older and less afraid to speak his mind.

During the time Bees, Clarafina and Klipp were all sitting around the kitchen table it consisted mostly of Klipp telling them about his time at school, the books he read and didn't read, the classes he took, the friends he made, the food he ate as well as learned to cook which was the topic of conversation on which the most time was spent considering Bees' weight gain as well as Bees pestering Klipp for ideas on how to better the farm.

After Bees went upstairs to go to bed, Clarafina and Klipp talked about how comically overweight he had become considering how much he values appearance, a thing which Clarafina attributed to the deteriorating state of the farm as well as the Brungle bank account which led them to having to spend quite a bit less money on drink and tobacco and so Bees looking more to cheap and unhealthy food to ease his sorrows.

The following morning Klipp got up, brushed his teeth and got dressed and went down to the kitchen to make himself a bowl of cereal after checking if Bees and Clarafina are still asleep and going over to the workers cabin to go and find Petrus, on his way there, he sees the children, about that age that he was when he left the farm, playing cricket in few feet away from the cabin, he asks them if they know where he might be able to find Petrus to which they reply by pointing him in the direction of the dam.

Klipp makes his way back across the lawn to the gate and out before stepping onto the dry and rocky terrain outside of the farm grounds back in the direction of the cabin to the dam across from it.

Unlike the grounds outside of the farm adjacent to the ground on which the dam is, the ground around the dam is somewhat moist and 'fluffy' almost, that if you blow on it easily separates, and from it grows in patches red flowers that the workers put in the hot water they use to wash clothes with along with washing detergent to soften the chemical smell that the washing detergent leaves and gives the clothes a more pleasant scent once dry, as well as letting the flowers soak in a cup of boiling water to drink to ease a stuffy chest.

Inside of the dam, mostly around the edges, are pieces of bamboo about five centimetres thick around a finger sized hole sticking out from the water that the children use to make rafts with by tying together many pieces of bamboo with the leaves from the stems of the crops of corn which are quite long and strong to hold together many pieces of bamboo for a long period of time; which they use to float or paddle around in the dam with another piece of bamboo as an oar.

As Klipp nears the dam, he looks around for Petrus but does not see him, he decides to trust the children's knowledge on the whereabouts of Petrus more than his point of vantage and starts around the edge of the dam and through the many long strings of petal leaves that 'fall' from the branches of the trees that grow around it to see if Petrus might be sitting under one of the trees.

Halfway around the dam, Klipp sees Petrus sitting next to a very dense patch of leaves and makes his way over to him. 'I was wondering how long it would be before you came to find me.'

Klipp walks around the patch of leaves and sees Petrus sitting on a sawn-off tree stump, his elbows resting on his knees busy carving something from a small piece of bamboo with a pocket knife. Petrus looks up at Klipp. 'It happened quite a bit sooner than I expected it would but I cannot say that I am upset about that.'

'How did you know it was me?'

'I haven't heard footsteps like that in almost 12 years now.'

Klipp laughs. 'That sounds exactly like something I would have thought you would have said.'

'Have a seat.'

Klipp sits down next to him.

'How was your first day back?'

'Good.'

'What did you do?'

'Sat with my aunt and uncle by the kitchen table and talked a little about the last 12 years or so.'

'Did you get on well with each other?'

Klipp nods. 'Yes.'

'That's good to hear, did you learn anything about what went on around here while you were gone?'

'Not really, they mostly wanted to know what I got up to.'

Petrus nods.

'I did hear from Scara a little bit about that.'

'I heard that you were writing to each other.'

'She said she wasn't going to mention anything about that to anyone?'

'I only heard about it a couple of months ago.'

'Oh.'

238

'Anything to tell?'

'What do you want to know?'

'How about you start from when you left to now?'

'Okay…' Klipp puts his hands in his pockets. 'I went to primary school where I made two good friends and read a lot of books, went to high school with the same two friends and read less books because I painted more, then I went to university to study art before going to work at an art gallery close by; before spending the last year at a friend's house painting and working for him at his restaurant.'

'When did you start painting?'

'Quite soon after I got to primary school.'

'How many paintings have you done up till now?'

'Maybe just more than 30.'

'That's not a lot.'

'It takes a little bit more time than you would think.'

Petrus nods. 'I would really like to see some of them some time.'

'I would really like to show you some time.'

'You should bring a couple of them here.'

'I will, they might not be much to your liking but if you can find something in them that you like, it will definitely make me feel better about them.'

'Looking forward to it.'

'Me too.' Klipp looks down at the carving that Petrus is holding. 'What's that?'

'It's a pipe for Dwendo.'

'Didn't know you did that.'

'I've been doing it for quite a while, it's very relaxing.'

'How long ago did you start doing it?'

'About two years ago.'

Klipp nods. 'How many have you made so far?'

'Maybe a hundred or so.'

'Do you still have all of them?'

'Most, others I sold in town at the flea market and some got lost or broke amongst other things.'

'Do you make all of them as detailed as this one?'

Petrus nods. 'Most.'

'Who buys them?'

'Farmers from around the district, they buy them for their workers.'

'How much do you sell them for?'

'10 Munto each.'

'That's not very much.'

'It's not too bad.'

'I think you should sell them for at least 20 Munto each, people might buy even more if they're a bit more expensive.'

Petrus nods. 'Something to look into.' He takes a breath and blows away the shavings from the pipe and holds it out to Klipp. 'Here you go.'

'Can I have it?'

'It's yours, just don't smoke tobacco from it.'

'What else would I smoke from it?'

'There are some healthier options.'

'Thanks,' Klipp looks over the pipe, in the shape of a rattlesnake with the bottom part of its open mouth as a holder for tobacco or any other kind of leaf and the tail where you smoke from. 'It looks very realistic for what it is.'

'They started to look that way quite recently.' Petrus picks up another piece of bamboo and cuts the first piece from it.

'Maybe you can bring a couple with you when I bring my paintings.'

'I will do that.'

Klipp looks down at the pipe. 'How many have you sold so far?'

'Half of what I've made maybe.'

'What do you plan on doing with the money?'

'Give some of it to Scara for her birthday and put the rest away to give to her when I'm gone.'

'I would have guessed that's what you would have done.'

Petrus laughs. 'Not a hard guess to make I would hope.'

Klipp holds the pipe out in front of him. 'Have you ever thought about making sculptures with bigger pieces of wood?'

'I have, but the wood is quite expensive.'

Klipp nods. 'Maybe there are some pieces lying around the house or in the garage maybe, I could ask my aunt, she might know where to get some for free even.'

'That will be nice.'

'Have you tried looking on the mountain maybe?'

'A couple of times.'

'Oh.' Klipp thinks for a bit. 'How about using a couple of pieces of bamboo together to make a bigger sculpture of, or you can make different smaller parts that fit together?'

Petrus nods. 'That sounds like it could be quite promising.' Petrus puts down the half-carved piece of bamboo and gets up.

'Where are you going?'

'To take you up on your advice, care to help?'

'Sure.' Klipp gets up and him and Petrus make their way to the edge of the dam, when there they reach over and grab a hold of a piece of bamboo and turn it from side to side to loosen it to pull out of the ground and the water and lays it down on the ground next them before they reach for another piece of bamboo.

'Petrus?'

'Yes.'

'I saw a box in my room filled with empty packets of cigarettes, do you have any idea where they might have come from?'

'From the farmhands that worked here for a while, your uncle found them in town and brought them here to help with the farm.'

'Scara told me about them, what were they like?'

'Didn't do much but cause trouble.'

'Do they still work here?'

Petrus shakes his head. 'No, they left more than a year ago now.' He lays down the second piece of bamboo next to him.

'Why?'

'Your uncle didn't like having them around anymore so he took them into town and dropped them off where he found them.'

'Did they cause any trouble when he told them they had to leave?'

'They day he took them back it looked like they were in a fight.'

'The two farmhands?'

Petrus nods.

'Why?'

'The one's face was bruised and bleeding quite badly.'

'I wonder what happened?'

Petrus nods. 'What happened is probably the reason your uncle wanted them to leave.'

'Probably.' Klipp and Petrus pull the second piece of bamboo out of the water and Petrus puts it down next to the others.

241

'Have you seen Scara at all?'

Klipp shakes his head. 'No.'

'How come?'

'Wanted to come and see you before, also have not had a chance to do so yet.'

'I am flattered.'

Klipp laughs.

'When do you plan on seeing her?'

'Whenever you give me permission to do so.'

'She is going to be at the old age home until five so she should be back around eight o'clock tonight.'

'What is she doing there?'

'She works there twice a month over the weekend.'

'For the whole weekend?'

Petrus nods. 'From Friday morning to Sunday night.'

'How does she get there?'

'She takes one of your uncle's trucks and drives herself.'

'He lets her do that?'

Petrus nods. 'The lady at the home said that your aunt and uncle can have rooms there for free when they come to be the right age, if Scara worked there for her twice a month over the weekend, and also on rare occasions that the lady might need her help with something when she is not working.'

'That's nice, they must really like her over there?'

'They do, after she was there the first time the people kept asking if she will be coming back, so the lady that looks after the place asked her if she wants to work there.'

'Does she like it?'

Petrus nods. 'She says the people are very nice, they give her things sometimes and she enjoys talking to the women about what they wore when they were her age and looking at pictures of what the style of dress was like when they were growing up and her age, she says she gets quite a few ideas for what she wants to do herself making her own clothes.'

'Has she made anything yet?'

Klipp and Petrus pull out another piece of bamboo.

'She has been drawing a lot of what she wants to make, the material to make it is quite expensive.'

'Have you seen any of them?'

'A couple, most she keeps to herself, shows me only when she wants my opinion on something.'

'I can imagine they look really nice.'

'I'm not too sure what nice clothes these days look like, but the children all seem to like them.'

They pull out another piece of bamboo and Petrus lays it down next to the others. 'Do you know what time it is?'

Petrus looks at his watch. 'Almost two o'clock.'

'I should probably get back to the house then.'

Petrus nods. 'Do your aunt and uncle know you are here?'

'No.'

'Will they be angry if they find out?'

'Not sure, that's why I should probably get back.'

'Off you go then.'

'I'll bring the paintings over soon.'

'Be sure to do that.'

'Bring a couple of the pipes too?'

'See you soon.'

Klipp waves Petrus goodbye and starts back toward the house while Petrus pulls out another stick of bamboo, before he gets very far Klipp stops and turns around. 'Do you think you'll manage fine with that by yourself?'

Petrus nods. 'Thank you for asking.'

'See you soon.'

Petrus holds up his hand and Klipp starts back toward the house again.

Chapter 14

At around eight o'clock, Scara pulls up in the driveway in front of the porch, she turns off the truck and gets out without locking the driver door as per Bees' instructions as he does not like having to open the door with the set of keys every time he has to go somewhere, which is not often anymore, and makes her way up the porch steps to the door and hangs the keys on one of five small hooks stuck to the wall right next to the doorway; before yelling inside the house for Bees or Clarafina that she is back. Another thing that Bees instructed her to do when she got back so that he might be able to see her, ever since her 18th birthday, he developed somewhat of a crush on her and made many a plan to see her whenever he could without raising suspicion on how he felt about her.

He spent many a night reading through the Bible with the hope of finding passages that pertained to interracial relationships so that he might be able to find clarity on his feelings, not finding anything he decided that how he felt was wrong and spent the next couple of days berating himself for how he felt, before starting to rationalise and coming to the conclusion that if he gave food and lodging to the person he had ill feelings toward as well as her friends and family, that his feelings might come more from a place of care than and he might be excused for how he felt.

After missing seeing her when she got back the first couple of times, Bees decided to start waiting for Scara on the couch in the living room so that he can hear the truck pull up in the driveway and meet her at the door when she hangs up the set of keys. The first time Bees met her by the door, having not yet seen him up so close in all her years, as well as having born witness to many of the heinous things he did to her father and friends over the years, she was scared to have him as close to her as he wanted to be, thinking that he might have some ill begotten intentions to punish her for things he wanted to punish her father for— as he is at the age that by doing so might cause his body damage to make him incapable to work.

After greeting her for the first time at the door, she realised that his intentions were to hit on her, his first attempt to do so based on him being by far the dominant of the two of them, beginning with scolding her for not working hard enough and doing so of poor quality and how important it is for a woman to work hard and work well seeing as it is the responsibility of the male to make money to support the two. Thus, the woman must work twice as hard to make up for not having to bear the burden of the male having to do the harder of the two jobs.

The following couple of times, Bees tried manners of approach grounded more in the idea that Scara might not be the type of woman to think herself the lesser of the sexes like most other women in Golden Heart and he went about telling her how much more she had to offer in terms of working outside on the farm and asked whether she might not want to come work more inside the house along with another female worker of her choice, another couple of times he tried to persuade her to have him photograph her for a men's magazine which he knew the editor of that, wanted for the first time to put a woman of colour on the cover as well as a couple of other ideas pertaining to him getting to photograph her.

After two months of trying to win her affection, he made her out to be, with the help of many hours of unjust scrutiny, a woman that likes to play with men's emotions as a means of being the less dominant of the sexes and took a couple hundred of much needed Munto and went to a brothel in town to have sex with a prostitute that most closely resembled her.

When the keys to the truck are hanging on its hook, Scara makes her way to the cabin where she is happy to find little to no one around so that she may have a shower more quite than in the mornings before getting dressed and taking from her bed her blanket, a notebook and pen and a couple of pictures and photos that she got from the women from the old age home and walks to the kitchen and pours herself a glass of red wine, before making her way outside and around the cabin to sit under the row of orange trees to sketch new ideas for clothes. A while later, she hears a knock on the cabin wall that sends a wave of shock through her body, she sits stiffly upright.

'Didn't mean to scare you.'

She puts her hand over her heart. 'You're meaning was lost somewhere between here and there,' she says pointing to her and Klipp.

He laughs. 'Sorry about that.'

She closes the notepad. 'Not to worry.'

A couple moments of quiet pass between them. 'So, this is what standing here 12 years later feels like?' Klipp looks around the area quickly. 'Not much different from how it was.'

'That's because the last time you were here, was 12 years ago.'

Klipp laughs. 'I guess so, only now I'm a lot better at reading.'

'And I'm not reading so much anymore, so maybe not so much the same then?'

'Maybe not, you look almost exactly how you did 12 years ago.'

'I'm not sure if that's a compliment or not?'

'Compliment.'

'You do too actually, only your face is a little bit less round.'

Klipp nods. 'Compliment.'

Scara looks down at something Klipp is holding. 'What's that?'

Klipp holds the package upward. 'It's something we talked about last time we were here.'

'Is it for me?'

Klipp nods.

'Come sit down then.'

Klipp makes his way over to her and sits down on the blanket next to her and gives her the present, she takes it from him and presses on it a couple of times. 'Is this a piece of red leather you said you were going to bring me?'

Klipp nods, Scara takes the wrapping paper off around it and holds the folded piece of leather in her hands. 'There's so much of it.'

'The lady at the store said that it's enough to make three jackets with.'

'Then there's more than 'so much' of it.'

Klipp laughs.

'And it's real leather?'

'Went to a place where they only have real leather.'

Scara turns to Klipp and gives him a hug. 'Thank you, this is the best present I've ever gotten.'

'Thank you,' Klipp mumbles.

'I have so many ideas with what I want to do with this I don't even know where to begin.'

'Can't wait to see what it is.'

'Can't wait to show you.'

Klipp reaches into his pocket and holds his hand out in front of Scara. 'I got this for you too,' Klipp opens his hand.

'The ring?'

Klipp nods.

'With the engravings on it?'

'Yep.'

She takes it from him and looks it over. 'It's got the teddy bears, just the one I wanted.'

'It was between that and the sowing machines, so I thought that the sowing machines have something to do with making things and the teddy bears also have something to do with making things because you can make it with a sowing machine and it also feels nice and you can sleep with it.'

'That might be the sweetest thing anyone has done for me.'

Klipp laughs. 'Thank you.'

'Where did you get it engraved?'

'At a small jewellery store close to the gallery I worked at. The owner is an old man who used to make bullets when he was in the army, growing up his father was a welder by trade and he used to watch him work as well as help out as he got older so he was quite good at it before he had to go to the army, one day as him and his base mates were walking the grounds on which they fought the night prior; he came up with the idea to gather as many bullet shells as he can during his time there and to make jewellery out of them as some were of materials that were quite expensive and somewhat rare, he then went on to make a small fortune from doing so and now owns a couple of small jewellery stores around the country.'

'Wow, that's quite the story.'

'What's his name?'

'Mr Flurmington.'

'That's quite the name.'

Klipp laughs. 'I thought so too.'

'Did he do the engravings himself?'

'Yep, I even watched while he was doing it.'

'How long did it take him to do?'

'Maybe a half hour.'

Scara looks at the ring. 'It really is very nice.'

'He makes lots of other things too.'

'Like what?'

'Ornaments that you put on the front of your car, things that you can put on wallets and other small things to make them look better, belt buckles and lots more.'

'Does he still make bullets?'

Klipp shakes his head. 'No, he said he stopped doing that when he got out.'

'Because he didn't like making those kinds of things?'

Klipp nods. 'He said when he saw one of his friends die from a bullet wound, he made a promise to not make things of that kind anymore.'

'I see.'

They sit quietly for a while. 'Can I ask you something?'

'Sure.'

'It's something not nice so if you don't want to talk about it just say so.'

Klipp nods. 'Okay.'

'How did your parents die?'

'They fell off a mountain.'

Scara's eyes widen. 'Were you there?'

Klipp nods. 'Yes, but I was very young, don't remember much about it.'

'What do you remember?'

'A couple of times a year, I went with my parents for a picnic up in the mountains close to where we lived, we walked to the top of the mountain and sat down under a bunch of trees on a red and white squares picnic blanket and ate lots of small sandwiches, potato salad, normal salad, some cheese and crackers and some fruit while my parents drank champagne and me sparkling grape juice so I wouldn't feel left out, when we finished eating we packed everything up and walked down the mountain again back to our car, about halfway down a snake sailed past us.

'I had never seen one up until then, so I was quite excited to see one sail past us so quickly, without having to care that it might bite us. A couple of steps further the snake sailed by us again, this time a lot closer so I got a fright and fell to the ground. When I got up again, I saw my dad holding onto a root by the edge of the mountain hanging off from it. When I looked a little bit closer, I saw that my dad was holding my mom's hand who also fell off the mountain, I remember my dad yelling at me not to move because he wasn't going to let go of my mother's hand no matter what, just then the snake sailed by again, stopping in front of me and looking at me for a couple of seconds, before biting my dad on his hand and making him fall off the mountain, after that I just stood there until another family found me.'

Chapter 15

The following morning when the first rays of the morning sun make their way up the foot of Klipp's bed to the space of shade over his face, that helps rest his mind causing it to brighten and him opening his eyes, when he gets out of bed he makes his way over to the window and breathes in as many lungs of clean morning air as possible which makes the sleep almost evaporate from his eyes within instant and sends subtle jolts throughout his body that makes it feel like the outside of his veins are freezing with every breath. Stepping away from the window, he feels more awake than he has in a long time because of the cold air as well as that he will get to paint again for the first time after leaving to come back to the farm.

In the cabin, Scara is getting out of bed just as Klipp is and as she had been for the last 12 years only with butterflies in her stomach so many that it feels like she herself didn't get her out of bed, another thing different from all the other mornings is that instead of lying out on her bed just one outfit she lays out three, something which she only realises she did after all three outfits were looking at her from her bed.

Stepping out of the shower, Klipp steps carefully out on the tiles to make sure not to slip as the shower mat that used to be outside of the shower, along with many other things in the bathroom that Klipp is in as well as the others and a couple of other rooms in the house are amiss and each bathroom now has only one towel and washcloth in it, both the shower and bath mats, two additional towels and washcloths, the mirror that used to hang above the bathroom sinks and the covers for the toilet lids are not there anymore as well as many other things from around the house—this because a couple of months ago Bees told Clarafina to gather everything from the house not necessary for them to get by from day to day as menially as possible so that they can sell it at the flea market in town.

He also added that before getting their money's worth she should be sure to sell everything the first day because it is more important that they get any amount of money instead of having to stand behind a stall, week after week trying to sell it for as much money as they are able to spend time there to get, late in the afternoon, the first Sunday that Clarafina spent at the flea market she brought back to the house 400 Munto.

The day after Klipp came back to the farm, Bees wanted to confront him about the empty state of the house thinking it to be uncharacteristic and even somewhat disrespectful of him not to have noticed it having lived in the house before it looked as it did now, before he was able to do so Clarafina came to him to complain, for however many a time again, about the house and how uncomfortable it is for her to live in it with so many things amiss and that they should spend less on drink and tobacco to save money to buy back with the things they sold a while ago—finding himself confronted with an argument much more sound than that which he was going to confront Klipp with Bees used Klipp's lack of mention of the derelict state of the house to get Clarafina to stop pestering him, telling her that if Klipp did not mention anything about it she should not have anything to complain about.

Walking out of the bathroom to his bedroom, Klipp hears almost floor trembling snores coming from both Bees and Clarafina's rooms, Clarafina's louder and more intense than Bees' almost, finding himself almost falling over halfway to his bedroom as their snores once 'sounded' almost perfectly in sync, after getting dressed he takes a clean canvas and a suitcase with his three favourite brushes and an array of paints out from under his bed.

Although he does have more brushes mostly he only ever paints with just the three, as well as only brushes of the same sizes that the three that he keeps in the suitcase, for reason that they are the same as the first three brushes out of the five brushes he bought for himself his first day after his first art class at primary school and because painting with just those three brush sizes, which vary in size quite a lot, gave the paintings that Klipp did a somewhat unique look and distinct style.

When he has everything that he needs to paint with he walks to the door, stopping there to listen for Bees and Clarafina's snoring hoping to hear it as it would mean that he can make his way outside without any bother, before walking down the stairs and out the front door, which is open throughout all hours of the day on most days besides the netted door cover left closed to cover the doorway, which gives him a feeling of security rather than the opposite having lived with his uncle for some time as a child.

As Klipp sets foot on the lawn, Scara is busy trying on her second outfit, a white sweater dress that comes down to just above her knees with short sleeves held together by six black buttons the size of the circumference of a milk cap stitched to one side of the garment the length thereof from the bottom of the chest area to the bottom seam of the dress, with a pair of black faux leather tennis shoes which together makes her most comfortable outfit other than her nightgown in her cupboard—in which there is a considerable amount of clothes, considering that she has barely enough money in her piggy bank, which is in the shape of a baby sheep, to buy three used books with from the used bookstore in town.

The reason that she has so much clothes is because three years or so ago, she came across a box tucked away in the garage filled with many different kinds and pieces of material and asked Clarafina if she gave her a third of what she had saved up over the years, who was in desperate need of money to buy herself a case of red wine which she wanted so that she might be able to write a song on the piano during the time she wanted to get a job playing at a restaurant in town.

She was able to use almost all of the material that was in the box a made maybe a dozen pieces of clothing with thread from a sowing box that was left to her by her mother and a sowing machine that was Clarafina's when she was younger that too was standing in the garage.

Just as Scara is about to make her way outside to go and wait for Klipp by the table, she hears him knocking, being able to tell it is him by the amount of the knocks on the door, knowing by now that when Clarafina knocks, she does so three times in a row three times over and Bees a considerable number of times in quick succession with various degrees of intensity, in no way gentle.

Scara opens the door. 'Good morning, you look pretty.'

'Thank you, you look quite nice too.'

'Thank you, are you ready to go?'

Scara nods. 'For a little bit now.' She steps out of the cabin and closes the door carefully behind her, Klipp holds out his arm for her to take before they start across the lawn to the driveway gate. 'I like your dress.'

'Thank you, and it's not so much a dress than a sweater dress, with short sleeves.'

Klipp laughs. 'It's very nice.'

'I made it myself.'

'I would have guessed.'

'Thank you.'

'I like the buttons on the side.'

'I do too.'

'Are they there just to look nice or do they keep the dress together?'

'If you had to guess, would you say just to look nice, to hold it together or both.'

'Good answer, can I ask you something else?'

'Sure.'

'Would you say that the buttons are off to the side for practical reasons or for reasons purely aesthetic?'

'Is there not a third choice?'

Scara shakes her head.

'The second one then.'

'Another good answer.'

They walk quietly for a while. 'Do you need any help with that.' She asks looking at the art supplies.

'No thanks, it's not that heavy.'

'What do you have there?'

'Canvas of course and some paints and brushes.'

'How heavy is the suitcase?'

'Not that heavy, why?'

'Trying to figure out how much paints you have in there?'

Klipp laughs. 'Oh, not that much, maybe two dozen.'

'All different colours?'

'Most.'

'How many different colours of pink would you say you have in there?'

'One, why?'

'Because that's my favourite colour.'

'I'm glad I know that I also have a couple of tubes of white in here so I can make different shades of different colours.'

Once out of the driveway gate Scara begins to hum a melody. Klipp listens for a while. 'That's nice,' he says.

'Thank you.'

'Where's it from?'

'Marana used to sing it to me when I was little while I was lying in bed to help me fall asleep after my mom died, for a while it was the only thing that made it, so that I could.'

'That must not have been very nice.'

'What?'

'Not being able to sleep.'

'Oh, it wasn't very nice, luckily Marana was there to help me through it.'

'Remind me to thank her.'

Scara laughs. 'I'll do that.'

'What song is it?'

'It's a song she made up.'

'Was it just a song that you whistled?'

'No, it had words and everything, a couple of them she even used when me and Finta and the boys were younger to sing various little melodies over what she sang to make it seem like there was a band playing behind her. She made up lots of songs like that while I was growing up, she kept them all in her head, never wrote down one, the one she used to whistle to me she said that my mom wrote for me through her after she died so that I could fall asleep.'

'That's one of the nicest things I've ever heard.'

Scara nods. 'I made up a story from it that I'm going to tell my kids one day whenever I put them to bed.'

'Maybe *that's* the nicest thing I've ever heard.'

'How many songs of Marana's did you hear?'

'I'm not sure, it was too long ago to remember, she did have a lot though.'

Klipp nods.

'Funny thing is, she had listened to very few songs throughout her life, and ever since she came here, she didn't have anything to listen to, whenever someone told her how good her songs were she always attributed it to not having heard many, I was about eight years old when I first realised there was no record player in the cabin.'

Klipp laughs. 'Of course, you didn't, you work on a Brungle farm, it's surprising you even have a roof over your head.'

Out of the blue comes flying a crow, it's screech so loud that it seems to tear apart the sky and sits down on wire stretched along miles of wooden poles sticking out of the ground that forms the fencing that separates the roads from the farmland throughout Golden Heart.

Scara puts her hand over her heart, 'That was scary.'

'I'm not even sure if I'm holding my art supplies anymore.'

Scara laughs. 'They're still there.'

'Good.'

When they reach the dam area Klipp puts down his art supplies. 'When do you want to start?' Scara asks.

'Whenever you want to?'

'Maybe we can cool off with our feet in the water for a while first?'

'Sounds nice.'

They make their way over to the edge of the dam, take off their shoes and socks and sit down with their legs hanging over the edge of the dam and their feet in the water. Scara kicks her legs lightly up and down, making waves that unlike those which them putting their feet inside did travel right to the very opposite edge of the dam.

Scara breathes in relief. 'That feels nice…' She says as she steadies her feet. 'Haven't had a day this hot for a while.'

'It is very hot, might not be able to paint in this weather.'

Scara laughs. 'What was the weather like where you were?'

'Colder the further away I went from the farm.'

'Having to wear gloves cold?'

Klipp laughs. 'Not that cold no, jacket over sweater cold maybe, the weather where I was the last couple of months before coming back here was very nice.'

'What was that like?'

'Maybe like how are feet are feeling now.'

Scara laughs. 'That sounds nice.'

'It was right by the beach which helped.'

'What was that like?'

'Like being on vacation all the time.'

'I can imagine.'

Klipp looks at Scara. 'Have you ever been to a beach?'

'No.'

'Should have known…' Klipp looks down at the water. 'It's not really that great, sand gets all over you most of the time.'

Scara laughs. 'Really.'

'A little bit.'

Scara takes her feet out of the water and rests them on the edge of the dam. 'Did you have to go there for your studies?'

'The beach town?'

Scara nods.

'I went to go stay there with a friend of mine to work for him and help him out with his restaurant.'

'Who is he?'

'His name is Milno, he judged the surfing competitions I entered sometimes when I was in primary school.'

'Is he older than you?'

'A little bit.'

'What was he like?'

'Like me a little bit, only older, if you saw him, you'd probably think he was in some kind of rock and roll music group.'

'Why?'

'His hair is very long and he has these things called inkies over his one arm which some of the guys in those groups have sometimes.'

'What's inkies?'

'It's this thing were someone draws a picture on your body with some kind of small machine that squirts ink into your skin that you can't get off, unless you have it taken off from your skin by a doctor with another special kind of machine.'

Scara frowns. 'What kind of pictures do they draw?'

'Anything you want, it's like a pen only it stays on your body forever, or until you have it removed.'

'So, it's like if I draw a teddy bear on my hand with a pen only you can't wash it off?'

Klipp nods.

'Why would people want that?'

'I don't know, it looks nice sometimes, also if you like someone you can get their name on your arm somewhere with a heart or any other picture that reminds you of them. So it's maybe like a reminder that you have of them with you all the time, like the ring you gave me almost.'

'I've never heard or seen any of those things.'

Klipp laughs. 'Not many people know of it over here.'

'Do you have one of those things?'

'No, I wanted to get one but it was quite expensive and I didn't want to get it in case my uncle might see it.'

Scara nods. 'He probably would not have liked that very much, what did you want to get?'

'A paintbrush.'

Scara pauses. 'Oh, I see, you do little things like that with it, I would get a sowing machine on my hand then.'

Klipp laughs. 'Exactly.'

'That's nice, where on your hand did you want to get it?'

'Between my thumb and my forefinger.'

Scara looks down at Klipp's hand. 'I think that would have looked very nice.'

'Me too.'

'When do you want to start painting?'

'We can start now if you want?'

'Okay.'

They get up.

'Where would you like to sit?'

Scara turns around. 'On one of those tree stumps maybe?'

'Sure.'

They make their way over to where Klipp's art supplies are and Scara sits down on one of the tree stumps nearby. When she is sitting comfortably, Klipp leans the canvas against a tall rock sticking out of the ground and puts the suitcase filled with paint next to it, opens the suitcase and begins to fill his paint tray with swirls of different colours of paint.

'How long do you think I will have to sit still for?'

'Until I finish doing the outlines, shouldn't be more than five minutes.'

'I thought it would be much longer?'

'It doesn't take long to do the outlines, after that you can move around as you want,' Klipp says and picks up a piece of sharpened charcoal and begins to draw the outlines of the painting.

'How long do you think it's going to take to do the whole thing?'

'I don't know, maybe two hours'

'Oh, can I watch while you paint.'

'That would spoil the surprise.'

'But I already know what you're going to paint?'

'I'm not going to paint what you think I am.'

'What am I going to do for two hours?'

'Okay you can watch.'

'Great, how far are you with the outlines?'

Klipp looks closer at the canvas. 'Maybe a quarter of the way?'

'Let me know when you're finished?'

'Okay.' Klipp keeps at the outlines.

'Do you usually paint people like this?'

'What do you mean?'

'Are most of your paintings of people, or things like animals or candles or bowls of fruit?'

'Oh, no, mostly it's just stuff I think looks nice, like the monsters I used to draw but a little more grown up.'

'What's your favourite thing you've painted?'

'When I worked at the gallery, I painted a picture for a guy whose dad was a banker in a suit and tie as a zombie.'

'Do you have a picture of it?'

Klipp shakes his head. 'No.'

'Was it a nice zombie?'

'He was smiling a little bit.'

Scara laughs. 'That's nice.'

'It's the biggest painting I've done so far, if I had to paint the guy's whole body it would be bigger and longer than he is even.'

'Did he pay you for it?'

'Yes, quite a lot of money.'

'What did you do with the money?'

'Bought more paints and canvases.'

Scara laughs. 'I should have known.'

Klipp steps back and looks at the painting. 'I think I'm finished.'

'Can I come look?'

'Sure.'

Scara gets up and makes her way over to Klipp. 'Wow, that's very good.'

'Thank you.'

'It looks almost like I'm friends with a real professional painter.'

Klipp laughs. 'That's nice of you to say.'

'I'm going to sit down here while you paint.'

'Great.'

Scara sits down on a flat rock close by and crosses her legs in front of her, fifteen or so minutes later she puts her feet back down on the ground. 'I think I'm going to go sit on the tree stump again, this rock is giving me a tummy ache.'

'I can go get one of the crates for you if you want?'

Scara gets up. 'That's okay, I like the tree stump better, it's a little softer.'

'Okay.'

She makes her way back over to the tree stump and sits down with her feet up. 'I think I'm going to try and take a nap.'

'Do you think you'll be able to do that?'

'You'll be surprised how soft my knees are.'

Klipp laughs. 'Hopefully I can find out one day.'

'Depends on how much I like the painting.'

Sometime later, Klipp looks at Scara out from the side of the canvas and sees her sitting with her legs pressed against her chest and her arms wrapped around them with the side of her face resting on her knees and her eyes closed and thinks to stop what he is painting and to just paint her as she is there. After sitting to ponder for a while, he hears something in front of him and when he looks up, he sees her with her feet on the ground, shaking her head. 'Couldn't do it.'

Klipp laughs.

She then brings her thighs together and places the palms of her hands on her knees and lays her head on top of her hands.

A half hour later, as Klipp is just about finished with the painting, a leaf that hung from one of the trees by the dam lands on and drapes itself over the top of the canvas, Klipp picks the leaf up off the top of the canvas and as he looks closer at the petals he forgets that he is busy painting, trying to make out whether the colour of the petal is either light pink or white as he looks at it from different angles, or while doing so an entirely new colour altogether.

So intrigued by this perception of colour he is that he thinks to take a couple of the petals to strain with the help of a sieve whatever liquid he can from them to mix with a clear paint-like substance to see if he might be able to replicate whatever colour he thinks he is looking at.

'Is this your first time seeing one of those up close?'

Klipp gets a fright.

Scara giggles. 'Sorry, didn't mean to scare you.'

259

'That's okay…' Klipp puts his hand over his heart. 'My heart is still beating.'

Scara laughs. 'Couldn't be happier.'

Klipp looks back down at the petal. 'It is.'

'Pretty, isn't it?'

'Very.'

'Have you marked the colour conundrum yet?'

Klipp nods. 'I did, it's quite amazing.'

'Never is not that way no matter how many times I look at it.'

'I can imagine, do you know what they're called?'

'Not sure what the scientific name is but Marana used to refer to them as fairy capes, she said that whenever fairies get permission to pass on, they fly around one of these trees until a petal or 'cape' attaches to the back of their neck so that it may start to drain the life from them as they slowly begin to float to the ground while they become before they reach it the dust from whence they came.

'She also said that if someone comes across or finds a whole of a leaf of which the petals are still healthy and able to be perceived as it's different colours, it is supposed to bring luck to whoever found it for however long the petals retain their healthy qualities.'

'Looking at it makes me believe everything you just said.'

Scara nods.

'Just one question, what do you mean when you say the fairies get permission to die?'

'As the story goes it is the duty of fairies to spread happiness, a task which weighs very heavy on their spirit and can drain it until it is no more, when whatever happiness they spread is taken full advantage of by whoever might receive it makes them happy in return and so replenishes their spirit and under certain circumstances they are able to live forever. We tend to take things like good deeds, luck and happiness for granted because we do not appreciate as we should, so fruitful is God with His generosity and love that we do not see it for what it is or should be anymore.

'Take the story of the leaf for example, if someone tells you how it can bring luck it would be silly, maybe even unappreciative, in your case of you to not paint or do whatever you might want said luck to affect as much as you can during the time it is said to do so if you are enamoured in any way however much you may be with what brought the notion, even if there might be no truth to the notion and no good tidings or luck might be gained from it; you will still end up with more paintings or answers to questions you might have had were you to not have come across the leaf, which in turn might be luck in itself.'

'Do they just fly around and spread happiness until they die?' Klipp asks completely unaware that he is doing so. 'That doesn't seem very nice.'

Scara nods. 'Yes, but their loss is also their gain, they know things that are far from our understanding and if they see but an ounce of the appreciation that it itself may expect among all the muck that surrounds it makes them very happy, if even one of them succeed in their purpose they all benefit from it, and when they are almost without spirit they come to fly around these trees while they wait for a petal or 'cape' to attach itself to them after which they drift away in every sense of the word.'

'How do they know when to come to the tress?'

'I think they just realise they are there when they are.'

Klipp sits quietly staring at the petal for a while. 'That's a very nice story.'

'Marana also said that it is luck in itself if you come to hear the story at all.' Scara pokes her head over the edge of the painting, she laughs. 'I see what you're doing.'

'It's not finished yet.'

'I guess I'm going to try and find another comfortable position to sit in.'

Half an hour later, Klipp looks over at Scara sitting upright on the tree stump with one of her legs hanging over the edge and the other tucked under her chest with her palms resting on top of her knee of her leg that isn't hanging over the edge of the tree stump, her arms outstretched and her chin resting on her shoulder and her eyes closed, Klipp picks up a stone and throws it into the water hoping to wake her up. As the stones reaches the bottom of the dam halfway, Scara opens her eyes and looks around her.

'Hey!'

'Hello, how long have I been sleeping?'

Klipp looks at his watch. 'Half hour.'

'Are you finished?'

Klipp nods. 'Yep.'

'Can I see?'

'I'll bring it over.' Klipp picks up the painting and walks it over to her, he holds it out in front of her, she laughs. 'Now I see what you mean by you weren't finished yet.'

Klipp nods. 'What do you think?'

'I think it's the nicest thing I'll ever get.'

The painting was of a poster of a Catin Gates film that was against the wall siding the girl's section of the side of the cabin where Scara and the rest of the children that grew up on the farm, along with other younger kids that were born while Klipp was away, slept and was of him and his leading lady's faces over a backdrop of a forest but instead of the leading lady's face next to his Klipp painted Scara's.

After gathering his art supplies, him and Scara start back toward the house. 'Where are you going?' Klipp asks.

'This way.'

Klipp frowns, 'Why?'

'You'll see.'

Klipp makes his way over to the edge of the clearing, when he looks down, he sees a ladder propped up against it, he looks at Scara. 'Did you know this was here the whole time?'

Scara nods.

'Why did we come here the other way then?'

'The walk seemed like a nice thing.'

Klipp laughs. 'I'm flattered.' He puts down his art supplies, climbing onto the ladder, he remembers how little he enjoyed the walk over the rocky terrain to the dam whenever he felt like spending time there, especially when he thinks back to all the times he heard Bees complain about how much of an inconvenience it is to get there and how much it pained him to wake up every day knowing that with all the good things the dam had to offer be it the shade, the water, the calming sounds of the chirping masses of birds that flock to the trees as well as the general atmosphere of the area.

The thought of having to walk there all the way from the gate on the other side of the farm, especially by means of the terrain that lends to making use of the area, plagued him so that it being there became more of an imposition than a source of relief, so agitated by it he was that he planned on taking palm sized stones from the ground itself and lying them out on top and in front of each other to make a path from the gate to the dam—so that he may more easily and comfortably walk there but never finished doing so when he realised how long it would take, he also never got around to asking the workers to do it for him for reasons unbeknownst.

Another way he thought to deal with the problem was to dig a smaller dam behind the house, after digging one much smaller than he first intended, he covered the bottom with a piece of plastic and began to fill it with water but stopped halfway through when he realised that having it does not have the same calming effect as the other one.

Once on level ground again, Klipp reaches up to get his art supplies from Scara and holds the ladder steady as she makes her way down it too, when she is standing next to him, he picks up his art supplies and they start toward the cabin.

'I love how soft the ground is up there,' says Scara.

'Probably has something to do with the fairies? I hear it rains cocoa around their parts.'

Scara laughs. 'That would be nice.'

'We'll never know until we find out,' Klipp says with a sly smile on his face.

'I guess we'll never know then.'

'It might be a nice detail to add to the story?'

'I think the fairies might get angry if we add potential falsities to their story.'

'I guess we *will* never know then.'

Chapter 16

On the morning of the second Thursday that Klipp has been back on the farm, Bees got out of bed with a heavy heart and sore stomach as he had to forgo his night of drinking the previous night so that he may be better off come the following morning. He took a shower, brushed his teeth, got dressed and went to the workers cabin to tell them that a very important guest will be arriving at noon the next day and that they should all be dressed in their work clothes and meet him, Clarafina and Klipp by the driveway at noon sharp to meet his guest when he arrives as well as to be of any assistance might there be need for it.

Back in the house he walks up the stairs to wake up Klipp and Clarafina, stepping inside of Klipp's room he finds him painting and tells him to make sure that all of his art supplies as well as everything that might pertain to painting is packed away before he goes to bed so that it cannot be seen by anyone who might come into his room as there will be a guest joining them the next day; who finds things of the artistic nature very unappealing and considers it the utmost waste of time.

The following morning as the sun began to light up the dark corners of the house, Bees gets out of bed feeling better than he has in a long row of mornings in a long time but too excited for the day of drinking that hopefully lies ahead of him to take notice thereof, after spending more time in the bathroom than he has ever before he gets dressed and goes to wake up Clarafina and Klipp and tells them to do the same right up to the detail of time spent in the bathroom before going downstairs to make himself a cup of coffee.

When Klipp and Clarafina greets him, he is already on his third cup of coffee to make up for the alcohol that should have been coursing through his veins at that point to help him get through the first portion of the day until he starts drinking again. After sitting down with Bees at the table, he tells them that the man that will be coming to visit them later should only be referred to as 'Leader' and that he does not like people knowing how old he is and that they may under no circumstances ask him about his age or talk about anything closely age related with him for any reason. After telling them more about 'Leader' he thinks they should know to make his stay with them as comfortable as possible. They rinse their cups, Clarafina's, Bees' three cups, and clean the kitchen and the rest of the house to the point of Bees feeling almost uncomfortable about having not seen the house as it was after in many a year. They make their way outside to the porch where the workers are waiting for them to welcome their guest, Bees walks down the steps onto the driveway from the porch.

'Thank you for meeting us here, everything today should go no less than almost perfect, I say *almost* perfect because I do not believe in perfect, the man that will be arriving shortly is however many years older than me but that does not mean that you should fear him less, in fact you should fear him more, why that is I cannot say for fear of having none of you standing here where he arrives. He also, more than me even, has a very strong dislike for the likes of you, so much so that he does not deem you even worthy of the simple worth to do hard labour for him and chooses to go as far as to demean his fellow brethren by having them do the work that most believe you should. He believes that you should all be dead and finds it very hard to understand why there is any of you around anywhere.'

Bees takes his pipe out of his shirt pocket. 'Not to worry, him and my grandfather were very close when he was younger so there should be an appropriate amount of respect between the two of us meaning that you will probably be treated no less than what you usually are around here.' Bees takes some tobacco out of the bag and stuffs the pipe butt with it. 'Also know that any one of you might be needed during any time of the day and night for something so do not leave the lawn at any time, is that understood?'

The workers nod.

'Good...' Bees puts the bag of tobacco back in his shirt pocket. 'Another thing you must know, and that I have already told to Ms Clarafina and my nephew here, is that under no circumstances must you address the man as anything other than 'Leader'. If you are so lucky as to be able to do that, if you fail to abide by this rule what will happen to you is entirely out of my control, something which I am very happy about because from what I hear he does to the likes of you I might not be able to stomach.' Bees takes a box of matches from his pants pocket. 'Also, and most importantly, know that if 'Leader' enjoys his stay with us, it can only mean good things for the farm and you too.'

Two tobacco filled pipe butts later, two trucks, both quite a bit bigger than Bees,' white, with the letters, in thick black plain font, 'WMP' over both doors on either side of the trucks as well as on the roofs, pull up in the driveway with as little dust behind them as Bees has ever seen any vehicle make when doing so.

In the first of the two in the front two seats are sitting two white men, a decade or so older than Klipp maybe, while the back is filled with suitcases and a box filled with firearms and boxes of bullets and another with a couple of bottles of brandy and a couple of glasses, the second of the two has again two white men of seemingly the same age as the others with 'Leader' and a young woman, about the same age as the men driving the trucks, sitting next to him.

When both trucks are quiet and standing still, the men in the first truck, wearing light brown button shirts of cotton with short sleeves, short pants of the same material and colour and black leather shoes, get out and walk back to the second and open the doors for the other two, wearing the same, which open the doors for 'Leader' and the young woman before the four men together begin to unpack the luggage from the trucks as 'Leader' and the young woman make their way hand in hand, to Bees, Clarafina and Klipp.

When 'Leader' is standing in front of Bees, he takes his head in his hands, turns his face up and down and from side to side to get a better look at the man he last saw as a young boy when he visited the farm. 'Leader' let's go of Bees' face. 'How very good to see you again my boy, it has been quite the time since we last met.'

Bees nods. 'Very much, almost 40 years if I have it right.'

'Quite the time indeed then.' 'Leader' looks down at Bees. 'I see that you have picked up a considerable amount of weight and wrinkles since we last saw each other?'

Bees' grin fades.

'Leader' puts his hand on Bees' shoulder. 'Not to worry my boy, you wear it well, just like I do.'

Bees nods. 'Thank you.'

'Maybe not exactly as well as I do but I do have a couple of years on you.'

Bees grins. 'I would say that you wear it better also sir.'

'Leader' looks at Bees suspiciously. 'You better not be fibbing my boy; it takes a special kind of man to wear it like I do.'

'Not at all, you look as I think all men should.'

'Leader' nods. 'Very good then, you might be exactly the type of man for what I am after for what I am here to discuss.'

'Thank you.'

'Or maybe the complete opposite.'

'Then believe me to be exactly what you are looking for, I am not this heavy because I cannot control my eating, I am this heavy because I choose to be so that I may learn to walk around this heavy comfortably.'

'How is that coming along my boy?'

'Not as good as you I can think, but quite good.'

'Happy to hear it my boy.' 'Leader' turns to Clarafina, 'And who might this dapper dame be?'

Clarafina smiles, 'Clarafina, sir.'

'Leader' takes her hand in his and kisses it. 'I know that, I simply wanted to pay you the compliment that you deserve.'

Clarafina smiles, more enthralled with 'Leader' even than she was with Mr Frappounne. 'Thank you, sir, that is very nice of you.'

'Quite the contrary, my dear, it would only be nice if it was not one of the easiest and most comfortable compliments I have ever come to pay a lady such as yourself, which it was, so it is in no need of a thank you, but thank you still.'

'Leader' turns to Klipp. 'And who might this be?'

'Klipp, our nephew.'

'Leader' nods. 'Very nice to meet you.'

Klipp holds out his hand. 'Likewise, sir.' They shake hands.

'Leader' puts his hands on Layli's, the young woman next to him, shoulders. 'This is Layli, she is my partner, or girlfriend as the young people say today.'

Layli smiles and waves Klipp, Clarafina and Bees hello.

Klipp holds out his hand. 'Nice to meet you.' They shake hands.

'You too,' says Layli.

'Pleasure to meet you, welcome to our farm.'

'Pleasure to meet you too, thank you for having us.'

'The pleasure is all ours but thank you anyway.'

Bees holds out his hand. 'Nice to meet you.'

Layli shakes Bees' hand. 'You too.'

'Quite the vision, isn't she?' 'Leader' says.

Bees nods.

'Beautiful.'

'Best part is she is not even 30 years old...' says 'Leader'. 'Which means that she might well could have been a daughter of mine, if that isn't winning, I don't know what is.'

Bees nods. 'Couldn't agree more.'

'Couldn't agree more with you agreeing more.' 'Leader' says with a sly smile, he turns around. 'Behind me, are four men that work for me, their names are too many to mention now; so, if we might come to need their help throughout the weekend just call for them, one or two will come running, as they always do whenever they come with me whenever I go somewhere.'

'Must be nice,' says Bees.

'It has its ups and downs.'

'I know what you mean.'

'You do?'

'Had two men of my own a while back for a while.'

'Do you not have them anymore?'

Bees shakes his head. 'Had to let them go.'

'How so?'

'They had trouble getting along.'

'I cannot say that I know what you mean.'

Bees nods.

'And happy to be able to say so.'

'Me too.'

'Before we go any further, I must ask that someone show my men to where me and my lovely young lady here will be sleeping so that they can bring our bags to wherever that may be?'

'Klipp will show them,' says Bees.

'Leader' nods. 'Am I correct in saying they will not be sleeping in the house with us?'

'There is a spare room upstairs but two will have to sleep on the floor because there is only one bed.'

'Leader' frowns. 'Why will only two have to sleep on the floor if there is one bed?'

'Because at the most only two people can sleep in the one bed.'

'My boy, there should never be space for another man in one bed if it already has someone in it.'

Bees nods. Somewhat unsettled that he might have given 'Leader' the wrong impression of himself.

'That cannot do Mr Brungle, I need my men to be well and rested come tomorrow morning.'

'There is another room at the back of the house…' Bees says pointing behind him. 'It has two beds and a couch, and a small kitchen and bathroom.'

'Leader' nods. 'Very good, they can take turns sleeping in the beds.' 'Leader' snaps his fingers and the four men pick up the luggage. 'Leave the box of brandy on the porch please.'

Bees turns to Klipp. 'Nephew, can you show the men to their leader and his lady's room please.'

'Sure.' Klipp and the men walk up the porch steps into the house and up the main staircase to the room in which 'Leader' and Layli will be sleeping.

'Very good, before we get to business can I ask that you ladies be kind enough to prepare us something to eat? A late lunch or earlier dinner perhaps, I for one cannot do business on a stomach that is empty.'

Clarafina frowns. 'Don't you want to speak to me and my brother about something?' Clarafina asks quite upset with the timing and tone in which 'Leader' asked of them what he did.

'No my lady, what I want to discuss I only want to do so with your brother, there is no place for you and my young lovely here when it comes to those matters, and very fortunately for you, so as those matters are quite uneventful and can sometimes be even tiresome, more suited for the male mind, I can assure you though that the duties you will find waiting for you in the kitchen will bring you plenty more joy than what we have to discuss.'

Klipp comes back outside with 'Leader's' men. 'Bags are in the room uncle Bees, anything else?'

Bees turns around. 'Show the men to where they will be sleeping, then you are free to do as you please.'

'Okay.'

'Also tell the workers that they are free to do so as well but to stay close by in case they are needed for something.'

Klipp nods. 'Not a problem.'

The men follow Klipp around the back of the house to their room.

'Leader' turns to Clarafina and Layli. 'How about that then?'

Layli holds her hand out to Clarafina; she takes it. 'Don't mind if we do.' They make their way over the driveway and up the porch steps and into the house.

'Leader' looks over at the table on the porch. 'Our place of business awaits us.'

Bees nods. 'After you.'

'Thank you.' They make their way onto the porch. 'Will you be so kind as to bring the box of brandy with?'

Bees nods. 'Will do.' He bends over and picks up the box and brings it over to the table and puts it down, 'Leader' takes a seat, Bees sits down next to him.

'What is all in here?'

'Take a look for yourself.'

Bees opens the box and takes a look inside.

'The finest brandy in all of this side of the world.'

'Can I look at it?'

'Go ahead.'

Bees takes a bottle out of the box and looks it over. 'What is better, the finest brandy in this side of the world or the one on the other side of the world?'

'Are you trying to be funny Mr Brungle?'

'No, I will really like to know.'

'Leader' nods. 'And it's 'would' really like to know.'

'Sorry.'

'Very well then, to answer your question, of that I am not sure, although this brandy might just be the finest from the other side too.'

'Then I can't wait to try it.' Bees puts the bottle down on the table. 'What must I do with the box?'

'You can put it down on the floor thank you, but take a glass each for us before you do.'

Bees nods and reaches into the box and takes two glasses out from it. 'Are all the bottles in here brandy?'

'Most definitely, brandy is the only liquor I allow to touch my palette.'

'Are they different kinds of brandy?'

'Leader' shakes his head. 'No, when the brandy is as good as this brandy is here then there is and more importantly, should be no need for any other.'

'Then I'm going inside to get us some glasses.'

'No need, I brought my own.'

'Oh, any specific reason?'

'Because I always do, I don't trust another man's glasses to be as clean as mine, to get the most from the brandy you choose to drink the glasses from which you drink, it must be as clean as possible.'

Bees nods. 'I will have to think about that myself.'

'Be sure to.'

Bees takes two glasses out of the box and puts one down in front of 'Leader' and the other in front of himself, before putting the box with the remainder of the bottles of brandy and glasses on the floor beside the table.

'Do you want me to pour a glass for you?'

'Leader' nods. 'Please, and without touching my glass if you can?'

Bees takes the cork out of the bottle, holds the neck end thereof over 'Leader's' glass and by tilting the bottle over begins to pour brandy into the glass.

'Just quarter of the way full please?'

Bees tilts the bottle back upward. 'Is that enough?'

'It will do fine.'

Bees begins to pour himself a glass. 'These glasses look very nice, where did you get them?'

'You buy them from wine and brandy stores, they're made specially to drink brandy from.'

'How is it special to drink brandy from?'

'The glass is curved as it is there to preserve the taste of the brandy, to ensure that whatever fumes may emanate from it once out of the bottle stays close to the surface of the liquid, so that it may float above and back into it to preserve said taste.'

Bees pours his glass of brandy full almost to the top. 'I've been drinking brandy for a very long time and I've never heard anyone say what you just said about it.'

'Leader' looks at Bees' glass somewhat disappointed. 'Filling the glass with that much brandy also disrupts the taste.'

Bees puts the bottle back down on the table. 'Should I pour some back.'

'No, what's in your glass now is much different from what is in the bottle, the brandy in the bottle would be spoiled if you pour yours back into it, the flavour molecules of the brandy in your glass are disrupted from pouring as much as you did as quickly as you did, if you pour it back in the bottle it will cause the same to happen to brandy inside.'

Bees nods. 'I'll drink really slowly so I don't waste it.'

'Not to worry, there is a lesson to be learned from every mistake made.'

'Thank you.' Bees holds his glass out to 'Leader'. 'To the future, may it be white.'

'Leader' laughs. 'Couldn't have said it better.' He takes a sip of brandy, tilts back his head and gurgles the brandy against the top part of his throat for a moment, before pressing his lips together and sucking in air in a long continuous motion before swallowing the brandy, Bees follows and takes a sip of brandy too and swallows before bursting out in fits of cough.

'Are you okay my boy?'

Bees nods, trying his best to hold back the burst of 'sharp' air trying to make its way up from his lungs.

'Not many cope well with a brandy so rich.'

Bees bangs his chest with the soft part of his fist to try and force out the remaining burning air out of his lungs. 'That caught me a little off guard.'

'What did?'

'The brandy.'

'How so?'

'It's very strong.'

'Leader' nods. 'That it is, for the hardened connoisseur only.'

Bees' coughing subsides.

'Better?'

Bees nods. 'Much, do you think I can maybe have a glass of water to help ease the burning a little?'

'That is up to you, but I must say that it will do the activity of drinking a brandy like this quite the dishonour.'

Bees nods. 'No water then.' He puts his hand in front of his mouth and as another fit of coughs push their way out of his lungs.

'Leader' takes another sip of brandy, tilts his head back again and washes it over his throat and sucks air in through pressed lips like he did the time before, and swallows.

Bees looks at him somewhat perturbed. 'Do you always drink brandy like that?'

'Like what?'

'Like you did just now? How you play with it before you drink it?'

'Leader' nods. 'The only way to do it.'

'I've never seen anyone else do it that way and I've seen lots of people that drink brandy?'

'You haven't seen any of them drink it the right way.'

'Do you drink it like that all the time?'

'Leader' nods. 'Every sip, there is no point in doing anything if you don't do it right.'

Bees nods. 'I think the same...' He wraps his fingers around his glass. 'Are you very sure that is how you have to drink it? Why do they drink it like that?'

'One very simple reason...' 'Leader' swills the brandy around in his glass. 'To enrich the taste, only true connoisseurs know to drink brandy this way and that is why it seems unusual to you.'

Bees nods. 'Now I know, thank you for telling me.'

'The first step in becoming a true connoisseur... Knowing about it.'

Bees nods. 'Thank you.'

'Leader' takes another drink of brandy, this time simply swallowing after doing so, Bees does the same and looks over the brandy in his glass.

'Are you sure doing that thing with your throat is a real thing?'

'Are you sure you want me to answer that question?'

Bees shakes his head. 'It's okay, it doesn't matter.'

'Leader' puts his glass of brandy down on the table. 'Of course, it matters, it is one of the great determinants of status in the world and for that reason it matters, take the two of us for example, which one of us is the most successful?'

'You.'

'Leader' nods. 'Of course, and which one of us drinks brandy in the manner we are talking about?'

'You,' he says nodding.

'Leader' leans somewhat more back into his chair with his glass of brandy by his chest. 'There you have it, must be a real thing then.'

Bees nods.

'Leader' takes another sip of brandy and tilts his head back to drink the brandy in the manner that almost two decades ago the man he worked for and aspired to be like told him to as that is how the upper class of society drink theirs, in order to enrich the taste thereof, in an effort to see if he might be gullible enough to make a habit out of it, after finishing what was in the glass of brandy

'Leader' picks up the bottle, takes the cork out from it and pours himself another glass.

'Why does the bottle have a cork and not a lid like the others?' Bees asks. 'Does that have something to do with the taste too?'

'It does not, but we say it does.'

Bees frowns. 'What?'

'Leader' nods. 'We tell people that it does, they will believe almost anything you tell them about a product if it is expensive enough, so we say that this brandy here comes with a cork instead of any other type of lid or cover, to allow the brandy room to breathe to retain as much of its original flavour as possible.' He puts the cork back in the bottle and puts it in the centre of the table. 'We also add 65 Munto to the price because of it.'

'Is this your brandy?'

'If by 'my brandy' you mean that me and a couple of other gentlemen from the WMP invested lots of money in making our own brand of brandy and are as we speak making a lot of money from it and will, in the near future make much more of it then yes, this is my brandy.'

'How long have you had it?'

'Not very long, it's my newest venture…' He dips his pinkie into the brandy and into his mouth. 'Well, not so much a venture seeing as there is no risk involved because everything the WMP undertakes will be a success, because, if need be, whatever it might be, can easily be the only thing thereof out there.'

Bees nods. 'Do you have a name for it yet?'

'Not yet.'

'Have you thought of any names yet?'

'Not too many.'

'Oh.' Bees pours himself another glass of brandy and holds it out to 'Leader'. 'To coming up with a name for it before we finish these glasses.'

'I like that toast even more than I liked the previous one.' 'Leader' holds his glass out to Bees.' They clink glasses. 'I must say Bees that you are surprising me in ways much more impressive than I first thought, you would coming here.'

'Thank you.'

They sit drinking quietly for a while, Bees staring at the bottom of his glass trying to find fumes of brandy floating around there and 'Leader' looking out over the lawn and the rest of the farm he is able to see from where he is sitting, which he last visited more than four decades ago. 'I have to say Bees, the farm looks quite a bit more sickly than it did the last time I was here.'

Bees nods. 'Things have not been going as good as they did when my grandfather was alive.'

'Why do you think that is?'

'I'm not sure, not enough workers maybe?'

'Leader' nods. 'Let me say this my boy, as vile a man as your grandfather was his work ethic was up there with the best of them which is something to be admired...' 'Leader' takes another sip of brandy. 'Although the work ethic might not have been his own, he still made sure that those under his whip had it in spades, no matter what the cost, and that is what kept the farm looking the way it did the last time I was here.'

Bees nods.

'Correct me if I'm wrong, it seems that his work ethic is somewhat lost on you and your sister?'

'Why would you say that?'

'It's not me saying it so much as how the farm looks.'

Bees looks out over the lawn. 'We have a lot less help than my grandfather did.'

'Why don't you get more help?'

'We don't have enough money.'

'Leader' nods. 'Find another way of getting help then?'

'How would we do that?'

'That's entirely up to you.'

'I did have two gentlemen work for me a while back but that didn't work out so well.'

'That's your problem, the workers you get are not of good quality, where did you find them?'

'In town, they were sitting on the sidewalk behind the gun shop, said they were looking for work and that they could work for very cheap.'

'Again, not only were they not of good quality, they were simpletons who live on the streets.'

'When I talked to them, they seemed like they would be very good at working here, they had clothes on that made them look very much like the job I wanted them to do.'

'At least your grandfather had the wherewithal to acquire workers of colour, specimens that were made specifically for it.'

'I don't know where to find any more workers of colour.'

'They're all over, so much so that they seem to look more and more like cockroaches as the days go by.'

Bees nods.

'I will say this, after you hear about the job, I am here to tell you about and agree to the terms, which you will, you will never have to worry about another worker again, or about money or anything that has to do with it ever again.'

'Really?'

'Leader' nods. 'Without a doubt.' 'Leader' holds up his glass. 'To a richer future…'

Bees holds up his and brings it to 'Leader's.' 'May it also be white.'

'In every way.'

In the kitchen, Clarafina and Layli are an hour into preparing the meal that 'Leader' requested, and the second biggest room in the house is warmer and lighter than it has ever been, warmer because of the plethora of pots, pans and trays on the stove and in the oven and lighter, because unlike Clarafina, Layli likes to cook with as much light as possible.

Standing already prepared on the kitchen table are two salads, the usual of lettuce, tomato, onion, olives and the added feta cheese and a potato salad along with a tray of an assortment of finger sandwiches and another with an array of different crackers and cheeses.

On the stove is a pan in which is cooking crumbed chicken fillets and another in which is cooking Layli's favourite fish, and one thing she is allowed to have a say in concerning the meals that she prepares for 'Leader' because fish is his least favourite food but he likes to have it on the table as an option while eating, as well as a pot in that is cooking a chili that 'Leader's' mother used to make for him when he was a child along with slices of pita bread cooking in the oven.

Along with that is a steel tray in which is cooking roast beef with a variety of vegetables, for the dishes to finish cooking will take about two hours, just enough time for Layli and Clarafina to make the pecan nut pie with either ice cream or regular cream, 'Leader's' favourite dessert, or at his request sometimes both, when he does not make a request as to what should accompany the pie, he leaves it up to Layli to choose.

On the porch, 'Leader' and Bees have just finished the first bottle of brandy, Bees is sitting more comfortably on the rocking chair than he has ever before with both feet on the front edges of the curved underside of the chair feeling very close to weightless, almost as he rocks slowly back and forth, as much a part of the chair as the wood from which it is made.

One hand clenching one of the arm rests to deter him from falling off, which is a very big possibility considering how much he has had to drink, accompanied with the fact that for the first time his feet are not up on the porch railing or planted on occasion on the floor beneath the chair to stabilise himself, while his other hand is resting casually on the opposing arm rest holding his glass of brandy.

Behind Bees is 'Leader' sitting in his chair with the butt of one of the rifles that he brought with him pressed to his shoulder and the scope over his eye moving the cross-air to and fro over the workers by the cabin.

Bees turns to 'Leader'. 'Are you planning on shooting one of the workers?'

'No, I'm thinking how easy it would be to shoot one of them and no one of any matter would care or even know that they are dead.'

Bees laughs. 'Something to think about.'

'Or...' says 'Leader'. 'Something to not think about at all.' 'Leader' moves the cross-air over another worker.

'You can if you have good enough reason to.'

'Can what?'

'Shoot one of the workers.'

'Leader' turns to Bees. 'What would be good reason?'

'I don't know, if they did something wrong maybe? Or if you want to shoot one of them so you can give me the job you talked about earlier you can.'

'That won't be necessary, but it is nice to know that you would allow me such a thing.'

'Not a problem.'

'Leader' turns the scope of the rifle onto one of the trees along the edge of the lawn. 'If I were to shoot that branch hanging halfway off from the seventh tree, down from where the cabin is will you drink a full glass of brandy in one go?'

Bees looks over at the tree of which 'Leader' is talking. 'If you can do that, I will drink the brandy.'

'Leader' lowers his rifle. 'You will drink it in one go?'

Bees nods.

'How drunk are you?'

'Not very drunk, why?'

'Can you remember how much you coughed the first time you drank the brandy.'

'A little bit, but I'm feeling much better now so I don't think the coughing is going to be a problem.'

'You might be right, but drinking a full glass, maybe three dozen sips in two or three will be much different than the first drink you took.'

'How much different?'

'Have you ever drunk boiling water?'

'No?'

'If you drank a full glass of that brandy in the amount of time you said you would I'm quite sure it will feel a lot like drinking a glass of boiling water.' 'Leader' lowers his rifle and turns to Bees. 'Having said that do you still think you will be able to do what we are talking about?'

'Why would you want me to drink a full glass of brandy if it feels like that?'

'It might be a lot to ask but I have seen a couple of people do it.'

'Then I probably have to do it.'

'Good answer.' 'Leader' holds up the rifle.

'I'm ready when you are.'

'You might as well pour yourself a glass now.'

'I think I'll wait a bit, not saying you're going to miss but if you do there won't be any brandy wasted.'

'Not a problem, just remember that when you do pour yourself a glass in a moment or two, I told you to do so before you did.'

'Not a problem.'

'Before we proceed, if I do manage to shoot the branch off the tree would you say that will be something you would admire?'

'Sure.'

'Then prepare to be amazed my friend.' 'Leader' brings the scope of the rifle to his eye and places the tip of his middle finger very gently on the trigger, a trigger he had fitted to all of his rifles with an action almost uncomfortably light and sensitive to make it feel like he was less so doing something of the shooting, and potentially killing nature, as well as using his middle finger to less do so as a way of getting across whatever message the combination of using his middle finger along with a firearm might send while repeating to himself a rhyme he does every time he shoots something that can breath and move, 'From peace to chaos, from chaos to peace, so is the message from man to beast.'

He repeats the phrase a couple of times before pulling back on the trigger with his finger more gently even than what it was when it came to rest thereon, moving the trigger from a state of peace to one of chaos as he explains to anyone, he talks with shooting about is the change of states when doing so, beyond that he had the words 'peace' and 'chaos' engraved on the part of the rifle that holds the trigger. Before Bees is able to take note of the shot fired, he sees the branch flying off the tree.

'I have to admit, I didn't see that one coming, you are pretty good with that thing.'

'Leader' sits down. 'I have shot these things for longer than you have been alive my boy, if I weren't good, I would be worthless.'

Bees laughs.

'Leader' lowers the rifle. 'Your turn.'

'Oh yes.' Bees picks up the bottle of brandy and pours himself a glass full. 'How is it that you shoot the branch off the tree but I get to drink the brandy?'

'Watch your tongue my boy, and I mean that literally.' He holds the scope up to his eye again and moves the cross-air over the workers. 'Now drink, and I trust you won't use my back to you against me.'

'Not a chance.'

'Not that you will be able to do so in the first place, if you pour it out onto the floor I will hear you, if you try and pour it back into the bottle I will hear you, if you toss it over the railing, I will see it and I also don't see any pots with plants here, so you won't be able to pour it out onto something that can soak it up.'

'No about those ones.'

'Leader' nods.

'Are you going to keep looking at the workers while I drink?'

'Who am I to bother a man when he is about to do something like drink an entire glass of brandy.'

'Here goes.' As quickly as possible Bees drinks the brandy hoping that the quicker, he does it, the less discomfort might await him after and almost as soon as he put the glass to his mouth, he puts it upside down on the table. 'Done,' he says through clenched teeth while trying to not cough as he feels doing so might bring up blood instead of fumigated air.

'Leader' turns to Bees. 'Impressive, now take a breath as long and as hard as you can.'

Bees breaths in as much air as he can, when the somewhat cold late afternoon air enters his lungs, it feels as if the fumes inside are being set alight and he begins to cough with a vigour not yet known to him as well as to 'Leader' who is looking at him out from the side of his eye both to make sure that he is in good spirits as well as to admire disconcertingly his coughing fit.

When Bees feels that all the burning air has left his lungs he turns to 'Leader'. 'It feels like someone poured melted metal down my throat.'

'Leader' laughs. 'You can forget about catching a cold for at least a month, every germ that was inside your body as of...' 'Leader' looks at his watch. 'Fifteen or so seconds ago is now more dead than a one-hundred-year-old coffin.' 'Leader' lays his rifle against the railing and picks up the bottle of brandy and pours himself another glass. 'You can thank me later.' He picks up the rifle again and holds the scope to his eye. 'The one in the yellow dress, who is that?'

Bees holds his hand over his eyes and looks out over the lawn to the cabin. 'I can't see very well from here.'

'She is very pretty.'

'Oh, it's probably Scara then, the priest's daughter.'

'Leader' turns his head toward Bees. 'You have a priest working here?'

Bees nods. 'Sure do.'

'Is that the tall older one by any chance?'

'That is him.'

'Leader' looks to the workers again. 'Does he give you a lot of trouble.'

'Not really, he's actually the best of the lot.'

'That's only because he's the oldest, don't let him not causing you trouble fool you into thinking fondly of him.'

'I didn't say that I like him.'

'Leader' glances at Bees. 'Good to know.' He goes back to peering out at the workers through the scope. 'Having said that his daughter is very pretty, very pretty indeed, I would almost go as far as to say that she is prettier than most of the women I know of our own colour.'

'Can't say that I have noticed.'

'I have...' says 'Leader'. 'And I like what I see, so much so that it makes me angry, so angry that it makes me want to shoot her dead on the spot.' 'Leader' lowers his rifle and turns to Bees. 'Do you think I should do it?'

'It won't bother me, but it will cause me a lot of unwanted problems.'

'Leader' holds the rifle up again. 'Don't worry my boy, I'm not going to do it, I'm just saying that she should be put down for making us feel the way she does, wouldn't you agree?'

Bees nods. 'I do,' he says. 'If you really want to do it, it probably wouldn't be so bad, in return for what might come this weekend.'

'Leader' lowers his rifle again. 'No better reason to start talking business than that.'

'I've been wanting to talk that since we sat down here.'

'Leader' leans his rifle against the table and sits down. 'A long time ago the WMP made a bid for office, we had everything we needed, the right people in place, policies drawn up to regulation and more importantly more money than we knew what to do with, that being said the party that was in power during that time had a problem with our policies saying that they were too aggressive and demoralising and because they still had the majority of the country's vote, they were able to put a stop to our efforts campaigning. Over the last 25 years though it came to be that all the money in this fair country of ours now belongs to only the people and all and any of their businesses that are affiliated with the WMP or any of its subsidiaries, are you following?'

'If by 'following' you mean that the WMP are going to take over the country then yes.'

'Then following you are my boy.'

'What do you need me for?'

'We need you to be the face of the WMP.'

'What does that mean?'

'In short it means that we want to make you president.'

Bees' eyes widen. 'President?'

'Leader' nods.

'How will you do that?'

'By writing your name down on the documents stating who the president will be when the WMP wins the election.'

Bees sits quietly for a while. 'What will I have to do if I'm the president?'

'In short you will have to act like you are making the decisions that we do for the country.'

'Why can't I make the decisions too?'

'Because you know nothing about politics.'

'How do you know about politics?'

'From spending years learning about politics from politicians.'

Bees nods. 'How will I have to *act* like I am making the decisions?'

'We will tell you what to say about whatever policies we need to address and you will tell the people about them.'

'On television?'

'Leader' nods.

'Will I be able to do that?'

'If the people who did it before you can, you might be able to do so even more.'

Bees sits quietly for a while. 'Is that all I will have to do?'

'Amongst other things.'

'Okay.' Bees sits upright in his chair. 'But if I get the job is the only thing I will be doing talking to people on TV?'

'Don't talk about the position, if you do get it, as a job, because it is not one, if you get the job, you will be a partner of the WMP and the last thing you will be doing is feeling like you are working.'

'What will I be doing then?'

'When you become president you will be more like a movie star than a politician, you will be on the front covers of magazines, you will drive and wear only the best and most expensive cars and clothes, you will eat at only the best and most expensive restaurants and drink at bars of the same quality, so much so that they will name ones after you, your wife that will stand with you will not be the type to be a teacher at a school or a receptionist at a dentist's office but a woman so beautiful that she herself will have been on the covers of numerous magazines or maybe a star of movies herself, heck you might later star in your own movies at a later point in your career.'

'Leader' picks up his glass of brandy. 'Does any of that sound like work to you?'

'No,' says Bees, not quite sure even what he is saying so to.

'Great, the odds are in your favour then.' 'Leader' holds his glass out to Bees. 'A drink to celebrate.'

Bees picks up his glass and holds it in front of him.

'Your life is about to change in ways you cannot imagine my boy.'

'Can't wait.'

'To Bees Brungle, the president of Famurantia.'

'To Bees Brungle.'

They click glasses, just as Bees is about to drink 'Leader' stops him. 'Before you do that, I think we need something a little bit more special for this occasion.' 'Leader' reaches into the box of brandy and takes out a bottle quite a bit smaller than the others and another brandy glass. 'This one is a bit older and more expensive, a bit more suitable, pour out the brandy you have there so you can pour yourself another glass of this.'

Bees throws his brandy out of his glass over the porch railing. 'Won't pouring the new brandy in this glass that had the old brandy in it spoil the taste of the new brandy?' Bees asks.

'Leader' looks down somewhat at a loss for words at Bees' empty glass, then back up at Bees. 'I'm not sure,' says 'Leader'.

'Shouldn't you know?'

'Why would you ask that?'

'Because you say that you know everything there is to know about brandy and so?'

'Leader' looks down Bees' glass again. 'This I do not know.'

They sit quietly for a while before 'Leader' almost jumps out of his seat at the thought that just came to him.

'And that is because it is not as you think it to be.' 'Leader' says. 'Brandy cannot spoil brandy, no matter if the one is of a lesser quality than the other, that's why I didn't know the answer to your question, because it was not a question to begin with because brandy cannot spoil brandy, so banal the question was to my cultured mind that I was unable to comprehend that it needed an answer,' he continues. 'Having said that, may I have your glass please?'

Bees slides his glass over to 'Leader' and he pours his glass a quarter of the way full with the new brandy. Bees slides his glass back over to him.

'Leader' and Bees hold their respective glasses out to each other. 'To accommodate the occasion.' 'Leader' proposes a toast.

Bees nods. 'To that.' Just as he is about to drink 'Leader' stops him. 'No...' he says. 'That's not right.'

Bees frowns. 'What do you mean?'

'The toast...' 'Leader' thinks, 'To consummate the occasion.'

'That sounds right.'

'Leader' pauses. 'I don't think it is.'

'To accomplish the occasion?' asks Bees.

'Leader' shakes his head. 'That's definitely not right.'

'What is it then?'

'To celebrate the occasion?'

'That sounds like it is the right one.'

'Leader' nods. 'It does, but it still isn't quite what I'm looking for.' 'Leader' looks down at his glass. 'To consolidate the occasion,' he says softly thinking.

Bees shakes his head. 'That sounds wrong again.'

'Leader' breathes a sigh of frustration.

'To seal the occasion,' Bees says excited.

'Leader' shakes his head. 'That might be the worst yet.' 'Leader' quickly drinks what is in his glass and pours himself another not realising even that he did so.

'To…' 'Leader' shakes his head. 'No.'

'To make the occasion.'

'Wrong again, to waving the white flag, for there comes a time in very man's life where he must make the defeated choice to do so in order to remain un therein.'

Bees nods. 'To the white flag, may it forever be the colour that it is.'

'That will do fine.'

They drink and sit doing so quietly for a while.

'Is it right that a black man might be president this year?'

'Leader' nods. 'That is correct.'

'I don't know much about the political way of things but how are we going to win against a black man if there are so many black people here?'

'Simple, wool.'

'Wool?'

'Wool.'

'What does that have to do with anything?'

'Instead of making sweaters with it we are going to use it to pull over people's eyes.'

'How are we going to do that?'

'The black man up for election this year is with the WMP.'

Bees frowns. 'What?'

'Leader' nods. 'He pretends to be with the opposing party but in actuality he is with the WMP, so no matter who the people will be voting for they will be voting for the WMP.'

'How did you get him to go with the WMP?'

'We paid him a large sum of money.'

Bees sits quietly for a while. 'So, I'm definitely going to be president?'

'At this point my boy, only you dying will stop that from happening.'

'Food is ready,' Layli says as she pops her head out of the front door.

'Leader' turns around. 'Thank you dear, we will be in shortly.'

'Okay, don't take too long, it just came out of the oven so it's still hot.'

'We won't.'

'Do you have any idea how long you might be because Clarafina and I are quite hungry?'

'It might be ten minutes, it might be an hour, when it comes to the things, I am talking with Bees with you never know.'

'If it happens to be more than half an hour can Clarafina and I eat so long?'

'What do you say?'

Bees nods. 'Fine.'

'Leader' turns to Layli. 'Unfortunately, I cannot allow that dear, what kind of people would we be telling Bees and Clarafina we are if we don't eat together, especially after it took the two of you this long to prepare it, try not to let the wait bother you, because if it wasn't for the two of us there wouldn't even be food to wait for.'

'Okay my love, we will see you when we see you then.'

'Very good.'

Layli goes back inside the house to the kitchen. Bees picks up the bottle of brandy to fill his glass but before he is able to do so 'Leader' stops him. 'Before you do that, I want you to come for a drive with me.'

'To where?'

'Not far, half hour or more maybe.'

'What about the food?'

'Like I said, it can wait, there is a couple of things I need to talk with you about.'

'We can talk here.'

'It will be better if we do it away from here, if you're worried about the food getting cold don't, I have to eat too.'

'Okay.'

'Leader' and Bees leave their drinks on the table and get up and walk down the porch to 'Leader's' truck closest to the gate, on their way there. 'Leader' takes his set of keys out of his pocket. 'Do you mind driving?'

'Sure.'

'Leader' hands Bees the set of keys and he makes his way to the driver door, him and 'Leader' get inside and Bees puts the keys into the ignition and starts the truck and puts it in reverse and does so onto a shaded patch of flattened plants next to the garage before turning toward the gate and driving out of the driveway onto the dirt road which since the first family of Brungles lived on the farm has been driven on less and less as time went on.

A couple of minutes into the drive Bees turns to 'Leader'. 'Where are we going?'

'Just for a drive around the area.' 'Leader' takes a small cigar, about the size of a cigarette, out of a box in his shirt pocket along with a box of matches. 'Do you mind?'

'No.'

'Thank you.' 'Leader' puts the cigar in his mouth and lights it. 'No that we've talked about it are you are up for the role of president?'

Bees turns to 'Leader'. 'Do I have the job?'

'Not yet, but Layli and I being here counts much in your favour, before you get the job, if you do get it, I want to make sure that you are up for it no matter what, because as much as it comes with everything a man can ever want it is not all diamonds and rhinestones.'

Bees nods. 'It still is impossible that my life now can be worse than if I become president.'

'Leader' nods. 'That is an impressive answer, it seems that you might be the right man for the job after all.'

'So, I have the job?'

'As soon as your eyes are back on the road.'

Bees quickly turns to look back at the road. 'Sorry.'

'Not to worry.'

'So do I?'

'Leader' nods. 'It seems that you do.'

'I don't know what to say.'

'And with that you've said all that you need to.'

'Thank you.'

'Just know that you have to be sure without any doubt that you will be up for whatever we put in front of you, you cannot after telling me that you accept the offer when I leave the farm tell me that you have changed your mind.'

Bees shakes his head. 'That won't ever happen.'

'I am glad we understand each other.' 'Leader' holds the front end of his cigar out over the top of the window to let the burnt leaves off it. 'You are going to be a very rich and powerful man Bees, anything you can think of will be yours, money, cars, clothes, jewellery, food, women, vacations, anything and everything you can want, everything your grandfather dreamed of will now be yours.'

'And all I have to do is be the president? Well not really, but...'

'As simple as that.'

20 minutes later Bees stops the truck at the side of the road in a part of Golden Heart that he had never been in before, one in much better a condition than where he lives as well as any other part of the district he has seen up until that point in his life. After Bees turns off the truck, him and 'Leader' step out onto the dirt road beside the wire fence that separates it from the green pastures that make up the land of all the farms in the district and make their way to the fence and stand looking out over it.

'Here it is my boy, your kingdom.'

Bees smiles, trying his best to stay calm to appear more so worthy of what is now his. 'I have never been out this far.'

'Now you have, and at no better a time than any, the very time that everything you are looking at became yours, every strand of grass, every bale of hay, every dime of dirt, it now all belongs to you.'

'It's about time,' Bees says again solely with the intent to impress.

'Leader' giggles at the sudden surge of confidence that befalls Bees. 'I will have to say that I agree.'

Bees turns to 'Leader'. 'So, everything, every farm here is now mine?'

'Technically speaking of course, yours and the gentlemen from the WMP. 'Leader' squeezes Bees' shoulder.

'Are the same people that live on the farms still going to live there after today, or when I become the owner of the district?'

'They are.'

'How can it be mine then?'

'It's yours in the bigger scheme of things.'

'What is that?'

'That if you were to want to walk onto any one of these farms here and cut yourself down a while tree of apples to take with you to your farm then you can.'

Bees frowns. 'How can I just do *that*?'

'Because it belongs to you of course.'

'But it's their farm?'

'Who's farm?'

'The people that live on it?'

'Leader' nods half-heartedly. 'In a way, but all the land that their farms are on belongs to the WMP, because we own the country.'

'How can you own the country?'

'Leader' pats Bees on the back. 'Don't worry about that my boy, just worry about what car you would want when we give you your first one.'

'How will the people that live on the farms know that it is mine?'

'They won't, you will, and you are the only person that has to know so.'

'But if I want to take something from the farms, how can I do that if they don't know that it is mine?'

'You give me a call, and I'll talk it over with the other gentlemen from the WMP and we'll take it from there.' 'Leader' squeezes Bees' shoulder. 'But the chances of you ever wanting to take a couple of apples from someone else's farm for no particular reason is not going to be very much now, is it?'

'Maybe?'

'If it does come to that be sure to notify me, with the permission of myself and the rest of the gentlemen from the WMP you can do just about anything you want around here, and also, considering what that would be, what can anyone do with something so big other than to make sure that it is taken care of and sit and marvel at it knowing that it belongs to you.'

Bees nods and quietly looks out over the land. 'Can I ask you something else?'

'Sure.'

'If I am going to be a part of the WMP I want to be so that I can make some of the decisions too, do some of the things that you do as well and not only drive around all the time.'

'Leader' turns to Bees unpleasantly surprised. 'Are you saying that if the demand you just made is not met you are willing to give up all of what you see around you?'

'No.'

'Then what are you saying Mr Brungle?'

'If I am going to be president, I don't want to sit in my house the whole time and just do what I'm still doing now, I want to do some of the things that you guys are doing too?'

'Leader' pats Bees on the back. 'Not to worry my boy, what you are referring to is more of a given than you think.'

Bees nods. 'Good, then I will be the president.'

'Didn't expect anything less.' 'Leader' turns around and walks to the truck.

'Where are you going?'

'To get something out of the back of the truck.' He opens the back passenger door closest to them and takes out a rifle from under the seat before making his way back to Bees, he frowns. 'What is that for?'

'Before I answer that I have a question for you.'

'Shoot.'

'Leader' laughs and shoves the rifle against Bees' chest and waits for him to grab a hold of it before letting go. 'When you look at what is before you are doing so at something that is close to perfection, would you agree?'

Bees nods.

'Good, having said that I would never give an associate of mine and the WMP's something which is less than perfection, that is something I frown upon and something I more so even pride myself doing the opposite, is that something you say you would believe, my boy?'

Bees nods. 'Yes.'

'Good, now I have to ask you why you think it is that I would refer to what I have given you as less than perfection?'

'I don't know.'

'Didn't think you would, now, would you like another guess as to why I referred to these lands as less than perfection?'

'Do I get something if I do?'

'Not this time my boy.'

Bees thinks for a bit. 'I don't know.'

'Leader' puts his hand on Bees' shoulder. 'The reason I do so is because other than looking as green and being as healthy as any farmland one would come to see on a postcard or magazine, they are spoiled by something, would you like to take a guess at why *that* might be?'

Bees puts his hand against his forehead and looks out in front of him. 'I don't see anything wrong with the lands?'

'Leader' laughs. 'I respect your answer my boy but unfortunately I cannot say that it is correct.'

'Okay...' Bees looks out in front of him again. 'There is not enough of it?'

'Not quite.' 'Leader' takes the rifle from Bees and holds it up against his shoulder with the scope to his eye. 'Allow me.' 'Leader' pulls the trigger.

As the pins and needles from the shot fired begin to work its way down Bees spine and he regains his composure he sees one of about a dozen farm workers working on the land in front of them drop to the ground while the remainder of the workers, far and near to him, run to his side.

Even though Bees had killed three workers while he was in charge of the farm it was always done, to his thinking, within the confines of righting a wrong, and seeing someone other than himself kill a worker which they knew in no way shook him to a core even he didn't know he had and upset him very much, the thought of losing everything that was promised him upset him more and he turns to 'Leader' with much the same demeanour as before.

'Leader' shoulders the rifle. 'Blacks Bees...' he says. 'Black people, they are what is wrong with this picture, they are the specks of dirt that ruin the picture that the land of the white man is supposed to look like...' 'Leader' shoves the rifle back onto Bees' chest. 'And for that reason, for making imperfect what is meant to be perfect, they must be taken out, one by one or group by group until there are none of them left and the picture we speak of, is returned to its former glory.'

'But if they are all gone who will do the work on the farms?'

'Leader' laughs, patting Bees on the shoulder. 'Good question, my boy, the answer to which is that lucky for me and you there are far too many of them and those standing on your land right now are a part of that, so much so that it causes a need for work that does not and more so even cannot exist, on another hand those of them that work need too much to take care of the part of the 'far too many' that is the 'too many' thus the compensation for what they do, far outweighs the amount and quality of work they do.

'For that reason, what I just did to the one of them on the ground needs to be done to the rest of them to even the discrepancy, having said that...' 'Leader' pulls back on the lever that loads the rifle. 'I need you to dot the last 'I' for me by taking out the remaining specks of dirt...' 'Leader' turns and looks over the land. 'And I suggest you hurry up because they are busy getting away.'

Bees thinks back to his life on the farm as of recent and how long it has been since he had a drink from a bottle that did not come in a box along with 11 other of the same, how long it has been since he had food brought to him by a waiter at a restaurant, how long, if ever, it has been since he put tobacco in his pipe; which you were only able to get if you knew to ask for it from the clerk and how long it has been since he had a roll of money in his pocket so big that it made it uncomfortable to walk. He holds the scope of the rifle to his eye, moves the cross-air over one of the workers standing still and pulls the trigger.

The drive back to the farm was more quiet than that away from it, so much so that Bees fell asleep halfway, a couple of minutes away 'Leader' broke the quiet, 'Young man?'

Bees opens his eyes and as 'casually' as possible moves to a more upright position as to try to not have 'Leader' think that he was sleeping. 'Yes?'

'I have a pressing matter I must discuss with you, something that when I got word of it upset me a great deal.'

Bees turns to 'Leader' unpleasantly intrigued. 'What?'

'It has to do with the priest that works for you.'

'Petrus?'

'Leader' nods. 'Yes.'

'What about him?'

'Before coming to the farm this morning Layli and I spent a while walking around town and while doing so, I came to hear that the priest has for a while now been preaching to the lowly black folk of the district when him and the rest of him go into town whenever for whatever reason.'

'How?'

'Apparently, they meet in an abandoned building near the edge of town somewhere where he preaches to them, I also heard that some of the workers that attend said meetings have gone as far as to pool whatever resources they have to acquire firearms and other weapons with which to protect themselves should circumstances arrive where they have to.'

'Where did you hear this?'

'From a very reliable source, one that will under no circumstances lie to me for reasons that he knows what will happen to him if he does will be much worse than what I am speaking of.'

Bees sits quietly for a while. 'I find that very hard to believe, I've known him my whole life and he has never done so much as take a speck of dirt without asking.' Bees stares blankly out in front of him.

'Any thoughts about what to do about its Mr Brungle?'

'No.'

'In that case I do.'

Bees turns to 'Leader'. 'What?'

'I propose that we kill him.'

'What? How?'

'Tomorrow night when everyone is asleep, we go to the cabin and kill him.'

'What about the other workers?'

'What about them?'

'If we kill Petrus, they will want to kill us.'

'Then we kill them all.'

'How are we going to do that.'

'I'll get my men to help us, that makes six of us together, I'm sure we can get our hands on two guns each...' 'Leader' turns to Bees, 'How many of them are there?'

'Children too?'

'Leader' nods, 'Yes.'

Bees counts on his fingers. 'Twenty.'

'How many adults?'

'Twelve.'

'Including the priest?'

Bees nods.

'Great, then within a matter of a second, we'll be able to kill them all.'

Bees turns to 'Leader'. 'What do we do with the children?'

'We can kill them as well, but the better thing to do would be to keep them to make money with.'

'How?'

'How old are they?'

'I don't know, some are quite young and others are about the same age as my nephew.'

'In that case we can sell them to farmers around the district maybe, or members of the WMP or men from other organisations that we know of, many of them will be willing to pay hefty sums of money for children their age—the younger ones and the older for that matter.'

'Why would they want to do that?'

'That my boy I would rather not tell you, but I'm sure being an adult, you can come up with plausible explanations as to why they would want to.'

Bees stares blankly off into the distance.

'It's settled then, tomorrow night when they are all asleep, we go into their cabin and shoot them, they won't even know what's happening.'

Bees nods. 'Okay, that sounds fine.'

'I didn't think it wouldn't.'

'Leader' makes the last turn onto the small stretch of dirt road that leads into the driveway of the farm where 'Leader' parks the truck, a truck that Bees thought on the way back to the farm, how he would want to look on the inside and out were he to get one as his first form of compensation for joining with the WMP, and him, 'Leader', Clarafina and Layli spent the next three hours around the porch table eating a meal that was fit for a president. While up in his room Klipp sat on the edge of his bed with a walkie talkie in his hand and his head slumped into his chest.

Later that day, when they finished eating the meal that Clarafina and Layli spent almost five hours making and another hour heating up again after 'Leader'; and Bees came back to the farm they went up to their rooms to take an afternoon nap while Klipp painted in his room with a mind and heart very heavy. What he painted was a portrait in the style of caricature of 'Leader' as an elephant standing on his hind legs wearing an outfit much the same as what he is wearing; with three rifles slung over his shoulder, holding a box of bullets in his trunk and a briefcase with money sticking out of it in one hand with the other over Layli's shoulder and a bunch of many different kinds of jewels on his tusks.

Next to him was Layli with her hair down to the bottom of her shoulder blades and her hands clasped together behind her back wearing a dress also much like she was wearing that with a bunch of bananas in one hand and a mousetrap in the other big enough to capture an elephant the size of which 'Leader' drawn.

When they woke up early that night, 'Leader' and Bees spent the remainder of it on the porch drinking while Clarafina and Layli where in the living room playing piano together until long after 'Leader' and Bees went to bed.

An hour or so after midnight when everyone in the house as well as the back room was asleep Clarafina got out of bed and stepped into her pair of slippers and made her way down the stairs to the kitchen to get herself something to eat and drink, at the bottom of the staircase she sees the living room light on and Layli sitting on the couch on her nightgown with a magazine on her lap and a glass of red wine on the arm rest of the couch, when Clarafina's shadow befalls her, she looks up. 'Couldn't sleep either?'

'Same story different night.'

'Right there with you, my boyfriend snores so loud that I have to be half asleep getting into bed if I want to do so.'

'That doesn't sound very nice.'

'The snoring or the finding it hard to fall asleep?'

Clarafina laughs. 'Both.'

'You get used to it.' Layli scoots over to the side. 'Care to join me?'

'Don't mind if I do.' Clarafina makes her way over to Layli and sits down next to her.

'Would you like some wine?'

'Don't mind if I do.'

'Great.' Layli picks up a bottle of red wine from the table and looks at Clarafina somewhat disappointed. 'We're missing a glass.'

Clarafina looks at the bottle. 'You can pour your glass full and I can drink the rest from the bottle, if you want?'

Layli thinks for a bit.

'If it's okay with you? I normally drink from the bottle anyway.'

'Okay,' Layli fills her glass and gives the bottle to Clarafina.

'Thank you.'

'Pleasure.'

Clarafina takes a sip.

'How do you like it?'

'It's very nice, where did you get it?'

'My boyfriend makes it, it's from one of a couple of wine farms he owns.'

Clarafina looks at the bottle again. 'Tastes like something that would come from there.'

Layli laughs. 'I'll tell him you said so.'

'Thank you, also ask him if he can maybe give us a couple of these boxes for free if you can?'

'I'll see what I can do.'

Clarafina takes a sip of wine. 'I have a couple of bottles of mampoer in my room, I can go get it if you want so you can try it?'

'What's that?'

'It's a strong kind of spirit like brandy or whiskey but not as thick and has a lighter colour.'

'Where do you get it?'

'I make it myself.'

'Really?'

Clarafina nods.

'How?'

'If I tell you, you have to give me almost all of the money you make if you want to sell it?'

'I don't want to sell it, I'm more of a red wine type of girl.'

'That's okay, we can leave it then.'

'Maybe tomorrow night?'

Clarafina nods. 'Okay.' She takes another sip of wine along with Layli. 'What are you reading?'

Layli looks down at the magazine in her lap. 'I'm more so looking, not really reading.'

Clarafina laughs. 'I also do that, what are you looking at?'

'I'm looking for ideas for a fashion brand I want to start.'

'Really?'

Layli nods. 'I've been pestering my husband about it ever since we got married.'

'How long have you been asking him about it?'

'Not too long, a couple of months after we got married, he came to me and asked if there is anything I would like to do, in terms of a job so I mentioned this.'

'What makes you think he's going to let you do it now still?'

'I don't know, a month or so ago he came to me and asked if I could show him a couple of pieces of material and their prices that I would like to use which he never did before.'

'Oh.'

Layli turns a page. 'Let me know if you see something you like.'

'I will.' Clarafina looks closer at the magazine and when she does so, she notices Layli's thigh, only a few shades darker than her white silk nightgown, coming out from the bottom of it and follows it down to her feet, inside of a pair of fluffy white slippers and her heart starts to beat faster and she begins to feel weightless almost, Layli looks up at her. 'Have you seen anything you like?'

Layli's question sends a jolt through her body and she puts her hand over her heart.

'I'm sorry, I didn't mean to scare you.'

Clarafina waves away her apology. 'Don't worry, I get more easily scared at night.'

Layli laughs, 'Me too.'

Clarafina laughs and takes another sip of wine. 'Did you know red wine is healthy for you?'

Layli nods. 'A little bit, it has something to do with some or other vitamin or something that's inside of it.'

'I know.'

After spending a couple of minutes drinking quietly and flipping through the pages of the fashion magazine, Layli asks, 'What time do you normally eat breakfast in the morning?'

'We don't really eat breakfast in the morning.'

'Oh.'

'When we did, it was usually at eight o'clock.'

'If you don't mind then it will be nice if I can make breakfast tomorrow morning around that time, my boyfriend likes his prepared in a specific kind if way?'

'Fine by me.'

'Great…' Layli puts her hand on Clarafina's knee. 'And also, because a lady like yourself deserves a break every now and then.'

'That will be nice, thank you.'

'I'll have everything ready at eight.'

'If it is anything like we had earlier today I can't wait.'

They continue to look through the magazine, after a while, somewhat unbeknownst to her, Clarafina closes her eyes and leans in to kiss Layli, when she realises this, she pulls away before Clarafina puts her hand over her mouth in a state of shock, they stare at each other for a while.

'I'm sorry, I didn't mean…'

Layli puts her hand on Clarafina's knee again. 'Don't worry about it, believe it or not it's not the first time something like this has happened.'

Clarafina shakes her head. 'Please don't tell anyone about this? My brother won't be…'

'I won't say anything, I promise,' Layli puts her hands on Clarafina's knee in an attempt to console.

'Thank you.' Clarafina takes Layli's hands off from her knee and quickly finishes what is left of the wine and puts the bottle down on the table and gets up and walks to the door. Before leaving she turns around. 'Looking forward to breakfast tomorrow,' she says before walking as quickly as she can up the stairs to her bedroom.

Chapter 17

The following morning 'Leader' is the first to get out of bed, he puts on over his boxer shorts and T-shirt a robe and gathers his bathing supplies and walks to one of two bathrooms not attached to a room and turns on the water to run himself a bath and takes off his robe and puts it neatly folded on the lid of the toilet, while the water is filling the tub he puts a small leather carry bag on the edge of the wash basin and takes out a tube of toothpaste, a toothbrush and a roll of floss and begins to floss his teeth.

After doing so, he brushes them, first with horizontal movements and a second time with circular before flossing them another time, after doing so he puts everything back in the carry bag and walks over to the tub, still being filled with lukewarm water, takes off his T-shirt and begins to wipe himself down with a washcloth held under the tap, this he does to dirty the bathwater as little as possible because as much as he bathes for cleanliness he does so more so for pleasure.

'Leader' got into the habit of taking long baths when he was still very young after his mother passed away, because she told him that the time, she got to spend by herself taking a bubble bath was some of her most cherished, other than the times she spent with him. 'Leader' grew up with both his parents until he was six years old after which his mother, Kimma, passed away in her sleep one night, she was not a particularly very pretty woman but she had a 'bright' sense of humour and very loving nature about her which drew very many well liked people to her, including 'Leader's' father, the people that knew her always talked about how positive an influence she was on those around her, though what people thought and said about her was not how she truly felt because she really had very few things in her life that brought her joy, much thanks to 'Leader's' father— which unlike with his mother, his relationship was very strained, so much so that growing up he never knew his father's name, only ever calling and being allowed to refer to him as 'sir' when he wanted to speak to him, and to this day still does not know.

When 'Leader' came into adulthood he was as most people referred to it 'a smudgy mirror image' of his father in that they looked similar, they spoke in much the same manner and with the same voice, had many similar mannerisms and ticks and had an unusually strong liking for guns, one of the few things that shone a different light on father and son was that 'Leader's' father grew up very poor and remained so throughput his life while 'Leader' only grew up so but became very rich very quickly after leaving school.

As a child, 'Leader' was no more than content with his life, but as he knew of nothing better having been made to live a very sheltered life. To him, his life was not much different from what he thought his peers' to be, what set his life apart from that of his peers', and in a big way, was that he never knew or came to, when he was old enough to understand the meaning of having names attached to people, known throughout his life his father's name and had to always address him as 'sir' whenever they spoke, which was very little as before he was born his father made the choice, were he to have a son, to never speak to him in consoling or helpful manners to raise him so that he may be as strong mentally as possible.

When he talked with others about it, he said that it was not so much that which caused him to detest his childhood but that after his mother passed away, he had to spend his formative years with a parent who much less than very rarely spoke to him and even more so after his mother passed, didn't speak to him at all other than the time he was seven years old and went to his father's bedroom and asked him why he never spoke to him; though to no avail, and went back to his bedroom and got into bed and made the choice, that from that moment on he would do whatever he could, still having to live in the house to do so as alone as possible.

When 'Leader' was around the age of six, a rumour started that his mother was killed by his father in an attempt to strengthen him around others although the rumour that sat most comfortably with people was that he did so because she was having an affair with the town dentist, although it was not true it was made easier to believe by the fact that she had a very close and comfortable relationship with the dentist, as he was very well liked and respected by everyone that knew him and everyone that knew of him.

The suspicion that his wife was having an affair with the town dentist behind his back was not enough to make him want to kill her but what happened on the night of her last birthday she would come to spend with her family was, they went out to dinner in one of the more expensive restaurants in town. The dentist heard from someone that they were there and having tried to get a hold of her throughout the day to give a present to her. He decided to go to the restaurant and wait outside until they were finished eating to give her present in person although decided against it, when he saw her sitting in the restaurant with 'Leader' and his father and drove to their house to drop it off in their mailbox. The following day 'Leader's' father found the present and after reading the letter threw it away.

Although 'Leader's' mother and the dentist did have feelings for each other; neither one was the type of people to act on them as 'Leader's' mother was married and the dentist was not the type of man to do so. The actual reason they did not act on their feelings for one another was because 'Leader's' mother wanted to give him the chance to grow up with both of his parents and more so because she was afraid that 'Leader's' father might harm him or her; if she were to leave him, and rightfully so because the day that 'Leader's' father found the present to his wife in the mailbox, he decided that not only was it justified to kill her but in the best interest of her, himself and 'Leader'.

A couple of years after 'Leader's' mother passed away, his father left to go and live with another woman, a week's drive away from the farm who he met in a bar in town a month before doing so. The night he did so he left 'Leader' a letter explaining why he raised him the way he did, that the only thing that makes a man what he is the amount of money in his bank account and that love was something made up by those who wrote the Bible to give people a false sense of hope in a hopeless world. He finished the letter by telling him why he left and with the words 'good luck' and 24 Munto, he purposely left out the address to the nearest orphanage as a last effort to teach 'Leader' a valuable life lesson.

After his father, left 'Leader' sought out the orphanage after a few of his friends' parents denied him a place to stay and the next five years he spent skipping school as often as possible to work various small jobs around town. After a while he had enough money saved to afford his own apartment on the outskirts of town next to the train station. Although the apartment was very cheap because of the noise from the trains coming in and out of town throughout the day and night it was still too expensive to live alone and he had to share it with a 42-year-old man who sold narcotics as his source of income.

He sold various kinds, all of which he made himself, the most popular being one by the name of 'Gangreene' which he made from various household cleaning products, all of which was in liquid form, which he poured in small amounts onto a glass table and dried with a hair dryer until in solid form and ground it up with a pestle and mortar until in powder form and mixed together in a small bowl with lukewarm water until it was of a thick and even consistency and shaped the mixture into small cubes about the size of a small marble which he then left to harden and sold separately or in bags of five and ten.

'Leader' and the man did not have a friendly relationship all the time they lived together but was rarely at the apartment the same time with the man sleeping mostly during the daytime while 'Leader' was working and vice versa.

The last job that 'Leader' held during his stay at the apartment was that of a manager's assistant at one of the biggest steel manufacturing companies in the country where he did many a menial job like filing papers, making calls to smaller clients and running various errands for his new boss, when 'Leader' came into work one day, he heard him talking over the phone to the owner of a rival steel company who threatened to kill 'Leader's' boss if he did not—as he accused him of doing—stop stealing his clients.

'Leader' had heard stories from other workers of this rivalry between the two companies but did not think much of it before hearing the two men talk over the phone, the following day after work, 'Leader' waited until his fellow employees left the premises and the owner of the company began to drink his afternoon brandy in his office and walked inside and shot him three times in the chest. After cleaning the floor, he wrapped the body in plastic and picked up the phone and called the owner of the rival steel company and told him what he did, in order to solve the problem between him and his employer and told him that in exchange for doing so, he wants him to buy the company he works for and give him the position of his former employer.

To his surprise, he wanted nothing of it going as far as to threaten to call the police and have him thrown in jail, a threat which 'Leader' responded to by laughing until the man put the phone down after which 'Leader' called him for a second time. When he realised, he had done so and told him that if he did not meet his demands, he would make it look like it was he who did it and that doing so would come very easily as he thought about doing so before going through with it. When 'Leader' put the phone down he sat back in his employer's chair, poured himself a glass of brandy and drank until the early hours of the morning, that day became the first day in the three-year string of days in 'Leader's' bloody and unjust rise to success.

In the bathroom, 'Leader' had just finished wiping down his body with a washcloth and after throwing it in the laundry basket he stands in his boxer shorts with his arms out and his legs spread to the side so that he can air dry himself while waiting for the bathtub to fill. When it is halfway full, 'Leader' gets inside and lays back to enjoy the lukewarm water 'wrapped' around his body and after three-quarters of an hour, after he waited for the skin under his hands to become the texture of a raisin, always doing when taking a bath as he believed that when that happened, it is the body's way of saying that the fluids that was lost throughout each day due to urination, perspiration and the like is replenished. He got out of the tub very carefully as he always does after suffering a bad fall doing so a couple of years prior, where he broke his tailbone and was unable to take the baths. He so enjoyed for almost a month and dried himself off and went to his bedroom to get dressed.

After doing so he wrote Layli a note to say that he had to go into town and will be back around two in the afternoon and put the note down on his pillow next to her and went down to the kitchen to make himself a cup of coffee that he poured down the sink after tasting it, because it tasted more like dirty water than coffee.

Before he left, he went to the back room, where the four men that work for him were sleeping and woke them up by clapping his hands and told the two who looked like they were sleeping in the most uncomfortable positions and probably had the most to drink the night before they had to come with him; so that they might be able to sweat out the excess alcohol in their bodies, helping him run a few errands. To the other two men, he told when they woke up that they could either go back to sleep or come with him to see what they would do, as soon as he told them they could go back to sleep they put their heads back down on their pillows and did just that.

While 'Leader' and the two men were away Bees, Clarafina and Layli had the breakfast that Layli told Clarafina that she would prepare for them the night before and turned out to be much less uncomfortable than Clarafina had thought considering what happened the night before after Bees, who for the first time in a very long time felt excited enough to want to drink more than usual while he waited for 'Leader' to return, Clarafina feeling relieved enough that the interaction between her and Layli the night before turned out to be much less uncomfortable than she thought it would do not want to drink and Layli enjoying time to herself without her overprotective husband looking over her shoulder.

When 'Leader' pulled up in the driveway he was pleased to find Bees on the porch with a drink in his hand and after greeting him put his head inside the door. 'Ladies, would you be so kind as to come outside, please?' He walks over to the table and pulls out a chair and sits down.

When Clarafina and Layli step onto the porch they are greeted with a wave from Bees, a nod from 'Leader' and two motioned tips of hats from 'Leader's' men before they went back to their room. Layli sits down on 'Leader's' lap, he puts his hand on the top of her thigh and pinches her skin between his fingers, something he only does when he is in high spirits and tells Layli that, even though she in no way could have been a fly on the wall and more so even wouldn't want to be given the chance as the nature of the conversations that 'Leader' had, during such occasions would send anyone with half a heart running up the same wall and through the roof, whatever he had to go into town to discuss went very well. When the eagerness from 'Leader's' fingers subsided, he takes his hand off her leg. 'Will you ladies be kind enough to prepare us something to eat?'

'Sure,' says Layli.

'Very good,' says 'Leader', thinking to himself that spending the day drinking and having conversations in town with potential business partners which consisted of nothing more than trying to better each other until one party had to succumb to the other's demands, the brunt thereof consisting mostly of putting forth pretences, to make it seem like neither of them had to give in to the demands of the other and Layli obliging so politely to his request makes him feel almost guilty for being able to ask it in so expecting a manner. 'Would you like the help of one of the hands?'

'No thank you dear, we'll manage fine.'

'Are you sure, they might be of some help?'

'I wouldn't have it to have help preparing you breakfast.'

'Leader' smiles. 'If that is what you want then that is what you will have...' he says with a somewhat sly smile. 'Now go and do your best to surprise the man who has everything.'

Layli kisses 'Leader' on the cheek and her and Clarafina make their way to the kitchen, just past the staircase Clarafina turns to Layli. 'Is he always so...?'

'What?'

'Scary?'

Layli laughs. 'Why would you say that?'

'It's how he talks. I've never heard a man ask things from a woman like he does and I have been very close with a couple of very bad apples in my life.'

'I cannot say that I know what you are talking about?' Layli says as they start toward the kitchen again.

Once inside after having started to prepare breakfast, Clarafina grabs Layli by the arm. 'If you want me to kill him, I will?'

Layli laughs. 'You're being silly.'

'I really will do it, even if I get hurt doing so.'

'You're being silly, let's just make the men their breakfast.'

After a couple of minutes, Clarafina asks, 'Have you ever thought about getting a divorce?'

'I think he'll kill me if I try to do that.'

Clarafina's eyes widen. 'Really?'

Layli laughs. 'No, I'm just kidding.'

'Do you think he will let you if you want to?'

'I don't know.'

'Do you want to?'

'No, why would you ask that?'

'I don't know, he just doesn't seem like the type of man that any woman would want to be with.'

'You don't know him very well then.'

Clarafina laughs. 'And I am glad.'

Layli laughs. 'Let's not talk about this now, we're having so much fun making breakfast.'

Bees turns to 'Leader'. 'Does 'WMP' stand for anything?'

'What would you say?'

'I don't know.'

'It does.'

'What does it stand for?'

'White Man Power.'

Bees pauses. 'That's very good.'

'Better than that even is that it can be read as a single phrase or three separate words.'

Bees nods. 'That's very good too.'

That night Klipp is in his room sitting on his bed with a backpack next to him, down the hallway the floorboards creak as Clarafina, who is usually the last to go to bed, makes her way from the bathroom to her bedroom to go to sleep. Klipp waits to hear her start to snore at which he gets up and slings his backpack over his shoulder and climbs out of his window and down the drainpipe next to it to the ground. There, he locks the back door by the kitchen and takes out of his backpack two pieces of rope and ties it around the door handle of the back kitchen door and the door to the back room where 'Leader's' workers are sleeping, before walking around the house and locking the front door with the set of keys hanging on the wall next to it and takes the other set of keys as well and puts it in his backpack, before walking over to the window from a room used as a storeroom opposite the living room and cutting the wire on a phone standing on a desk standing by the window with a pocket knife and closing the window.

which took longer to do than tying ropes around both the door handles at the back of the house seeing as they have been closed maybe two or three times since before Bees was born, and tying it shut with another piece of rope and walks to the living room window and does the same with the phone by it as well as the window—before making his way along the edge of the lawn to the cabin.

Inside, the workers are sitting with suitcases packed by their feet, Klipp knocks on the door and they get up and pick up their belongings and make their way to the door, where they meet Klipp and together they make their way—at the suggestion of Petrus—up the ladder against the rise in ground next to the cabin, to lessen the chances of them being seen by someone from the house might they wake up. When they are all standing with their luggage on the rise in ground next to the cabin, they start the walk toward the driveway gate.

Once there, Klipp, Tynum and Dwendo take as much of the luggage as they can and begin to load it into the trucks before Klipp makes his way to the truck standing behind the first to start it so they can begin their getaway. When Klipp opens the driver door, though what he sees makes any thought of an escape a very sudden impossibility. Upon opening the door, he sees, with much help from the light in the roof of the truck, 'Leader' in his pyjamas and slippers in the

305

passenger seat, his penis exposed and erect, with a pistol in one hand and Lumeo knelt on the driver seat with his head positioned over his 'Leader's' crotch.

The moment the door opens, 'Leader' gets such a fright that he inadvertently pulls the trigger of which the bullet of the shot fired grazes Lumeo's ear bursting his eardrum before going through 'Leader's' foot and the floor to get lost somewhere in the mechanics of the truck. 'Leader' quickly pulls his pyjama pants up over his still erect penis and 'rips' another pistil from a holster around his waist and pushes himself out of the passenger seat and onto solid ground.

Klipp ducks for cover behind the driver door as Tynum and Dwendo rush toward 'Leader' who brings them both to a screeching halt when they see his pistols pointed to each of their heads. 'Leader' smiles a sly smile. 'Well, hello, Goliath and Goliath,' he says. 'Not so scary when you have guns pointed to your heads now, are we? Now take two steps back each of you, so I can be more sure of my safety.'

Dwendo and Tynum take two steps back each. 'Leader' nods. 'Very good.' Now…' 'Leader' lowers his pistols and shoots Tynum and Dwendo in one of their knees each. They go down. 'Leader' laughs at both Tynum and Dwendo on their backs holding onto their injured knees. 'Hurts, doesn't it?' he asks. 'They say the knee is one of the most painful places to get shot, abbra kadabra, I shoot you each in one of your knees.'

Just then Klipp comes rushing around the front of the truck and tries to tackle 'Leader' to the ground but fails to do so as 'Leader' heard him coming and knocked him down on the head with one of his pistols. Klipp takes a couple of steps back as the knock he took sends him to mild disarray. Tynum and Dwendo both 'scurrel' to get up in an attempt to do the same to 'Leader' as Klipp wanted to but because of their injuries are unable to do so in time and 'Leader' shoots each of them in their other knees as well. 'Stay down, will you?' He says without any hint of bother.

Dwendo and Tynum fall back down on the ground onto their backs again. 'Leader' turns to Klipp. 'You, lights out, make your way slowly over here and go and stand next to your two dogs so that me and my two friends here, can make sure that you lot don't get up to any funny business.' With his hand on his head, Klipp makes his way over to where Tynum and Dwendo are. 'Leader' takes a step back and closes the passenger door of the truck with his back and stands up against it. 'Now that we are all a safe distance from each other, I can casually kill you.'

'I don't think that will be a very good idea,' says Klipp to 'Leader'.

'And why would that be?'

'Because if you kill us, you'll surely be killed yourself.'

'How so?'

'If you shoot us, you'll have to shoot Lumeo and my aunt and uncle when they come outside, which they probably are right now because of the shot you fired.'

'I have more guns in my truck.'

'The rest of the workers are all by the gate, they are waiting there with weapons in case something like this happens.'

'I'll kill them too.'

'They're more than you think they are.'

'I have more guns than you think I do.'

Just then they hear a shot fired from inside the house and turn around and see the door being kicked open and Bees, Clarafina and Layli stepping out onto the porch, Bees with a rifle to his shoulder and Clarafina two pistols out in front of her. 'What is going on here?' Bees asks.

'I caught your nephew and the two you see lying in front of you as well as another in the truck behind me trying to break into it.'

Bees walks down the porch steps points his rifle at Klipp. 'Is this true nephew?'

'No uncle Bees.'

'Then why is Mr Gultherton saying it is?'

'I don't know.'

Bees points his rifle at 'Leader'.

'Don't point that thing at me.'

Bees lowers his rifle. 'Who is lying here?'

'Who do you think is lying? Or better yet who do you want to be the one lying?'

Bees frowns. 'What do you mean?'

'If your nephew is lying, you get everything I promised you, if I am lying you get nothing.'

Bees points his rifle at Klipp. 'Why are you lying nephew?'

'I'm not.'

'Are you saying then that he is?'

Klipp nods.

'The point is not to find out who is lying but to make a choice as to who you think is lying.'

'I don't know who is lying.'

'Then I might as well shoot you right here.'

'If you do that my sister will shoot you.'

'I'll shoot your sister before she is able to shoot me.'

'Then Klipp or Tynum or Dwendo will shoot you.'

'They don't have guns.'

'They can use mine or Clarafina's.'

'If you shoot me, you'll die here a poor man on a farm that will be dead before you are.'

'If I don't shoot you, you will shoot me.'

'Why would I want to do that?'

'What do you want to do then?'

'I want you to give your nephew the hiding that he deserves and for us to go ahead with our plan as we would have.'

Bees looks at Clarafina from the corner of his eye.

'What plan?' Clarafina asks.

'Leader' looks at Bees. 'Do you want to tell her?'

'I don't know what he is talking about.'

'Then why did he say you have to tell me something?'

'I don't know.'

'Leader' lowers his pistol. 'Your brother and I planned on killing the priest and the rest of the workers because they are causing us unwanted problems.'

'What problems?'

'That is none of your business.'

Clarafina points one of her pistols at 'Leader's' head. 'This is my farm Mr Gultherton, and whatever happens on it is my business.'

'Not when it concerns someone of my stature.'

'What are you doing out here than Mr Gultherton and why do you want to kill our workers?'

'I told you that is none of your business.'

'What's to stop me from shooting you right now?'

'Why do you want to shoot me in the first place?'

'Because you want to shoot our workers.'

'Supposedly.'

'Do you, or don't you?' Clarafina turns to Bees.

'We have to kill the workers because Petrus and they are running amuck in town every time they go there,' Bees says reluctantly.

'Running amuck how?'

'That is none of your business...' says 'Leader'. 'What is your business is this...' He pushes the nose of the barrel of his pistol against Clarafina's chest... Just then the four men that work for 'Leader' come running around the house with a rifle each pressed to their shoulders, they stop a couple of feet away from where 'Leader' is standing.

'Are you okay, boss?' One of them asks.

'Not quite, I caught Mr Brungle's nephew and the priest trying to break into my truck.'

The men point their rifles at respective targets. 'Do you want us to take care of them, boss?' Asks another one of the workers.

'No, keep the two on the ground and the sister and the nephew here, while I go speak to Mr Brungle for a bit.'

The men nod and make their way over to where Clarafina, Klipp and Tynum and Dwendo are.

'And make sure the one in the truck doesn't get up to any funny business.'

'There's one of them in the truck?' Asks one of the workers.

'Yes,' answers 'Leader'.

'What is he doing in their boss?'

'He was trying to break into it.'

The workers nod. 'I'll take really good care of him boss.'

'You better, I pay the four of you enough.'

'Dear, I think it's best you come down here where it's safer.' 'Leader' calls out to Layli. She makes her way down the porch steps and stands next to Clarafina.

'Make sure they don't go anywhere while we're gone.'

The men nod.

'Come with me, Mr Brungle.'

Bees follows 'Leader' to the opposite side of the truck. 'Do you still want to be president, Mr Brungle?' He asks as he takes a rifle and a pistol out of the truck.

Bees nods.

'Then follow me.'

They start toward the cabin.

One of the men points his rifle at Klipp, 'What were you trying to break into my boss's truck for?'

'He wants to kill the workers so we wanted to get away.'

'Why does he want to kill the workers?'

'I'm not sure.'

The worker pushes the 'nose' of his rifle against Klipp's forehead. 'Then think young buck because I want from you an answer.'

'Sorry but I don't know.'

'I said I want an answer.'

'Now, now guys, let's just stay calm and wait for Rutther to come back,' says Layli.

A third of 'Leader's' men points his gun at Layli, she holds up her hands. 'The boss said not to talk.'

'No, he didn't,' says Clarafina.

The worker turns to Clarafina. 'Not with words, but he definitely wanted me to tell it to you if you did.'

'No talking then,' says Layli. 'Got it.'

After almost ten minutes, everyone standing by the porch hears a shot fired from inside the cabin and turn their attention to it. The workers look at each other. 'Are you thinking that is what I'm thinking it is?' Asks one of the workers to the other.

'If you think it's boss taking out one of the couple of others, then yes, I think it is what you think it is.'

'Do you think we should go check it out?'

Another of the workers look at the two currently talking with one another. 'Of course, you should go check it out, boss might be in need of our help, you know how many of them are there.'

'Which one of us is going to go? I don't feel like dying tonight.'

The four workers look to and fro between each other. 'I'm not going.' They say in unison.

After a couple of seconds of silence, one of the workers respond. 'We'll flip a coin to see who goes?'

'Good idea, does any one of us have a coin in our pockets?'

The workers check their pockets. After a while, one of them holds out in front of him a gold coin.

'Great,' says one of the workers.

'Who goes when?' Another asks.

'If it falls on tails the two of you go and if it falls on heads the two of us will go.'

The workers nod. 'Go ahead.'

The worker with the coin flips it into the air with his thumb, catches it in mid-air and places it on the top part of his other hand. He looks down at the coin and then up at the other workers. 'It's heads,' he says.

Two of the workers nod and hold their rifles steady to their chests. 'Are you sure you'll be able to handle this lot here, only the two of you?'

One of the workers hold up their rifles. 'Look at the size of this thing, I'll think we'll be fine.'

The two workers that are going to the cabin nod. 'Wish us luck.'

'Good luck.' The other two say as the workers that picked the side of the coin that was tails make their way to the cabin. The two remaining workers turn to Layli, Clarafina and Klipp. 'Don't think that because we are now just two that you can try anything funny?'

Layli shakes her head.

'No two worries about it,' says Clarafina.

After a while Clarafina's eyes widen. 'Bees?' She mumbles. She steps past 'Leader's' two remaining men.

'Where do you think you're going?'

Clarafina turns around. 'To see if my brother is okay.'

'You're not allowed to do that.'

'Are you going to stop me?'

'If you walk any further, yes.'

'Sorry to hear that,' Clarafina turns around and runs as fast as she can over the lawn to the cabin.

The two remaining workers look at each other. 'Should we just let her go?' Asks one to the other. They stare back at each other for a while. 'Let Jummert and Jush take care of her.' They laugh.

Running her way to the cabin, a bullet flies past Clarafina. So startled she is by it that she ducks to take cover almost automatically. After looking around very nervously to see if she might be able to tell where the bullet came from, she gets back up and continues toward the cabin when she deems the grounds and dark sky clear of any trouble. A couple of steps later, she sees 'Leader's' two men that went to go help him standing a few feet away from her with the scopes of their rifles pressed to their eyes readying what it looks like to her to shoot her.

She stands still and holds up both of her pistols, just as she is about to pull the triggers, she hears another shot fired, this one not from one of the rifles of the two of 'Leader's' men standing in front of her. Perturbed by where the shot might have come from, she moves to one side to see if she might be able to make out where it did.

Just as she is about to step new foot on the ground, she sees one of the men standing in front of her fall to the ground. Just as she wants to make a run for it, she hears yet another shot fired and sees after the second of 'Leader's' two men standing in front of her fall down on the ground next to his comrade. After regaining whatever of her composure that was lost from witnessing two men get killed in front of her, she sees 'Leader' with his rifle out in front of him walking toward her. Just as she wants to shoot him 'Leader' fires at her and hits her in the chest. Her vision goes blank.

When 'Leader' reaches the driveway again Klipp, Layli, Tynum and Dwendo are still where they were when 'Leader' left them with his two remaining men still watching over them with their rifles. 'Boss, what is going on?' Asks one of the men.

'These people planned on pulling one over on us from the very beginning, when we got to the cabin Mr Brungle tried to shoot me.'

The man's eyes widen. 'Did he?'

'Leader' frowns. 'What do you mean did he?'

'Sorry boss, glad you are okay.'

'What was going on here while I was gone?'

'These lot were causing a lot of trouble.'

'What were they doing?'

'They talked too much.'

'Who was talking too much.'

The man points his rifle at Layli. 'What was she saying?' 'Leader' asks.

'She was just talking too much.'

'Talking too much how?'

'Just saying things that make us angry.'

'Leader' holds his pistol to the man's head. 'What did she say to do a thing like that?'

Just then they hear a groan coming from the truck, the men along with 'Leader' point their guns at the truck. 'What was that?' Asks one of the men.

'I don't know...' says the other. 'Let's go take a look.'

'What are you idiots on about?' says 'Leader'. 'Didn't you hear me say to you to keep a watchful eye over the one in truck besides the two left here?'

The workers look at each other and laugh. 'Oh yes.' They say in unison and look back at 'Leader'. 'We remember boss, sorry about that.'

'Leader' waves away their snickering. 'Just keep quiet and keep watch.' He says and opens the passenger door and shoots Lumeo in the head.

His men look at him with wide eyes.

'You've seen worse.'

'Where is my aunt and uncle, sir?' Klipp asks.

'They're dead, now, here is what is going to happen, the two of you are going to go to your room and pack your belongings, while Layli goes to ours and packs the same, then we'll meet back here in ten minutes.'

The men nod. 'What about this one?'

'Leader' looks at Klipp. 'Get a rope and tie him up.'

The men nod.

'In the truck there should be some.'

The men walk to the back of the truck and rummage around to find a piece of rope, when they have it, they walk back to Klipp and tie his hands and feet together. 'Now what?'

'Now you go pack.'

They walk around the house to the back room.

'Leader' looks at Layli. 'Dear, ten minutes.'

'Okay.' Layli makes her up the porch steps into the house to their bedroom.

Inside the back room 'Leader's' men are packing their belongings, one turns to the other. 'You know that thing we've been talking about?'

The man nods.

'Now might be the time to do it.'

Back outside 'Leader's' two men are packing their and his and Layli's luggage into the back of the truck, once finished they walk over to 'Leader' and Layli with their rifles in hand and point both at the back of 'Leader's' head.

313

'Leader's' eyes widen. 'What are you doing?'

'It has come to our attention boss that you have not been paying us enough for how you have been treating us.'

'Your point?'

'You have to pay us more.'

'And if I don't?'

'Then we'll have to shoot you.'

'If you shoot me what is going to happen to you?'

'We'll take the money you've been talking about?'

'Where are you going to find that money?'

'You're going to tell us.'

'And if I don't?'

'Then we're going to shoot you.'

'What's to stop me from shooting you, now that you've threatened to do the same with me?'

'If you say you're going to kill us we're going to kill your boss.'

'If you kill me now, you'll have no way of knowing where the money is, and after killing me, you'll have to kill everyone else here or they'll probably kill you, and after that even if you do find the money, you won't be able to make use of it because there will be too many questions surrounding how you came to want the money.'

The second of 'Leader's' men presses the nose of his rifle onto the back of 'Leader's' head. 'Then we'll just kill you now.'

'Leader' turns around. 'If you do that you won't be able to work for me anymore and you'll have no way of making money.'

'We'll get other jobs then.'

'That might not be as easy as you think after doing what you plan on, and even if you do, they won't pay nearly as much as I do.'

'What do you want us to do then?'

'Leader' turns around. 'You're going to drive us away from here and when we get back, I'm going to give you more money than you can know what to do with and then you're going to leave and make sure that I never see you again.'

The men look at each other and back at 'Leader' and nod. 'Okay.'

'Sounds good,' says the other.

'Get in the truck then.'

They turn around and get into the truck.

'Not the same truck, you over here and you over there.'

One of the men get out of the truck and start toward the one behind it.

'And put your rifles in the back here,' 'Leader' says to the workers.

He nods and does so, as soon as he gets into the truck 'Leader' takes a pistol out from under his pyjama pants and shoots the worker sitting in the front truck.

The remaining worker yells to 'Leader' from the back truck. 'Boss?'

'Leader' walks to the second truck in the line of two behind each other and puts his head in the window. 'Yes, number whatever your name is?'

'What happened?'

'I shot your friend.'

'Why did you do that?'

'To make it easier for me to kill you when the time comes.'

'When are you going to do that?'

'Right now.'

The man reaches over his shoulder for his rifle that is usually slung over it.

'Leader' laughs. 'I told you to put it away remember?'

The man looks back at 'Leader' and nods.

'Get the other one of you out of my truck so we can leave.'

The man nods. 'What about this one?'

'Leave it.'

The man walks over to the first truck and lifts the other man off and out of the driver seat and gets inside.

'Get inside dear.'

'I think we should stay here for a little while longer.'

'Why?'

'I don't trust him to keep us safe.'

'Leader' holds up his pistol. 'That's what this is for.'

'How are you going to know he wants to do something to us? He might have two or more guns on him now, you know how many they keep with them?'

'He won't dare, he'll probably forget how to walk if he kills me.'

'I don't know,' Layli says somewhat worried.

'Leader' looks at her suspiciously. 'Are you saying that you would rather stay here than come back home with me?'

'No.'

'Then what are you saying?'

'I'm saying that it might be better if we stay here for a little while for him cool down, he just lost three of his friends and is probably angry about it.'

'This is definitely not the place for him to do that, then.'

'Why don't you go check if he has any guns on him?'

'He might shoot me if I do.'

Out from the corner of her eye Layli sees Petrus.

'It will be much harder for him to shoot us if he's driving.'

'How so?'

'Because of what you're holding.'

'I'll be holding it in the truck as well.'

'You'll be more easily distracted in the truck.'

'He might be wondering why you have your pistol with you, it will be harder to keep a close eye on him, we might need to pull over somewhere for some reason and that could turn out to be problematic somehow?'

'What will be different if we stay here?'

Just as Layli is about to speak, Kolos puts his arm around 'Leader's' neck and chokes him until he is unconscious and lays him down on the ground. The last remaining worker jumps out of the truck and tries to get away but falls to the ground almost immediately when he steps outside. He hits the ground with a loud thud. A few feet in front of the driveway gate stands Petrus with a piece of material in one hand and a couple of small rocks in the other.

Shortly after two in the early morning, 'Leader' and the man that works for him are sitting by the kitchen table, on the table is a bullet proof vest with two compressed bullets sticking out from it and 'Leader's' pistol in front of him, with their hands tied behind their backs behind the backrest of the chairs on which they are sitting and their feet tied up by their ankles to the bottom of them. Around the table is standing Clarafina with two pistols, one each pointed at 'Leader' and the man that works for him, Klipp with 'Leader's' rifle, Petrus and Kolos and Dwendo beside 'Leader' and his worker respectively.

'Are you just going to stand there, Ms Brungle, or are you going to do something?' 'Leader' asks, agitated.

'I'm going to stand here until we figure out what to do with you.'

'And how long do you think that is going to take?'

'As soon as you tell us where the money is that you came here for.'

'I will be dead before I do that.'

'No, you won't, you'll be working for me here from morning to night until you tell me what I want to know or until you are as you just said.'

'How are you going to make that happen?'

'Look around you.'

'I'll be dead before I let any of them tell me what to do.'

'Fine by me, Mr Gultherton.'

'If you kill me there's going to be a lot of people after you, I told many an associate of mine where I was going before I came here.'

'I'm not going to kill you, Mr Gultherton.'

'You'll have to, if you want any more out of me other than sitting at this table.'

'Where is the money, Mr Gultherton?'

'I don't know what you are talking about.'

Clarafina lowers her pistols. 'Have a good night then, Mr Gultherton, see you in the morning.' She turns to Klipp, 'Do you and Kolos and Dwendo mind staying here with Mr Gultherton and his friend for the night to make sure they do not get up to any trouble?'

Klipp nods. 'Sure, auntie Clarafina.'

'Thank you, nephew, see you in the morning.'

'You too, goodnight.'

She gives a pistol each to Kolos and Dwendo. 'In case you need it.'

They nod.

'Goodnight Petrus, see you in the morning too.'

Petrus nods. 'Goodnight, Miss Clarafina.'

Clarafina picks up 'Leader's' pistol… 'If you don't mind, Mr Gultherton?' And makes her way out of the kitchen and up the stairs to her bedroom.

An hour or so after Clarafina fell asleep, Klipp knocked on her door to wake her up to come down to the kitchen, when she got their 'Leader' and his worker was sitting on their chairs just as they were when she left them, 'Leader' with his hands hanging by his sides, both him and his worker sitting face down on the table with a bullet wound to the side of their heads.

A couple of minutes after she went to bed, 'Leader' managed to free himself by his hands and from a holster attached to the bottom of his leg pulled out a pistol about the size of his hand and shot his worker in the head before shooting

Dwendo twice in the chest, before turning the gun on Kolos but realised he was out of bullets when he pulled the trigger, when Kolos tried to take the pistol from him he grabbed the one that Clarafina gave him and turned it on himself.

Chapter 18

Two years later, the farm looked much different from how it did the weekend 'Leader' came to visit, the morning after he shot himself and his worker Petrus and Klipp buried him and the worker he shot as well as the others and Bees and Lumeo behind the house under a bunch of lime trees.

Later that day Klipp, Petrus and Desta, a 70-year-old man who lived on the farm before Petrus came to, walked around the decaying fields of crop in order to see what they would be able to salvage. After an hour they decided that they would strip the cornfield and the vineyard and plant on its wheat too, it took a month to do during which they did the same with the wheat, a quarter of which was used to grow it over the entirety of the three pieces of land while the remainder was used to make flour with.

Other than the changes with the crops, another was an addition of a second workers cabin, quite a bit bigger than the old one and consisted of a sleeping and bathroom area adjacent to each other on one side of the cabin, a kitchen in the centre and a living room with a television set and a couple of couches around it next to it.

Along with the cabin, many changes were made to the house—in that the pieces of wood that were not as healthy as the others, in that they had cracks in them and were heavily deteriorated were replaced and the new as well as old pieces of wood were painted over white on the outside while all of the inside other than the various rooms, which was painted different colours, the bedrooms and bathrooms the same light yellow and white respectively, the kitchen and pantry light brown and the living room a light yellow too, the other rooms were left as was before.

Other than the changes to the immediate surface décor of the rooms the living room, which was before the renovations the most spacious room in the house because of the many things from it that Bees and Clarafina had to sell, underwent the biggest change aesthetically with additions of two new couches that matched the remaining one to a degree that made it look like they were a set.

In between the couches, that sat half rectangular to each other the width of the living room, was a flat piece of wood which Tynum and Kolos found at the bottom of the mountain one day while they were out looking for firewood, about knee height and the size of a piano in front of the television set next to the fireplace across from where the piano stood, where now is standing the same piano that Clarafina had to sell a couple of years prior that Klipp found in a used music store in town; after the lady who it was sold to had no more use for it.

Many of the floorboards around the house were also replaced with all of that which made up the kitchen floor being so due to the blood from 'Leader' shooting himself and his worker as well as the curtains and a couple of the windows from most of the rooms as well as the bedding from all.

In the bedrooms, slept Klipp, in the one he did when he first came to the farm, Bees' room is standing empty, Clarafina is sleeping in her room next to Layli sleeping where her and 'Leader' slept while the fifth room is still the guest room.

When it came time to harvest the wheat after almost two years, half of it was used to make flour with while the other was sold to an associate of 'Leader's'. Three-quarters of the flour was sold to various people for various reasons, while the remainder was used to bake bread with over a large fire that Tynum and Dwendo built behind the cabin, it came out very well and whoever tried it said that it was of the best bread that they had had.

Even Layli, who on various vacations with 'Leader' throughout their time together, tried many a type of bread from many a country around the world, mostly due to that instead of harvesting the wheat when needed to let dry as usual, they let it do so for three months after harvest time while still in the ground so that it may be more moist before putting it within a certain proximity by a fire to let it dry quickly so that each seed may retain its moisture qualities better and do so in a more hardened and buoyant manner after being harvested to give the bread when finished baking, a more airy texture than usual.

After which Nleeclo, who had the idea to use the flour to bake bread with as well as to harvest and care for it in the manner in which they did, said that her and the rest of the women, would they want to, should bake bread on a bigger scale to try and sell at the flea market every Sunday.

That following Sunday Nleeclo, along with Lavetta, Varieda and Xhema and Scara and Finta used the remainder of the flour to bake more bread with, this time with more thought put into it in terms of what they planned on doing with it as well as what they used to bake it with which was two ovens built from various stones found in the mountain that made up the physical foundations of the ovens as well as smaller stones or pieces of rock as they are when pulled or dug from the walls that make up various parts of the mountain behind the cabin.

The Sunday after the second batch was finished, they drove into town and set up a table at the flea market and after five hours, came back with everything they took with them. During the following week they baked another batch of bread, which they drove into town with again on Sunday and set up the same table as the Sunday before and set out all of their baked goods along with a container filled with red wine. they gave away to people for free during the day, to their surprise many people came back for more as well as wanted to buy various and different loaves, buns and rolls and after the day was over, they went back to the farm with a couple of loaves of bread and an empty container of wine.

The week after the second Sunday, the workers were at the flea market. They spent the entire week baking as many bread rolls, buns, sticks and various kinds of loaves of bread as they can before putting them in brown paper bags and tying a string around each to keep them fresh, that Sunday, the workers had on their table an example of each of the kinds of bread they baked along with a tray of butter, a jar of honey and a jar of apricot, strawberry and fig jam along with a small spreading knife for each jar; as well as the tray of butter and a spoon for the honey. Within four hours all that was left on the table was the tray of butter, pot of honey and the three jars of jam.

They made 1080 Munto and with it after packing up they went to the deli in town to buy various small ingredients such as olives, pickled onions, cherry tomatoes and the like as well as a couple of different kinds of spices and herbs to bake the next batch of bread with.

Over the coming two weeks, Nleeclo and the rest of the women decided on three different combinations of flavours of the various ingredients and extracted from each their primary source thereof and made, along with a thickening agent, three different flavours which they used to knead the dough with to make three different types of flavoured bread with.

Over the next three months, every time the workers went into town to the flea market each Sunday, everything they brought with them sold out long before the day was over with people stopping by for a second time even to buy more. Because of this they started to take orders from various families in the district as well as those surrounding, which they filled within a week or two before they went back. A year or so after the first Sunday they set up their table, it became somewhat of a staple to have a loaf of bread made by them on the table, be it sweet or savoury, along with butter or honey or any kind of jam or other savoury or sweet spread, to be had during breakfast, lunch and dinner as a starter or dessert.

Despite all the success of the baking venture, the downside was that the business of the only two other bakeries in town declined quite quickly after the first year the workers spent their Sunday mornings to afternoons at the flea market and the owners developed ill feelings toward them and tried many a ploy to stifle the workers' venture. Both bakeries were almost a hundred years old and family owned and were called 'The Golden Heart Bakery' and 'The Bakery of Golden Heart,' each was opened on the same day by a couple that used to be best friends.

One Friday night after work, they were having dinner to celebrate the end of the work week as they did every other Friday night each week discussing business ideas, back then, the people of Golden Heart baked everything that needed to be themselves and so did either of the couples. When they hosted the other for dinner and so the idea to open a bakery entered the conversation, both couples immediately grew very fond of the idea and wanted to do about what they were talking. After quite some time arguing about the idea, the couples went their separate ways and two months passed between them without any contact.

After both opened their respective bakeries on opposite ends of town and for the next almost hundred years, two generations of both families supplied the people of Golden Heart with various baked goods savoury and sweet and a service of sorts which they were not used to as well as created a divide of much insignificance between the people of Golden Heart.

After almost a year, the workers took their profit along with money that Clarafina lent them to rent a small space in town which they wanted to use to open the bakery considering the orders they were getting became too much and they needed a bigger space to accommodate all of it. a little more than two weeks after Nleeclo went to Clarafina to ask for money to open the bakery; 'The Baker's Blanket' opened its doors to the people of Golden Heart.

A couple of months after the bakery opened, Layli and Scara had the idea to start a clothing line, this happened when Layli found Scara in the garage making a dress which led them to talking about how much they enjoyed flipping through the pages of fashion magazines and how they have both entertained the idea of starting a clothing line which led them to talking about doing so, even if it was just for themselves.

Around this time, Scara came across a string of petals that made its way from one of the trees to the ground next to the old cabin of which the petals were very dry having laid there for quite some time. When she picked a petal from it, she found that it can be easily pulled apart and becomes almost like wool when done. She took the string of petals to Layli and asked whether she thinks it will be possible to make wool or yarn from it, upon looking closer at it, she found that it will be possible as the petal becomes almost like fluffs of cotton when pulled apart when dried out and that when rolling together the fluffs in certain ways, it becomes quite easily like wool or yarn.

They then went to the dam to count how many strings of how many petals hung from each tree, after almost half an hour they counted about 250 strings of petals with 900 or so petals on each and figured that with the leaves from each tree they will be able to make 125 spools of thread of 300 meters each, and the same amount of yarns of wool of 100 meters each, around the dam there are five trees and once plucked each leaf grows back within three months.

The following day, Layli and Scara sat in the living room discussing and sketching ideas for various pieces of clothing, the first being a denim dungaree but instead of having two pant legs it has a skirt that comes down to the middle the thighs, the second was a leather top with sleeves unusually short, of which the body leaves the midriff exposed and a collar quite big with buttons that closes the top, the third was a loose fitting T-shirt that comes down the just above the knees made from wool, while the fourth was a dress, the sleeves of which was layers of dress straps that hung over the shoulders with the bottom of the dress coming down the just above the knees, enclosed by a set of buttons so it may be worn open or closed in that manner.

After they sketched the ideas for the four pieces of clothing on four separate pieces of paper they started to talk about a name for their brand and after five minutes they decided on the name 'Layli Scara' and right after started making patterns for the clothes, two for each piece of clothing, one in Layli's size and another in Scara's, who is considerably shorter than Layli.

The following day, they went to town to look for materials other than the yarn or wool, they would be able to make from the petals to make the clothes with, after getting all the material they needed and a couple of other necessities they bought a second sowing machine and loaded everything into one of 'Leader's' trucks and drove back to the farm to set everything up in the garage.

The remainder of the day they spent, with the help of the rest of the women, picking each and every leaf from all five of the trees by the dam and letting them dry for a day, before pulling each petal apart into its cotton like fluffs and rolling it into wool as well as making thread from it which they did by using a heap of the petal fibres of which a small amount is made into a piece of thread by pulling it through the eye of a needle before being soaked in a bowl of ice water to strengthen the fibres, a method which they forewent seeing as it took too long to make too little thereof.

After three months, when the trees around the dam looked as they did before, then Scara and Layli plucked them once more and laid them out to dry and picked them apart into many bundles of fibres and put into a couple of boxes and went to the post office with to have them shipped to a textile company a week's drive away from Camel's Neck to have yarn and wool made from them, three weeks after they went to the post office they went back to collect their order and drove back to the farm with five boxes of 325 spools of thread of 300 meters, 200 of which was used to make a sheet of material with, and 60 yarns of wool of 100 meters each.

Once back at the house, they got to work behind their respective sewing machines and after almost a week of working ten hours a day they ended up with 12 pieces of each of the items of clothing they wanted to make. a month after that, three clothing stores in town had a couple of items from 'Layli Scara' on their racks.

The money for the renovations to the house as well as the second cabin and other additions to the house came from the suitcase full of money that 'Leader' came to the farm, to find out where it might be. Coming there to talk to Bees about joining the WMP, a couple of years before Grandpa Brungle passed; he buried a suitcase full of money that he stole from 'Leader's' office because he felt that him and other men high up in the party made unfair use of the people that helped them establish it and also because he claimed that some of the policies that Grandpa Brungle put forth was his own.

Grandpa Brungle broke into his office late one night and took from the safe whatever money was there, the following morning when 'Leader' went into his office and saw the safe broken into and all the money as well as other valuables that was inside, missing. He was not able to implicate anyone but knew that it had to be someone from the WMP because if his office were ever to be broken into, it could only have been someone from the WMP or someone very close to him.

Later that day, after the sun had set, Grandpa Brungle walked up Camel's Neck Mountain and buried the suitcase full of money three-quarters of the way up, a quarter for each letter in 'WMP,' so that he can more easily remember where he buried the money were he to lose the map he drew of where he buried it, which he did. A couple of days after he drew it, Bees found it in his office and thought it to be a plaything of sorts and took it to his room and put away in one of his drawers after not being able to figure out where it might be of.

During the renovations of the house, Layli came across it in Bees' old room and showed it to Clarafina who recognised Grandpa Brungle's handwriting as well as that it is of Camel's Neck Mountain and also what area on the mountain. A couple of days later, Klipp, Dwendo and Tynum walked with the map to where it showed them on the mountain and came back with the suitcase which after being cut open had one million Munto inside of it.

A year or so after the weekend, 'Leader' came to the farm, Klipp called Milno to hear how he was doing. After talking for a while, they made plans for Milno to come to the farm in a month or so's time, a week after they talked Milno was standing on Klipp's doorstep with Auburn, holding their daughter, a young girl by the name of Indigo, on the side of her hip. they greeted each other and Klipp introduced them to Layli and Scara and whoever else was living in the house. He helped them carry their bags up to the spare room where he watched enamoured how quickly and in sync, they unpacked their belongings before showing them around the farm and introducing them to the rest of the workers.

Klipp, Milno, Scara, Layli and Auburn along with Indigo went to sit around the porch table to drink a couple of glasses of beer from a couple of champagne sized bottles which Milno brought with, the beer is one which he had brewed to specifications that made it to be of a much lighter consistency than the average beer, the bitter and bland flavour more intense and the amount of alcohol three times higher than that of the average beer—intended to be drank in a manner similar to brandy or whiskey at a brewing company, in the city next to which Coral and Shell and two other beach towns much the same as it 'sits' and plans to have it branded as 'Bilno's' and wants to try and have it stocked at various liquor stores around town as well as the rest of the country, if all goes well.

So much everyone from the farm liked the beer, most of the workers walking over from the cabin to try it as well, Kolos and Dwendo being so fond of it that they asked to come and work for Milno were he ever to produce the beer on a grander scale, an offer to which he obliged quite excitedly after seeing them drink the beer at the pace at which they did and with expressions on their faces after doing so.

The remainder of the day was spent playing a drinking game, which Auburn taught them, and Scara asking about Milno and Auburn's inkies, the latest being letters across the top parts of their fingers that when held together spells 'True Love Forever' with a picture of a small red heart on Auburn's pinkie. Altogether Milno, Auburn and Indigo spent 30 days at the farm and every day after the first day that they arrived was spent much like the first.

Around that time, the Brungle farm workers began to hold church services, led by Petrus every Sunday, in an underground bunker of an abandoned train station building near the outskirts of town for anyone that might come to hear thereof and want to attend. Over time, many people, mostly workers from Camel's Neck as well as some from surrounding districts, began to show up to the services and about six months or so after the first service was held, which consisted of only Petrus and the rest of the workers from the Brungle farm and about a dozen or so from others, almost three-quarters of the bunker stood filled.

Over a period of the following six months, more and more workers and their children from surrounding districts began to show up to the services, along with a few farmer families as well. Very soon, Petrus had a place in the hearts of many people from Golden Heart, reserved for very few.

Printed in the USA
CPSIA information can be obtained
at www.ICGtesting.com
LVHW021641091223
766064LV00007B/49